Can I Borrow
Your Skin

Other Books by Angelique Clemens:

The Guide to the Mirror, companion guide book to Can I
Borrow Your Skin: Learning to be the Fierce Person You See
in the Mirror

Can I Borrow Your Skin

Learning to be the Fierce Person You See in the Mirror

Angelique Clemens

I would like to dedicate this book to those I hold dearest. Specifically, my parents – Columbus and Geneva, my sisters – Chamira and Dominique, my nieces – Jada, Simone, Madison, and Olivia, my nephew – Andrew, and my loving husband, Jeff – without you I would not have been inspired to write this novel.

Thank you to my proofreaders – your job was not thankless!

Thank you to Shawn T. Blanchard, my mentor!

Cover design by University of Moguls

Edited by Adept Workforce Solutions

Author photography by Lifetouch Inc

It was cold and early. Nicolette walked to her car bundled up in her large coat stepping gingerly across the ice; down the winding walkway from her front door to the car. "Fuck", she sighed watching her breath dance before her mouth. Nicolette slid into her prewarmed car. It was 5:10am on Christmas morning. She drove her car from 23 Mile Rd and Avon down Rochester Rd to her parents' home in Detroit. Most of the radio stations that Nicolette tried to tune were all playing Christmas music, "No thank you!" She landed on 90.9, the classical music station in an effort to miss the commercials and "holly, jolly Christmas" music. Pulling into the driveway at her parents' at 5:53am; "Perfect. Seven minutes to spare." Nicolette stated to herself as she made her way to the front door. As she unlocked the screen and deadbolt, Nicolette could hear the music, a Temptation's Christmas, blaring from inside. She pushed through the door and addressed her father, Alexander, that was walking from the wood stack. "Hey dad. Merry Christmas. Where's mom?" she remarked. He pointed to Ernestine, Nicolette's mom who was sitting in the living room near the fireplace rocking in her chair almost bursting at the seams waiting to start Christmas festivities. "Hey mom. I am here. On time. Seven whole minutes before the deadline. Am I last?" Nicolette asked. Ernestine shook her head and remarked, "No. You are first. Your siblings and cousin Dana are late." Nicolette could hear the edge in her voice so she just nodded and started texting all who were listed missing. 'Mom is pissed' was the only content of the text. Two minutes late, Dana was knocking on the door. Nicolette let her and Erich, her husband, into the house. "Hey Nici! Thanks. How are you? How's Aunt Ernie and Uncle Alex?" She hugged Dana and Erich. "Not good. Can you explain how my siblings, who both lives three doors down, literally walking distance, are late? You drove ten minutes and I drove forty-five and yet Steve and Charles are nowhere to be found." Erich sighed and pushed past Dana and Nicolette, "So I could have slept in?" Erich went to address Alexander and Ernestine while Nicolette and Dana exchanged an annoyed look.

A little later, Steve and his family arrived. They marched in a little disheveled and Steve announced, "I am here. Sorry that we are late, but you know new baby and all. Hey Nici. Dana. Erich. Mom and dad. Ok. We can open gifts now. We are last right?" while hugging everyone. "No", Nicolette smirked. "You are not late Steve. Of course, Charles has to be last. He is so selfish. Speaking of which... What is up with this house? I thought you said it was an investment property. How did Charles move in?" Ernestine hushed Nicolette, "It is Christmas. We are not doing that today." Steve defended Nicolette to their mother before Nicolette could, "Nic has not said anything anti-Christmasy. We are all thinking it and I suggest we should talk to Charles after we open gifts. You and dad bought that house as an investment. I thought you didn't want to be a landlord for them again?" Nicolette defended their mother's decision, "It is cool, Snick. I will leave it alone. I have other things to talk to Chuck about anyway." Charles and his family walked through the door as Nicolette was finishing her sentence. "Merry Christmas Everyone!" Charles spoke more to announce himself than anything, "Sorry that we are late." "Yes, both of y'all were late though I had to drive forty-five minutes to get here. Hell, even Dana made it and she is not even a child." Dana laughed and took a sip of the Captain Morgan rum and Coke she just mixed, "I was on time. So, I got more brownie points today. Child or not." Charles' children rushed the gifts, ignoring the adults. Ernestine begun passing out gifts and all attention shifted to Christmas and the laughing, smiling children. It did not take long for all the gifts under the tree to be distributed and opened. Ernestine, Steve, Charles, and Nicolette went to the kitchen to begin the pancakes, bacon, and turkey sausage. "So...", Steve started, "You moved in down the street last night?"

Before Charles could answer, Nicolette added in, "Yeah, I heard congrats are in order. Did you sell your other house?" Charles looked annoyed and exchanged looks with Ernestine. "Yes, I moved into the new house yesterday. Thanks for the congratulations. And no, we have not sold the other house, yet. We actually have not finished moving." Nicolette nodded along to Charles' statement. "I see. Can you guys afford to carry both houses? I know you are back working, but I did not think you were making that much money..." Nicolette's voice trailed off. Steve commented before Charles could answer, "Shouldn't your extra money go to your medication since Andrea's insurance just kicked you off?" Nicolette looked confused. "Wait, what?" Charles sighed and looked at Steve very angrily. "That was not common knowledge," Charles remarked looking angrily at Steve then turned to address Nicolette. "It is not a big deal, Nici, but I maxed out on my insurance through Andrea's job. We cannot afford all my anti-rejection medication so we are rotating between the ones that I am taking." Nicolette threw her hands up in the air, "If you cannot afford your drugs, then you cannot afford a new house. This is ridiculous! Dad is retired and mom is looking to retire. They cannot pay for this house for you. You need your meds to live. Why don't you move back around the corner and focus on your health. How short are you? I just got a raise at work. I can help." With a stark face, Charles said firmly, "I am not moving back. Mom and dad are not paying my bills. We are paying for things ourselves. I should be able to rotate until my insurance kicks in at work. I do not feel well and am not going to stand here and be lectured at." Ernestine was watching the kids argue and having heard enough, she said, "Ok. Either help me cook or leave the kitchen. In fact, I do not need help except Nicolette. The rest of y'all leave!" Charles gladly left the kitchen and Steve followed behind him. Nicolette turned towards he mom and said softly, "Mom, you guys cannot carry that house for them. Aren't you being laid off by the Board?" A little uneasy, Ernestine muttered, "I do not know. I have the most seniority so I will be the last to go, but I know cuts are coming. I do not plan on paying for that house. Charles and your father have worked out some plan. It's his money, his son. I am not involved in that house. I am not being a landlord again." Ernestine waved her hand to signify that she was done with the conversation. Nicolette nodded in agreement and dropped the topic. The women finished making breakfast and served the family. As the family started the meal, Steve addressed Nicolette, "Are you off tomorrow or are you working through this entire holiday, as well?" Nicolette replied with a grin, "No, I am off. This is the first time in several years since being on this project that I have the next two days off." Alexander jokingly replied, "Wow. You are no longer working like a Hebrew in Egypt? That means everyone is off tomorrow, except Charles. We should get together and do something." Charles made a face, "Maybe, I can call in. What are we doing?" Steve and Nicolette commented almost in unison, "You cannot call in. You are still in your probationary period." Charles looked at them and snarled, "I would call in because I do not feel well. Not because I want to just hang out with you guys. What are y'all going to do anyways?" Ernestine replied sharply before anyone can answer Charles' question, "If you do not feel well then you should go to the hospital and not worry about what we are doing." Charles did not dare continue down that path of conversation. The family watched the children play with their gifts and relaxed in the living room in front of the fire. Erich fell asleep on the couch and Nicolette tidied up the mess. Nicolette left for home when her siblings left to go to their in-laws house. She preferred being at home alone with a glass of wine rather than sitting around with her parents. Friday morning came in like a whisper. Nicolette spent the morning lounging around and she arranged for ali, a subservient male, to visit that evening. Over the years while exploring the lifestyle, ali was a constant in her life. He was the first person that introduced Nicolette to the BDSM scene

9

in metro Detroit and he continued to serve her since they first met at a house party in Ann Arbor eight years earlier. After her schedule was set, Nicolette touched bases with her mother early in the afternoon and learned that Charles did call in, but he was also sick and went to Henry Ford Hospital emergency room. "Typical Charles" Nicolette thought.

Ali arrived around eight and started Nicolette's laundry while she relaxed. Nicolette was sitting on her bed talking on the phone to her best friend, Joshua, venting about how her brother, Charles, is irresponsible and takes advantage of their parents. "You know Charles cannot afford that damn house my parents bought. He takes advantage of them every chance he gets. I'm sick of it," Nicolette snapped. "Nici, I hear you. It's been this way forever and it's probably not going to change," Joshua replied. "Charles just moved into a house that their parents bought as an investment that he decided was for him because he loved the home and more importantly the address." Nicolette replied. It was on one of the coveted neighborhoods in the city of Detroit. Charles was always trying to be a nouveau riche kid and this address would signify that he made it. Neither Charles nor his wife had the financial ability to purchase the abandoned house for cash, but it did not stop Charles from convincing their parents to let him live in that home that they bought as a real estate investment. Nicolette was lying against the headboard and swearing about Charles' inconsideration and his failure to take care of his health, while Ali folded laundry in the other room. "Charles is just so fucking inconsiderate," Nicolette fumed. "They bought that home as an investment. Now his entire family is living there. And he's not taking care of himself!" "Are you sure his medical benefits are maxed out?" Joshua inquired. "Charles and his wife Andrea, were informed a few weeks before that Charles had reached the lifetime maximum on Andrea's job provided insurance. Charles had started working again a couple months prior but had not reached his mandatory probation deadline for health insurance. Therefore, they decided that they would rotate the kidney transplant anti-rejection medication they would buy for Charles instead of him taking all of them since they could not afford all the required medication." "Damn. I know they cost a lot. Too much for life and death situation." Joshua commented. While Nicolette was speaking to Joshua, her mom called. "Hang on. My mom is calling."Nicolette says as she clicks over. Her mom explained that her dad and Andrea were summoned to the hospital where Charles had been admitted. Nicolette switched over and told Joshua. "Andrea and my dad were called to the hospital" Nicolette stated. It was after 11 o'clock in the evening. She started crying and reasoning with God while talking to Joshua explaining "Oh God, I was being a bitch. I cannot lose my big brother. Charles cannot die. I did not mean what I said. Oh my God. Josh I cannot imagine life without my brother." Joshua said everything he could think of to calm Niclolette down then the call waiting line alert went off again. Nicolette looked at her cell phone and dread immediately overtook her as the contact name "Parent's Home" displayed on the screen. Nicolette asked Joshua to hold and she took the call. "Hello? Mom?" Her mother just sobbed "Charles is gone, Nicolette. Charles is gone." "I am here, mom. I am on my way." Nicolette reassured her mother and hung up the phone with her. Nicolette went back to the call with Joshua. "My brother died. I was a bitch and selfish. And my brother died. My last words to him were veiled contempt. I am a bitch and I cannot undo my words to my brother. Oh my God. I have to go be with my mother. I have to get dressed." Nicolette cried to Joshua as she frantically found clothes to climb into. Nicolette chastised herself for berating Charles as Joshua tried to console her. Nicolette got off the phone with Joshua, dismissed Ali, and began the 45 minute drive back to Detroit. Nicolette had road rage worse than she ever had and was driving at least 90 mph to get back home to be with her mom. She made her way down I-75 barely being able to see through the tears that fell from her guilt and her pain. She made it off the highways and to her parents' house in less than 20 minutes; it was all a blur. She kept reminding herself that she had to be the strong one for her family. As Nicolette drove down the familiar street winding along the rows of trees, she could feel the sense of anxiety setting into her being. Christmas lights are still lit on the houses; ice and snow was still on the lawn and homes. Tears rolls down her face, while the words of her mother still play in her head. "He's gone, Nicolette. Charles is gone." Nicolette's older brother, Charles, died in the hospital after rejecting his liver transplant. He and his wife were just turning the corner on his health or so Nicolette thought. His family of four had just moved into a home on one of the coveted street in the city of Detroit; just doors from her parents and next door from their youngest brother. Nicolette remembered Christmas morning at their parents' house just four days earlier discussing Charles' finances and how he couldn't afford a new house prior to selling their current home. He had his heart set on providing a better home for his family with more space for each child. He always felt behind in his professional life since his friends were all college graduates unlike him. This was mainly due to his congenital liver disease; Charles felt as if he was on borrowed time for over ten years since the transplant at 21 years old. Many organ recipients do not live longer than ten years with a donor organ. So Charles pushed himself much harder in his 20s than most his age ensuring that not only was he known professionally, but he was revered as exceptional. He was a bright man, a self-trained chef who started his degree at Central Michigan University in Business Administration. Charles owned his own professional kitchen prior to getting so ill, but he had to let go in order to have the transplant. He fought hard to be able to work again, to be able to provide for his family although Andrea was the sole breadwinner for the family for most of her relationship with Charles. Now just over nine years after getting the transplant and fighting to regain his strength,

Charles was lying cold at Henry Ford Hospital. Nicolette pulled into the driveway at her parents' home still replaying all the recent conversations with Charles, Andrea, and other family members in her head. She got out the car and was greeted at the door by cousin Dana, who was more like a sister to Nicolette, and her youngest brother, Steven. "I don't know what to do", Steven exclaimed through tears,"Charles was my best friend. My son will never know his uncle." Nicolette nods her head, "I know", she manages to mumble through the fog. Nicolette works her way through the house to the kitchen where her mother, Ernestine, was making a cup of hot tea and chain smoking a pack of cigarettes. Nicolette hugs her mother and whispers that she is there continuously in her ear.

Soon, Andrea returned from the hospital with tears in her eyes. She sat their children down after hugging them, and explained that their father died because his liver stopped working. The eldest of the two children, their daughter who was nine years old, asked "but why didn't Daddy just get a new liver like last time?" Fighting back more tears, Andrea explained, "there was not enough time and usually people only get one liver. Your dad was lucky he got two and had this much time to spend with us." "I miss my daddy", their six year old son cried. The three of them hugged for a few minutes and then Andrea walked away while Nicolette, Steve, and Ernestine tried to comfort the children and answer the additional questions that they had. As the day progressed, people began to come to the home offering their condolences; each blending into the tapestry of the moment and making no true impression on Nicolette. Nicolette waited until 6:30am to make her way into the office; she had a list of things to accomplish at work after already informing family and friends of Charles' death. Nicolette was running on pure adrenalin and desire to ease the burden for her family. With Charles' phone in hand, Nicolette sat at her desk and began calling family and friends. Her colleague's began showing up with kind words and the occasional hug as Nicolette pushed through both tasks at hand. As the day droned on, Charles' phone began ringing more and more frequently as people were returning Andrea's calls on Charles' cell phone. Nicolette had the grueling task of informing all of Andrea's family and their mutual friends of Charles' passing. Nicolette recognized most of the names, as she and Charles had many of the same friends growing up being only one year his junior. With tears streaming down her face, Nicolette completed all the calls by 2:00pm. Having only a few items remaining for the merger, Nicolette pressed on until nearly 4:30pm. At that time, Nicolette decided she needed to inform Charles' job that he had pass. Charles had called off work on Friday after Christmas when he checked himself into the hospital. His job did not have Charles scheduled for work that day, Saturday, but he was due back to work on Sunday. Nicolette received a call from her cousin Bridget as she was walking to the parking garage; she was heading into the city to be with the family and wanted to know if Nicolette needed any help. Nicolette informed Bridget that she was going to Charles' workplace to inform them of his passing. Bridget insisted on accompanying Nicolette. They arrived almost simultaneously at the call center in Southfield, MI, where Nicolette identified herself to the security guard and asked for Charles' supervisor. The security guard informed Nicolette and Bridget that Mr. Smith will be out to see them momentarily. A tall, attractive, slender man approached the guard desk and addressed Nicolette, who in turn introduced herself and Bridget. Nicolette tried to keep her composure and addressed Mr. Smith, "My cousin, Bridget, and I are here to inform you that my brother, Charles Guyere, passed away at the hospital early this morning. I know that there is a process that must be followed, but I wanted to ensure that he is not terminated for not calling or showing tomorrow. Andrea, his wife, will file whatever paperwork that is needed." Mr. Smith started shaking his head in disbelief and the bright smile on his face quickly turned to a scowling frown, "I am so sorry for your loss. Charles was a great guy and awesome co-worker. I will send information over to HR and I will, personally, ensure that everything is taken care of on our end. I was hoping that this was not the reason you were here. I am speechless. He was so young and full of life." "I know," Nicolette responded with tears running down her face. "You never know when it's your time. Thank you for the information and I will be sure to pass along the arrangements." "Yes, absolutely, please do", Mr. Smith commented as Nicolette turned to leave with Bridget helping her along the way. "Brig, I do not think I can do more of this. I am just so drained. I need to go see my parents. I need to make sure the kids are ok." "Nici, you cannot take care of everyone and let yourself go", Bridget warned. "I will be ok. I have to be because they need me," Nicolette muttered. "You cannot give what you do not have, though, Nici." Bridget rebutted. "I can try. I can try." Nicolette responded as she climbed into her car and headed to Detroit with Bridget following closely behind.

Nicolette used work to distract her from Charles' death; she worked long hours at the chemical company and then drove the 25 miles from Southfield to Detroit in order to make dinner and help with Christmas break homework for Charles' family before heading home another 40 miles to Rochester Hills. Nicolette was up for 18-20 hours each day; running herself nearly ragged. Ernestine, Nicolette, and Andrea planned the funeral, services, and handled the estate. Charles and Andrea did not have much money but Andrea was adamant that everything be perfect. Alexander, Nicolette's father, picked the most expensive options for his first born son, which Ernestine insisted on obliging. Nicolette provided whatever people needed from cooking most of the meals and ensuring her parents and brother ate, to financially contributing to Andrea's household. Steve and Theresa, Steve's wife, just had their first child, a son named

Sebastian, and were not able to contribute. Steve had the most difficult time just getting out of bed without the begging of Theresa who was still nursing their four month old son. They buried Charles the first week of January after a standing room only funeral Mass. Nicolette had friends from all over the country deliver flowers, attend the funeral, and send messages of support. Their support was so she could give her all to her family. Nicolette put together a photo tribute and wrote the eulogy. With a deep breath and Steve by her side, Nicolette recited an oral history of Charles with antidotes and stories outlining his thirty-one years. At the repast, Steve drank so much that he danced until he fell out. Nicolette cleaned, served, and made sure her dad and mom were doing as well as possible. Andrea walked around the repast taking photos recalling how much Charles loved his family and how when the family gets together, it must be documented. Around 4 o'clock in the morning, family had cleared out of Andrea's house and Nicolette did one finally lap of cleaning and then left for the 45 minute drive home.

After the funeral, Andrea fell into a deep depression while the kids returned to school. Andrea had a hard time managing the household including the bills as Charles maintained the budget, therefore, Nicolette took it upon herself to provide for the short falls in their home; she even bought the house they vacated just before Christmas from Andrea for a price much more than what it was worth. Nicolette worked to fill the emotional and financial gap for her parents, brother, nephews, and niece. People who had not spoken to Nicolette in the years preceding Charles' death called her to tell stories and have her play the role of Charles in their life. Friends that Charles and Nicolette shared as a child with whom Nicolette have not spoken to since leaving high school started calling her with invitations to meals and events. While Nicolette and Charles were very close growing up, Nicolette's interests diverged more when she moved away for undergrad. Nicolette had not seen or heard from any of their mutual friends for years before Charles' death. Stepping back into those friendships would have been easier if the expectation was not for Nicolette to act as Charles in the friendships. Nicolette was disappointed when some of their cousins and even her father started asking Nicolette to fill Charles' role in their respective lives. Steve slipped when inviting Nicolette to events by listing what Charles would have done. As the weeks passed, Nicolette worked on the needs of her family and renovated the home she purchased from Andrea. As the simple fixes were coming to a close, Nicolette sold her suburban townhome for $700 above what she owed and planned her next chapter.

Chapter Two

The weeks passed slowly and quickly at the same time. Nicolette had not yet found a good routine during the last several weeks as she was working on the needs of everyone, but her own. So much was changing for Nicolette after Charles' death with supporting two households and being thrust into helping fill the void in the lives of Charles' daughter, Adrianna, and son, Jude. Nicolette had just completed the oversight on an acquisition by the chemical company she worked for and requested an inter-company transfer to a position that was less demanding with reduced travel. After interviewing with her current supervisor and the Vice President, General Counsel, Americas, Nicolette was informed that 'she was too valuable in her current role for the transfer, but care will be taken to reduce her travel time from 40% to 25%'. Frustrated that traveling so much would be detrimental on Adrianna and Jude, Nicolette left her position with the Fortune 100 Company as Lead Attorney of Acquisitions, and took a position with a small law firm working on patent law, intellectual property, and mergers to ensure that she would travel less. Her supervisor at the chemical company was quite upset at the decision of the executives to allow Nicolette to leave so she gave her a huge bonus and threw her a going away party catered by her favorite Mexican restaurant. Nicolette's final day of work was filled with gifts and well wishes and she dreaded that she was making a horrible career decision as she drove away from the building for the last time. The new company was a much different format than anything that Nicolette had ever experienced before; it was owned by a very well known emeritus professor and attorney from Wayne State University. He was brilliant in the letter of the law and set-up the firm as a boutique catering to even smaller firms and industry clients that did not have the legal expertise in-house for some of their patent applications, IP infringement cases, and government investigations. The firms' CEO was a medical doctor who thought Nicolette's undergraduate degree in Chemistry and her years with a top chemical company made her the perfect fit. Nicolette reported to an attorney who was part-time at the firm and studied under the owner. Nicolette loved almost everything about the new position: their flexible hours, the normal 40hr work week, 100% company paid benefits, and their contributions to her professional organization fees. The only downside was the financial compensation before bonuses; the bonus schedule was neither well defined nor guaranteed. The pay cut was not significant so Nicolette could still enjoy the lifestyle she had become accustomed with only slight modification. She started the new position just a few weeks before her birthday and she was just getting settled into the position when the big day arrived. Nicolette had turned 30 on a Thursday in March and she barely remembered the day, but she does recall her father calling her at six o'clock in the morning singing in a baritone that always managed to make her smile. This milestone was the first birthday since the passing of Charles and no one felt like celebrating, especially Nicolette. Alexander ended his rendition of 'Happy Birthday' by asking what time Nicolette was stopping over their house with cake so they all could sing to her. Nicolette never understood why she always had to provide her own birthday cake, but she obliged. After working only nine hours, Nicolette stopped at her favorite bakery and got a tuxedo cake, then began the rush hour bumper-to-bumper drive to her parents. It was unseasonably warm out so her niece and nephew where outside playing when Nicolette pulled into the driveway. Adrianna and Jude came running up the street to hug their aunt and wish her a happy birthday. They walked into Nicolette's parents' house where Steve and Sebastian were already inside. Ernestine called Andrea to come down and Alexander searched for candles. The family exchanged pleasantries and confirmed the meeting time for dinner the following night. Nicolette held Sebastian while Adrianna and Jude stood on each side of her and the family sung. The cake was cut and ice cream was served while Nicolette played with Sebastian. Steve asked Nicolette if she was going to forego her diet for one day and enjoy cake with them, to which she just shook her head no. Once the cake was eaten and she cleaned the kitchen, Nicolette started her trip home to Rochester Hills as she had to get up early the following day to ensure she could depart in time for the birthday celebration she had planned. Nicolette arrived earlier than normal to the firm to ensure her departure time. She was surprised by a bouquet on her desk from the office staff. There was also the standard company gift of $100 gift card. Nicolette smiled to herself and she worked diligently to accomplish the days' tasks. The winter weather had returned making the dress she had hanging in her closet at work for dinner not the best option. As the work day came to a close, Nicolette changed into her cocktail dress and hoped that the wind would stop being completely disrespectful. She exited straight from work for the planned fancy dinner with family and friends at a local steakhouse, while being pushed along the road by the fierce wind.

Everyone in her immediate family attended as well as her closest friends. The meal was quiet with little reminiscing and much less talking. Time was passed along by Nicolette's family complaining about having to cook their own steak on the hot stone, having to drive to the suburbs, and the cold weather outside. Dinner was otherwise eventless with her work friends from previous employer relating well with her family and other friends. Nicolette planned a dancing outing after dinner, but she stopped by her townhouse to change to flat soles in order to dance the night away. Dancing after dinner was only attended by her two close friends, Joshua and Carol, and Andrea; everyone else went home. Andrea and Joshua did not dance, but the club scene was a good distraction for a couple hours for Nicolette. In addition to dancing, she and Carol got to catch up on life; Carol was nearly finished with her second year of law school at Wayne State University and was dating Joshua for almost two months. Nicolette jokingly gave Carol to Joshua as a 30th birthday present one week prior at Charles' burial proceedings. They both were in attendance and quite supportive. Nicolette had been trying to get Joshua to consider dating Carol for almost four year and he finally ignored the six year age difference and took her on a date. Both Carol and Joshua were huge supports for Nicolette during her difficult times and she was happy to be able to be needy even if just for a few hours. The evening ended early because as Nicolette's guard came down, the exhaustion level of her body increased. She hugged Andrea good-bye and was dropped at home by Joshua and Carol. Nicolette hugged Joshua and Carol and told them that they were the family she chose because they meant much more to her than 'friends' do. They departed and Nicolette got her first full night's sleep in two months.

The next morning Nicolette was awaken by a text alert on her phone from Ryan, a male who claims to be submissive who gets off on breath play and total power exchange, which she has known and played with from time to time. Nicolette felt refreshed, renewed and more like herself than she had since Charles passed. She laid looking at her ceiling and thought to herself "Is this 30?" She looked at the text from Ryan and smiled. "I need to start getting back to the Nici I was before, but a new improved Nici", Nicolette said to herself as she sat up in the bed with her phone in her outstretched hand. Ryan was in his mid-30s, with short brown hair that was curly and a swimmer's body. He was sweet, attentive, and mostly into facesitting, but he was also a service-oriented submissive. Ryan enjoyed the power exchange of facesitting; that the Dominant woman dictated if and when he would draw breathe. Nicolette enjoyed her play with Ryan not only for the power exchange of his main kink, but also for the additional tasks he did for her. His text was inquiring how Nicolette was doing and if she got the flowers he sent for her birthday. The flowers, 30 stems of daisies, were sitting on the dining room table and were delivered when she was at work. She smiled and responded that Ryan was quite sweet and the flowers were lovely. Ryan was courting Nicolette to collar him, make him her personal submissive. Nicolette did not want to settle down with Ryan as most of their kinks or non-kink hobbies aligned well, but she found going through the death of her brother alone to be more difficult than she imagined. Ryan was always kind and there whenever Nicolette needed a distraction from life. Ryan responded that he would like to bring breakfast and perhaps provide her with a chair. Nicolette looked over at her watch trying to recall if she had any plans; she stretched as wide as she could in her sleigh bed and responded that she wanted eggs, bacon, and toast with mimosas. Ryan sent only a smile emoji. She went to the bathroom, brushed her teeth, washed her face, and prepared her shower. The water cascading down her torso was relaxing and stimulating. Nicolette's hands ran over her body and the loofah with Shea butter body wash rolled down her spine. Fully cleansed and thoroughly relaxed, Nicolette emerged from the shower and dressed simply in a tank top and bra with panties set. Nicolette made her way to the living room and started watching recordings from her DVR when the doorbell rang. Nicolette walked to the door and peered out, seeing Ryan standing there shuffling slowly side to side; she opened the door to his bright smile. Ryan walked into the door allowing it to close behind him and addressed Nicolette with respect and reverence. "Mistress, which would you like for me to do make you a drink, make breakfast, or provide you a chair, first?" Nicolette answered," I would like both a beverage and a chair. Please put the groceries in the fridge and make me a mimosa; did you get the nectar that I prefer?" Ryan nodded, removed his winter outer wear and khaki slacks, and made his way to the kitchen and prepared the drink, walking past her smotherbox along the way. Ryan presented Nicolette with a mimosa and immediately positioned himself into the box. Nicolette took a long sip of her beverage and smiled down at Ryan in the box, finally sitting down onto his face. Nicolette was grinding slowly onto his face, feeling his breath against her panties as he released a deep, glottal moan. Nicolette kept a mental count of two minutes, ensuring that she allowed Ryan a breath every 125 seconds. Ryan would start wiggling around 100 seconds and he was nearly bucking underneath Nicolette by the time she allowed him to breathe. Each breath that Ryan was allowed smelled of Nicolette; he knew that she controlled whether he lived or died. Both were turned on by the power exchange of smothering and breathe play. Ryan's erection was growing in his basketball shorts as his penis dancing vigorously with each struggle. Nicolette rocked back on the smotherbox and displayed her empty glass to Ryan, who groaned his disappointment in the pause in the play. Ryan scurried from beneath Nicolette and made her another mimosa. He presented the drink to her and gestured that he wanted to return into the smotherbox. Nicolette looked Ryan in the eyes and took the longest sip as he tried to adjust his rock hard member. Nicolette pointed at the ground between her legs and Ryan crawled back into place. She spent the next twenty minutes while finishing her second drink allowing Ryan only twelve breathes. His struggle only fueled his excitement and Ryan begged if he could masturbate while being smothered, but Nicolette denied him released.

Nicolette stood and exclaimed "I'm hungry"; Ryan got up and started making an omelet, bacon, toast and mixed fruit. Nicolette ate breakfast while Ryan massaged her feet. Ryan then cleaned up the dishes, hugged Nicolette, and thanked her for the play. He handed her a birthday card, donned his garments, and departed. Nicolette put the card next to the flowers he sent, changed into her lounge clothes, and settled into the rest of her weekend. Monday morning arrived quickly and Nicolette made her way through the weekend tidying up the home and doing laundry. She, also, had periods of vegging on the couch watching TV and reading a book. The weekend ended with a murmur, quietly coming to a peaceful end. Nicolette seemed more prepared to start the workweek than in the preceding weeks.

Nicolette was becoming familiar with the procedures at the new job relatively easily, often times being the lead on small cases. Suddenly, her direct supervisor, Julie, was called away urgently leaving Nicolette in charge of the entire operation. Nicolette received word from the CEO, Richard who went by Dich, that Julie would not be in for several weeks due to a family emergency and Nicolette would have to pick up the slack. Nicolette learned that Julie's daughter died unexpectedly at the age of twelve; she had meningitis. Nicolette sent flowers and sent word that Julie should not rush back as the firm could make due until she was ready. Julie attempted to return to work after a few weeks but the loss left a vacant place in her heart and her work suffered because of it. Julie would spend hours locked in her office crying and day drinking, while Nicolette continued to carry the work load of two senior attorneys. Mourning herself, Nicolette bounced between pitying Julie and resenting her lack of ability to perform. Other attorneys, both junior attorneys and senior counsel, as well as the paralegals were not as supportive of Julie, many making comments on her decreasing quality of work. Working as a bridge between Julie and other staff, Nicolette was trusted by all levels of the firm. As such, Nicolette naturally moved into the role of staff supervisor; she had a dominant personality and was confident due to her amazing educational background and professional experience. A month passed and Nicolette's new normal of supervising all the firm's staff was settling in. Nicolette noticed that she was overseeing all of the firms cases so she approached Dich about her increased workload; before she could outline her reasons for a raise, he presented her with an envelope dated six weeks prior. Inside the envelope was a bonus check for one month's salary, Nicolette gave Dich her natural 'I'm from the Eastside of Detroit and you got me fucked up look'. He smiled and responded "the increased effort was noticed, but as they say the squeaky wheel gets the grease. Enjoy your oil!" Nicolette could not decide if she wanted to categorically explain why that adage would fail him or just appear grateful in the short-term so she nodded and replied, "The oil I am looking to buy is Champaca Essential Oil." Dich looked perplexed and went to perform an internet search on the oil as she left his office. She could hear him chuckle, "Wow. $2, 300 per ounce, huh?!" Nicolette thought that the extra monies would go a long way towards the renovation of the house and other needs as she drove home that evening. She budgeted monies into her finances for Charles' family and made sure she took Adrianna and Jude on at least one outing a month. Nicolette's main focus was caring for her niece and nephew. She tried to get them into grief counseling or camps for children who lost a parent, but Andrea did not see the value in the activities. Andrea even took the children out of the Detroit Area Pre-College Engineering Program (DAPCEP) programs that they attended for years prior to Charles' death. Nicolette thought that once she moved into the adjacent neighborhood as her entire family, she could be more helpful in their healing and spend more time with them.

Chapter Three

Finally, in August, Nicolette moved onto Seneca St., eight months after burying her big brother. The four bedroom, four story house was historic and beautiful, though not in the coveted subdivision of Indian Village. The walls were plaster with decorative plaster ceilings in a few of the rooms. There were walnut baseboards, crown moldings, and chair rails that added a regal touch to the home. The large picture windows in the living room and master bedroom allowed the morning light into the home. The common rooms all had custom cherry wood floors that Andrea installed, while the bedrooms had the original pine floors. The third level had a bamboo floor and baseboards. The basement was fully finished with an epoxy floor except the wine cellar, which was polished concrete. The bedrooms and two of the bathrooms still had the pipe for the gas lights that illuminated the home decades earlier. Nicolette was determined to turn Charles' former home into her house. She cleaned out all the belongings that Andrea and Charles left, renting a dumpster for the bulk of the items, and imagined different uses for the space. The family came over to help Nicolette empty the house; she was adamant that her house wouldn't be a shrine to Charles. As the family was clearing out the clothes, dishes, furniture, and knick knacks that were left behind, they would come to Nicolette explaining a story of importance between the beholder and Charles completing the story with "So where do you want me to put this?" Nicolette would listen intently to the stories, smiling and asking details – overall reminiscing about Charles. She would always end each conversation with "It sounds like it means a lot to you. You should have it. I insist as I do not want it. Otherwise, just throw it in the dumpster." Each item that Nicolette insisted went into the dumpster gained ire from her family and loved ones as if Nicolette was asking them to discard Charles himself, and not his abandoned belongings. Eventually, Ernestine was very upset and she sat on the porch swing with Alexander discussing whether they were going to stay and continue to help Nicolette. Dana joined the conversation and

Nicolette overheard Dana say as she was walking out to discard another bag of clothes that was not worth donating, "Look, bounce if you feel you need to, but Nici did not do anything wrong. Charles left these things. He and Andrea did not want them. Why do you think it is fair for Nici to have to keep them when the owner did not even want them? C'mon. Y'all are being a bit unreasonable." Nicolette was returning from the dumpster and joined the conversation, "It is getting late and I have to go figure out something to eat as there isn't a stove or refrigerator here. Can I buy you all dinner for your help today?" Ernestine and Alexander used the out that Nicolette provided and excused themselves to go home, while Dana suggested ordering in. Andrea and the kids finished gathering the few items they wanted to take home and left immediately after Nicolette's parents. Dana and Nicolette finished the night sitting on her living room floor telling stories, catching up on their careers, and discussing their love lives.

Nicolette had the wall color changed, bought all new kitchen appliances, and changes the fixtures for the home. The kitchen was complete with a chalkboard wall and new door for the pantry. The cabinets were from Ikea and had a decorative glass cabinet door; Andrea installed them for Charles when he reopened his business out the home a few years earlier. The kitchen was complete with brushed nickel finishes and butcher block countertop. The first floor bathroom had a custom frosted glass sliding door wall installed along with a green roof and skylight. The wine cellar in the basement had a bright yellow barn door and racks for 256 bottles. Also in the basement, there was a completely renovated and expanded bathroom, storage under the stairs, pantry complete with a chest freezer, exercise room, and a laundry room. The bathroom had travertine stone walls and floor, a shower with several water jets, and a giant three-person soaker tub. The dining room boasted French doors on two walls leading to the kitchen and to the living room. Nicolette installed a shelving unit to hold her two paintings; one by a little known street artist that did an abstract portrait of Nicolette when she was in college and the other a reproduction of the Woman in Gold painting by Gustav Klimet. The deep burgundy accent wall of the dining room complimented the gold of the Klimet painting well. Nicolette sets up her radio tower in the foyer. The tower has, in addition to her radio system, all of her board and card games. The lone picture hanging in the home is a collage of her parents, Charles and his family, and Steve with his family. It is the first item that she sees whenever she enters the home through the front door. Also in the foyer, there is a bench box which holds all the sporting equipment that Nicolette uses as well as the cushions for the front porch swing. On the front porch, there is a swing while on the back deck there is a table with four chairs. There is also a deck box which had the cushions for the chairs and several quad chairs for when additional guests were present. When Nicolette moved, she purchased a very nice charcoal BBQ grill with a built-in smoker. Prior to his death, Charles planted a miniature apple tree that sat in the nook between the two stairways for the backyard deck. The home was erected in the early 1900s, before motor vehicles, which meant that there was not a driveway, but there was a horse barn that was converted to a three car garage. Nicolette looked for unique items while redecorating the house that honored the character of the home. Originally, it was a stately home of a Ford Motor Company Executive complete with leather floors in the kitchen. She was determined to add her personal touches to the home so that her family and friends would think of the house as her house and not Charles' home. Nicolette flirted with adding fordite to the home's interior decorations but only wanted Corvette fordite that was rare and very difficult to locate in enough quantity to make a statement. However, she was able to find a Cadillac fordite sculpture for the side table of the living room. Making the home that much more exquisite. Alexander had retired from GM, spending most of his time in a Cadillac plant which made the sculpture even more special. In addition to the knick knack decoration, Nicolette ordered a new bedroom set for the guest room, a mahogany closet system from John Louis Home for the bedroom that she converted into a dressing room, a couch and a chair and a half for the living room, and an oversized suede ottoman for the dressing room. The dressing room had two walls of shelves and hanging racks, one wall of mahogany shoe racks and small dresser, and full length stand-alone mahogany mirror. The bare wall had the heat register and the bedroom door opened onto it. The ottoman sat in the middle of the room; providing seating that allowed a focal point for the entire room. The third floor had a sitting area off the master bedroom that afforded the room a suite-feel between the two levels. It was equipped with a futon, entertainment system, La-Z-Boy chair, and caged bed. The caged bed was for Nicolette to have a human pet restrained under a bed that she slept upon or provide space for a kept human to sleep. The third floor bathroom was just a simple commode of all white porcelain.

Most of the rooms did not have much furniture as Nicolette's townhouse was less than half the size; however the house was still full with memories of her brother Charles. Each empty room held a vivid memory of times past. The boxes that Nicolette did move into the Seneca St. house were piled up in the living room. Nicolette had one of the four bedrooms turned into a dressing room, the master was selected out of the two larger rooms, and the smallest of the rooms was converted from an office to a guest room. The master bedroom was naturally bright with the picture windows so Nicolette focused on light when decorating her room; she moved her sleigh bed into the new home, but all the other furniture was new. The king-sized sleigh beds was deep cherry wood looking almost brown to the untrained eye, but look much deeper red against the bright, light blue-gray walls in the morning light. The room was furnished with a bench against the far wall, a night stand next to the bed, and entertainment stand for the television. The guest bedroom was bright and welcoming, but not too welcoming with orange walls that complimented the multi-colored bed comforter, a dresser, side table, and rich drapery. The light in the guest bedroom would bounce off the orange walls making the room literally glow. In making her mark on the home, Nicolette decided that the largest spare room would be the playroom. Each home Nicolette owned since she finished law school in Boston had a space for her to train and discipline the person under her thumb. This playroom overlooked the backyard and had two walls of windows. The floor and molding was made of an Australian Cypress. The walls were a deep chocolate brown with light blue piping details. The drapes are crème linen hung from brushed nickel ball rods. The room had an oversized dark brown leather chaise lounge in the corner farthest from the door next to the rear window. There was a walnut side table next to the chaise that held a vase. There was a plush brown rug in the middle of the room flanked by the furnishings of Nicolette's trade. These furnishing included a St. Andrew's Cross, smotherbox, spanking bench, and a wall shelf with accompanying hooks. The St. Andrew's Cross was customized, built of pine wood to comfortably fit a 6'8" person while allowing access to the entire torso and head for Nicolette's 5'5" stature. The same carpenter made the smotherbox which allowed Nicolette to sit on a face for hours without needing to stand. It was constructed of brown elk hide and Australian Cypress wood with accompanying detachable head and back support for the person sitting. The spanking bench was the sawhorse style made of brown elk leather and pine wood. It had rings for bondage attachment on each of the legs. The wall shelf and hooks held all of Nicolette's implements including her blue and black rose flogger, black suede nunchuck flogger, blue leather cat-o-nine tails, handball paddles, bamboo canes, and other assorted implements of corporal punishment. The playroom was the only place in the new house that was uniquely and completely Nicolette's. On lonely days when she missed Charles, she would curl up on the chaise and cry to herself. It was both comforting and lonely being in the home of her deceased brother because each room made Nicolette think of Charles, but unfortunately each room made Nicolette think of him especially the master bedroom where Charles had scrolled his name on the ceiling in glow-in-the-dark paint. Mourning Charles was impossible when every turn in the house reminded Nicolette of him, deep down she knew she would have to deal with her feelings of loss, but Nicolette did not feel loss when all she had to do was enter another room and there was Charles anew.

Chapter Four

It was the weekend before her parents' 35th wedding anniversary, their first anniversary since losing their first born son, when Nicolette moved into the Seneca St. home. A large shindig was planned, Charles was going to cater. The party plans evolved since his passing from a dinner party to a BBQ; and the day had finally arrived. Nicolette was not certain what to expect and was tired from moving the week prior and then spending the current week unpacking the boxes that were piled up in the living room every night. Nicolette was in need of a washer and dryer since she had to buy all the appliances for the home and started with essential refrigerator and stove first. Nicolette spent the early morning on the Saturday of the party at the local laundromat. After hauling all of her clothes home and putting them away in the dressing room, Nicolette went appliance shopping before making her way to the family gathering. After those few errands, she could no longer prolong her appearance at the event so she went home to get ready. Her shower was long and the water beating against her back provided Nicolette with a much needed massage. Fresh from the shower, she dried herself off and laid upon the ottoman staring up at her clothes deciding what to wear. Looking over her clothes,

Nicolette picked to wear a strappy, ankle length sundress of an orange and yellow geometric pattern and basic flip-flop. She arrived at her parents' anniversary party moments before Steve and his family. Relatives were already there and packed the house and yard celebrating, dancing, eating, and drinking. There was a DJ spinning some of the popular dance songs over the last few decades and the eclectic mix never left the dance floor empty. Nicolette went to find her parents to give them her gift, a personalized wooden family tree which included pieces from all persons her parents helped raise completed with photos and messages. After giving them their gift and explaining that the tree represented all their children and people who lived with them; people that they raised as their surrogates. Alexander jokingly wiped a tear from his eyes and hugged both his wife and his daughter. Ernestine hugged Nicolette and whispered "I did not need a wooden tree to remember that we supported so many because I loved all my children, grandchildren, nieces, and nephews. One supports people out of love. Nothing more, nothing less. That is what family does." After the presentation of the gift, Nicolette and Ernestine went for a slice of the vodka watermelon that Nicolette made the night before, toasting the celebration. Also the eve before, Nicolette made a specialty drink recipe specifically for the occasion, drawing on her bartending background. It was sweet, but strong therefore appealing to both her parents. After the toast, Nicolette made a glass of the drink and made her way to Dana and Steve. Sebastian was nearby, dancing along to the music in Frankenstein's monster style due to his new found ability to walk. Dana was the sister that Nicolette always wanted and their relationship had grown even more since Nicolette moved back to the City of Detroit less than a mile from Dana. "Nic, your brother and I were talking about going out clubbing next week. A pre-Fall shindig. I know Michigan Football does not start yet so are you free?" Steve added, "I have not been out like that since Tre had the baby. She is excited to get loose." Nicolette thought about her schedule answering, "I pretty certain I am free. Are we going straight chicken-head style or classy?" Theresa overheard the question and yelled from across the room. "Straight class of 95 – old school, tennis skirts and K-Swiss, six different length hair, popping lip gloss, around-the-way girl, B-boy style." Nicolette laughed, "Straight up? That jitting and percolating on them niggas, huh, Tre?" Dana let out a very deep, belly laugh, "In 95, I was in grad school in Tallahassee, it was all that country grammar rap – no jitting, but I am sure I have some Cool James-inspired outfits left over." Steve just shook his head and chimed in, "I will also include De'Andre, Lawrence, and Nate. We may have been 12 or 13 in 1995, but we know how to robot or Pee Wee Herman or something." Nicolette chokes on the laughter and smiles at Steve, "Pee Wee Herman huh?" Dana started singing the notes of the hook. Tre shakes her head, "Hell naw. We are not doing the Pee Wee Herman." Steve started dancing the moves, "why not?" "I need a new drink", Dana announces and starts looking for her husband, Nicholas. Nicolette walked away searching, also, for another drink and some food. Steve's friend from high school catered providing a whole pig roast, grilled chicken, and all the sides. Alexander made steaks on the grill because Ernestine wanted some red meat. Nicolette made herself a heaping plate of food and enjoyed it slowly as she sipped on her second drink and played dominoes with two of her cousins on her dad's side and one of her aunts. Nicolette usually does not play bones at family events because people take the game too seriously, but the only open table where she could eat was the bone table. Nicolette played dominoes a lot online when she was living full time in Ann Arbor, MI, after law school so she knew the mechanics and settled in for a fun night. The table was friendly, no money was waged, but the cred that was on the line made the game enticing. On her father's side of the family, none of Alexander's kid really fit in; they were resented for their accomplishments and not having children early in life. Being able to excel at the family game of bones was just the thing Nicolette needed to fit in. Nicolette was the third to play and she was able to get 15 points on her first play. She set her domino down quietly, announced her points, and continued to eat her plate. As the second and third rounds of play went similarly, Nicolette quickly watching the game, getting points where she could, and eating her dinner. Nicolette's aunt laughs loudly when Nicolette scored her next ten points, "Look at Harvard over here. Kicking our asses all nice and quiet. Probably counting cards or something." "I know right. Her brain is probably working over time she can't even talk shit and do it", one cousin exclaimed. The next round plays on with most of the people passing because they were blocked. Nicolette dominoed. Finished her plate and drink and walked away from the table. "Aren't you going to give us a chance to beat you or at least give us a rematch?", the table calls from behind her. Nicolette turns and smiles, noticing her dad was standing next to the table talking shit for her, and she responds," Naw. I am apparently way too good for you amateurs. It's best that I give up my seat. It's a friendly game. But thanks for the chair to eat my dinner." "That's my daughter", Alexander declared, "y'all should've known you were going to get your asses handed to you. Now move over. I will take her chair." Nicolette made her way through the party for a while longer, talking, dancing, and observing her family. It was a jovial event with laughter echoing into the night air. Her parents' hosted so many joint events over the years that both sides of her family were very close to one another; most of them claiming the other side as family. Nicolette used the distraction of family partaking in dancing, drinking, and eating great food to help lift her spirits and take a night off from looking after everyone else. With the exception of cleaning the kitchen and picking up some of the yard, Nicolette enjoyed the night of being a guest amongst her family. As the night wound to a close, Nicolette made her way back to her new home. She walked into the house and felt the familiar sense of dread settle upon; the brief respite at her parents' party amplified the pain. Nicolette drew a bath, lit a few candles, and turn on the radio in bathroom. Soft jazz was playing on WRCJ 90.9 when Nicolette slinked softly into the basin. She soaked in the bath, allowing the stresses of the house to melt away as melodic tune enveloped the room. Clean and relaxed Nicolette mixed herself a Bloody Mary and decided to waste some time on her tablet. Nicolette checked her email on collarme.com and saw she had fourteen new views and four new messages. The inquiries were mostly persons from other countries but there was a message from ali. ali was at Nicolette's townhouse folding laundry when she received the call from her mother about Charles' death. It had been over six months since Nicolette has heard from him. Ali stated that he was uncomfortable with death and mourning, but he wished Nicolette well, hugged her close, and exited. ali was younger than Nicolette and on occasion his immaturity was apparent. In contrast, he was professionally in a fairly powerful position being a brand manager for a well-known athletic line. ali was commanding, articulate, and responsible in his professional life. Nicolette's frustration with his inconsistency was subsided by his impeccable servitude, besides he was also easy on the eyes. He was of average height and build, but the muscles he had were very tone. Nicolette assumed he was a wrestler before leaving school. ali had hazel eyes, black hair, and simple features with the most beautiful smile. While ali was always dedicated in the services he provided, he was constantly nervous about his kinks for fear of being found out as submissive. ali was raised in a conservative, traditional Muslim family and his submission would be viewed as extremely negative by his family. Nicolette opened the email fondly thinking of ali's past years of service and his fetishes. The email was brief; it read "Hello Mistress. I have missed you. I hope are getting better with missing your brother. Please call me if you need my service. ali". Nicolette smiled and mumbled to herself and then began to type, "you miss Me? Well lucky for you that you have memories. Isn't that something you said instead of comforting Me when Charles died?" She sent the email and continued to read her email. Nicolette opened the next email; it was an oral slave begging to service her. Nicolette responded with her standard 'thanks, but no thanks message'. The third email was from a financial slave in Germany inquiring about the process of flying Nicolette to Germany for a weekend of service. Nicolette replied with the standard 'I am not your fantasy fodder message'. The fourth message was from an age appropriate slave with compatible kinks in Northwest Ohio. His message was kind, thorough and he was polite. Nicolette went to read his profile and was impressed by the content. She message him her thoughts on his efforts and offered an option for them to meet at a local event for the lifestyle. Nicolette browsed the profiles that viewed her account and found no one worth contacting. As she was completing her time on collarme.com, Nicolette received two new messages; one from ali and one from a slave named uwe. ali begged for consideration," Mistress, please do not take me trying to give You space to be with family and heal as being unsympathetic to Your needs. i love serving You. my tongue loves Your taste and i would do anything to massage and worship Your feet." Nicolette thought for a moment and responded, "I have not heard from you in literally six months. I currently do not have space for hollow promises, but I will reach out if that changes." uwe's message was kind and straightforward, "I play professionally with the NHL and I am off for the summer. I am in the United States several months of the year, but I am currently in my hometown in Germany. I am not a flake and I have no problem flying you here and paying for EVERYTHING." Nicolette responded, "I do not have a problem with playing in general, but I do not play with persons I have never met." uwe responded," If you come here I will meet you at the airport and provide you with enough money to stay for a week (or two) and you can decide if you want to play or not. No pressure. Financial domination is part of my kinks. I am also into corporal punishment and enjoyed looking at the photos of your handiwork." uwe had emailed Nicolette before in the past and they have corresponded off and on for about two years. When he first contacted her, uwe was working to move from a German hockey team, to the NHL. She noted to herself that he did, indeed, make it to the US and plays for the NHL. Though his background and story were familiar to her, Nicolette read over uwe's profile again and responded, "We can Skype tomorrow. I am MzNicolette on there. We can talk about this in more detail. In the meantime, please provide more information on your two kinks." Nicolette signed out of the website. She brushed her teeth and turned in for the night.

Nicolette awoke on Sunday morning around 8 o'clock in the morning. She stretched and yawned loudly in the bed. Nicolette looked at the clock and reached for her vibrator. Devinn Lane's Wicked Pearl Dolphin has been the most reliable toy since Nicolette learned to reach orgasm only a few years earlier. After making herself come thrice, Nicolette decided it was time to start the day. She reached for her tablet and looked up email on collarme.com. uwe wrote another message to Nicolette. It detailed his experiences with financial domination; mostly horror stories of women taking advantage of him and his fame. Blackmail was used in the past as a tool. He mentioned that he is fairly new to the lifestyle as he was not into hardcore pain and permanent marks like many of the German dominants that he had met. uwe mentioned wanting something long-term and ultimately wanting to find love. He has been divorced before and wants to have both kink and kindness in his relationship. Nicolette smiled at his message because she, too, was looking for kinky expression in a long-term relationship.
Sundays are lazy days for Nicolette since she usually spends most of her time preparing for the upcoming work week. She anticipated the upcoming work to be hellish with two pending depositions for the sell of the construction chemical

brand with the company that she was contracted to assist. Nicolette begins her household chores of polishing and dusting the wood. Nicolette takes a brief break from the chores to sit on the porch swing and listens to the traffic on nearby Mack Avenue pass by. She makes easy work of the remainder of her chores with one rug to vacuum and one bathroom to clean. With the chores of the weekend complete and a few hour before she has to start prepping dinner, Nicolette turns to her favorite distraction of finding a subservient mate. uwe appears to be online and when Nicolette signs into her computer, a Skype call is initiated. She checks her hair in the webcam feed and answers, "Why hello. Persistent I see." uwe smiles and responds, "Ja, sicher…I mean, yes. I am persistent. It is the only way to get what you want." Nicolette smiles back at uwe and responds with a wink, "Geduld ist eine Tugend." uwe perks up in his chair, "Herrin, sprichst du Deutsch?" Nicolette shakes her head slowly while smiling, "Nein, ich spreche kein Deutsch. Habe gerade genug gelernt, um durchzukommen. Besides if I speak only in German this conversation would be over very quickly as I am limited." uwe nods in agreement, "well, I definitely want this conversation to last as long as you would permit. So, if I pass this conversation, what would be the next steps on being able to meet you, Mistress?" "The steps would include setting the boundaries we both are comfortable with. Ideally, I would prefer that you come to the States prior to considering any overseas travel."

After twenty-five minutes, Nicolette ended their conversation with well wishes; smiling to herself, she could not help but think he was too good to be true. She went to prepare herself a meal, after a weekend of indulging her cravings, Nicolette decided to make a Cobb salad with balsamic vinaigrette. After grilling the chicken and chopping all the vegetables, she assembled her salad and settled in on the couch and watched some network television. Nicolette completed her dinner and television show and went to wash dishes and clean the kitchen. As the last dish was placed into the drying rack, she was startled by the sound of a thunderstorm rolling into the city. Nicolette decided to pour a glass of wine before retiring to her room. The flash of lightning brightened the entire home as she ascended the stairs. Nicolette walked into the dressing room, placing the wine on the dresser, and begun undressing herself. Looking at her watch, she determined that she had about an hour to waste before she could retire to bed. Nicolette selected a crème and navy blue pants suit for work tomorrow and ensured that her briefcase and gym bag were packed, thereby, making the morning as smooth as possible. Nicolette picked up her glass of wine and walked to the master bedroom. Sitting on the bed, she checked her cell phone and found a two surprising text messages from ali. Nicolette laughed aloud and read the messages which outlined all the ways that ali had served Nicolette and included words of thanks and pleads for Nicolette to reconsider because "She has to feel the connection that they have." ali was the most consistent play mate that Nicolette has had since discovering the lifestyle five years earlier, but she was unwilling to compromise her feelings for a few moments of exhilarating play. In the long run, Nicolette's goal has always been a long term relationship with a BDSM component, preferably Dominant/submissive relationship (D/s relationship) with full power exchange. Nicolette took a sip of the Zinfandel and placed the phone on its charger. On her tablet, Nicolette checked collarme for a few moments. There were a few new profile views and six new messages. One of the messages was from ali, he was informing Nicolette that he texted her and he hopes to hear from her soon. Nicolette also ignored that message. There were three messages complimenting Nicolette on her profile, photographs, and looks. She replied her thanks for the kind words and compliments. There was one trolling message from someone accusing Nicolette of stealing her webcam screenshots from a profile from New York. Nicolette sent the troll message a note of appreciation for their keen eye in finding the person who was stealing her photos and then attached the original video of her for proof. There was a message of thanks from uwe for the Skype conversation and as instructed, uwe's list of needs from a D/s relationship. It also included questions that he had for Nicolette including inquiries about her likes on face sitting/smothering, how is face sitting different from oral service/oral sex, what types of corporal punishment are required in her relationship, and when can he meet her. Nicolette started her response to uwe addressing his questions in order, 'in reviewing your list of need from a D/s relationship, I must say that I find none of the requirements to be too far off from what I want. I, too, want mutual respect, honesty, and fidelity. I am not into having multiple relationships at a time and do not share fluids or play in an unsafe manner so you do not have the same issues that broke up the last D/s relationship you attempted. I think that the summers in Germany would be trying on any relationships; moreover, I dated someone in the NFL before when I was in law school and I found the infidelity in that league to be rampant. I have never dated anyone who played hockey so I do not know what it is like in the NHL. I have, however, found that men with very large egos will always seek others outside of their primary relationship until they mature. Thus far, I find that you are, at least, mature enough to move forward with getting to know one another, but I have reservation based on my experiences with other professional athletes. Just know I require fidelity and without it there is no relationship – I do not give second chances. As for your questions, first, think about the basic things that human need to live and your list will include air, water, food, and expelling waste. Everything else is nice, but not required. With face sitting/smothering, the person beneath Me is entrusting Me with one quarter of the things that they require to live. There is an intense power exchange in being entrusted with someone's life, literally. This is called dolcett slavery and it is the deepest form of love and dedication as the person serves with their literal life. All day on this site you can read profile after profile where the person is either seeking to dedicate their life or have a life dedicated to them, but most are just playing a role. The true power exchange from someone who means it is a turn-on. There is a big difference between sitting on a face and having oral sex. I sit on faces in no less than underwear, but the most I have sat on a face in is a fur coat; the slave had a furry fetish. While I do enjoy oral service, I do not have sex of any sort with any and everyone. I have not had sex with any of the people under my ass and do not plan on sleeping with any of them unless I am in a committed long term relationship with that person. Oral service can include anything from oral sex to body worship. I absolutely LOVE corporal punishment. I enjoy all kinds of implements from whips and canes to floggers and crops. Overall, it is my essential, required fetish that needs to be indulged. While I require and enjoy corporal, I do not believe in permanent marks or damage. I am a sadist; my sadistic nature is not just for punishment but I am truly aroused by the moans of both pleasure and pain that come from my work. Overall, I enjoy using crops the most, as it gives you best of whips and floggers. You can administer both severe stinging pain and thud-like massaging pain. I have mastered the use of bull whips of many lengths, different styles of floggers, and other styles of punishment including wax, chastity, and cupping. What types of things do you enjoy that can also be viewed as painful; there is a little masochist in many of us. Do you enjoy having nails dig into your back while you are balls deep in some woman? Do you enjoy being nibbled upon or bit during foreplay? Do you enjoy spankings? Have you had your balls massaged or pulled and enjoyed it? Some are into ball busting. What about wax or ice cubes during your amorous activities? You see, there are numerous ways that a sadist can express themselves and the same scene will never be repeated even if the activities are the same. As for meeting, I am just getting to know you before I will be comfortable going on such a journey overseas, since you will not be in the States for another two months. I was speaking to a financial slave that I know in Germany who has been begging Me to come there for quite some time, but finding time since I no longer work for a German company has proven difficult. I know that the German Passion BDSM is coming up in November; that seems like a great event to meet and have an amazingly good time.' Nicolette sent the email and noticed she had two new unread messages. One was received from the aforementioned German financial slave who used to take Nicolette shopping whenever he was in Michigan. The message read, "Mistress, I am traveling to the U.S. soon and would like to take you out. Do you have any use for me?" Nicolette checked the clock and noticed that she was nearing her bedtime so she sent a brief response, "That might be possible. What days are you here and what are you looking to do? I am also thinking about attending Passion this year in Germany. Can you look into an itinerary for me so I can decide if I can attend? Also, can you gather information on what I need to do in order to have a play space with a cross in it?" The other message was from ali asking why Nicolette has not responded to his multiple attempts to contact her. Nicolette sighed and responded, "ali, you made the decision that I needed to spend time with family and loved ones. I am taking your advice. I am working on finding My happy again. I wish you luck in finding an emotionless Dominant who does not have any issues, problems, and no one in Her life dies." Nicolette closed out the app, finished her wine, stretched, brushed her teeth, washed her face, and turned on the television in her bedroom to watch ESPN. Sportscenter highlighted the day's games and previewed some of the upcoming seasons for college football. University of Michigan, Nicolette's team and alma mater, did not have a promising year ahead given that their head coach retired and the school brought in a nobody to be coach. After hearing enough disappointing news about her squad's chances in the upcoming year,

Nicolette switched over to Fox Sports Detroit to watch a preview of the Red Wings season. Filled with excitement about the Fall and its sports, Nicolette had yet another restful night of sleep.

Chapter Five

After attending Mass at Charles' church for his funeral, Nicolette promised herself that she would try the Church again. She has not tried attending church regularly since St. Thomas in Ann Arbor. Nicolette woke without her alarm early Sunday morning, plenty of time prior to the 11am Mass. She styled her hair into a low profile bun and donned a pants suit. Steve was attending the service as well. Nicolette walked to service enjoying the morning air arriving ten minutes prior to Mass. Steve was already in the pew, Nicolette addressed Sebastian and Steve. Sebastian was bouncing in his seat and once Nicolette sat down he climbed onto her lap. Sebastian liked bouncing on Nicolette's lap and singing along to the music in Mass. Nicolette was sitting just four rows behind where she sat when Sebastian was baptized with Nicolette as Godmother, and where Nicolette sat when Charles received his final rites. Sitting in the church, Nicolette felt a calm that she only finds when she is asleep. Fr. Dave gave a stirring homily that touch Nicolette's heart. She was moved and experienced an oneness with God that she missed for over a decade. Nicolette hugged Steve and Sebastian farewell then walked the long way home thinking about the messages in the homily reflecting on her life. Nicolette was having such a difficult time with being back home, a place she never thought she would live again. Nicolette walked through the door of her home and decided to spend the day outlining a plan and budget to accomplish the goals she had set for her life. Nicolette crafted s a ten year plan; she wanted to find love again, excel at her career, and spend more time with family. After spending some time making a short-term plan, Nicolette started browsing washing machines and dryers on the internet.

Nicolette awoken on her couch a few hours later, the television was in sleep mode as was her laptop. Checking her cell phone for the time, she got up from the couch to make herself something to eat because she slept through all the meals of the day. Nicolette decided to make vegetable pasta with garlic bread. After putting water on to boil, Nicolette went to change out of her clothes from church into something more comfortable. Dressed in a lounge outfit, Nicolette completed making dinner and sat down at the dining room table to dine. Nicolette disliked sitting at her dining room table alone as it exemplified how lonely her life was, but she made an exception this evening. Learning herself was part of the process of finding love again; she wanted to ensure that the hopeless romantic in her could find someone that the sadist in her could enjoy while still pleasing the pious schoolgirl who yearned for the white picket fence and 2.4 children in the suburbs. She began crying at the dining room table trying to figure out what traits she needed to have and what qualities about herself she needed to work on in order to find the unicorn she sought. She was comfortable with her physical shape since she started working out consistently. Nicolette was often told that she should smile more; she found the statement condescending, but as a single woman of 30, the time is ticking for her to procreate. She has a lot of interests that males find desirable including football, hockey, and baseball. She was very successful, which is unfortunately is deemed as a negative since 'most men do not want a woman more successful than them'. Nicolette went over additional pros and cons in her head for the duration of her meal. After, Nicolette quietly cleaned the kitchen and turned in for the evening knowing she had a doctor's appointment tomorrow, Monday.

The next day passed quickly with Nicolette running from appointment to appointment. She was content to finally be home after work, errands, and the doctor's appointment. She climbed out of the shower after washing off the long day and walked across the floor into the dressing room where she begins to massage Shea butter into her skin. Nicolette stood tall, nude in the full length mirror. Her hair is pulled into a messy ponytail atop her head. It has been seventeen months since she decided to cut most of the processed and fatty food from her diet. Nicolette sighs to herself as she feels the soft abs that has hard spots beneath them. She sees the progress, but cannot help but wonder if she will always be "cuddly–thick" as the men she grew up dating would call her. At 5'2 and 185 pounds, Nicolette is still obese. It boiled her blood the way Dr. Smithson hissed the word in her direction as he mentioned things she could try. 'Cut candy, soft drinks, and fatty snacks,' he said. Nicolette did cut those items from her diet ten years ago. 'Try eating fish and chicken instead of red meats,' was his rebuttal. Nicolette has been eating fish, chicken, or vegetarian six-to-seven days for all meals for almost twenty years. 'Well, you have to be active!' he snapped. With a raise of the eyebrow, Nicolette listed her daily gym routine as well as the volleyball league games she attends one night, a week as well as bike riding on the weekend. 'Regardless, you are obese', he hissed. Looking at her full breasts now which laid prominently against her stomach, Nicolette thought to herself how losing these forty pounds of breasts would change her from obese to normal. But, alas, she has never been unnatural in her entire 30 years – never worn a weave, fake nails, fake lashes, no surgeries to correct or enhance, Nicolette does not even wear make-up regularly – all natural including these forty-plus pound 38KK breasts Nicolette has had since she was 19 years old. Her hands run over stretch marks and old scars from being a tomboy. Her hands reach her neck and Nicolette closed her eyes and rolls her neck. A satisfying cracking noise is produced. Nicolette opened her eyes slowly and took another long, hard look at herself. The biggest smile comes upon her lips. Flaws and all, today in that moment, Nicolette felt perfect. The curves of her body had a beautiful sun-kissed glow and her muscles were defined and striking. It was nice to finally appreciate herself: body, mind, and spirit; especially after the trying dinner criticizing herself the evening before. Nicolette finished massaging Shea butter into her skin and went to relax after the long, hard day. Nicolette logged into the collarme website from her laptop and found four new messages. The first message was from ali asking Nicolette to reconsider her decision to no longer see him. He was not trying to push her away or be insensitive, but wanted to get her to spend more time with family and friends. Nicolette was thinking of ignoring the message and stopping the back-and-forth with him, but decided to send one final message simply stating that her decision was final and the constant badgering would not benefit his goal. The second message was from uwe which stated, "Thank you, Mistress, for taking the time to respond to my message in such a thoughtful manner. I, first, want to inform you that I am a faithful man; I have never cheated on anyone I have been in a relationship with. In fact, I think I may have been cheated on before, but I did not stray. Being in the NHL, I guess, is not like the NFL as most of my friends are in committed relationships and we spend our time when we are traveling hanging out in groups watching sports and practicing. I know that there are guys who may not be on the upmost, but I am not in that group of guys. I love what you said about the power exchange in a BDSM relationship. I have had several fantasies about having a Dominant Woman in my life that can be my everything in a full power exchange. I have never heard the term dolcett before, but I do appreciate you teaching me about that. I will look into that further. Thank you. I have had several compliment me on my oral fortitude so if we are ever in a long term relationship and that is something you seek I know I can definitely please you in that way. I have never thought about corporal punishment as a turn-on but I do enjoy biting people and being bit, spankings are sexy, and definitely have enjoyed being scratched. I re-read your profile and saw that you are into anal play. What does that entail? I would love for you to come to Germany. I have never been to Passion, but I see that is in November. I will be in the States then as my season starts in October, with pre-season and reporting being in a couple weeks. If you cannot make it here before then I would love to fly you out after camp." Nicolette looked up his team and saw that the Red Wings do play them in preseason and started making mental plans to attend the game. Responding to his message, Nicolette wrote, "I do hope that you find information on dolcett to be interesting and forthcoming, not the porn scenes of men strangling women because they are psychopaths. I hope you are open to more ideas on corporal punishment. As for anal play, I enjoy fucking ass. It is a huge turn-on and the idea of bending a man over and taking their anal virginity is pretty nice as well. I am gentle to start, but I can be quite vigorous in my anal fucking. Are you an anal virgin? Have you ever had anything in your ass…fingers, toys, other men? I looked up your team's schedule and you play my Red Wings; I might have to come to your game I will secretly cheer for you, but I am a Wings fan through and through. When do you come stateside?" The third message was from Heinrich, the German finslave, who Nicolette tasked with gathering information about Passion. Heinrich's message was very informative, "Mistress, I will pay for you to come to Passion. It is in Munich and I can put you up in a very nice hotel in downtown and provide you with spending money. While you are here playing at Passion, can you please use me?" Nicolette smiled at the message and sent the response, "Thank you for the information. I am rethinking Passion though it sounds like an awesome party. It falls during Michigan football season and I do not want to miss any games for a kink party especially when we have a nice scene here. Perhaps in May for the Fetish Ball. When are you coming here in the next few weeks?" The fourth and final message was from Nicolette's favorite boy of all time, a 60

46

year old accountant from Niagara Falls. His name was James and he was charismatic and funny. James has been a fan of Nicolette's for her entire time active in the BDSM lifestyle; he had been emailing, chatting, and video chatting with her since she entered onto the scene. She was not certain if he was a submissive, switch, or just a fetishist. He always deferred to her, but he carried himself differently than the other men she chatted with on collarme. James sent his usual greetings and asked Nicolette how she was fairing after the death of her brother and the subsequent move. Nicolette sent James a kind note of greeting and wished him well. Included in her message was the reminder that he promised to meet her that summer which was drawing to a close. Nicolette browsed through some of the videos and photos on the site for about ten minutes before she received notification that she was requested for an instant message chat with James. Nicolette accepted the chat with James.

cunninglinguist: Hello Mistress. How is your evening treating you?
MzNicolette: hi James. My evening is going ok. I had a long weekend. you?
cunninglinguist: my weekend was good. Thank You. Why was Your weekend long?
MzNicolette: Just being around family with the party and all. It was good but tedious
cunninglinguist: I understand having a tedious family. mine was not a cake walk. What all did you do today? i went to the gym and played handball. It was a very fun.
MzNicolette: Today, I went to work and the doctor as well as the gym. Had dinner and now here I am. I am heading to bed soon so I do not knock off My schedule.
cunninglinguist: well I just wanted to say hello. i will not keep you. have a good one.
MzNicolette: Good night James. I look forward to your plans to visit within the month"

Nicolette did not have any new email so she logged off the website, turn off the television, and prepared for the next day. Nicolette briefly cleaned up the house and headed to bed. Though she did not sleep well due to the tossing and turning, Nicolette was not tired the next morning. Nicolette's work week went by quickly with her assisting on the cases of the firm. She seemed to always be in meeting after meeting, shuffling through the hallways of the building. Nicolette had a pattern of going to work, working out at the gym, and returning to her empty home to cook, clean, and be alone with her thoughts. As the week was drawing to a close, Nicolette's routine was much easier since moving around the corner from her family. The commute to the new job was also shorter and much more manageable from the home in Detroit as she was always traveling the opposite way of traffic. Those little changes gained Nicolette an additional two hours in her daily schedule. As the summer drew to a close, Nicolette found herself shopping with Adrianna and Jude for uniforms for school. She helped with school supplies lists and books, as well. Adrianna was moving from her elementary school to the local middle school. She was nervous about changing schools, but Nicolette helped her see it as a way to find more friends and learn different topics that interest her. Jude would be attending the same school as the previous year that was three doors from his new home. He was excited about being in the school by himself and going to higher grade. He was always a good student to this point, even managing honor roll the semester after his father passed. Jude had a grief counselor at the elementary school that also attended church with the family that helped him feel grounded, which was imperative for his continued growth. Nicolette was determined to be the best support system and aunt that the kids had.

Nicolette was reviewed for her work at the firm and was given sizeable 18% raise in recognition of her increased workload and responsibility. Nicolette was getting into a groove with her work and her home life. She got home after work on Friday and reviewed her mail; it was a large envelope from the appraiser. She wanted to refinance the house's debt into her name. She opened the envelope and her heart sank; the house only appraised at 27% of what Andrea and Charles owed on the home. This was the Nicolette's third and final attempt to find an appraiser who knew the homes in the area. Taking a deep breath, Nicolette ascended the stairs to her dressing room where she removed her suit while talking to herself about how she can pay off the debts of Andrea and Charles. The quit-claim deed that Andrea had signed for Nicolette allowed her to put all the utilities and taxes in her name, but she could not even get her credit union to refinance the house. Fully nude, Nicolette slumps down on her ottoman and just sobs. Nicolette felt defeated; she had done everything right and has been unselfish with her money, time, and life since Charles died and she felt like she is being punished. Looking over her bank book and bills portfolio, Nicolette wipes tears and begins determining a reasonable budget that will help pay down the debt to a level that she needs to be able to refinance. After having a plan in mind, Nicolette takes a deep breath and calls Andrea, "Hey Andi, I got my third appraisal and it, too, is nowhere where it needs to be to refinance the two mortgages you guys had on this house. I do not have enough saved to pay off the debt. I will continue to pay on the debt, in some cases, paying more than what you owe to the principle so that I can get the debt down." "Oh. Well that is not convenient. I do not want this debt in my name anymore. Is there anything else you can do? This is annoying. It is no longer my house. Should I file a complaint with the banks or my credit report?" Andrea responds. "If you dispute the mortgages, I will have to fight to keep the house. I already sold my home and do not have anywhere else to land. I will pay the bills so it will not negatively affect your credit. I am hoping to pay 60- 70% of your debt off in the next three years." Nicolette says laying out the plan she just determine. Andrea is silent longer than a pause and then sighs. Nicolette continues, "Andi, the market has crashed. You and Charles took every dime you could out of this house. You will not get anything if you try to sell the house independently. Letting the house fall into foreclosure would not end well for you. At least this way, you get all the positive credit from me paying the bills off quickly and on-time. This is the best option we have. I will even allow you to write off the tax credit. This is nothing but a win for you. I do not understand the hesitation." Andrea finally responds, "Nici, you can try this plan, but know in three years, I am done regardless of where the house is. I do not want to continue to carry this debt. It doesn't matter if you pay it or not." "Ok," Nicolette replies coldly, "Thanks, I will talk to you later." Nicolette hangs up the phone and bounces between extreme anger, utter disbelief, and helplessness. Talking to herself, Nicolette paces the house, replaying the conversation and looking over her budget which was a five-year plan. "What an ingrate!" Nicolette screams. Tears roll down her face as she paces faster through the house. Nicolette eyes catch her kickboxing gear. As she begins to gear up to workout to release her frustration, the phone rings. It is Steven calling. "Yes, Steve," Nicolette manages through her fog. "What's wrong?" Steve can hear the distress in Nicolette's voice. "Nothing. I just have so much going on. Unless this is important, I have to go." Nicolette responds pushing him off the phone. Nicolette finishes dressing and her phone rings again. It is Ernestine calling from her cell phone. "Hello, mom", Nicolette begins. Before she can finish, Ernestine informs Nicolette that she is on her porch and coming into her house. Nicolette can hear Ernestine on the stairs of the porch and the alarm alerts to the door being opened as Nicolette reaches the landing. Nicolette wipes her face and addresses her mother. "Hey, mom. What's up? What made you want to stop over?" Ernestine looks at her daughter who has made it to the first floor, dressed in her workout gear. "You've been crying. What is wrong? Steve called me," Ernestine responded. Nicolette handed her mother the appraisal and begins, "Charles and Andrea took every penny and then some from the house. I have paid for three appraisals. None of them came in within 45% of what they owe. My credit union will not refinance the house, none of the appraisals that they would accept came in higher than 33%. I let Andi know and it took some serious convincing for her not to force default. She is giving me three years to pay off enough of her debt to be able to refinance. I am just tired. I have been spending ALL my extra money taking care of her family and now, even with the raise I got today, I do not know I can meet the three year deadline because I cannot put every dime I have into this home. I am unsure of what to do. A large part of me wants to walk away. Another part of me wants to make sure I am here for Adrianna and Jude. I am lost. And I just want to hit something." Ernestine puts the report on the bench by the door and hugs her daughter. "Nicolette, no one would blame you if you said 'fuck it' and took care of yourself. You have done so much for all of us. You are not a super woman. Take care of yourself. Andrea is an asshole. First, she had the house in default when she did the quit-claim deed. Now this, she does not even pay rent for the house your dad and I are letting her live in. She got two life insurance policies and only your dad, you, and I paid for the funeral. She is not wanting for money. Stop doing so much for her." Nicolette wipes some of tears away, "Thank you, mom. I need to know that you all will not hate me if I pull out of helping those Guyeres as I need to work on paying off this house." Ernestine smiles and hugs her daughter again, "Take care of yourself. We, all, are doing too much for those Guyeres. We all love Charles but we cannot do everything for Andrea or she will never learn to be self sufficient again." Ernestine departs and Nicolette follows behind her to go to the gym. Nicolette gets to the YMCA and jogs the track. She runs into her favorite fireman, Tony, who is doing his intense kettle bell workout. Watching Tony's chiseled body sweat and move through his motion is a major motivator for Nicolette at the gym. He acknowledges Nicolette at the gym and asks how her week went. Not wanting to explain the drama of her life, Nicolette just shakes her head "no" and smiles at Tony. Nicolette hit the weights hard, squatting heavy weight trying to push herself. Tony spotted Nicolette on some of her late repetitions and helped her lift more than what she averages. Nicolette made her rounds for legs and back getting the help from Tony on occasion. Nicolette used fantasies of Tony to motivate her throughout her workouts in the months previously; his chiseled physique glistening with sweat, dimples, sweet smile, and kind demeanor made him the perfect candidate to get Nicolette to the gym on those long days and winter evenings. Through her headphones, Nicolette could hear Tony grunt and growl as he benched his final reps of 325. Exhausted, Nicolette stretches her muscles and walks a mile on the indoor track for a cool down. The workout helped refocus Nicolette's mind away from the appraisal issues and helped her have a much better plan which included decreasing her financial contributions to Charles' family. Nicolette exited the track and started her way to locker room to gather her personal items at the same time as Tony. "You went hard, today. I have not seen you push like that in quite a while," Tony remarked. Nicolette responded, "I had a lot of frustration to get out. It has been a long week and I needed these sore muscles to have something positive to focus on." "I understand that. Have to go hard some days just know you are human and alive." Tony said with a nod as he moved towards the exit. Nicolette nodded pack and continued down the stairs to the locker room. Nicolette went home and took a long, hot shower. Completely unmotivated and defeated, Nicolette went straight to bed without dinner or checking her phone.

The phone was ringing in the other room startling Nicolette from her sleep. Nicolette looks at the clock and notices that she slept only three hours and it is only 11:30pm. Nicolette rolls back over and attempts to go back to sleep when the phone starts ringing again. Nervous and scared that something horrible has happened, Nicolette jumps from bed and answers the phone. It was Dana. "Hello, Dana, what's wrong? Is everyone ok?" Nicolette rushes out in her half-awake, panic state. Dana laughs, "Nici, it is 11:30pm on a Friday. Most 30-somethings are getting ready to go out! Hence my call. You are hibernating! Have you done anything fun that was not family related in the last six months? You need to get out." Nicolette rubs her head and sits down onto the bed silently weighing the pros and cons of going out. Dana continued, "I am on my way to your house and I will be there in twenty minutes. Erich has plans with his friends. We are going to AT LEAST go to DBC and have a beverage. C'mon girl. No excuses." Nicolette begrudging agrees and hangs up the phone. She walks slowly to the bathroom, being reminded with each step of how hard she went at the gym, to wash her face and brush her teeth. Completing her hygiene tasks, Nicolette makes her way to the dressing room where she decides on a simple sundress and flip flops. Nicolette rubs in a Shea butter bug repellent into her skin, grabs her wristlet, cell phones, and keys and makes her way to the door where Dana is standing preparing to knock on the front door. "Perfect timing, D. You want me to drive?" Nicolette addressed Dana as she opened the door. "I can drive. Is DBC good or you want to go to your spot?" Dana responded. "Either or. I just need a place that sells food. I am starving. I did not eat dinner yet." Nicolette replied. "Nici, you were in bed for the night when I called.", Dana shook her head, "Ok, let's go. We can get you food at the bar." Nicolette armed the alarm on her home and made her way to Dana's car. Inside, Dana was bumping the latest Eminem album and they started towards downtown. The Detroit Beer Company, or DBC as it is known to locals, is located across from the Detroit Opera House and just steps from Comerica Park. It is a microbrewery with pub fare and good atmosphere. Dana's husband Erich was good friends with some of the bartenders, that's why Dana knew them well also. There was a normal crop of regulars at the bar at

DBC, many of them are Michigan State University fans; University of Michigan rivals, which made the bar less than perfect in Nicolette's eyes. They parked on Broadway across from the bar and headed in to find Rony, one of the aforementioned bartenders. Rony was a beautiful, shapely black woman who stood 5' tall. She was very personable and very good at mixing drinks. "Hello, Dana, how are you, doll?" Rony addressed Dana. "Good, Rony. Hope you're well. Do you have space for my cousin and I? This is Nicolette." Dana replied. "Hello, Rony," Nicolette addressed her while pulling back a chair, "Can we sit here?" Rony nodded and asked Dana, "Red?" She nodded yes in response and Rony walked off to pour the DBC amber lager for Dana. While she was pouring the beer, Nicolette and Dana took two of the hightop bar chairs on the right of the center of the bar on the first level. Rony returned with Dana's beer and pointed at Nicolette who commented, "I will have the black and white dip, a gimlet, and a Dagwood to follow, well done, with a side of BBQ sauce. Thank you." Rony went and entered the food order and then preceded to make the drink. Nicolette turned to Dana, "You are going to have some of the dip, yes? I was craving salt and only saw the dip as a viable option for salt intake." While rubbing her thighs she continued, "I know better than to try to lift that much but I was in a mood." Dana responded, "Yes, I can fuck with some cheese and bean dip. I might have to get a sandwich, too, because Erich did not cook tonight, so I am winging it too. Maybe I will get some wings." Nicolette laughed, "Menses coming, eh?" Dana looked pensive for a moment and then sad. "I guess so," she finally uttered. Dana and Erich have been trying to conceive for about a year now and have been unsuccessful. Nicolette, now realizing that fact, tried to change the subject she unthinkingly started, "Or you are just hormonal. Lord knows when it will happen, but it will. Besides Dana, you cannot live your life by others' standards. If we listened to what people think we should be doing then I would be an old maid. Who gives a fuck? You are, at least, beating me; you found a man! Be happy that you have successes. You *will* have a family. I am confident in that. Now let's order a round of shots and toast what a bad bitch you are!" Nicolette smiled at her cousin knowing all too well what it was like to be expected at 30 to have a husband and family. The ladies drank, watched sports, and overall just had a relaxing time. After finishing dinner, Nicolette and Dana left DBC and headed home. Dana pulled up in front of Nicolette's house, "Thank you, D. I did not realize how down and out I was until you made me come out. I will do better, I promise. At the very least, I might go to Germany. I will look up your dad's family if I go." Dana, who is half Swiss-German, smiled and commented, "It is lovely this time of year. I will give you my aunts and uncles info and let them know to look for you if you head that way." They exchange pleasantries and Nicolette head for the door. Once inside, she is energized and feel wide awake even at the late hour of 2:30am. Nicolette decides to check email and see that she has 12 new messages on collarme. Half of the messages received the standard form message of no interest. One of the messages was from MstKat's pet kel who was inviting Nicolette to their party in two weeks. Kat and kel were the relationship that Nicolette looked to in the lifestyle to imitate. They were both educated, compassionate, loving people who also had a D/s component. Nicolette have attended several of their parties and have looked up to Kat as a Dominant Woman mentor and envied her relationship with kel. When Nicolette interviewed pets she always, on some level, compared them to kel. Nicolette looked at her calendar and noted that the weekend of their party was a Michigan home game, having season tickets she knew that she would be coming straight from the game to the Southfield location of the party. Nicolette usually took a hiatus from the scene in the Fall due to the conflict of football season, but she was excited to be around the Ladies in the group she frequented. Nicolette responded to the message that she will be present, but later in the evening around 8:30pm as the Michigan game was at 12:00pm. One message was from ali first begging for reconsideration and then accepting the decision that Nicolette made. One message was from Ryan thanking Nicolette for the play recently, and asking if she was settling into the new place well and if she had time for him to be her chair for one of the upcoming away games. It was common knowledge amongst the persons in her community that Nicolette took the Fall off from play and parties due to the demand of football Saturdays in her life. Ryan has been known to spend an entire away game in Nicolette's smotherbox being smothered for 12-16 hours that day. Nicolette responded that the first away game was against the Irish on the 13th and she was not certain if she will be going out for the game or not but as the games play out she will make the decision and perhaps some facesitting and corporal will make the day worthwhile. There was a message from uwe checking in, he had made it to Ohio where he plays in the NHL and was hoping Nicolette made a positive decision about coming to the Red Wings game even if she cheered against him. Nicolette responded that most teams do not let their team's block go to the opposing team. "I will cheer for you, but I will be wearing my red & white and definitely bleed the octopi," Nicolette added to her message. She included thoughtful messages of not wanting him to be shunned by his teammates if she was in their seats being a Wings fan. Lastly, Nicolette welcomed him to the States and said they can make time to hang out now that he is stateside. Heinrich sent his itinerary for coming to Michigan in 4 days and left time to take Nicolette to dinner 4 of the 6 days that he did not have work obligations; in addition, he has sent aside one entire day to take Nicolette to Somerset and purchase whatever she wanted. Lastly, he wanted to know how much in American dollars did she require from him to ensure her time one date. Nicolette skipped that message and read the message from James. James was uncertain why Nicolette would make time for him and definitely unaware if he should drive there to see her. Nicolette responded that

James was overdue on yet another deadline and if he was just using Nicolette for wank fodder then he should be upfront and honest because online service was not her thing and she "is a grown ass woman and no amount of age gap would change that fact." Nicolette returned to the message from Heinrich and responded that she could make time for him and would love to go to Somerset. She, also, included the note that, "I never advertise a rate as I am not for sell, silly boy. If one wants to pay homage, one can determine the importance of my presence in their life and pay homage accordingly." Nicolette was getting ready to logoff for the evening when a new message came through. It was from uwe. It read," I am buying tickets with my discount outside of the player's visitors' block. I can get January 27th tickets, but I will see you in Detroit in November…if not before?" Nicolette looked at her schedule and calendar and realized that uwe had cleared both the first home and away Wings game for her. Nicolette smiled and responded, "Yes, you can see me before then if your schedule allows. I would assume practice, games, and other obligations are strict. Either way November is a date. Can you come ahead of the game on the 27th? I know you are off that day and given that it is a holiday here, so am I; perhaps we can go out." After hitting the "send email" button, Nicolette had new emails and a chat request. The emails were from uwe and Heinrich. Heinrich was providing his flight and hotel information for when he arrives in a few days. Nicolette did not respond to Heinrich's email. uwe asked permission to send a chat request which Nicolette permitted. The chat requests were from a submissive from Utah and a new request from uwe. Nicolette accepted the request from uwe.

germanpet: hello! Thank you for taking my request.
MzNicolette: No problem, uwe. How are you? When did you get stateside?

germanpet: ok, thank You. got in yesterday late. Cannot believe that we are only 3 hours away from each other. We are going to meet soon – so excited!

MzNicolette: Good to hear that you had a safe trip. Yes we are close and it is fun that we will be able to meet and potentially play soon. Where do you live in Ohio?

germanpet: I have a condo that I rented out to some teammates during the off-season. So we have practice for the next couple days but can I come after that?

MzNicolette: absolutely, I look forward to meeting you. I am fading fast, we shall talk later. Send Me the details when you have them.

Nicolette logged off the chat and returned to bed after a full night of socializing. It took a moment for Nicolette to get comfortable; she looked up at the ceiling staring at Charles' name on the ceiling. Nicolette tossed and turned most of the night and could not quite get rest.

Chapter Six

Nicolette woke up at 6 o'clock in the morning after maybe two hours of steady sleep. She felt tired but could not will her eyes to close again. At least in the daylight of the morning, Charles' name was difficult to make out on the ceiling. Nicolette decided to try to paint over his name yet again – this would be the second attempt and fifth coat of priming and paint. Nicolette brushed her teeth and put a mask on her face before donning some old sweats. Making her way to the basement, Nicolette looked for the Kilz Primer and light blue paint for the master bedroom. Locating the paint and supplies, Nicolette placed a drop cloth over the bed and climbed onto the cloth and edged the border with blue painter's tape. Ensuring that she had the room sufficiently protected from the current task, Nicolette added primer to the paint pan, started her Pandora channel, and begun painting. The plaster ceiling took the primer very well sending Nicolette to refresh her roller more often than needed with drywall. Once the ceiling was sufficiently primed and dry, Nicolette put another disposable paint pan on top of the empty primer pan and added the light blue room paint. Nicolette worked her way around the ceiling ensuring that the each area was covered with two coats of the blue paint. Complete, Nicolette carefully removed the painter's tape and cleaned up the drop cloths and disposable materials. Hoping that the ceiling will dry without Charles' name on the ceiling, Nicolette cleaned up herself as well. Content with the job that was done, Nicolette lounged on her couch to watch some of the recordings on the DVR. Nicolette started a recorded show, got comfortable and fell asleep in the first 15 minutes of the show. Nicolette was awoken from her nap by the noise of an intense scene in the show Nicolette tried to watch. Looking at the time on the television, Nicolette noted that she got another 40 minutes of sleep. Deciding that it is too early to try and sleep, Nicolette decided to try to watch a different television program but while sitting up.

Nicolette deleted the program and rummaged through the refrigerator, she grabbed a bowl of berries and return to the couch. Nicolette checked her phone and saw she had emails. Logging into her email, Nicolette read through correspondence from her close friends and deleted a variety of spam messages. Included in the spam were notifications from collarme, so Nicolette logged onto the site to read the emails she received there. There were only four new messages. Looking at the mail screen, Nicolette smiled to herself, "looks like ali is finally getting the message." The first message was sent at 6:23am from James, it read "Mistress, I am scared. I have imagined finding someone as intelligent, kind, beautiful, and compassionate as you to dominate me for several years. I began this quest over thirty years ago after mourning the passing of my wife. I have been selective all my life never wanting to settle and at last, it seems that my patience has paid off. When I first contacted you four years ago, I never thought you would give me a second glance. I have been trying to convince myself for the past three years that I do not have this yearning from deep within my soul to serve you with all my being. I have had the normal, and not so normal, sexual fantasies that a man my age has of a completely delicious woman of your age. But more than that, I have wanted to just sit with you and have a meal...or simply a glass of scotch. I get excited, mentally and physically, when I see an email notification from you and my employees all say my entire demeanor changes when I take a call from you during my day. I debated and fussed all summer about driving the four hours to see you. I have promised, made plans, and canceled them enough times that I know you think of me as nothing more than a penpal. This morning, I woke up with determination. I have booked a hotel room at the Book Cadillac hotel, packed my bag, and after sending this I will depart. I anticipate getting to Detroit late morning. I will see a couple friends and would like you meet you. I know this is short notice, but it was only way that I could force myself to take the chance. I look forward to hearing you and until then I will wait on pins and needles." Nicolette picked up her cell phone and dialed James. The phone rang and went to voicemail. She shrugged and hung up. The second email was from Heinrich; it contained an Amazon gift code for $500 with no message. Nicolette responded with a simple two-word phrase of impolite thanks, "Um, ok." Nicolette finds Heinrich desire to gift her things without a message to be rude and impersonal and she does not prefer them. The third message was from david, a submissive with whom Nicolette met through a non-kink networking event, that she had played with off and on for six years when their schedules would align. The message read "Are you going to MsKat and kel's party? Was hoping to be your pet for that evening and any other evening you have need of me soon; I am in need of some corporal that only you can give me. I know I am horrible about keeping in touch, but we both remain too busy." david was busy, but thoughtful; he sent Nicolette a bouquet of flowers and an orchid when Charles passed. Nicolette responded, "I am sure I can make time on Wednesday after the gym and grocery shopping. What is your schedule like on hump day?" The final message was from Ryan inquiring on how Nicolette was settling into the new home and if she has forgotten about him. Nicolette laughed as she ate another large handful of the berries and responded, "How can I forget about my favorite chair? As for the house, I am mostly settled in. It has been a long few months. I have so many changes in my life and there are times when I look up and several weeks have passed. Thanks for always checking on me." Nicolette decided to respond to the message from James, "I received your message. I do hope you made it to the hotel safely. I tried to call. Drop me a line or a call when you get this." After deleting the email she had read, Nicolette had three new messages. She immediately opened the new email from James it read "Hello, Mistress. I just arrived to my room at the Book Cadillac hotel about twenty minutes ago. I left my phone in the car as I am roaming in this part of the world though I am sure I can probably pick up Rogers Mobile here as well. I have internet and was hoping you would send me a note. May I please take you to dinner tonight?" Nicolette weighed her desire to not leave her house against wanting to have a nice meal with James. Literally scratching her head, Nicolette responded, "I can meet you for a dinner, but I do not want anything über fancy like Roast. Are you comfortable driving in the city? There is a nice Thai restaurant not too far from there called Sala Thai that I enjoy. We can meet there in forty minutes." The other two messages were from persons whom Nicolette did not know; one message was complimentary to which she responded politely her usual message of thanks, but no thanks. The other message was a random male dominant, so he claimed, that demanded that Nicolette should serve him because "that is a woman's place." Nicolette read and deleted the message without a response. James responded that he was not comfortable driving in the City, but he would try and get directions if Sala Thai was a requirement of dinner. Nicolette responded, "Not a requirement. I can get fancy enough to go to Roast. I do not want you to feel lost in the city. Give me an hour."

Nicolette walked up the stairs and took a quick shower. She picked a maxi dress and heels to wear, pulled her hair up into a neat bun, and put on some lip gloss. Nicolette then grabbed her purse and checked her watch. "Perfect," Nicolette exclaimed after noted she had twenty minutes to get to Roast; the restaurant was fifteen minutes away. Nicolette pulled up to the valet parking at Roast with seven minutes to spare. She walked into the restaurant and James was standing there with a bouquet of flowers for Nicolette. James was an attractive man; a mix of Pierce Brosnan as 007 and Peter Falk. He has dark hair, curly salt and pepper hair, and the most amazing six pack. His spin on machismo was appealing; he frequently has women approach him both in the lifestyle and in the vanilla, non-kink, world. She hugged him hello and they were shown to their table. James stumbled over his words once they were seated at the table, "I…I cannot. I am surprised that you came. I, mean, I knew you were going to meet me. I…you are so stunning. I know we have done video chats, but you are sitting here more beautiful than I expected. Wow." Nicolette smiled at James, "You realize that I am just a human person. Perhaps, an amazing, human person, but still human and I am still the person who you have been speaking to for literally four years." James took a deep breath and relaxed noticeably, "You know, I have not been this nervous in decades. Thank you for making me feel youthful." The waitstaff approached the table and asked for their drink orders. Nicolette and James, both, got a scotch on the rocks. "Thank you for the flowers; they are quite lovely", Nicolette started, "How was your drive in?" "The drive was full of anticipation. I drove faster than the speed limit a few times, but I got here without a ticket though." "You seem to be relaxing – that is good," Nicolette tried to reassure James. The waitstaff returned with their drinks and took their dinner orders. "I wish I could have you for dessert, but I am glad that at least I can enjoy your smile," James complimented Nicolette. She laughed aloud, "you are the only person I know that can make a cheap come on sound sweet." "In my generation, we called that being smooth. But your laugh, does that mean I have a chance at dessert?" James says with a sly smile. The two settle into conversations that they have shared for the past several years picking up just like old friends. After enjoying their dinner and commenting on their dishes and tasting small portions of the other's meal, Nicolette and James sat and chatted for almost an hour. Repeatedly sending away the waitstaff as they did not need any additional assistance; they were just enjoying the company of the other person. "So, where did we land on dessert?" James asked, hope in his voice. Nicolette looked James closely in the eye and said, "Dessert? You want to taste me? Perhaps that will get you here more often." "Touché. Let me get the check. I hope to see you again soon and I will do what I need to make that happen. Perhaps I can have you out to Niagara." James paid the check and escorted Nicolette out to the valet stand to fetch her car. James had the charges added to his hotel room, kissed Nicolette sweetly on the cheek, and thanked her for her time and consideration. Nicolette returned home and placed the flowers in water. She then ascended the stairs and changed into lounge clothing. Nicolette was tired due to lack of sleep the night before, so she grabbed her tablet and climbed into bed. She turned on the television and checked email.

There were five unread messages on collarme including one received from James ten minutes earlier. Nicolette opened the message from david who verified he was free on Wednesday but did not want to limit his time with Nicolette and asked her for the grocery list which he will shop while she goes to the gym. Nicolette sent her list to david and she commented that she will text her new address on Tuesday. There was a message thanking Nicolette for her polite rejection. The message from James was complimentary and reiterated that she was invited to visit Niagara whenever Nicolette wanted. Nicolette thanked him for a lovely evening and informed James that she was safely at home. Ryan responded that he wanted to see Nicolette and he sent his schedule of availability. Nicolette decided that she will check her schedule and respond later. The last message was from the same rude dominant from before; the message was vulgar and ruder than before. Nicolette blocked him and deleted the message. Nicolette yawned widely and turned off the television, put the tablet on the nightstand, and went to bed. Sadly, Charles' name still glowed faintly on the ceiling above.

The rest of the weekend flew by with Nicolette trying to catch up on her sleeping. She has established a routine for her life that was working outside of her not having a particular person in her life. The work week was typical, as well, with nothing new to note. Nicolette was working on a portfolio of cases for the firm and was impressed by the variety she was able to experience with no two days being identical. Nicolette, in addition to working every day and seeing Adrianna and Jude a couple days a week, was working out after work every day. She was trying to establish a habit as well as make Dr. Smithson happy. Wednesday arrived and Nicolette left work slightly early recalling her date with david. She went to the gym and made her way through her upper body workout. After driving home and showering, Nicolette prepared dinner. Her diet was never unhealthy and true to form she picked a healthy meal that was low in fat and high in Ω-3 fatty acids. After finishing dinner and brushing her teeth, Nicolette checks her watch. david will be arriving at any moment with her groceries. She selects a matching bra and panty set, then a flowing chemise to go over them. She enjoyed the way her body moved in the chemise- her breasts and hips clinging to the soft fabric drawing in attention. Nicolette ran her hands over the shoes on the rack against the wall, debating which to don. First she tries a strappy three-inch sandal, but decides to be more casual. After trying four pair of shoes of varying heights and styles, Nicolette slides into her comfortable, well-worn house shoes. She glances at her wrist; it is 8:30pm. Right on time, there is a buzz at the door. Nicolette heads to the back door to unlock it. david carried the groceries into the house and placed the bags onto the counter. david is the epitome of tall, dark, and handsome. He has a muscular 6'2" frame, defined cheekbones, and chiseled chest. His cocoa complexion is radiant with hints of red. In addition to his amazingly good looks, david was smart and accomplished. He graduated top of his class at University of Pennsylvania Wharton Business School and is now the COO of a Fortune 500 company based in Southfield. david and Nicolette complimented each other; both smart, attractive black persons. david finished bringing all the bags into the house. He promptly kneels in front of her, his head bowed towards the ground. Nicolette walks to the counter and inspects the groceries. "Oh, they had the key limes I wanted for the potluck event on Saturday," Nicolette expressed thumbing through the bags, "oh and the red quinoa from Bob's Red Mill. They were out for, what, like a month." david slightly nods at her inquiries knowing that Nicolette was addressing herself more than him. She completes her inspection of the groceries. "Did you forget the wine I requested, david?" she asks with a slightly nod of disappointment in her voice. "Ma'am, they did not have either of the vineyards that you requested in red or white," david replies. "Shame." Nicolette responds, "Run to the cellar and bring a bottle from bin 32." david stands slowly and proceeds to the wine cellar to retrieve the requested wine. He returns and opens the bottle. He pours the wine into a decanter and places a glass next to it. He glances at his watch and returns to his kneeling position in front of Nicolette. Walking around him slowly, placing her hand softly on his shoulder, Nicolette pulls his head upwards forcing him to look into her eyes. Peering down at him, she states," you can put the groceries away, now." david murmurs, "Thank you Ma'am." He rises slowly to ensure he does not pull himself from her grip and begins to place the groceries in their proper place. As he is unpacking the groceries, he also begins to clean up the remaining dishes from the dinner Nicolette prepared for herself. He packs the leftover salmon, couscous, and asparagus into one counter to make them easily portable. Nicolette retires to playroom where she lights candles and awaits david. When he completes the tasks, he checks his watch to verify the wine had enough time to breathe. He pours a glass of wine and walks to the playroom. david hands Nicolette the glass of wine and kneels in front of her. "Such a good boy," Nicolette says in a singsong voice. She takes a sip and places the glass on the table. Nicolette motions for david to stand and she removes his shirt taking care to unbutton each button. Her hands run slowly and deliberately over his chest, her nails scratching along his skin. david moans his pleasure leaning into her gasp, yearning for more pain. Nicolette slides the shirt off his shoulders and allows it to drape from his hands binding his arms allowing him only a 45° angle of clearance on each side. She angles his body to the bench wear she positions him face up and lying flat, with his shirt pinned under his torso he cannot reach his hands forward. The definition of his abdomen is more apparent with him horizontal and Nicolette admires his frame as she loosens the button and zipper of his fly exposing david's pelvic region. Picking up one of the candles she lit earlier, Nicolette moves next to his chest only 27 inches from his torso and drops a drop of wax onto his chest. david jumps upon impact of the wax burning his skin releasing a groan. Nicolette drops three more drops of wax in sequence along his midline while david wiggles and jerks with each impact. david grunts loudly and groans, "Thank you, Mistress." Nicolette runs her free hand nearby the wax, allowing her nails to scratch him as she goes, david moans in ecstasy increasing his tone as she passes. Nicolette continues the path of her nails towards his pubic crest, dropping wax every few seconds as she traces his body. david was fairly hairless so the removal of the wax is mostly painless so Nicolette ensures to enjoy the wax droplets as they are the height of her sadistic thrill. Nicolette had twelve different colors of wax that she used on david and as she covered his torso with drops. As Nicolette's free space on david's torso started to thin, there was zero thrill for either of them to layer wax on top of wax. So she removed david's pants and underwear completely on his urging exposing his penis, which was dancing and erect from the pain he enjoyed. As his penis swayed and dripped with precome, david exclaimed "Mistress, can you please put some wax on my member?" Nicolette thought briefly and decided to make his shaft look like a Chianti candle. She went to her linen closet and gathered some additional items for the new scene. She took care to clean up the oozing head of his head; it was swollen and he groaned his thanks to her touch. Nicolette dabbed a drop of aloe cream to the urethral opening to prevent wax from clogging the urethra. She, also, rubbed a thin layer to the length of his member as david arched into her touch. "Your touch is electric, Mistress. It is so satiating that you know my body." Knowing that the skin of the penis was sensitive, Nicolette had to blow on the wax as it fell on his member to prevent burns. The first drop made david contract his body into the bench and grunt his pleasure and surprise at heat. Nicolette started with white drops; it was one of the hottest colors for body wax. His erection did not decrease due to the unexpected pain from the intense heat of the wax on his penis. After the base layer of wax was complete, Nicolette did continue to drop beads of wax as the aesthetic was appealing. She continued first with blue, her favorite color, and followed that with yellow and purple. Nicolette was allowing the red, orange, and light blue to collect an entire pool of wax so that she could run it down the length of his shaft. Once she felt she had a good multi-colored base, Nicolette started to run long lines of wax from his head to his balls. The wax worked into the gaps in the drops and settled on his testicles. The wax was still quite warm as it trickled down his skin; david moaned and wiggled as the wax tingled against his skin. He was surprised at some of the gaps in the wax causing his erection to throb. It took Nicolette almost forty minutes to completely accomplish the Chianti candle in david's crotch. "This is picture perfect", Nicolette said looking at her work and admiring it. "Then you should capture it, Ma'am," david commented with a smirk, "Can you also send the photo to me as well?" Nicolette located her camera and took a few photos in varying light of her artwork and forwarded them to david. Once all the candle wax was used and the photos taken, Nicolette began the usually fun process of pulling the wax from david body. There were a few places, especially near his nipples and penis that had hair that elicited a yelp or two for Nicolette's delight. david asked for a photo of wax cascading down his dick before Nicolette removed the wax and she captured the full ten inches of wax in brilliant color. Disposing of the used wax into the trash in the room, Nicolette rubbed aloe vera lotion into david's chest, stomach, and genitals. His already relaxed demeanor became nearly a stupor of joy. david laid on the spanking bench for five or ten minutes after Nicolette informed him that she was done with aloe. Once he did sit up he thanked her profusely. "Are you done? You do not want to be caned," Nicolette inquired as she was used to more than one scene whenever they played, "I have a new crop from the saddlery." david smiled at Nicolette, "I have never felt this good after playing in my entire life. I know I have been hesitant of wax play because of the burns I got from the woman before you, but Oh My God that was cathartic! I probably would have come if I did not think it would have stopped the scene. Thank you deeply." Nicolette nodded her understanding, "If you can, try and come tonight. I did put a dab of Vaseline at the urethra opening, but I cannot guarantee that there is not a blockage." "Trust me; I will come tonight and probably a few other times to this scene's memory. Fuck, you are hot!" Nicolette handed david his pants, "You say that now, wait until you see if I ruined your pants." Nicolette laughed as david dressed slowly. He hugged her tightly and thanked her yet again. Nicolette extinguished all the candles in the room and walked david to the back door where he departed. Nicolette wiped down the furniture with antimicrobial and polished the wood and leather. She checked her clock and noted it was nearly time for bed. Nicolette showered and retired to her own masturbation from the memories of the scene with david. Just as Nicolette was climbing into bed she received a text from david again thanking her for her time and the orgasm he just experienced, the text included a large puddle of semen with few bits of wax on his abdomen. Nicolette responded that he is always entertaining and that she hopes he enjoys his evening. Nicolette and her dolphin vibrator capped the evening quickly.

Nicolette was awaken at 4:30am by the sound of her neighbors. She glances at the ceiling for a few moments hoping the chaos on the street will subside. After what seem like an eternity, Nicolette glances at the clock; it was 4:33am. Whatever commotion on the street did not appear to be ending soon therefore Nicolette arose and prepared herself for to the gym. Nicolette washed her face and brushed her teeth all while plotting against the apparent dope house across the street. Nicolette growled to herself that she will be glad when it gets cool so she does not have to deal with them as they seem only to be around during the warm months. She grabbed her bag and headed off to the gym; at least working out before work will afford Nicolette ample free time in the evening. Nicolette arrived at the gym right before it was scheduled to open but the door was unlocked. Nicolette hit the floor with her Pandora blasting in her ears. As soon as Nicolette walked onto the floor, she was addressed by Tony. He was smiling and waved as Nicolette ran on the elliptical stair stepper; she usually walks. Nicolette average just over a nine minute mile and burned a few hundred calories; she did not realize how much pent up frustration she had already this week but she reveled in doing her personal best. Nicolette stretched once she dismounted the stair stepper and went to the weights. It was an arm day so Nicolette rotated through exercises for biceps, triceps, abdominal, deltoids, and latissimus dorsi in thirty minute circuit with only 5 seconds of rest between repetitions and 30 seconds, at most, between exercises. Nicolette felt that pushing herself harder on limited sleep would help her power through the day. She greeted a few of the regular ladies at the gym; they asked if Nicolette had plans in the evening since early morning workouts were not common for her. "No, my neighbors were extra this morning so I decided to not waste the daylight. How are you ladies?" Nicolette asked instead of fully breathing through the bicep curls she was performing. "Good. When are you going to come running with us?" The eldest of the ladies answered. "I do not run. I am not built for running between my ample bosom and sloped knees that is a recipe for disaster! I am trying to join a Fall volleyball league if you know of anything," Nicolette responded while walking to a new machine. "You are good at volleyball. I recall seeing you on the court downstairs a few weeks ago; did you join the league here?" Denise, an acquaintance of Nicolette's from the gym asking as Nicolette continued to power through her circuit. "No, I did not join the summer league here, but I take full advantage of the nets when they are up. I miss the sport. Played intramurals at Michigan and fucked around in high school," Nicolette answered through strained breath as she rested for her thirty seconds, "They do not have a Fall league." "I see. I think Come. Play. Detroit. does have a fall league. I have a friend that plays in it, but you have to have your own team. I can ask her if she needs another play. What position do you play?" The eldest of the ladies answered. "I am not a blocker," Nicolette laughed, "I play setter and leo. I would love to know more. Denise has my contact information." Nicolette started another exercise in her cycle program after waving good-bye to her companions. Once she completed the circuit, Nicolette was stretching next to Tony. "You are here early," Tony greeted her, "You must have plans later." "No, I do not have any plans. I was awaken by my neighbors and could not go back to sleep. I did not have laundry or cleaning so I decided to work out before work." Nicolette commented with a shrug. "Good plan. Frees up your day. It was good seeing you," Tony said as he gathered his things and cleaned his mat. "You too. Have a good one." Nicolette completed her stretches, cleaned her space, and showered.

Walking out of the gym, Nicolette felt every step as she pushed herself hard at the gym. It was a great burn and she noticed that her clothes were fitting loosely. "Maybe, if I continue the circuit and do two-a-days three days a week, I could strive for overweight instead of obese." Nicolette said aloud to herself. Nicolette climbed into her vehicle after dropping her gym bag in the trunk and headed up I-75 to the firm. Nicolette was able to single-handedly expand the firm's business by providing approved continuing education modules through the firm's website. Therefore, Nicolette has been given permission to expand her team and set out to hire two junior associates and a paralegal. She arranged to start interviews that morning and had four candidates arriving for first rounds. The first candidate had zero real-world experience in scientific law through his resume stated that he had five years; Nicolette discovered the lie when he referenced her mentor from Michigan, but he did not know his other graduate students or his administrative assistant. The second candidate also attended Michigan and she was six years Nicolette's junior. Becca was a perfect for a junior associate for Nicolette as she had an open mind, was eloquent, and had four years' experience researching for patent applications for a drug discovery pharmaceutical company. Nicolette scheduled a second interview for Becca to meet both Dich and Julie. The third candidate called and canceled his interview fifteen minutes prior to its scheduled start. He did ask to reschedule, but the office assistants knew that Nicolette would want to make that discussion herself. The fourth candidate arrived ten minutes early for his interview and was dressed quite sharply. He was polite and his references were impressive. Nicolette asked him several hard questions and he handled the hypothetical situations in ways that would be appealing to the problem as well as Nicolette. She was surprised that Jim was only applying for a junior associate's position as he had as much, if not more, experience than Nicolette. When questioned about the decision to not try for a partnership in a larger firm, Jim stated that he cannot do long hours or the stress that comes with the larger firms and partnerships therein. He enjoyed working independently for six years after being a junior partnership at a large firm, but he could not sustain the aggressive advertising needed to keep his expected salary. Jim was honest and could help Nicolette expand her portfolio at the firm even more; therefore Jim was also scheduled for a second interview with Dich and Julie. After the fourth interview, Nicolette enjoyed a salad with chicken, avocado, cucumber, tomatoes, and lettuce. Nicolette decided to browse through her Amazon wish limit to see what was left available for purchase; she had the $500 from Heinrich to spend. There were some boots that she had been eyeing hoping it would drop below $250 and she noticed that the Pleaser Fantasia 2020 Black Chrome boot was $256. "Oooh, close enough", Nicolette purred before adding them to her cart. As she looked at the other shoes and items in her wish list, Nicolette picked few other items including a petticoat. Nicolette quickly spent the $500 from Heinrich, but was excited about the boots she had been wanting for almost a year. They would arrive in time for the party at Kat and kal's party.

Nicolette mulled through the rest of the day including a video deposition for one of her cases and researching embryonic stem cell treatments in the US and the world looking for precedent for the case her firm was considering. The deposition was for patent in neuroscaffolding. The complex system of a bioabsorbable matrix to help with spinal cord injuries of paralysis patients was new and the information needed to secure multiple patents was immense. Nicolette has to understand the entire process including the way the human body regenerates neurons and neural pathways. She spent time each week learning new topics in chemistry, biology, physics, and statistics. She felt that she needed to understand the jargon and science in order to be successful at the firm. The case was extremely interesting for Nicolette as her brother, Steve, had worked at the stem cell core at University of Michigan in undergrad under Dr. Mattie O'Morse. Nicolette knew if she needed, she could get factual information from Steve without disclosing any information about the case. In the case, the facility at Wayne State University was being sued because a patient was denied care using stem cell to aid in the reconstruction of heart valves because of US law had not yet caught up to the scientific break-through. The physicians and researchers at Wayne State University were joint faculty members on the University of Michigan stem cell core. In the case, the patient felt that the physicians were not using all available options to help treat their congenital, fatal heart defect. Nicolette had just finished looking into the details of some of the success stories of using embryonic stem cells from the umbilical cord to promote repair of the heart muscles as well activation of the adult stem cells in the patient. Nicolette has found cases in South America, European Union, Thailand, and Canada. Nicolette compiled the cases together and forwarded them to her client to allow them to provide information on the similarities and differences between the patients. Nicolette also found a few studies which cautioned against activation on the adult stem cells as they do not produce the healthy cells needed to repair the damage that was present. She stretched her back and shoulders and walked the halls of the firm to increase the circulation in her legs. She thought about the candidates for the positions on her team as she walked. Nicolette was the only black person at the firm and one of only two women attorneys. Granted the firm is small, Nicolette thought, but having one minority and only two women was not ideal for her. Nicolette had additional interviews to conduct throughout the week and she hoped to be able to add more diversity to the firm through her team. Nicolette completed her rounds with a brief conversation with Julie about the firm's case load and priorities.

The drive home for Nicolette was quiet. She did not even turn on the radio as she was reflecting on the events of the day and the plans for the weekend. Nicolette had to complete all her household chores by Friday night so that she could accomplish what she needs in order to attend the end of the summer party. Nicolette arrived home and walked in the house feeling mentally exhausted. She changed into something more comfortable and lay down on her bed for a few moments just to relax before jumping back into the go-go-go style of her day. Nicolette was awaken at 7:00pm when her alarm went off to remind her to take her medication. "Shit," Nicolette moans to herself, "I guess I was much more tired than I thought I was." Nicolette tried to shake the cobwebs from her head. Nicolette takes her meds and checks the refrigerator for something easy for dinner. "Fuck! Vegetables, fruits, and bunch of stuff that takes effort. Healthy smealthy." Nicolette looks over the massive amount of ingredients and notices that nothing is appetizing. She closes the doors of the fridge and grabs a pot and makes popcorn. It may not be a complete meal, but it is better than not eating and going to bed. Nicolette snacks on the popcorn while scrolling through her email. Once she read all her mail, she logs into collarme.com and sees that she has 14 unread messages. Nicolette browses the senders and decides that she can read the messages another day. Nicolette eats a few more handfuls of popcorn and straightens up the kitchen and heads back to bed.

The rest of the week flies by with Nicolette going through the rest of the round one interviews, providing a position statement on the stem cell case to the plantiff's attorneys, and drafting one of the patent applications for the neuroscaffolding. Nicolette, also, finally got to her email on collarme.com which had 22 unread messages. She was able to clear more than half of them by either thanking the writer for their compliments or by her standard thanks, but no thank you message. One message was from Ryan providing his schedule for the next month asking for time with her. Another message was from James asking to provide Nicolette with a hotel at Niagara because he wants her to visit. Nicolette responds with her availability and asks for a list of tentative hotels for her review. The second email from James was hoping Nicolette was well as he sees that she has not been online often in the past week. There was a message from uwe coordinating the trip to Detroit. Nicolette answered the necessary logistic questions and he sent some creative photos about his kinks. Nicolette commented on the photos and asked if he had ever taken any nudes and gave some specific types of photos she wanted to see. There was an email from kel with logistical information for the party on Saturday. david sent an email to coordinate for the party on Saturday since he is attending as Nicolette's play thing. Nicolette finished outlining a plan with david. She ended the week with a hearty dinner and folding laundry.

Chapter Seven

Nicolette stirred late on Saturday for a game day, sleeping in until almost eight. She felt so well rested that the tasks before the party seemed too few. Nicolette took her time getting to the gym as it was one of only four things scheduled. Her workout was not an intense one, but it was enough to break a good sweat and keep her on path to her health goals. After the gym, Nicolette took a long, hot bath; she soaked in the tub for almost twenty minutes in an effort to soften her skin. Nicolette prepared a tub of coconut milk and Epsom salt. She emerged from the tub and dried herself.

Taking care to massage lotion into her newly washed skin, Nicolette spent time looking at herself both longingly and critically in the mirror. It was part of her health routine; looking at the changes in her muscle tone and altering the scope of her regime as needed. There was a new slight dig at her pelvis where the hip meets the crest. Nicolette loved that dip and enjoyed seeing it form on her own body; "look at you getting all sexy, Nici!" With a smile upon her face, Nicolette could not find anything negative to state about her body as she finished massaging lotion into her skin.

Next on Nicolette's list was packing her toy bag for the party. The party was moved to kel's condo in Livonia so Nicolette could not carry her cross, but would be able to take the smotherbox. Considering that she would be playing with david, Nicolette packed several implements for administering pain. david was a total pain slut who brought out the best in Nicolette's sadistic side. She picked out a couple floggers, three canes, and two crops. Nicolette also packed a bag of clothes pins and some silk rope for CBT. CBT was not a favorite for david, but would allow play in that realm if already elated from other pain play. In all the years that david played with Nicolette he has never had to use his safe-word so he trusted her completely. Finally, Nicolette packed some nail polish and essential oils for the men who would attend the party that have foot fetishes. The bag and smotherbox would not be too cumbersome for Nicolette to carry together to her car but since david is meeting Nicolette at the party as he would be able to carry it for her.

Nicolette went to the kitchen to prepare and eat something before the drive to Ann Arbor. She wanted to eat something healthy but not overly abundant because she did not want to have gas while she was facesitting later. She picked a simple chorizo breakfast burrito as it would be filling without too much weight on her stomach. Nicolette begun chopping vegetables and browning the meat. In the oven, she warmed the wheat tortilla. She chopped green, red, and yellow peppers, onions, and added them to a pan with oil olive. An egg was beaten added to the cooked vegetables and tossed with the cooked chorizo. Nicolette rolled the meat, vegetables, cheese, and egg into the warmed tortilla. Nicolette took the plate to her dressing room where she ate as she donned the maize and blue. Nicolette pulled her hair up and put on a ball cap. Once sufficiently ready and dressed for the Blue, she finished her burrito. She then cleaned the kitchen and headed to Ann Arbor.

Nicolette met her college friends for a tailgate. It was the first game of the season. It was a chill tailgate and boring blowout game. However, the buzz of the new season was evident. There were excited people all around the stadium, high-fiving each other and smiling wherever you looked. Nicolette stayed to watch the band; she always enjoyed the pomp and circumstance around the Michigan Marching Band. She left after watching their entire post game performance, as usual. She headed back to the highway, heading northeast to avoid the normal post-game traffic. Nicolette got home only an hour after the game and headed to her dressing room to get cleaned up and turned around for the party.

Nicolette looked over the three options she had selected for the evening trying to decide what to wear. There was a corset, decorative cut out underwear, and petticoat option. There was a sheer night shirt, thong, leggings, and thigh high boot option. Finally, there was a spiked bra, leather jacket, and liquid hot pants option. Usually, Nicolette's body shaming and perceived issues dictate her outfits, but she was feeling particularly sexy this evening. She tried on all three and loved each, so she sat on the ottoman in distress. She checked her cell phone and had four messages from ladies who were attending the party. As she scrolled through their messages she found one with a photo that cemented for Nicolette. "Corset, liquid leggings, and thigh high boots. I will take the best from each outfit and be FIERCE!" Nicolette dressed while she put away the items she did not

77

select. Placing the once worn undergarments into the laundry; "ten minutes or ten hours; it is all the same." Once dressed, Nicolette did one last check over her outfit and was quite pleased, "Those tits are right and tight." She grabbed her toy bag and the smotherbox and packed the car. Nicolette decided to grab some snacks and head to the party.

Nicolette arrived at the party right around 9:00pm. As she parked and started to pull her items from her car, david walked up. "MzNicolette, please allow me to carry those items for you." Surprised that he was waiting in his car for her to arrive, Nicolette smiled, "of course, david. I will grab the food bags from the car. Thanks. I have some surprises for you in there." They approached the house and entered the garage to go into the house. "Hello, lovely people", Nicolette sung as she walked up the stairs with david trailing behind carrying the items from the car. Kat walked to the top of the stairs to see Nicolette and david walking up; Kat waited for her to reach the top of the stairs to hug her. Kat then turned to the room which had five other women and seven men and announced, "This is Mz. Nicolette. She is a spitfire with loads of furniture and skill. And..." she turns to david. Nicolette added, "And this is david. He is a yummy little maso who craves to please." Nicolette smiles at david. He adds, "And I belong to MzNicolette so please get her permission before approaching me. We have a code word." Nicolette gives david a look so that he knows he went a bit too far, but she recalls his experiences with dominants in which he thought he was not protected enough. david set-up the smotherbox and picked out a chair for MzNicolette and got her silent approval and sat on the floor next to the said chair. Nicolette sat in the chair and took in the scenes that were going on including Mistress Tina doing cupping with her pet named kevin. Tina is very experienced with cupping and is doing a combination of fire/wax play and cupping. She only uses glass cups. MsWhip was there and she was playing a switch, a person who is both dominant and submissive, named Brian. Brian is an extreme foot fetishist and he was massaging Whip's feet. Coleen was a switch who was sitting on the couch with Bridgette when Nicolette came in. Bridgette was now doing some cutting and bloodletting on both kyle and switch/dominant Henry. Henry was trying to learn the skill and Bridgette was known for her skill in the SE Michigan/NW Ohio area. Mistress Rosa was doing ball busting on michael by kicking him in his balls and when he takes a rest she pulls on each of his individual testicles. timothy and phillip were sitting around looking to be of help to one of the ladies. Kat was playing hostess in between scenes with kel, timothy, phillip, Brian, and Henry. Nicolette had david get into the smothebox where she sat on his face, much to the delight of the crowd as most of them have never seen one before. This was david's first time in the box and he was not certain that he would enjoy it, but the almost immediate dancing of his penis let Nicolette know he was very much into the scene. To further intense the scene for david, Nicolette placed clothes pins on his nipples. david moaned his approval almost immediately squirming against her leggings as Nicolette flicked his nipples. Nicolette allowed david a much longer breath than anyone she normally sits on because he was not accustom to facesitting. phillip asked if he could massage Nicolette's feet and worship them while she sat on david's face. Nicolette explained that she would allow phillip to paint her nails when she is done sitting on david. david grunted from the lack attention but Nicolette flipped a clothes pin off his nipple making him buck into the smotherbox. Nicolette laughed with glee and scratched her hands over his stomach and pinched his nipple that did not have the clothes pin on it any longer. Nicolette was enjoying her scene while also watching kel be trampled by Kat. Nicolette admired Kat and kel. They were the perfect combination of vanilla and kink in Nicolette's opinion. Kat was a physician that also got her degrees from Michigan, but she is slightly older than Nicolette. She was practicing in oncology at Henry Ford Hospital and she was both a mentor in kink and a good friend of Nicolette. To say that Kat was beautiful does not do her justice; she was hands-down stunning, petite but powerful with an infectious smile. kel was a construction foreman; he was the perfect mix of brawn and brain. He had a degree in engineering from Wayne State University and degree in construction management from Eastern Michigan University. He was a body builder who has won Mr. Michigan and placed second in the Arnold Classic in the past. Watching their scene was like poetry in motion; their chemistry was apparent to any on-looker. Kat carried herself with poise and even when crushing kel's cock and balls under her heeled foot she commanded admiration from all. Nicolette learned in their previous outings that Kat and kel started in the lifestyle years ago; when she was new onto the scene, he was an experienced slave in search of a dominant. They were introduced through a mutual friend and they took a shine to one another almost instantly. Nicolette watched half in awe, almost longing, and half with the eyes of a student as Kat walked over kel's torso, back, and legs. Nicolette's eyes were briefly pulled from Kat and kel when she heard the crack of a whip. MsWhip was using a short bullwhip on phillip who was standing spread eagle against the cross that kel set up for the occasion. MsWhip's form was different from Nicolette's as she used her biceps for power and did not turn or twirl the whip. MsWhip was exclaiming various insults at Phillip as she worked over his body; for example MsWhip asked him "are you always such a whiny little bitch? I am barely striking you and you are jumping and whimpering." phillip was jumping and moving from the whip. MsWhip was laughing and running her hands over the welts on his skin as she continued her questions and inquiries, "Does this hurt? I am trying really hard here to not get bored with this scene. phillip, can you take more? Are you man enough to take all that I can give you or are you going to bitch out?" phillip did not answer and MsWhip hit him with a series on his back and legs. phillip tensed up with each strike and finally murmured, "Yellow. I am sorry

80

MsWhip, but that is too intense. I need a break. Thank you, but yellow." MsWhip put down the implement and helped phillip from the cross to the couch. He sat down gingerly onto the couch and again thanked MsWhip for her attentiveness. Bridgette was finishing up her scene of bloodletting and she and Henry were cleaning up their area. Nicolette was, also, finishing up her scene she got off david's face who was quite attentive to her especially with the clothes pins on his nipples. He smiled at Nicolette and commented that he did not know that he would enjoy the pain from the clothes pin that much. Nicolette just smiled with him in response and instructed him to catch his breath. While david was resting, Nicolette signaled for phillip to massage her feet if he was still interested to which he jumped at the opportunity. He removed her left boot and begun working his fingers around her toes and deep into the muscles. Nicolette moaned her approval. david sat on the floor nearby and awaited his next order. Kat finished up her scene with kel and noticed that there were a number of people not playing. She decided on a game that they can play. "I would like all the guys who are playing the game to line up over here in front of the television. The game is simple; we are going to blindfold you and have you on your hands and knees. We have this obstacle course set up and each task will be timed. The boy who completes the course the fastest will win a prize from the Dominant of their choice, with her permission of course. The tasks include bringing Mistress Tina to orgasm with foot play; she gives amazing direction whether you want to use your tongue or your hands. Taking MstrKat on a pony ride", she says as she points to the saddle Nicolette helped her purchase, "Next in the Play Olympics, you will endure ball busting with Mistress Rosa; she will define the time, but nothing to exceed fifteen minutes. To give you something simple and since you will already be on your knees, Coleen and Bridgette will require your upmost attention on their ropes course. Coleen was a girl scout and a Navy veteran so she

81

will get you right and tight while Bridgette, who has been doing artistic rigging and rope work for the past two decades, will tie you in some creative scenes voted on by the other Ladies. Finally, MsWhip and Nicolette have their implements of torture. MsWhip and Nicolette both have their favorite bullwhip on hand and will perform a tag team which will either bring you to a frenzy of ecstasy or to your knees in pain. Each event has a maximum score to be determined by the dominants. They will, also, determine your score. At the end, the boy with the highest score will win." Nicolette and MsWhip started discussing how they wanted to construct their dual scene while the other dominants also started setting up their events as well. Kat had told them ahead of time that she wanted to have a competition so they had the needed supplies for the Olympics. david walked over to Nicolette and asked for her permission to participate in the Olympics, "Excuse me, MzNicolette? I do not know how well I will do, but I wanted to play. May I please?" Nicolette smiled and nodded her approval. She returned to her conversation and finalized the scene with MsWhip. All the guys present participated in the Olympics and Coleen also participated in a few of the events. She wanted to see both sides of some of the scenes; half of the Ladies that were now identified as dominant at the party had been submissive in the past. Nicolette, however, only identified as dominant and has never been submissive in a BDSM relationship. Similar to a gymnastics meet, the boys started on different events and rotated through all the events thereby everyone was occupied and playing. Nicolette took a few moments to steal glances at the other scenes while she was allowing Whip to take the lead with the sub under their control. The looks on the faces of her companions was priceless while the subs were moaning, groaning, and in some cases screaming in response to the scenes. Nicolette has been keeping an eye on david when she started whipping michael. He was a huge pain slut and craved intense pain; Whip had tired trying to get him into this subspace. michael was blasé about the repeated thudding-stringing pain of the whip. Nicolette alternated pinpoint, precise whips with digging her nails into his skin. It surprised michael and he groaned his pleasure in the sensations. michael slipped easily into subspace after the combination of pinpoint, intense pain and raking, digging pain. Nicolette was starting to slip into her own domspace when she heard david yell red. Nicolette quickly turned to see that Rosa was standing over him with her foot cocked ready to kick him again. Nicolette turned and made eye contact with Whip who begun imitating the combination Nicolette established with michael. Nicolette made her way across the room to where she kneeled down next to david and while stroking his head she whispered words of reassurance that she was present. He murmured a few things in response to Nicolette and slowly made his way to his knees. He laid his head on her shoulder and continued listening to the things that Nicolette was saying. Rosa exclaimed to Nicolette, "C'mon you are babying him which is why he cannot take anything from others. Either you let him play or have him sit out." Nicolette ignored Rosa, for the time, and continued to comfort and reassure david. Once she was content that he was ok, Nicolette ran her hands over his head and stood to address Rosa. "You must have lost your fucking mind. He told you that he does not enjoy or usually participate in ball busting and asked you take it easily upon him and your response was to kick him as hard as you can? That was not him trying to top from the bottom," Nicolette says with air quotes, "but it was him letting you know his limits. You're done playing with him." Nicolette turned to david, "Come, you can be by me until your next rotation." Rosa tried to interject her opinion but Nicolette dismissed her with a wave and returned to her scene.

david took up a place near the chair that Nicolette was using to rest in between rotations. Rosa had a look that was a mix between anger and bewilderment; she went to discuss with Kat what had happened. Rosa kept looking over her shoulder at Nicolette in between her sentences. Kat threw up her hands and commented, "He said 'red.' You cannot go against his wishes and she *is* his owner, even if it is just for tonight. Red is stop; there is no question here. If you want to play with him more you will have to go through Nicolette that, too, is not debatable. I have no dog in this fight." Nicolette and Whip were finishing their scene with michael; they were slowly bringing him out of his subspace. If you bring a submissive out of subspace too quickly it is usually accompanied by a shock to their senses and it can be quite mentally and physically painful. Nicolette usually does aftercare of affirmation and providing water after an intense physical scene like she and Whip had with michael. michael's breathing was returning a normal cadence and he was responsive to their inquiries unlike when he was deep into his subspace. Whip seeing Rosa waiting to talk to Nicolette, she took over the aftercare duties and started massaging aloe lotion over some of his welts which helped bring him completely out of subspace. michael sipped his water and nodded at david, "you're lucky, bro. Mistress Nicolette is amazing at punishment." "Yes, she looks after me and I would not have come here with anyone else. She is the only dominant I trust." Nicolette looked at Rosa trying her best to be understanding and hide her utter annoyance, "Yes, Rosa, how can I help you?" Nicolette failed, her words cut and there was no veil. Most people in the room where done with their scene and almost everyone turned to look at the exchange between Rosa and Nicolette. Rosa started, "I know you think I was being overly difficult on david, but I was being gentle. I am not good with pets who cannot take pain. For that, I apologize to you and", Rosa looked past Nicolette at david, "to you david. However, I think that your", Rosa returned her gaze to Nicolette, "approach to me was very uncalled for." Nicolette took an audible deep breath and replied, "Rosa, your opinion on my approach is just that. An opinion. I have opinions as well, but I will respect Kat and kal, their home, and this event. But if you want to get together at a separate occasion, I will be glad to let you know *exactly* what I think of you." Nicolette turned to david, "you have a new scene or are you dropping out of the game, dear?" Nicolette turned to see that Rosa was still standing near her so she addressed Rosa again, "We are done here. Thank you." david was looking at Nicolette with wide-eyed admiration, "I would like to do my next rotation if that is ok. I think I am ready to play again, Mistress. Thank you." david scurried off to do foot play with MistressTina. Rosa was setting up her next scene as well; it was apparent that she was not in a good head space so before she started Kat gave her a reassuring nod and pat on the small of her back. Rosa smiled at her and stole a glance of Nicolette, who too, smiled at her. Nicolette knew that Rosa was experienced in play and did not wish her ill will, but she also needed and wanted to protect david who was not comfortable playing with her. Rosa visibly calmed down and slipped back into her a comfortably space and introduced herself to the next pet in the rotation. He was very much into ball busting so he was the perfect pet for Rosa to play with to regain her confidence that evening. Nicolette and Whip begun their usual inspection of the pet that they were getting ready to play with. Whip noticed that he had several skin tags and moles which can bleed or be whipped off from an intense scene. Whip and Nicolette explained the risks of the tags and moles with impact play and they decided to do a spanking scene instead of a whipping scene. Nicolette slipped quickly and easily back into her Domspace. She used her favorite crop and paddleboard paddle, which allowed her more impact play. MsWhip focused only on her billy club. The remaining scenes blurred together with Nicolette using ever implement she brought with her. The ladies work through the Olympics just over two hours. At the end, the Ladies took a much needed rest while they discussed who should win the prize. After about thirty minutes of snacking and discussing the performance of the males, it was a unanimous decision that none of the males was exceedingly better than the others. As such, all the pets lost…or won depending on your perspective. It was nearing two o'clock in the morning when Nicolette was ready to head to her home. david loaded all of her gear into the car while Nicolette did her rounds to say good-bye to her friends. Once david completed loading the car, he thanked MstrKat and kel for their hospitality. He addressed the others in the room and then they exited. david followed Nicolette to the highway to ensure that there were no issues; he then went to his home while Nicolette headed down I-96 back to the eastside of Detroit. Nicolette carried her gear into the house and left it near the back door while she headed up to bed. The next morning, Nicolette awoke too late for Mass; she laughed to herself about how after a night a debauchery and she misses her opportunity to repent like a good Catholic and thereby not receive all her blessings. It was the first time Nicolette had missed weekly Mass in quite some time. Nicolette enjoyed the rest as she was more than just physically tired because, usually, intense play and being in domspace for an extended period of time is exhausting. She had a combination of both very intense play and spent several hours in domspace the previous evening. Nicolette stretched and laid in bed a bit longer before starting her Sunday. While she was laying there, Nicolette received a text from Steve inquiring if she was making it to church to which she responded that she was out late and will not make Mass. Steve responded that she was lucky because their normal priest was not present and the replacement was especially difficult to understand. Eventually, Nicolette started her day with cleaning her playroom and disinfecting the furniture and implements that she took to the party. She disinfected the implements after each scene last night, but she did another disinfection before adding the items back to her stock. Taking care to oil and condition all her leather toys, Nicolette displays pride in the items in her collection, some of which were unique. After getting the smotherbox and toys back into their place, Nicolette turned her cleaning regime on the second floor bathroom and master bedroom.

Nicolette dusted, polished wood, and mopped the floor in the master bedroom; taking time to change the sheets on the bed. After completion, she turned her attention on the bathroom. Nicolette scrubbed the toilet, sink, and basin on the second floor bathroom. She mopped with floor with a disinfectant and cleaned the mirror with vinegar.

Taking a break from the cleaning, Nicolette checked her phone to see she had a voicemail from david, "Thank you so much for such an amazing night. It was one of the best releases I have had in such a long time and I owe it all to you. I do not know how lucky I am to have you in my life but I am quite grateful for the time that I get to spend with you and in your presence. I emailed you my schedule for the next few weeks; hopefully you have time for me. Take care beautiful". Nicolette smiled and exclaimed aloud, "if only that man wanted the type of BDSM relationship I sought. He is perfect is so many ways, but fails in the most important ones. Nicolette grabbed her tablet and sat on the chaise lounge in the playroom and scrolled through her email on collarme.com. There were 18 new messages; much more than can be expected after a private play party. There was a message from Rosa and Nicolette let out a very audible sigh and opened the message. It was a bunch of wingding type characters and nonsense language. Her iPad prompted her to open an untrusted application to which Nicolette denied and shook her head. It appeared as if Rosa was trying to give Nicolette a computer virus as an attachment. She promptly reported the potential computer virus through the website to the admins and blocked Rosa. Shaking her head in anger, Nicolette decided to screenshot the message and call Kat. "Hello, lady. How are you? What time did you get to bed?" Kat laughed, "Hey Nici, we were up until about 6 a.m. It was a hoot. Hope you are well. How is david? I had a talking with Rosa after most everyone left. She seemed remorseful." "Funny you should bring her up, I just received a computer virus from her on collarme. Fortunately, I accessed the message from my iPad and not my phones or computers. I was over the incident with david, but this added fuel to my fire. What is her problem", Nicolette replied. "She sent you a WHAT? Oh my! kel, you were right," Kat excitedly replied, "kel was saying that Rosa is known for being over-the-top and seeking revenge when she feels disrespected." "Wow. She felt disrespected?! She disrespected david, me...you...kel...hell, just about everyone at the party. Well, I blocked her, but I am thinking that some of these 18 messages I received from people that I do not know will be deleted unread. I will have to look into them and see if Rosa is in their photos. I do not have time for this childish ass behavior, but what are you going to do? I take looking after someone very seriously. You're a doctor. Did you explain the damage she could have caused?" Nicolette inquired. "Yes, I did discuss with her about the recklessness of kicking someone in the balls without any prior experience in the scene and disregarding their limits. She did not seem to take it well; she implied that I was disrespecting her expertise as a dominant. Oh shoot, I wonder if she sent me a virus, too", Kat said with a loud chuckle. "Well, if you do have a message from her I would delete it unread. She and I will have our conversation, but it will be worst than she thinks." "Girl! Nothing illegal, Kat, but she will know that trying to give someone a computer virus is a federal crime. I am done playing with her," Nicolette interjected. "I know. Here, she is pulling rank on medicine with a doctor and giving a lawyer proof of laws broken. She is not very bright is she?", Kat replied. "No. No, she is not. Well, girl let me get through these messages. I will catch up with you and kel later. Thank you again for an amazing evening," Nicolette said ending their conversation. Looking through the emails, Nicolette saw that only four were not planted on the behalf of Rosa. One message was from James, he was again inviting Nicolette to visit Niagara Falls; she decided that instead they should meet up at the Hershey Hotel and Spa. Nicolette made the reservation and forwarded the details on to James,

who in turn sent her a chat message on Yahoo! Messenger.
They started chatting about their weekends and other
pleasantries while she returned the other three emails. The
second email was from Heinrich stating that he has checked
into his hotel and was looking forward to seeing Nicolette
when her schedule allows. uwe had also wrote his email with
his Yahoo! Messenger information so that they can chat
while he is in the States. The last email contained david's
schedule. Nicolette spent about thirty minutes chatting with
James and she also added uwe on the application. She ended
the conversation with James with the plan outlined for
meeting in Pennsylvania in a few weeks.

Nicolette decided that dinner Monday night would be perfect
for Heinrich and she left that message with his front desk:
Sunday before bed. She would enjoy seeing Heinrich as their
dinner dates usually ended with shopping and sometimes
physical play. Heinrich was not into the physical play side of
BDSM but he enjoyed doing what he needed to ensure
Nicolette would continue to entertain his fetish of financial
domination. When she arrived at work, Nicolette arranged
her Monday and Tuesday work schedule to allow her to
leave early on Monday and arrive later on Tuesday. Nicolette
picked her favorite restaurant for dinner that evening with
Heinrich; it was a wonderful Italian restaurant that served a
full multi-course meal standard. The restaurant also had live
music on the weekend and some of the weeknights which
provided a wonderful atmosphere without being too
pretentious. Nicolette arrived at the restaurant a few minutes
prior to the dinner time wearing a long, flowing summer
dress in deep brown. The dress had gold and metallic
ornaments which made Nicolette look more ethnic than she
usually comes off. Her sandy brown hair and freckles made
Nicolette appear more European though her complexion and
high cheek bones are clearly black and this dress spoken
fluent African though Nicolette did not even remember her
Swahili lessons from Cass Tech High School. Nicolette

always stood and sat higher, like true royalty, whenever she wore an outfit that inspired African tone and rhythms. Today was one of those days. Nicolette was naturally graceful, but today she had an air of affluence, royalty that is not always present in the way that she carried herself. The valet driver provided his hand as Nicolette exited her vehicle; she nodded her head slightly at him and he grinned exaggeratedly. Heinrich, who was waiting outside the restaurant, met Nicolette at her vehicle and he offered his arm to escort her into the restaurant which she obliged. Once inside the restaurant, Heinrich and Nicolette were shown to their table which was on the side of the restaurant with the stage. Once seated, Heinrich expressed his appreciation for Nicolette's time. "Thank you, Ma'am, for taking time out of your day for me. I appreciate all the time you have for me. I am a bit confused by the selection of a restaurant far from any shopping venues. Do you not plan on using me?" As he was speaking, the server came to the table. Nicolette looked up from the menu and smiled at the server and ordered a bottle of the '99 Gaja Langhe Sito Moresco. Once the server walked from the table, Nicolette looked Heinrich in the eye, "Dear boy, I do not need a mall to spend your money." Heinrich sat stiffly upright in his chair with a huge grin on his face, "Yes, Ma'am. Thank you for correcting me." Nicolette nodded and went to looking over the menu. "I am thinking Chateaubriand for dinner. Are you in the mood for some cow?" He nodded in agreement, "Whatever you want is fine. I can go for a good steak. I prefer mine rare to med rare." Nicolette laughed her typical boisterous roar, "I am not watching you eat bloody ass meat. I will not force you to eat well done steak so I will look at something else. Maybe I will do salmon or a surf & turf. It is still cow, but it will not be table side service." "Mistress, I can eat the rougher meat. I am fine with that. I want you to be pleased." "Well done steak does not mean it is rough. You can have juicy well done steak. I eat juicy steak and the temperature is never rare or medium. People who cook all the juice out of the steak under the guise that it is required for well done meat does not know how to cook, in my opinion. I would imagine that raw meat is chewy and tough to get to," Nicolette says with a shrug, "I will get the surf & turf lobster steak duo. I am content with my choice. That way you can get your meal and I will have one I enjoy." Heinrich nodded in agreement. The server presented Nicolette with bottle of wine. She examined the label to ensure it was the correct vintage and assented to the opening of the bottle. Nicolette was presented with a taste of the wine; the wine was complex with a nice woody finish. She approved the pour for the table while contemplating the lobster's ability to stand up to the wine. They ordered their dinner and enjoyed typical dinner conversation about their jobs and Heinrich's trip to the States. When their antipasto course arrived they were discussing the current project and the amount of time that Heinrich expects to spend in Michigan. As they enjoyed the salad course, Nicolette was recapping the challenges with being contract attorney for some very complex cases. With pasta course, they were discussing their respective plans for the Fall. Nicolette, being a huge fan of football, focused mostly on her season tickets and the rebuilding year for her teams. As dinner was served, Heinrich was getting antsy about how Nicolette was going to spend all the money he brought that evening and she could see that he was getting impatient with her process. It amused her that he was nearly begging to be used. "How is your dinner? Is the Marsala sauce as rich as the menu made it sound? I think the wine should pair well with that sauce", Nicolette asked. "The sauce is lovely. I would offer you some, but I recall you do not eat mushrooms. The wine does, indeed, pair well with the meal. I did not expect such a long meal or such a slow bottle." Heinrich replied. "Well, one does not gulp down a $200 bottle of wine; it is designed to be savored", Nicolette said then taking a sip of the wine, "It surprisingly also pairs with the lobster. I was concerned that it would be too powerful for it. But I stand corrected." Heinrich almost choked with surprise which then quickly turned to glee. "$200?!? I did not know that the bottle of wine alone was that expensive. You are correct, Mistress. Right when I think I know, I am shown to not understand. Not you or your ways. You keep teaching a slave who is set in his ways. I should know not to question your motives and ways, but I am a fool. This is why you are in charge. This is why, indeed." Nicolette winked at Heinrich and continued to eat her steak and lobster. As the meal was nearing completion, the server asked if there was room for dessert. Nicolette ordered a scotch and peach flambé for the table. Heinrich said he would finish the wine. The presentation at the table side of the peach flambé was impressive; it was something that Nicolette always enjoyed. After completing dinner and the cordials, Nicolette and Heinrich departed the restaurant. He was pleasantly surprised at the cost of the meal and how he was able to satiate his fetish in an unexpected way. As they waited for their cars to be brought around by the valet parking staff, Nicolette made plans to see Heinrich in three days, the evening before he departed. The plans were vague, but did not include a meal. Nicolette's car arrived first and Heinrich met the valet paying him a tip, while Nicolette situated herself into the driver's seat. The valet smiled at Nicolette one last time, as Heinrich turned to her to say his farwell. He reached into his jacket pocket and handed her a card, "it is to express my thanks for a lovely evening". Nicolette tossed the card onto the seat and as she said good night, Heinrich's rental was pulled up behind her. "Seems your chariot awaits and it is past time for me to remove this bra. Thank you for dinner and the card. I will speak with soon. We can coordinate Thursday via email or text. Good night." Heinrich closed her car door and waved as Nicolette pulled away. She drove home via Mack Avenue, making it home in just under fifteen minutes. Nicolette pulled into her garage, removed her card from the car and noticed that it was thicker than a greeting card. She sighed and walked into the house. There was a trail of clothes of shoes leading from the backdoor to the alarm keypad. Nicolette disabled the alarm and collected her items off the floor and put the clothes in the laundry. She took her shoes up to the laundry room and opened the card from Heinrich. It was a thank you card with a handwritten letter that explained that in the twenty years before meeting Nicolette, he had a hard time finding a woman that enjoyed financial domination but did not need her bills paid. Someone that enjoyed the act of taking money without feeling required to have sex with the slave. That he, for once, felt truly in subspace due to the financial play and did not feel like a john with a prostitute. The letter was sincere and Nicolette smiled at the sentiment. She had heard that she was unique and rare in financial domination expressed previously by other slaves with the fetish. Nicolette was expecting that the envelope would have money wedged into it, but she was content that it did not. Nicolette placed the card and envelope into the trash and smiled to herself for the ego stroke. She took a quick shower and headed to bed. She texted Heinrich to thank him for the polite card and that she was home safely. She checked her email to ensure that there was nothing pressing; she saw that she received an email from the admin of the collarme.com site. It read that they looked into her complaint and they deleted and banned the IP address of Rosa and her submissives that sent the virus over the website. There was an apology and thanks for reporting. There were two additional emails, but nothing that Nicolette thought required checking that evening. She set her alarm, stretched out, and headed to sleep. The next morning was slated to be a very busy one at the firm and Nicolette wanted to be well rested.

Tuesday, Nicolette made an offer to two of her four finalists for the position on her team. She picked a graduate of Michigan with a degree in Chemistry, who despite some social anxiety issues, was a brilliant lawyer and a paralegal who was related to her brother, Steven's wife. The paralegal was very hardworking and a graduate of Wayne State

University. Nicolette was pleased with her decisions and both accepted the positions under Nicolette. Both agreed to start the position with the firm in two weeks. Nicolette began outlining the project for both Kamilah, the paralegal, and Michael, the attorney. Nicolette knew that she would need much help on the filing of the patent for the neuroscaffolding project as well as the patent for a pending client. The stem cell negligence project will take a lot of leg work interviewing patients all over the world both in person and via electronic methods. With the neuroscaffolding project, the research of competing patents and defining the overlap would be imperative to a successful application. Nicolette was going to assign to Michael the tasks of researching the applicability of neuroscaffolding in the US and look for competing patents in the field of neurobiology, neurochemistry, and medicine. She also is going to assign him the tasks of looking for additional precedence in the stem cell project. Kamilah will be tasked with filing all inquiries in both projects as well as conducting some of the preliminary screening interviews for the stem cell project. Nicolette read over some of the requests and prepared her subpoena list for the stem cell project. Once she had all the requests and subpoenas complete, Nicolette checked the clock and it was almost 7:00pm. It was time for her to go to the gym. She arrived at 7:30pm, just in time to hit around the volleyball with some of persons arriving for league play. Nicolette wanted to be active, but was not in the mood to workout in a traditional sense. She was not sure why she was so tired, but taking time to bump and set balls was enough for her to get her heart rate increased. Nicolette headed home and poured a large glass of wine and sat on her couch to relax over reruns of forensic crime dramas on TBS. She sipped the wine and got immersed in the show and the cares and stresses of the day seem to melt away with each passing segment. Nicolette poured her second glass and went to her dressing room to undress, placing the glass on the dresser. Once nude, Nicolette went and took a short shower and spending some time under the warm, pounding water. The water against her body felt like a much needed massage; Nicolette realized how tight her muscles were and made a mental note to schedule an appointment with her masseur. She stepped out of the shower, dried her skin, and walked back into the dressing room. Nicolette massaged lotion into her skin, then brushes and then braids her hair. She takes another sip of her wine and walks into her bedroom and sits on the chair with her tablets. Nicolette turns on the television to more reruns of the forensic drama and logins into collarme.com. She had four new messages. One of the messages was from david who wanted to know if Nicolette received his message about availability and wanted to check in with her to ensure that things were going well. Nicolette checked her sent mail and noted that she read but did not respond to david about his schedule. She noted that he was probably nervous that she was disappointed in him; it did not help that Rosa was spamming and trying to hijack everyone's accounts that crossed her. Nicolette drafted a thoughtful message to david that first apologized for the oversight in getting back to him sooner; she thought she had emailed him, but she must have just replied in her mind. She outlined the actions of Rosa against herself and Kat, explaining that she has been subsequently deleted and banned from the website. She reiterated that david did nothing improper and that her concern was and will continue to be his safety when he is playing in scenes and at events as her invited pet. Nicolette outlined that she has a few trips upcoming, but she is looking at her schedule and will earmark some time for david. She thanked him for reaching out and she hoped he has a good week. david read and responded almost instantly asking if Nicolette had time to speak on the phone. She granted him permission. The phone rang almost as soon as she sent the message. "Hello." "Mistress, thank you for taking time to speak with me. I am eager to see you again. Each time we are together, I feel something new and the experiences take me to new heights in my submissive. The release is amazing and nothing I have ever dreamed of. I crave it. I do not think there is a day that goes by that I do not think of you. Please find time for me before your trips. I would do anything for you. I…I do not know what I can say to convince you to use me," david exclaimed in haste, almost so excited that the words would explode in his mouth if he did not get them out. "david, you would not do anything. I appreciate the excitement and the desire to be under my thumb, but I do all things deep in realism. I, too, enjoy the time that we spend together. You are a good pet, but ultimately you are seeking ways to get release and to play while I would one day like to find a loving relationship with someone into the fetishes that I enjoy. A true BDSM relationship that survives in the real world. I have been making time for you in the remaining time that I have for my pursuit. Unless something has changed for you since things have not changed for me. I cannot give you a top priority in my life because we play well together, as our compatibilities end once play ends." Nicolette explained in a kind, sympathetic manner. david sighed and took a long pause, "I know. I wish we wanted the same things in the vanilla world, but I cannot deny that I am only attracted to you because of the emotions you stir in me during our scenes. I will admit that I have fantasized about you and not just in a BDSM scene.…I have imagined what sex with you would be like. I have not had sex or a relationship with a black woman in over a decade. Maybe I could try…we could try." Nicolette laughed audibly, "david, I do not need any favors. I have never in my life had to force a man to want to be with me. As I said, I schedule you into the time I have available. While I may not be your cup of tea, there are dozens of men that I am wading through to see if I can find someone I might want to spend the rest of my life with. I am not, nor have I ever been, desperate. I would rather be alone than in something that is not good for me. Thanks for the offer to try, though." david let out a frustrated laugh mixed with a sigh, "So, you have no time for me this week? I guess I may have to reach out to others if you will never have time for me…" Nicolette's tone went from cheery to cold, "Well if the time I have for you does not work, you, by all means, should seek someone that has enough time for you in the capacity in which you require. I wish you luck in your endeavors. Bye david." "Wait! Why, bye?! I wanted someone to fill the time you do not want, not to replace you." david stated. Nicolette took a long sip of her wine and weighed her options in her head, "And I wish you luck in filling your time. Why not search for a white dominant that can be everything that you want. Why waste your time with black women like me?" "Race is not important to me…well except, when it comes to a possible wife. And I see myself with someone Asian or Indian…not necessarily white. I want a woman who will be subservient and cater to my every need. I guess I am saying that I do not want to have a relationship with the woman I serve because I plan on being the dominant force in my marriage. A man's place in a marriage is on top. I enjoy serving you, Mistress. I was so hesitant when I started down this path to understand my fantasies. You were patient and loving in your dominance. I needed that. So many are either too soft or too hard – you are the perfect mix of dominant and loving. I needed you to help get me out of my shell. For that, I crave you and more of your time. I did not see it as a negative until you drew parallels in my mind to marriage. I know you want a relationship that leads to marriage. I don't, well not necessarily. Can we find a happy medium between my desires and yours?" david reasoned. "This schedule that we currently have, it *IS* our happy medium. It does not seem to be working for you. I do not have any requirements for fidelity from you. I, also, do not have any delusions of relationship." Nicolette responded still quite cold in her tone. "Ok, I guess then we do not have a problem. You are content where we are and I love our play and want more of it. You cannot give me more because you do not have more time for me. We have reached our impasse and it is what it is." david responded with a calm hoping to thaw Nicolette's demeanor. "Yes, it is." Nicolette continued her tone. "Great. So about my schedule that I sent via email, do any of those days work for you? I would love to see you this week." david asked with hope and anticipation in his breath. "I have plans on Thursday, but I am free this week after football. If I am not too tired then we can possibly play. You know Fall is difficult for me since I spend 12-16 hours in Ann Arbor on Saturdays." Nicolette responded. "Does tomorrow work for you? You did not mention Wednesday and I am free tomorrow." His voice was increasingly annoyed, "I feel like I am begging for time as if I am not important." "Tomorrow would be hard to make work as it is my only free day this week to do things for myself around the house. I am exhausted and the Fall is just starting. You enjoy impact play which is difficult on me and I cannot perform well if I am already exhausted," Nicolette explained. "I know my fetishes lay, generally, in impact play, but watching different scenes at the party over the weekend have opened my eyes. I want to try other things. Maybe I can come over and help with your chores and if you are so inclined you can indulge me other play," david insisted. "I will see how I feel tomorrow, but if you need a definite, now it would be no" Nicolette stated. "I do not need a definite now. I will check in with you tomorrow," david said with pride and joy. "I will speak to you later. I am going to go back to my email on collarme. It was nice speaking to you," Nicolette ended their conversation. Two of the messages were from persons who were either commenting Nicolette or insulting her. She responded to the complimentary message with her standard message of thanks, while she just deleted the insult. It was always funny to her why people took time from their day to be insulting to a person that they did not know nor cared about their opinion. The last message was from Ryan who was just checking in and stating that he wished he had time to be Nicolette's chair, but did give her the option of using him for the first away game. Nicolette replied that it will have to be the second away game as she already had plans for the first. With no new messages, Nicolette finished her glass of wine, brushed her teeth, and turned in for the evening.

Chapter Eight

Wednesday came in like a storm with Nicolette waking up in pain from her premenstrual cramps. Usually she has back pain, bloating, and intense pain during her menses; it was confirmed by ultrasound a few years earlier that she had endometriosis. Nicolette made her way to the bathroom to take a warm shower to allow the gentle, thudding massage of the water against her back and legs which provided relief of the premenstrual cramping, even if only temporarily. After the shower, Nicolette brushed her teeth, combed her hair, and dressed for the day. The drive seemed longer for Nicolette as she made her way into the firm. She was not particularly motivated to start the day and the pain coursing through her midsection did not make things any easier. She arrived at the firm and walked directly into a heated discussion between the owner and Dich. They appeared to have a difference of opinion about the direction of the company; Dich was allotted a majority share in the company's board so his opinion carried some weight with the other managing directors. Nicolette tried to avoid being pulled into the conversation, but those attempts failed as did her hopes of a light, under-the-radar day. "What are your opinions about the future of the field, strictly looking at remaining solely a small business' bouquet legal firm?" Dich asked Nicolette in a leading manner. "I do not have enough information on our marketing strategies, share of market, or other available markets to answer that question in any informed manner. Can you let me know any significant information so that I can, at least, make an intelligent statement about the future of the firm?" Nicolette answered trying to avoid the obvious pitfalls of the topic. "We have an overabundance of companies who reach out to us to help just within the State of Michigan. We have awards and well-recognized methods that are highly sought after. While we are not the only firm of this type in the country, we are the only one in southeast Michigan, and one of only two in the entire state that is not attached to a scientific company. We used to have a marketing team that went around the state to recruit jobs for the firm, but we no longer have a marketing team so we rely mostly on word-of-mouth and referrals." The owner added, in a matter of fact manner in response to Nicolette's request. "However, there are so many other scientific companies throughout the country, hell world, that could use our company and our expertise. I do not want to limit us," Dich added. "The laws change as you move state to state, and definitely as you look internationally. Would it be a great use of our resources to bring on clients that we may not be able to service? Most of us are only admitted to the State of Michigan Bar; a few of us are also admitted to the Federal Bar. I do not know anyone who has several memberships to multiple state bars or can practice in other countries. Devil's advocate. What is the plan for ensuring that we can fully participate in cases in other states and countries?" Nicolette pushed back against Dich. The owner smirked at Dich and it was obvious that some of the things that Nicolette mentioned were points that he had mentioned in their discussion. "We can always contract with other attorneys in other states and countries; they can file briefs and assist on cases that we bring. Developing a network of private practice attorneys is the easy part. If we have so much work that it needs to be outsourced then I would welcome that. Also, you or one of the other attorneys can sit for other bar exams." Dich stood his ground. Nicolette laughed, "I do not have plans of taking additional exams. It has been years since I had to study for the bar. My life is not set-up for that amount of studying anymore. I am one of the youngest lawyers here; I am sure the older attorneys feel similar to me. I would poll the staff before trying to require them to study and take another board. It may be a very rude awakening." Dich's face deepened to a bright shade of red, "You are saying that you would rather be fired than gain new skills?" Nicolette's demeanor change quite quickly to sobering one as she checked her tone, she replied, "Firstly, my contract does not have any continued education requirements above and beyond what is required to maintain my license. Second, requiring that I obtain new skills on threat of termination is akin to coercion. Third, I highly doubt you want to approach others in that manner as you run the risk of losing your entire team and the backbone of your company. Lastly, if for one moment..." "Nicolette, do not take this conversation as a threat, coercion, or any contract violation. Dich does not like to lose and he has found this conversation to not go as he was expecting." The owner interjected. Dich grinned and laughed, "I love it when you get fired up. I am not threatening you. I just think that we can expand the business and hate being tied. Do you have any friends looking to supplement their income in either California or Florida? We have a possible case in those states and I want to explore what our expansion would look like." Nicolette gave a flippant response, "Nope", and walked to her office shaking her head. Nicolette could not understand how Dich could be so reckless in his behavior, especially when he has contracts with all the attorneys. Nicolette sat at her desk and opened her email box and saw that she had almost 45 new emails; hovering over the sender information they all seemed legitimate emails. Taking a sip of her water, she started looking through the emails and noticed that majority of the messages had a similar theme. There were testimonial emails about the neuroscaffolding techniques that were used on them. One of the messages was from a medical doctor who described using the neuroscaffold matrix to grow skin cells for a patient who had a Methicillin-resistant Staphylococcus aureus (MRSA) infection that caused extensive necrosis of the neck after a motorcycle accident. Using the matrix to grow the cells allow for a graft that was not prone to another infection since the cells were cloned, but selected to not contain the MRSA bacteria. Another message was from the patient of the aforementioned motorcycle accident. Also included in the mailbox were members of the care team from this patient. Nicolette, in the course of the emails, had emails from four separate cases that used the neuroscaffolding techniques for patients. Nicolette printed and compiled all the information from the four separate cases and made notes to look into the regulatory compliance of the cases to ensure that the letter of the law was followed to clear them for inclusion in the patent application. Two of the cases were through University of Michigan Health Systems, one was through St. John Medical System, and the final case was through Boston Children's Hospital. Each case would have been considered a Phase IV clinical trial which would require informed consent, institutional review board approval, and surveillance. Nicolette checked her clock and noticed that she was due to be in a meeting in ten minutes so she grabbed her notebook and headed to the conference room. Nicolette walked into the conference room where she was introduced to a Singapore man named Oisin; he was one of the principle members of the Board and an individually wealthy man. Oisin introduced the reason for his visit, "Nicolette, it is nice to meet you. I have heard some wonderful things about you and the work that you are doing here at the firm. I have been an active member of the Board now for five years. I initially made my money through a hedge fund investment and now I invest in interesting companies, large and small, and look to make a positive impact on the world. I was always impressed by the Rockies Law and Consulting Firm from the beginning due to the unique, niche market that it belongs. When I found Rockies, it was doing small time work and through my investments they have been able to expand their footprint. With your addition, we are hoping to push the Company firmly into the black. I am excited to have you here. I hear you are working on some very intriguing cases, specifically the neuroscaffolding case you provide me some more information on that case?" Nicolette sat for a moment and listened to Oisin while Dich just looked on. Nicolette went to speak but instead sat back more into her chair. Dich looked at Nicolette and then at Oisin and started to speak on her behalf, "The case is still in the discovery phase. I am not sure if Nicolette has much information, but we do know that we will be applying for multiple patents on the behalf of the client. She will have more information in the coming months, but I am sure she can hit the highlights for you." Dich turned to Nicolette and motioned that she had the floor. "I respect your position on the Board and I would love to learn more information about the structure and interactions of the Board and Rockies. Can you elaborate on that?" Nicolette stated changing the subject. Oisin looked confused, "The Board is technically the Board of Directors for Warwickshire Law Practice, which as you know owns Rockies. So, technically, my role is in Warwickshire, but I do have some free reign here as well. Legally, Warwickshire and Rockies are separate entities." Nicolette sat forward in her chair, "With all due respect, we, as a Company and myself personally, have a non-disclosure agreement in place with the inventor of the neuroscaffolding matrix. As you said, your role is not with Rockies and therefore you are not privy to any information about this case and honestly, any case that I am lead attorney on." Dich started to interject, he was again a deep shade of red, "Nicolette, I need you to" Before he could finish his thought Oisin raised his hand to pause Dich, "That is true. I do not have a legal right to know the information. I find the information that Dich provided me already interesting. He provides me with a synopsis of all the cases. He does that out of respect to the investment I have made in the Company…effectively paying your salary. I, however, respect your conviction." "It really is not anything personal. Ethically, I cannot disclose anything about the matrix, the case, or our legal strategy. When we submit information that is under the Freedom of Information Act or

103

deemed public information, I can let you know that, but otherwise my hands are tied," Nicolette concluded. Oisin sat back and smiled at Nicolette. The room was silent for a moment. Nicolette looked from Dich to Oisin, neither seemed to be ready to break the silence. Nicolette also sat back in her chair, pushed her hair behind her ear and stared at a space on the wall behind the two. After nearly five minutes of complete silence, Nicolette stood and extended her hand to Oisin and offered the pleasantry of how nice it was to meet him. Oisin chuckled, "You can sit back down. I see you will not crack even under the hardest amount of pressure. I like that about you. Please close the door as we have something very important to talk about." Oisin motioned to the chair. Nicolette closed the door and sat down in her chair. "What important thing do we have to talk about?" Nicolette asked, still very skeptical. "I am in need of legal help here in Michigan. I have another company that I invest in that is having legal troubles with the Department of Health and Human Services. Before I continue, I will require a NDA and I will work solely with you. None of my information or anything about my case will go to your staff. I have already spoken to Dich and I will require 25% of your time." Oisin started addressing her question. "This company, Compliance Assured Testing, is being accused of dry labbing. I do not even know what that means. I need someone to defend me against the lawsuits; I did not incorporate the company well under Michigan law." Nicolette listened intently and begun taking notes, "How much of a percentage do you own in the company? What way did you incorporate? Who are the principles of the company? Are they also being sued?" Oisin answered the direct questions quickly, "15%, LLC, Hullerbrandt and Kochery. No, they are not currently named. Hullerbrandt owns 55% but through a few layers of protection. Kochery owns the remainder, but he personally just filed for bankruptcy. I think of the three of us, I am the only one with assets that can be attached. Luckily, the tools that they use in the US to seize assets do not apply in Singapore." "Okay. So you are being pulled into something civil or criminal? Dry labbing is usually a criminal prosecuted case. Are your employees being prosecuted? Or is this just a money grab for those who were prosecuted by your lab results? How long are we speaking in the terms of dry labbing? And, most importantly, was there results that were dry labbed?" Nicolette asked trying to get a handle of the scope of the case. "We mostly did drunk driving and drunk driving vehicular homicide cases. The person suing me was sentenced to prison for driving under the influence and causing an accident that lead to the death of another. The employee who testified that he ran the samples later admitted that he never truly tested the specimens. He stated that he felt that the information accompanying the case specimens proved the guilt of the donor," Oisin stated. "So, was that employee still working for you? Are there charges against you him? Is the donor still in prison?" Nicolette pondered. "He does not work for me anymore as he has been indicted and is held over on bond. The government is looking through all the cases that our laboratory has tested and looking at the results and trying to find the raw data to ensure that the samples were truly analyzed. The donor is still in prison, but there is an appeal in process and the paperwork for a mistrial has been filed." Oisin answered her questions. "Who is handling the appeal/original case?" Nicolette inquired to determine if Oisin would stand a chance in his lawsuit. "The law firm of Rothfield, Fielder, and Childmenship. I know they are a tough firm in California. I do not know what their record is like here. I guess they specialized in cases where the defendant was railroaded," Oisin says while doing air quotes, "railroaded. Why would I railroad anyone? I have no personal stake in the outcome of the cases that come through the laboratory. Honestly, I do not pay attention to the day-to-day workings of the company. I live in Singapore." He sighed. "Railroaded." Nicolette took a long pause to evaluate her next group of questions, "I am not aware of the firm of

Rothfield, Fielder, and Childmenship. I understand the sentiment that the donor felt railroaded. What information, if any, can you tell about the donor?" Nicolette asked. "One of the best ways to defend you, Oisin, is to see the case that the defense is building." "It is a younger male. I am not sure if he is black of Hispanic, but he is a minority. I want to say he is under 30- maybe under 25 and he was driving a newer model Honda. It was crushed almost beyond recognition. I know that it was also determined that the driver did not hit the vehicle where the victim died. There was also blame placed on Honda; the dealership near the accident, where the car was purchased, was also indicted as there was a recall that the driver was not made aware that caused the car to not brake or the brake lights not to work. Something along those lines. That information was not made available to the laboratory. We only received that a young, minority male was driving home from a nightclub. There was drug paraphernalia in his vehicle though no drugs were located. He admitted to having one beverage at the nightclub and he was a reluctant designated driver. He passed his field sobriety test, though the Drug Evaluation and Recognition (DER) officer said he did not pass his nystagmus test." Oisin recalled slowly. "Oh, also, I know there was something medical that was only mentioned behind closed doors that was not included in the public record." Nicolette leaned forward in her chair, "Ok. There is a lot here. I do think we can build a defense. I, also, think you need to exercise more oversight on your companies if they are going to have such a financial impact on you and your life. We will need to sit and do a deposition on this case. I also need to talk to the employee who dry-labbed and his direct supervisor. Someone should have reviewed that case work. All in all, I will try and devote 10-15 hours a week to this case until we have to go to court. When is your court date?" "I have a preliminary hearing in two days," Oisin stated trailing off and leaning back in his chair. "Two days? Alright then," Nicolette sighed while massaging her head.

"I need you to provide me with the contact information for the employee, his direct supervisor, and I need copies of all information you are privy to. Moreover, I will need a bonus for all the extra time I will be devoting to this case. I need that information before lunch and I have one rule. Lie to me and we are done." Nicolette said quite brazen. Oisin reached into his bag which was under the table and pulls out a file that is almost two inches thick. "This is all I have. The contact information you requested is in the file. I will not lie to you. I will compensate you above and beyond your salary. I like the confidence." "I am not promising any outcome, but I am stating that my time is important to me and it desires to be compensated at a rate much higher than my normal rate due to the amount of my time being sacrificed." Nicolette commented frankly. "I will begin looking through this and see if I can move up the start date of my staff to work on my other projects as they cannot stop for a few days to prepare for your hearing on Friday. I am assuming the summons with the pending charges is included in this stack?" Oisin nodded. Nicolette shot a look at Dich and left the conference room and headed back to her office. Her cramps are getting worse and so Nicolette noted that she needed to stop at the restroom soon as to not bleed through onto her clothing. Nicolette grabbed a glass of hot tea after leaving the restroom. Sitting at her desk, she plugged in her heating pad and began pouring over all the documents in the file. In addition to the information that Oisin provided in the meeting, Nicolette learned by reading through the documents that the employee, John, was reprimanded for the dry-labbing internally by his supervisor, Erin. Erin did not approve or release the results; John sent them out without the proper review because he knew that they would be flagged as not real since the laboratory information management system (LIMS) that laboratory used included a graph of all positive results. The internal quality management system caught the discrepancy and issues an updated report once the sample was rerun; it was negative. The updated report is what spurred the lawsuits and the appeal. Nicolette also noted that Oisin was not in the States for the time period two months before the incident and for seven months after the incident. Emails were obtained via search warrant that proved that Oisin did not have prior knowledge of the dry-labbing and did not have any role, oversight, or input into the disciplinary action due to the dry-labbing. There were financial records of Oisin included in the file; he contributed $276, 000 to the laboratory in the past three years, but nothing in the last year book-ending the incident. The funds were used to purchase equipment that was needed; there was even a proposal from the laboratory which outlined the need for the funds á la grant proposal. On the surface, so far this case is a slam dunk, Nicolette thought as she continued to thumb through the files. The next group of files were all the lab results both falsified and corrected. It was noted Oisin name was not on the report or contained in any of the files. Nicolette decided to call Erin and take her statement to get a better idea of the case because the files did not explain why Oisin was being sued. Nicolette dialed the supervisor of the laboratory; she answered the phone sounding a bit annoyed. Nicolette introduced herself and informed that she was representing Oisin; Erin soften her tone tremendously. "I am sorry. I have been bombarded with interview requests, lawyers, and everything in between. How can I help you?" Nicolette started with an easy topic and group of questions, "Honestly, I am trying to build a defense for Oisin. Can you start by giving me some background on you and how you came to work at Compliance Assurance Testing?" Erin let out an unnecessary, but fairly audible sigh, "I am a chemist. I studied chemistry, specifically physical chemistry at the University of Pennsylvania. After graduating from Penn, I studied under Dr. Besty Ford-Gunn at Penn State University where I received a MS degree in Toxicology. I am board certified and have been published several times in the past two decades. I am a respectable member of several societies and I am respected in my field. This *person* has ruined all that I spent the last two decades of my life building. I came to Michigan to be with my husband; he is from here and he wanted to be near home to get help with the kids. My ideal job would have been at a larger laboratory or working for one of the many mass spectrometer companies. They all do a lot of research and I would have resources at my disposal that I do not have here in Michigan. Sadly, now my career is over because of a selfish, racist little twit." Nicolette was taking notes as Erin spoke, "Ok. Great. Thank you for that background information. Why do you think John is racist?" Erin was quiet as she realized she allowed her frustration to get the better of her, "My apologies," she said quite sternly, obviously trying to cover her tracks, "that is opinion, not fact. I would rather, if possible, focus solely on fact." Nicolette agreed that facts were the only important aspect of the case, "Switching gears back to the case, would you classify this as dry-labbing? And can you please define explicitly what dry-labbing is? Erin stated very simply, "Dry-labbing is when a specimen is not run in the instrumentation, but results are reported as if the sample was run. It is called dry-labbing because the specimens are wet and analysis of a dry, i.e. nonexistent, sample indicates that a sample was not run. In the Rodriguez case, it was indeed dry-labbing as the specimen was not analyzed until six months later. It was negative, but specimen degradation becomes a factor. We have done some, but not a full validation to six months on the ethanol, ethyl sulfate, and ethyl glucuronide analytes." Nicolette noted the information that Erin provided on the phone matched the information in the file. "Great!", Nicolette exclaimed, "Let's talk about how you found the dry-labbing." "I review all results. I am supposed to review results before they are released to the client. The quality manager was doing an audit and noted that there was a group of results that were released without my approval as my signature was not on the released results tab. The quality manager dug deeper and noted that the results that were missing my signature were all for criminal cases where a minority male was on trial for either manslaughter or drug facilitated sexual assault. There were a total of seven cases over the entirety of his career with the laboratory. Luckily, he is a newer employee and has only been employed here for 16 months." Nicolette heard the devil on her shoulder yell 'Oh, hell No!' but she had to keep her composure, "There seems to be a pattern here of delinquent behavior by John. Sixteen months is quite some time to have the power he wielded. Can you provide more information about these other cases that were dry-labbed? Erin, did you go back and run those samples? Were any of them positive?" Erin pauses for a moment, "Nicolette, is it? I want to provide you with all the information you need to defend Oisin, but I cannot disclose information about other cases as they do not have any bearing on this case." Nicolette understood her point of view and did not push it, at this time, "Okay. Since you cannot provide me information on that, can you let me know how did John become employed at the laboratory? How is Oisin involved in the hiring?" Erin laughed a bit before slowly describing the way that John was hired, "John is the fraternity brother of one of my colleagues. I run the production laboratory, but he runs the research & development team which works with the same staff as we are small. They went to Lehigh University together. I was not consulted in his hiring, but when we got this new account that needed their backlogged tested it was all hands on deck, so to speak. Once I got to review his resume his degree was not in the hard sciences, but in general studies. He said he took 'a few science classes and did well in them'. His friend, my colleague, reviewed some of the work that was dry-labbed. He was not authorized to do so under our ISO quality management system. Oisin has zero input in our hiring practices. I did not know he existed until this lawsuit. I have been working here five years." Nicolette thanked Erin for her time and stated that she will be I touch and went back to reviewing the files. She was searching for the name of the colleague of Erin who attended college with John and was responsible for his hiring. In the files of the test reports, Nicolette saw the name Robyn Clementson. Nicolette looked for the contact information for Robyn in all the files and saw that the number was the same as the number for Erin, but with a different extension. On the phone, Nicolette introduced herself to Robyn. He avoided all pleasantries and jumped directly into the conversation, "You are calling about John. I plead the fifth. Thank you for your call. You can reach out to my lawyers." Nicolette interjected before he hung up the phone, "Sir, I am Oisin's attorney. I am looking for general information about hiring." "Oh. I am sorry, but I have been bombarded with calls about John and his dry-labbing. This has been a complete nightmare and career ending," Robyn said apologetically, "How can I help Oisin. He is a very cool dude." "How do you know Oisin?" Nicolette asked surprisingly since Erin seem to not to know him as well. "Oisin is a shareholder of the company. I met him about a year or so ago; he has ensured that we get our paycheck when times are rough, I learned. We had some tough times over the last few years. We were on an up-swing, but this dry-labbing shit will ruin us." Robyn commented. Dissecting his statements, Nicolette believed that Robyn did not know Oisin very well either. "I see in the files that Oisin provided me that you released the results of the dry-labbing. Can you walk me through how you review results and how you did not catch that the results were dry-labbing?" Robyn sighed very audibly, "Yes, I am noted as the person who reviewed the results, but as John has testified I never actually reviewed the labs. I trust the people who work for me and I took him at his word. I am disappointed because he is a Delta Up brother; we were close. I was his big brother. Our motto is about justice…" Nicolette could hear in his voice that he felt betrayed. She saw from the files that he was not being indicted, "I see. So you did not know that he was dry labbing samples, until when?" "I was the person who discovered the other samples that were dry-labbed. I reviewed all his results. I spoke to John and got him to confess. I spoke to him about our principles as brothers and as scientists. I know he is not truly a scientist, but he worked with us for almost two years and he took this job seriously. I do not know what lead to the dry-labbing. I tried to talk to him about it and he disregards my inquiries." Robyn stated sounding as if he was trying to resolve the situation in his mind. Nicolette had only a few more questions for Robyn, "Did Oisin know about the dry-labbing? Do you know if Oisin ever met John? And finally, how do you still have your job?" Robyn sounded indignant, "I have my job because I have a Master's degree in chemistry from a good university. I am published and worked at a renowned pharmaceutical company. I was not involved in the dry-labbing. That has been proven. And despite what Erin may think, I am good at my job. I wish Oisin the best. He had nothing to do with this. Good day." The phone line went dead and Nicolette went back to the files.

Nicolette thought she had a good defense for Oisin in the case in which she was contracted. She completed looking at the files and while she had not contacted John yet, Nicolette felt confident in the information about the case. She checked the clock and decided to get Lebanese food for lunch. There was a wonderful restaurant near the firm that had good lunch specials that allowed her to get hummus, chicken shwarma, rice, and crushed lentil soup without breaking the bank. Nicolette enjoy the meal though it was much later than she preferred. At 3:00 p.m., she decided it was time to speak to John. The call was placed to the prison and a message was left with both the prison and the attorney defending John. A return call was received just before 4:00pm. With his attorney on the line, Nicolette was granted an interview with John. "Thank you for returning my call. My name is Nicolette Guyere and I am representing Oisin Chua in a lawsuit that was filed against him in response to the actions of your client, John P. Day. Those actions are in regards to the testing of the Rodriguez case, where Mr. Day has admitted to reporting results without testing the samples. I have spoken to Ms. Erin Nixon and Mr. Robyn Clementson already and wanted to get information from Mr. Day." Nicolette started the conversation in a very standard manner as she did not know what to expect from John Day. "Thank you, Ms. Guyere, for reaching out to Mr. Day and myself. He is happy to answer any questions that you may have, but please note there are some topics that I will advise him against. Please start your questions. Wayne Daniels, the attorney. "Thank you Mr. Daniels. Mr. Day, can you please provide me, first, your background and how you became to work at the Compliance Assurance Testing?" Nicolette started with a softball question, looking to corroborate what she already learned. "Sure. Thank you for getting my side of the story. I appreciate you wanting to talk to me as so many people are painting me to be a villain. I am just human, so again, thank you. I got the job at Compliance Assurance through my fraternity brother, Robyn. As you know, I am sure, I am not a scientist. I did take numerous science classes at Lehigh, but my degree was in general studies. I was not a specialist like many in college – I loved so many topics that I took as many classes as I could on so many topics. My college advisor kept trying to get me to declare a major, but I did not know what I wanted to be when I grew up. I did well in all my classes, but there was not just one topic. Robyn told me about the position after he posted it on the frat's job listing board. He was my big brother and he knew that I was idle and just floating between dead end jobs. He was looking out for me. He is a good guy. I can get you a copy of my transcripts if it would help in Oisin's defense. To be honest, I do not know why he is even on trial. I have never even met him." Noting that all the items he stated matched what she already knew, Nicolette bounced on the fact that John did not know Oisin, "So you never met Oisin, but was he involved in your hiring or any of the cases that you tested during your tenure at Compliance Assurance Testing?" "No, I learned about him through Robyn. He explained that he was kinda like Bruce Wayne – a rich young guy that wanted to improve the world by using his money in a positive way. I never communicated with him, met him, or have any knowledge of him having any say in what I did day-to-day or my employment as a whole. To be honest, I do not understand how he is even related to the Rodriguez case" "Thank you for that background, John. Can you give me some background on the Rodriguez case and how we got to where we are today?" Nicolette asked expecting an objection of Mr. Daniels to the topic. "Sure. It is already documented that Mr. Rodriguez had failed his field sobriety test and was being tested for causing the death of three people. We received two samples from him; an A sample and a B sample. That was uncommon in simple test cases so I knew something was up. Plus his samples came escorted by State Police. I already admitted that made a mistake and reported based on my assumptions and not the results, but what people do not know is that I did not report these results on my own." John started. "Mr. Day, you cannot reveal that information as that is protected as part of your deal. Trend lightly," Mr. Daniels interjected. "Ok. Thanks, Wayne. The bottom line is that Erin and Robyn may not have signed off on the results, but they are not the only persons in the laboratory to have input in results being released. Half of our instruments were down and we were being pressured. Oisin may not have any impact on this case, but Dich is his right hand. Here. There at your company. And everything else that Oisin touches in the US." Nicolette kept her composure as she weighed what John was alleging. "Ok. So Dich released the falsified, dry-labbed result?" "Yes." John stated flatly. "Did you know that he was releasing the result? Did he know that the result was not run?" Nicolette probed trying to understand the situation better. Mr. Daniels interjected. "Okay, let me clarify my question. Can you walk me through how Dich is involved with Compliance Assurance Testing?" Nicolette backtracked to ensure that she stayed on track. John simply stated that "Dich is the CEO. He comes here four to five times a week to check up on the laboratory, ensure we are making money, deal with any personnel issues, and he does approve/release results. Erin and Robyn both argue with him about it, but he is a physician. I knew that Dich promised that results to Sgt. Romeo, but I told him that we had instruments down and that it was not scheduled to be run. He asked for my opinion about the sample and the case. I gave him the facts that we had and he said that was all he needed to know. He thanked me and left. I did not know the result was released until" "John, you are off track again" Mr. Daniels interjected again. "I see. So how is Oisin related to any of this?" Nicolette asked drawing the conversation back to her client. "Dich was hired by Oisin at the laboratory," John stated matter-of-factly. Nicolette thanked them for their time and asked for them to schedule a call tomorrow morning so she can ask some follow-up questions. They agree and she went to find Oisin to ask some difficult questions. Nicolette found Oisin in Dich's office and she asked if he had time for her to ask some questions of him. Dich motioned for her to join them in his office, but she declined and asked for him to join her for a few moments in her office. Dich raised an eyebrow as he stood to join them. "Alone," Nicolette stated flatly in Dich's direction. Oisin waved Dich off and followed Nicolette to her office. Nicolette motioned for him to sit and she closed the door. She walked around the desk slowly and sat. Nicolette was motionless and quiet for a moment. "Oisin, I researched your case, as you asked, and before I give you my opinion and we discuss your defense I have a couple of questions about the structure of Compliance Assurance Testing. First, who runs the day-to-day dealings of the laboratory? Who signs the checks for the laboratory? Who makes the hiring and firing decisions?" Oisin sat back in the chair; it seemed evident that he knew that these questions meant that Nicolette had all the information and just wanted confirmation. "Yes, I am being sued because Dich falsified

115

the results and I sign all the checks even though I have no input in the day-to-day activities. Dich makes all the decisions about the laboratory." Nicolette leaned forward in her chair, placed her hands together in a pyramid, and looked into Oisin's eyes. "You are aware that Dich falsified records. You know John took the blame, probably on Dich's insistence, and now you are being sued. What am I missing here? I am certain there is probably a paper trial because you have full audit trial at the laboratory." Oisin leaned back in his chair, "They need a scapegoat and John fit the ticket. His attorney is trying to throw out the confession, but it is already accepted and being used to release Rodriguez from prison. I did not know about the falsified results until I got the notice that I was being sued when I got to the States for this visit. They apparently went to serve me at the laboratory. I had my IT firm pull emails and I know Dich and Sgt. Romeo were communicating before the result was released saying how the Rodriguez person deserved to rot in prison. Apparently, Sgt. Romeo was friends of the parent of one of the decedents. I learned from the emails Dich promised to help him. I have already confronted Dich and under the terms of his contracts, I have little recourse because gross negligence is not defined as dry-labbing in the contract. I have sought opinions and most lawyers say that if he is prosecuted then I can remove him, but not until then. This is why I am here." "So, why did you ask me to get involved? I am new here and I left a good job to come here," Nicolette asked. "Well, I know you are a free thinker and you would not let his opinions or threats move you to betray your morals. Your job is safe regardless of the outcome of this case. I just want to clear my name and move forward," Oisin stated. Dich knocked and walked in without waiting for a response. "My apologies for interrupting, but I need Oisin. We have a conference call that we need to be on in five minutes. I am sure that there is nothing earth shattering going on in here. You can pick this up tomorrow." Nicolette looked at Dich with contempt. Oisin smiled at Nicolette and thanked her for her hard work. Nicolette looked over the case file and sighed. She decided that she needed a large scotch and went straight to the bar for happy hour.

Chapter Nine

Nicolette found the bar to be very full. There was only one bar seat available when she walked in. She noted that the empty chair was next to the gentleman that most women do not like sitting next to because he is relentless when he hits on them. His persistence is not attractive though he is an attractive man, with the exception of his teeth. Honestly, he would be attractive if he sought out a dentist to fix his teeth; some of them were crooked, some of them were discolored, and a few were broken. Nicolette walked slowly down the bar noting the fullness of each persons' glass. Being happy hour, most were either drinking as much as possible or nursing the beverage so that can drive home shortly. She sat down next to Peter and he smiled heartedly at her, she nodded her greeting and he complimented her. "How are you this evening, young lady?" Peter asked and then sipped his beer. Nicolette ordered a long island, her drink of choice, and turned to Peter, "I am in need of this beverage. It has been a long confusing day. How are you, Peter? How are the kids?" Peter, who was a public school teacher in Detroit, answered, "I'm good. The kids are good. Doing my best to teach them the sciences; I have a couple students that tell me that they want to be scientist because of me. It is sad that the school year is drawing to a close and I have yet to get the funding that I was promised at the beginning of the year. So I have spent a lot more of my money than I anticipated at the beginning of the year so the date I would take you on will not be as grand." He smiled big and leaned into Nicolette. She tried her best to not roll her eyes too hard. Peter laughed before she could respond, "WOW. That is one hell of an eye roll. Was it that bad of a line? I thought it was a pretty sweet tie-in." Nicolette laughed, "I am not seeking to date at this moment. But I appreciate the laugh." "I am just trying to make you laugh, Mama. I do not need an eye roll that hard. We get along. All the years we sit here talking Tigs, Wings, hell, even Stones. I hope you know that I am not trying to hit on you. You're not even my type," Peter responded. Nicolette immediately felt offended thinking to herself that this man that no one wanted was rejecting her. She did know what to say so her rejection spoke for her, "oh, I am not good enough for the likes of you? Good to know! Not that I was interested but it makes me happy to know that I, a lawyer with years of experience and a good person, was not good enough for a teacher, who most women at this bar reject." Peter seemed to smile to himself and Nicolette realized that she walked directly into his trap and he was quite pleased because he took her reaction to mean that she had feelings, even if just lust, for him. "It is not that you are not attractive, Nici." "Nicolette" she interjected. "Nicolette. I find you very attractive. I just am not into black women. I would gladly take you home and fuck you. Hell, I would enjoy fucking you; that I am sure. But I am want something real, long-term. I just do not see me dating a black woman. I do not see the benefit of that. So I am sorry if I offended you, but you aren't my type." Peter continued in a very apologetic manner. Nicolette felt like an idiot. First, she did not see that Dich was holding all the cards at work and was pulling her strings and now she is sitting at the bar feeling rejected by a man she never even wanted her. Gathering herself, Nicolette responded to the situation, "Peter, I do not care if you find me attractive or not, but I do thank you for the compliment. I must come off pressed for you, but let me assure you that I am not. I have *zero* desire to fuck you." Nicolette shook her head and took a long sip of her beverage to allow for the pause. "I did not think so; I thought we had a mutual non-desire for one another." Peter responded. Nicolette nodded. As they were speaking William, a Detroit police officer that was, also, a regular at the bar, walked into the bar. William had been courting Nicolette at the bar and the gym for months. She felt he was kind and attractive, but Nicolette did not see anything long-term with him. William waved at Nicolette and Peter and came and stood next to them. They watched and discussed the Detroit Tigers game for about twenty minutes before Peter excused himself. He had class the next morning. William sat in Peter's old seat and they discussed the game and the events of the day. Nicolette did not know if it was his job or him being understanding, but he listened to her plot and was very sympathetic. They spoke for an additional thirty minutes or so and from the bar they walked back to his apartment. Nicolette thought it would be nice to watch the end of the game at William's apartment. When they entered the high rise off of Adams Street in downtown Detroit, overlooking Comerica Park, Nicolette walked around and saw a clean, safe looking apartment. It was two bedrooms, one bath that she could see. She walked briefly through the rooms that William was pointing out to her; it was a quaint home which included space for William and his son that he had part-time. After the tour, she sat on the couch while William turned on the game. He took her presence in the apartment as a signal that she was open to his advances. While they have spoken briefly here and there, Nicolette made it clear that she was celibate and her only sexual releases are experienced from Domme space and masturbation. William said that he could serve her well, but Nicolette did not see him in that space. He sat next to her on the couch and pointed to her heeled feet. She placed one of her feet in his lap and he started massaging her feet and sucking on her toes. His technique was enjoyable, but Nicolette had a hard time reaching Domme space with William as she did not see him as someone she wanted to own or play with. He continued to massage and worship her feet, while she tried to enjoy the game. He informed her that the game was over; he heard the muffled cheers from the ball park from the apartment windows. He was aware of what the sounds were, but Nicolette did not. She continued to watch the game waiting on the television delay to catch up.

Nicolette resolved herself to the fact that the game was over and that the Tigers had won, but she wanted to see the ending for herself as it was a close game. William went to remove Nicolette's underwear, asking if he could lick her. "What do you mean by lick me?" Nicolette asked. "I am not trying to make you uncomfortable, but I can make you feel pleasure you will never forget," William said. Nicolette did not think it was fair of her to use William as she had no plans of sleeping with him or reciprocating. "William, I am celibate. I have not had sex in years and I do not plan on having sex again until I am confident in the relationship. I, also, do not give blowjobs. I do not know what you are looking to do here, but if you want to orally please me, I think I am open to that." William tried to remove Nicolette's underwear, but she did not respond. Nicolette stopped his advance and reiterated, "William, seriously, what is your end game?" "I wanted to make you feel something that you will soon never forget," William stated yet again. "Yes, you mention that, but you have failed continually to answer my inquiry." Nicolette exclaimed again. William was starting to sound as if he was angry, with a mix of frustration, "It is not like you are a virgin. I am not going to make you do anything you do not want to do. Either you want to come on my tongue or you don't. Your choice." Nicolette peered at William as he continued to oscillate between worshipping her feet and trying to remove her panties. Nicolette finally granted permission for oral sex so William slowly removed her panties while slowly sinking to his knees. Expecting him to perform cunnilingus, Nicolette was taken aback when he started to perform analingus. He was very much into the act going as far as pushing Nicolette over the chair in the living room of the apartment to gain better access to her asshole. Nicolette was enjoying the sensation of his tongue darting in and around her anus and she was getting turned on by his action. The television was still on the Tigers game coverage and she, by reflex, cheered for some of the highlights of the game that she did not see live. William was upset and stopped trying to please her with his tongue; sighing to himself as he stopped his oral worship. He expressed ire by Nicolette's lack of focus of their sexual encounter. She apologized, picked up her panties, and made her way towards to the exit. William tried to stop her, physically by grabbing on her and pushing her back against the wall in the hallway towards the door. Nicolette could feel his hands grind into her arms as he forcefully tried to keep her in the apartments. She was not sure why, but a feeling of being unsafe washed over her and so she laughed it off, "I think it is getting late and I have work in the morning, but please text me this weekend. Maybe we can go out sometime." William sighed and expressed his desire to continue their sexual encounter and pushed Nicolette forcibly towards the apartment. Every red flag that could sound was going off in her head and Nicolette's fight or flight reaction started in her head. She started once again to leave the apartment; the hallway to the door seemed much longer than it did when she entered. William grabbed her by the arms again and tried to push her towards the apartment, but Nicolette braced for the initial impact and pushed back, advancing the both of them towards the door. "Damn! You're strong! I guess you have not missed as many days at the gym as I have," William said as he tries to push her into the apartment, but to no avail. Nicolette was stronger than his advancements, truly fighting her way past him, and reaching the door. He puckered for a kiss and she kissed him lightly on his cheek as she finally pushed past him and left. Nicolette reviewed the evening in her head trying to ensure that she did not lead him on; feeling guilty she texted an innocuous message letting him know that she made it home. He responded that he had a lovely time that evening and that valued their friendship. There were not any answers for the questions that were running through her head. Nicolette could not shake the feeling that she avoided being raped just a few moments earlier.

Nicolette went to bed hoping that Thursday at work would be leaps and bounds better than her Wednesday. At least, she had plans to hang out with a financial submissive after work; if need be Nicolette could focus on that all day to distract her from the hell of the day. Nicolette woke up to 14 messages on her phone, where more than half of them were from Dich. Nicolette yawned, groaned, and started getting ready for the day. She decided to get all her items ready for later and take them all to work with her since she was anticipating a long day. Nicolette donned a simple suit with an A-line skirt and short waist jacket. She packed her briefcase, lunch, and then headed for the office. When Nicolette pulled up she could see that Dich was waiting outside of her office; he was speaking to Oisin. She sat in her car and said a prayer to both St. Ives and St. Thomas More, the patron saint of lawyers. Nicolette asked them for strength and patience. She stepped out of her car and walked into the building. Nicolette nodded a greeting to the men and tried to walk past them to her office, but Dich started in, "Do you not answer text messages from your boss anymore?" Nicolette held tightly on her "eastside" and responded as she removed her phone, "Oh. It seems I have fourteen new messages….and eight are from you, Dich," Nicolette opened the messages and started reading them as she walked into her office with both Dich and Oisin in tow, "No, I do plan on handling the Oisin case tomorrow. I do think we have a viable defense. I do know your role in this case….and no, it is not part of our defense. I do not have any files from the other cases and I, honestly, do not want to know about all that unless it becomes impactful on my case. I do not have any opinion on the laboratory or its employees. Yes, I am aware that there is an appeal in the works for John which he and his attorney are confident about, but no they did not divulge the aspects of their appeal." Nicolette started scrolling faster, reading the spiral that Dich was typing last night, "And…that covers all your questions." "Well, you have to defend me against whatever John and Wayne Daniels have planned," Dich interjected emphatically. "While I appreciate the confidence you have in me and in my skills, it is clearly a conflict of interest for me to represent you, Dich, and Oisin. Your interests are in direct conflict. So unless you have any other questions for me, I really need to review the information I gathered yesterday and perform a couple more interviews this morning." Dich looked extremely angry so Oisin, who had been surprisingly quiet, stated "Dich, I think Nicolette has a point. She cannot do her work here as well as all the items she has to do to defend me if she also has to research your cases. You are being pulled into several areas, but I am just being restricted to the one case. Perhaps someone with a smaller case load, like Julie, can defend you. As you said, your cases could resolve themselves and Julie is competent – her work has billed more hours than almost any attorney here." "Julie is not my attorney; she is an incompetent fool," Dich yelled. Nicolette just peered at them; she was not going to give the conversation any traction as she knew she would not defend Dich. Oisin stated flatly, "Well, Nicolette cannot do both. We have liability insurance for the laboratory; they will assign an attorney and I am sure that they will be adequate. Let us allow Nicolette to start her day." Nicolette was able to keep her head under the radar and worked her way through the rest of the day with interviews for the case and preparing for the new hires she has starting that she wish were already on the job. She did receive some probing from the stem cell case; Nicolette was hoping to put it on hold long enough to get through the hearing with Oisin. After responding to the email inquiry which was requesting immediate scheduling as the plaintiff was very ill and wanted to see the end of the case. Nicolette stated that she did not have enough time for discovery and that immediate scheduling would be detrimental to her client's case, but did agree that she could start the jury selection process in order to speed up the case for the plaintiff. Around 6:30pm, Nicolette received a text from Heinrich stating that he was on his way to Somerset

Mall. They had a prearranged outing and she started to pack up her items to go shopping.

Nicolette arrived at the mall only ten minutes after the planned time. She changed into some flat dress shoes that matched the suit she was wearing and walked into the mall to meet Heinrich at the arranged meeting place. Heinrich, too, was coming from work and he was looking quite dapper in a fine pinstriped suit, overcoat, while holding his hat. Nicolette took a moment to enjoy his aesthetic; he was tall, attractive, and reminiscent of the footballer, David Beckman. She does not always take the time to enjoy him physically, but as he grinned at her as she moved through the mall towards him she could not help but to enjoy the view. "Good evening, Mistress. Thank you for meeting me here. I appreciate being able to provide you with whatever your heart's desire. Would you like to shop first or go to dinner?" Heinrich asked once Nicolette made it to his side. "I would love to get dinner and a very LARGE drink, first. Then we can go to my bra store first. I need several new bras. Next I want to get some bath bombs and make-up." "Ok, Mistress. Where would you like to go for dinner? There seems to a number of good restaurants here at the mall." Heinrich asked as he walked, slowly, with Nicolette to the map that was nearby. "PF Chang's is a good option as they have a number of great entrees and some decent beverages. Plus it is around that corner and there does not seem to be a line as I passed by it when I got here," Nicolette answered passing the map and heading in the direction of the restaurant. Heinrich followed closely behind her. They reached the restaurant and they were seated immediately. "So, I guess I should not ask how your day went, huh, Mistress?" Heinrich pondered after they took their seat. "I noticed that you were not on Yahoo! messenger nor have you logged into collar me in a few days. Is everything ok? I noticed you were late. That is not like you, Ma'am." Nicolette ran her hands up to her forehead, holding it briefly, before proceeding to run her hands over her entire head towards the base of her neck where she paused to massage her own shoulders. "It has been a very long, difficult week and it is only Thursday. I need this distraction badly so for that I appreciate this shopping trip." The server approached the table and inquired about drinks; they both ordered something and returned to their discussion. "So would you like to discuss what is ailing you or is this something that is privileged?" Heinrich asked trying to provide her an outlet. "I appreciate the listening ear, but this is not a topic that needs to be discussed. Work will get easier in the next few weeks as I hired people to reduce my workload. So what do you usually eat with Chinese food? I am thinking we can get two dishes and share them, family style. I love sesame chicken and Mongolian beef. I enjoyed both brown and white steamed rice. I do not enjoy PF Chang's fried rice. Does that work for you or do you want to order something else?" Nicolette stated changing the topic from work. "I do enjoy both sesame chicken and Mongolian beef. If I had my choice, I would prefer white steamed rice. Also, can we have fried dumplings as well?" Heinrich inquired. The waiter returned to the table with beverages, "Ma'am, here is your top shelf Long Island Ice Tea. Sir, your Macallan 18 year. Are you ready to order?" Nicolette looked at Heinrich and nodded. "Yes, we will start with an order of fried dumplings. We will then have both the sesame chicken and Mongolian beef, to share. We will prefer white steamed rice. Thank you." "Ok. Thank you, sir. I will put in the order right away." The server stated as he gathered the menus and walked away from the table. "So how was your trip? Did you get everything done that you wanted at your Auburn Hills and Ann Arbor facilities?" Nicolette asked of Heinrich. "This was a very productive trip as we were able to vet the system that we will be expanding to all our plants here in the US. We are ahead of schedule and we tested the entire concept. I will be able to use this stepping stone for the promotion that I have been trying to get for the past four years. The criticism of me in the EVP role has been that I have not run a successful, large scale project from conception through proof of concept. This was that earmark project and we have exceeded my modest projections for ROI. I am quite excited to return to Germany and speak with my superior. We already have an appointment scheduled." Heinrich answered with a beaming of pride and excitement. Nicolette considered his answer briefly, "So, you would not be traveling back to the US much anymore as EVP, correct?" Heinrich answered quickly, "No, I would be limited in my travel. But, I will have vacation time and you are my favorite Dominant. You use me in ways that make me crave more. I would gladly send you a monthly stipend, especially if I get the increase in salary that comes with the promotion." Nicolette sighed, "I am not really into getting money, no matter how great, in the mail randomly. I enjoy the interaction as I do not need the money." Heinrich frowned. It was clear from the pensive look on his face that he had no response to the Nicolette's desires in regards to financial servitude. The waiter returned and dropped off the fried dumplings to the table, both ordered a second round of their beverages. Nicolette picked up her chopsticks and cleaned the slivers off the wood by rolling them between her hands, while doing the task mindlessly she addressed Heinrich, "Where in Germany are you? I love to travel and have yet have a finslave that could afford to fly me to them. I am assuming an EVP could afford such." Heinrich's demeanor perked up considerably, "Oh, yes, Ms. Nicolette." He said with a growing smile, "my salary now allows for such an arrangement. I never knew you had a desire to visit Germany. I am outside of Mannheim. There are so many wonderful things to go and visit in Germany – not just in Mannheim." Nicolette picked up a dumpling, dipped it in the sauce provided and bit into the morsel. It was the perfect mixture of salty, meaty, and sweet. She has always enjoyed the dumplings at PF Chang's. Heinrich also begun enjoying the dumplings as Nicolette placed the second half of her dumpling into her mouth. She sat back in her chair as the server dropped off their second round of drinks. "I have not been to Germany since leaving the chemical company. They are headquartered in Ludwigshafen. I enjoyed my time there. I know the two towns are very close. I would love to travel there again. What city, if you do not mind sharing, is your home in? Where would my hotel be – closer to your office or your home?" Nicolette asked. "I am in Baden-Württemberg, Germany as well- in the town of Limbergerhof. It is very close to both Mannheim and Ludwigshafen. There is a lovely 4-star hotel in Limbergerhof and it is fairly new. You can stay there or one of the American chains in Mannheim. Mistress, I cannot fib as my mind is racing with you taking control of me at home. I must not leave my chair." Heinrich beamed with pleasure. Nicolette smiled and continued to eat the dumplings. Their entrée arrived at the table before they had finished the dumplings, but both continued to enjoy the appetizer and prepare mounds of rice for dinner. "Well, Heinrich, that trip is at least a few months in the future. Let us enjoy this meal and the shopping tonight and go from there." Nicolette stated very matter-of-factly. The rest of the dinner conversation was polite, not in-depth. They conversed mostly about the taste of the meal and who wanted which dish passed/placed on their plate. As they ate, Nicolette begun searching her mind for the details of Heinrich profile that she had not read in months. She has been allowing him to cater to her frivolous wants for almost one year, but she did not remember why their relationship was solely financial in nature. "Is everything ok, Mistress?" Heinrich asked, peering at Nicolette, attempting to make eye contact. Nicolette noted that she was lost in her thoughts for much longer than she anticipated. "Yes, everything is fine, Heinrich. Thank you for asking. I was lost thinking why our relationship was purely financial. I tend to at least friend those under my thumb in some way, shape, or form. It has been a year of you buying me things, taking me to dinners, sending me gifts, and generally being one of the best finslaves I have ever had. Not to look a gift sub in the mouth, but why have we only gone this far? Like, what is your goal in BDSM? Are you content?" Heinrich turned from beaming with joy over the potential German rendezvous to turning almost ashen white, "I...I am not...I cannot...I do not...Mistress, I am not able to dedicate myself to a relationship. I have tried. Both normal and kinky. Each time the woman always want more than I can give. They are disappointed. I am heartbroken. With work and travel, I work up to 80 hours a week. By the time I am done with that, I have nothing for anyone each. I am beyond spent, but I am content with just a relationship where I help financially, we enjoy each other's company, and help fulfill desires. I can become fulfilled with just getting release from being needed." "When was the last time you had sex?" Nicolette asked abruptly. Heinrich choked slightly on his dinner, took a sip of his beverage, and replied, "It has been years. I was able to orally please my last girlfriend in the last months of our relationship, but I have not been able to get an erection from sexual contact or thoughts for almost a decade. I do experience erections; I am most erect when I am being used financially. Most women, even dominant women, do not understand how their nude, often gyrating, body does illicit a respond. Are you looking for sex?" Nicolette shook her head 'no' as she finished chewing the bite in her mouth. "No, I, generally, do not engage in sex with those under me with the exception of pegging. On even rare occasion, I have contact with someone on a personal level and I use their face as a grinding post. Fucking their mouth, as it were. I have noticed your erections with me, often if I am being modest. I find it interesting that you do not receive pleasure from an attractive woman grinding on you," Nicolette shrugs. The waiter returned to the table to check on their progress and satisfaction with the meal. Heinrich expresses their contentment and the server departs. "Yes, Ma'am. You are correct. I have often had a very erect member in your presence. I have, also, pleasured myself to the thought of you using me. But I have never imagined that use to be sexual.

Maybe I am a broken toy. So, I guess we have the perfect relationship. I am spending 95% of my available funds on you; there is a young woman, she's in her mid-twenties, that I do buy things for in Germany. Do you want an exclusive relationship? I can easily cut her off. I would be glad to be owned again," Heinrich commented with a slightly giddy tone. "We can discuss that in more detail later. Let's finish this meal and start shopping." Nicolette stated simply as she finished her dinner. They both completed eating their meal, Heinrich paid the tab, and they made their way to Intimacy. They entered the store and Nicolette walked directly to the drawers that carried her size. Heinrich took a pause to look around, while she looked through the drawer and started picking several bras from the drawer. There were Panache and PrimaDonna in several colors and styles. Nicolette selected one of every color and style for purchase and at least $70 each; Heinrich spent $600 on lingerie. Heinrich smiled wide while the store clerks tried to make small talk and discern their relationship. Nicolette was pleased with the variety of bras that she was getting; they were a blue one with purple flowers, a plain tan one, two black ones with different designs, a red and black 'demi-bra' only a couple size too small that will allow for a full cup, red bra with a leaf design, and orange and pink bra with a leaf design. Heinrich completed the transition and they walked out of the store. "Mistress, what is our next store?" Nicolette pointed across the mall, "We need to go to Lush now." They walked to the store where Nicolette picked out four different bath bombs including the avocado one, two massage bars which include shea and cocoa butter, and one shower scrub. Heinrich spent almost $70 on bath products. He was beaming with pride and his erection was obvious in his pants and they walked to the store next door. "I just need to grab a lip balm and a face scrub before we leave the mall." Nicolette stated as she walked to the shelves. "Whatever you want, Mistress." Heinrich responded, clearly deep in subspace. Inside Origins, she got a bottle of United State, a beet lip balm, and a lip liner in a color of purple-red. Heinrich paid the bill and they made their way to the exit as he carried all the bags. At Nicolette's car, Heinrich placed the bags in her truck and hugged Nicolette long and hard. "Thank Mistress. This has been one of the best days of my life. I appreciate all that you have done for me. I will leave the States tomorrow knowing how amazing you are. Should I consider myself owned?" Heinrich asked pensively with hope in his voice. "Heinrich, I would love to have you as My personal wallet. We will have to iron out the details, though. Have a safe trip home. We will talk soon." They hugged once again and Nicolette made her way home. Placing the bags in the dressing room without unpacking, she prepared for bed. Nicolette washed her face and brushed her teeth. She went to bed much more content with her evening than she was with her entire day.

Friday morning was unseasonably warm. Nicolette stretched after her alarm went off- post snooze. She had been having a difficult time stirring that morning. It was probably because she felt the impending doom that the hearing would bring in the case for Oisin. Nevertheless, Nicolette went to the bathroom and started her morning tasks. She decided to wear her hair with curls instead of a bun in an effort to look less stern during the hearing. Bouncy curls tend to soften most lawyers and judges when dealing with her; Nicolette theorized that the curls made her look younger and therefore less threatening to some. After showering, cleaning her face, and brushing her teeth, she begun putting large barrel curls in her hair. She sighed as she expressed her disdain with the amount of new growth in her hair. "I guess some creamy crack is in my future." Regardless, Nicolette was able to get her hair to lay fairly flat even with the bushy roots. Sitting on the ottoman in her dressing room, Nicolette selected a cream pants suit with dark brown pinstripes, 4" platform stiletto heels in chocolate brown, and a satin brown camisole. After dressing, she took a glance of herself in the mirror and was content with the selection; it was natural and muted enough to not be considered flashy or unprofessional. She knew that regardless of what she wore, there would be critical, judgmental eyes on her. Nicolette used to file things in the 6th circuit for her previous employer and she always looked 'like a child playing dress-up' according to the judges and magistrates she appeared before. She was always prepared and argued all her cases well, but Nicolette was the one of the youngest attorneys in the district; definitely the youngest in her senior roles. "You are smart. You *earned* everything that you have professionally. You deserve every accolade and accomplishment you have. Do not let anyone knock you off your mark. You got this, Nici." Nicolette stared at herself in the mirror after her affirmations and finally felt ready for work. Nicolette gathered her files on Oisin's case and headed to the 6th circuit courthouse. With fighting through traffic to get downtown Pontiac, she arrived thirty minutes prior to the docket call time. Oisin arrived within minutes of Nicolette with Dich in tow. Nicolette reviewed the discovery items with Oisin again to ensure that he was comfortable with the defense she had laid out. Dich interrupted their discussion fourth times for clarification on how their defense would affect the cases he had pending. Nicolette continually replied that her focus was solely on Oisin and his case. She was not versed in all the details of the case against him and she could not responsibly comment. Dich's attorney arrived five minutes before the call time and introduced himself. He was appointed by the liability insurance company and had over thirty years experience practicing law. He was dressed very well in a dark blue suit, light blue shirt with jeweled cuff links, Swiss watch, and Italian shoes. He spoke briefly in private with Dich and returned to Nicolette asking for a summary of Oisin's defense. She tried to not look or sound frustrated when addressing him, "Mr. Coleman, our case starts in two minutes. I do not have time to give you a summary at this time." Mr. Coleman looked at Nicolette with disdain in his eyes, "Young lady, I have been doing this for years. They never run on time. You have a moment to provide me a summary of what you found in discovery as my client feels it negatively impacts our defense. Isn't he your boss? Why are you not prepared?" Nicolette raised her eyebrow at the attorney and before she could speak their case was being called into the courtroom. "As I said, I do not have time to hold your hand through the case you are about to defend." Nicolette led Oisin into the courtroom. Oisin was directed to sit on one side of a long table that had stenographer and audio recording equipment. Usually there was a magistrate that runs the depositions that are taken as primarily to determine if a case was going to be moved over to a judge trial, but this case was so egregious that the court determined that the deposition would be part of the trial itself. Therefore, there was going to be a judge assigned to deposition and final decisions could be made. Judge Samuel Johnson, who worked exclusively on the Federal docket, introduced himself. Nicolette had heard about him before the trial; he is described as fair and down-to-earth. She was looking forward to arguing the case before him. The prosecutor, on the other hand, was known for being ruthless and under handed. Nicolette and Oisin sat on their designated side of the table, given that this was a deposition, there were not opening statements, but other rules of orders apply. Judge Johnson introduced the case for the record, as he was speaking the prosecutor, Mr. Montgomery Bonds, asked to have Dich and his attorney removed from the courtroom. "Your Honor, I apologize for interrupting you, but the presence of Mr. Richard Hansen is very detrimental to the cases that are being brought against him later this day. I would like to have him removed and barred from these proceeding. n addition, I would like to request that all of his counsel be removed and barred. Ms. Nicolette Guyere, I hope you informed your client that that includes you," he said as he sat up in his chair and smirked at Nicolette. She was prepared for that move and commented, "Actually, Mr. Bonds, I am not and nor have I ever represented Mr. Hansen.

As you know, I am employed at a company in which he manages, but I have not and will not work on any of his liability cases. I know it is surprising to you, but that is what liability insurance covers. Your Honor, if it pleases the court, I did bring a detail list of the cases that I am covering under my employ." "Ok, I expected this case to be complicated, but I did not expect to be interrupted in my introduction. Mr. Bonds, do you have any proof that Ms. Guyere has worked on the defense of Mr. Hansen?" Judge Johnson asked. Mr. Bonds just shook his head 'no'. "Ok. Ms. Guyere, I will take that outline of your cases for the record. I know you submitted them to my office last week so I have already reviewed them. I will not ban Ms. Guyere from these proceeding as I have reviewed all the cases that she is working on and there are not any conflicts. Moreover, it is clear that Mr. Hansen has a legal team outside of his employment. It seems that Ms. Guyere's involvement in this case is also outside of her employment as well. As for public presence in these proceedings, I agree that the presence of potential defendants in related cases could make for an unfair advantage. Deputy, can you please clear this room with the exception of the persons seated here for the deposition." Dich was not pleased with the decision, "I am taxpaying citizen; according to the county charter, the public can sit in on these types of proceedings." Turning and addressing his lawyer, he continues, "C'mon, do your job! You said it was important to know what is going on in here!" The deputy escorted Dich and his attorney, one of the scientist from the lab, and the three other members of the galley from the room. The door was secured and Judge Johnson continued his introduction and statement of the decorum that he expected in his courtroom. "I, generally, introduced counsel to one another in an effort to ensure that proceedings are cordial, but it seems that you two are familiar enough. So let's jump right in.

Mr. Chua, are you aware of the reasons that you are here today?" Oisin looked at Nicolette who nodded for him to

133

answer the question. He proceeded, "I received a subpoena which stated that I was being sued by the States of Michigan, Florida, California, and New York. It is alleged that I was part in a conspiracy to defraud the aforementioned governments by costing them in court, rearing, and other costs by falsifying laboratory results through my laboratory, Compliance Assurance Testing." Judge Johnson motioned to Mr. Bonds, "Mr. Chua understands the charges pending against him, please begin your questioning." Mr. Bonds started quickly and pointedly, "Mr. Chua, what role do you play at Compliance Assurance Testing?" Oisin looked to Nicolette who arranged a system with him that she would write the number "2" if she needed him to stop talking. The system also included only answering the question that were asked of him and if in doubt, ask first. On the notepad in front of him she jotted the number zero. Oisin started to address the court, "Technically, I do not have a role at Compliance Assurance Testing. I am on the Board of the parent company, Science Initiative United, to several companies owned by Mr. William Sunner. I met Mr. Sunner through a mutual friend who went to school with him and traded with me. I funneled monies into his companies. I received return on many of many investments into his company. Compliance Assurance Testing is just one of many companies I invested in. I believe in the model that he and Dich, Mr. Hansen, outlined for me." Mr. Bonds continued his questioning, "So, you funded the ponzi scheme?" Nicolette objected, "Objection. Leading Question. Baseless. Seriously, Mr. Bonds?" Judge Johnson interjected, "Sustained. Mr. Bonds, please stay on course." Mr. Bonds restarted, "Mr. Chua, what do you do for this company on a day-to-day, week-to-week, month-to-month, year-to-year basis? What do you contribute?" Oisin responded, "My role is as an investor. I rarely have any input into the companies that I invest in around the world. I have zero input in the direction of the companies here in the States. I invest in the concept and hope to reap benefits from them if they are successful. I do not invest in companies if I do not see potential. I am a multimillionaire because I made good investment decisions, not because I threw my money away." Mr. Bonds seemed skeptical and continued his questioning, almost working with kid gloves, but Nicolette knew he was leading up to something, "Do you have any input in the Board of Directors in which you sit?" Nicolette wrote a two on the notepad. "I do not understand the question. Which Board of Directors are you asking me about, specifically?" "You do not understand my question? It was such a simple question. Judge Johnson, please compel him to answer the question." Mr. Bonds responded with disdain slightly veiled in his voice. "Mr. Chua, do you truly not understand Mr. Bonds' question?" Judge Johnson asked calmly and kindly. "Judge Johnson, I sit on the Board of several organizations. I am active in several organizations in so many countries that I did not want to volunteer something that was not the goal of the question. I want to be forth coming, but I also did not want to volunteer information that would do me harm. I know I have done nothing illegal or wrong, but I am not a fool." Mr. Bonds shifted in his chair, "What is wrong with volunteering information if you did nothing wrong?" Nicolette pounced, "Objection. Is Mr. Bonds presenting a case or fishing for a case? Seems he is badgering my client." Judge Johnson nodded and turned to Mr. Bonds, "Can you clarify your first question?" Mr. Bonds was becoming more red and is visually frustrated that his normal tactics were not working. "At Compliance Assurance Testing, do you, as a Board member, have any input into the daily workings of the company?" Nicolette wrote the number three onto the pad in front of Oisin. "I have never tried to have any input. I, in the several years that I been a Board member of Compliance Assurance Testing, have not had any input into the operations whether day-to-day or major decisions." Mr. Bonds look at his notes and looks pensively at Oisin and Nicolette and finally sits back in his chair. He signed loudly. Everyone looked at him as they awaited for him to continue.

After a pause of almost fifteen minutes, Judge Johnson prompted him to speak, "Mr. Bonds, do you have additional questions or does the prosecution close?" Mr. Bonds sat forward, "I do have one more questions. Mr. Chua, I do not see fault in you, but I need to know, are you covering for Mr. Hansen? I mean, are you part of this conspiracy?" "Objection!" Nicolette exclaimed. "No, what is the conspiracy about? What do I have to gain?" Oisin asked confused. Judge Johnson sustained the objection and after the prosecution rested, dismissed the cases against Oisin. They were informed that though the cases was tried in Michigan, all of the other jurisdictions deferred to the Michigan case and Oisin was free and had no other pending prosecution. Before Judge Johnson dismissed the participants, he made it clear that they were under a gag order and could not discuss the outcome of the case against Oisin. Both Nicolette and Oisin acknowledge that they understood the parameters of the gag order. They walked out of the court room and Oisin thanked Nicolette and stated that she would receive payment from her work separately from her normal pay. Dich walked up to them purposefully as they exited the room, "What happened? What was said? Are you ok?" Nicolette nodded at Oisin and walked towards the exit. Oisin, when in earshot of Nicolette stated, "Sorry, we cannot speak about it. We have a gag order. Good luck on your case. If what you told me was true then you should be ok." Dich's first case was called as Nicolette hit the exit door. As she walked through, she looked back and saw Dich entering the courtroom and Oisin halfway to the exit as well.

Nicolette made her way to her car and was angry because this case was what she hoped it would not be, a way to put Oisin out on a limb. She unlocked her door and sat in the driver's seat and let out a large sigh. Nicolette noted that she should not get comfortable in the position as it might be very short lived. Oisin knocked on the window, briefly startling Nicolette. As Nicolette rolled down the window, Oisin began speaking. "Sorry, I did not mean to startle you. Thank you again for the work you did on this case. So what do you think this means?" Nicolette managed a smile and replied, "Oisin, you have won all the pending cases against you in the matter. You will no longer be called as a defendant. I, also, highly doubt that you will be called as a witness in the cases pending and soon to be opened about Dich. You have been absolved of any wrongdoing. I do not know what Dich has told you, but my advice as your counsel would to be not discussing any of the pending cases against Dich with him or his counsel without your own representation." Oisin nodded as Nicolette spoke. He replied, "Do you think this is bad? Is the firm in trouble? Or the lab?" Nicolette looked Oisin in the eye as it was clear that he was truly on the outside and not fully aware of all the things that were going on, "Oisin, in discovery, I learned a lot of things and I only looked for one day. These prosecutors have been working this case for six month or more. I am sure things will be coming out that will not be good for the laboratory. I did not find anything that would jeopardize the firm. Protect yourself." He nodded and smiled. "Thank you, Ms. Guyere. I owe you a debt of gratitude." He reached into his pocket and handed her an envelope. "That is the going rate according to all my friends. I appreciate your help in this matter. If I am contacted by anyone in regards to this, I will direct them to you. Otherwise, I hope the remainder of our communications is pleasant and light." He smiled and turned to walk to his vehicle. Nicolette rolled up her window and started the drive to the firm. She pulled into the firm just before noon. She opened the envelope to see a personal check for $9, 600 with a note on the memo line, "saving my ass". Pleased with the fee, Nicolette tucked it into her purse and headed to work on her cases for the firm. She walked through the door to yet another brush with chaos. Julie walked up to Nicolette quickly, "Where have you been? George has been looking all over for you! We were served a subpoena for all of Dich's computers and some of the files for laboratory." Nicolette followed Julie towards the owner's office, "What agency served the paperwork?" Julie shook her head, "I do not know. Only George saw it." Nicolette and Julie arrived at George's office who was pacing and barking at his secretary to call Dich again. "He will not answer. He's in court. I just left there. He, Oisin, and I anticipate the laboratory as a whole are being sued by the State of Michigan. I know other states were also looking to sue them so this may turn into a federal prosecution." Nicolette spoke as she entered. Julie's jaw dropped open as Nicolette was speaking and the owner spun around, "Close the door, Jules." Julie closed the door tight and exclaimed, "*That* is why Oisin made an unscheduled trip to the States. I knew we were not expecting him for another couple months. Nicolette, how long have you known about the legal troubles of the laboratory and Dich?" The owner interjected, "Or better yet, why did you not tell me?" Nicolette quickly gathered herself, "I learned about the case against Oisin on Wednesday when he asked me to represent him. My knowledge of the case against Dich and the laboratory came during the investigation of the case against Oisin. I cannot share any details that are not in the paperwork you received due to privilege. I learned most of the details I have this morning. As for where I was, my calendar is public as the requirements state. It states my location and case number. While technically, this is not a firm case, I did include all the docket information on my calendar so that accurate updates could be gained by contacting the courthouse." The owner handed Nicolette the paperwork presented by the prosecutor's office and she read through the information they sought which were digital and physical files that would link Dich to a conspiracy to defraud the States of Michigan, California, Florida, and Ohio by knowingly producing false, untrue laboratory results in fifteen cases. Moreover, it included another charge of hate crime. Nicolette thought to herself, 'yup, federal' as she read through the counts and the subpoena which was very specific including times of the conversations. It made her believe that there was a mole in the laboratory; that made the protection of John by the attorney make much more sense. "On the good hand, none of the information being sought or any of the damning evidence has to do with the firm. In fact, it literally lists the firm as rented office space therefore not being prejudice against the work being done here. George, do you own any part of the laboratory?" Nicolette asked pensively. "No, Dich and I are only partners here. I am not even on the Board as it is made up of bankers and hedge fund people like Oisin and Dich. I sold parts of the firm to him because he wanted to have a diverse portfolio and I was cash flow poor. You cannot run a successful law firm on credit alone. That would be like robbing Peter to pay Paul. I do not want this scandal to take down what I worked so hard for. My wife and children are also part owners." The owner sighed and motioned everyone from his office as he paced the room. Julie turned to Nicolette, "What side are you on? You will need to pick. If you choose to keep the company of Dich, it may negatively affect your job here." Before Nicolette could address her question, Julie walked away angrily, shaking her head. Nicolette walked back to her office slowly, going over the previously few months at the firm in her head. She was not certain if she would continue to at the firm long term, but at that moment she felt compelled to help the owner who was blindsided by the lawsuits and subpoena. Nicolette sat at her desk and started to check email before getting a call from the owner. He wanted to go to lunch and talk frankly with her about the case and perhaps hire her as his family's personal attorney on the case. Nicolette agreed and jotted down information of the restaurant before departing for the bank. Nicolette had a small business account for the Limited Liability Company (LLC) that she started when she passed the bar for freelance work that she would take from time to time. After making the deposit in the account, she headed to the lunch. When she arrived at the country club dining room, Nicolette was escorted to a table in the back hall where the owner, his wife, and two adults, who were close to Nicolette's age, were seated. She addressed the table as a whole, making her presence known as they were deep in conversation when she approached. "Hello, George. All. I am Nicolette Guyere." The owner who was partly startled, stood and continued the introductions, "Nicolette, this is my wife, Julianna. My eldest child, my daughter Pauline. My youngest son, Pierre. And on the way is my middle son." Looking past Nicolette, the owner perked up, "There he is, that is Stefon." Stefon reached the table quickly. The owner motioned for the two to join the table. "Nicolette, I have filled in my family to the lawsuit. At least, the information that I am privy to. I explained to them that you will not break privilege, but they had some questions about the impact that this case might have on their own financial stability. First, for Julianna and I, can we be personal sued due to this case?" Nicolette answered frankly, "None of you, personally, or the firm, collectively, are mentioned in the lawsuit. Moreover, the lawsuit is for the laboratory not the firm. You do not have any ownership in the laboratory. Legally and operationally, there are separate entities. The subpoena was served at the firm because Dich has files at both facilities and does answer calls in both locations about the laboratory. If you want to clean anything up, insist that he does not do laboratory business at the firm under no circumstances." Julianna breathed a sigh of relief, "Great. George was saying the same thing, but he has a habit of protecting us from everything. Then this is a celebratory lunch and not a working lunch. Drinks?" Before the table could respond, Julianna's hand went into the air and made a circular pattern, "Drinks, Maestro!" Nicolette laughed as did Julianna with glee. She ordered lunch and had a pleasant lunch in which she outlined ways to ensure the constant separation between the laboratory and the firm. She further discussed ways to protect them from the reach of the federal government when they come to seize Dich's assets. "Civil lawsuits do not have the strict lines as criminal cases. I know that Dich has some

140

ownership in the firm so be prepared to buy him out if you have to. I would move my accounts to retainer; I am surprised how many people you bill hours. The collection of retainer funds will quickly build your cash reserves and give you the option to approach Dich with an offer to buy him out. I am assuming your current contract with him has a moral clause." The owner nodded his head in a positive manner. "So, outside of the possible civil liability, you should be okay. Please note your liability insurance will cover a fair bit of it without the need to buy him. My advice to build your reserves is a strong one." The rest of the lunch conversation was a continuation of the limited advice that Nicolette provided. The lunch ended late in the afternoon and Nicolette went back to the office to ensure that Human Resources had all the information that was needed for her two new hires that start on Monday. When she finally started the way home that evening, Nicolette was looking forward to sitting around the house all evening before going to the game on Saturday. It was a home game and though the season is projected to be bleak at best there was nothing like Michigan Stadium on a Saturday.

Chapter Ten

Nicolette was meeting her ex-boyfriend at the stadium for the game, he already had his ticket. Michigan was playing a small MAC school, Nicolette felt this was a winnable game and wanted to tailgate and enjoy the atmosphere. Nicolette walked into the house and stretched and dropped her briefcase into her home office. She undressed and put her suit into the hamper for the dry cleaner. After, she changed into some shorts, a t-shirt, and ankle socks to lounge around the house. Nicolette poured a scotch over ice and looked at the options in the refrigerator and freezer and decided that she did not want to cook. She ordered a pizza for delivery and grabbed her laptop and looked at her email on collarme.com. Nicolette had not logged onto the webpage in several days so there were several emails that she had to tend. One of the emails was from James, who had been working out the details of their trip to Hershey, Pennsylvania. Nicolette read through the details of the trip which outlined her reservations and provided her with the options to either drive or fly to the spa; she had decided that she wanted to make the eight hour drive instead of spending the same amount of time driving to the airport, waiting at the airport for two hours, the two hour flight, and then driving another two hours after clearing baggage claim. The added benefit of making the drive instead of trying to fly is that Nicolette has full access to all the toys in her toy box instead of having to ensure that they are checked luggage safe. Looking at the Michigan football schedule, Nicolette noted that the trip to the Hotel Hershey was next weekend. James was a mystery to her as he wanted a long term, Female-led relationship; Nicolette found almost everything about him ideal. They were friends and their compatibility was undeniable when they were in each other's presence. She was looking forward to this vacation as it will be the first of a few that she had planned, and its timing was almost perfect with the implosions at the firm. There were messages from uwe, Heinrich, and Ryan. uwe was outlining the trip of his time to Detroit in the coming weeks while Ryan was looking to attend a Michigan game with her. Heinrich was trying to coordinate the possibility of Nicolette traveling to Germany to visit him and use him at home. There was also a message from Jeff; he was a married painslut who was very much into spanking. Jeff and Nicolette had been corresponding for years, but she refused to meet or play with him because she made a habit of not entertaining the idea of submissives that she could not correspond or meet their spouse. Nicolette was caught in the middle of an infidelity issues when she first found the lifestyle because the submissive male was not upfront and honest with his wife and she was caught in the middle. Deception of another woman was not something that Nicolette wanted, and she made it her business to not have that happen again. Therefore, if the person trying to correspond with her was married, she made it clear that she had to speak to the wife prior to any play or meeting. The message from Jeff was asking if she would allow him to be her friend as he was trying to prove himself worthy of her kindness. As Nicolette neared the end of her email, there was a knock at her door; it was her pizza delivery. She was looking forward to the Italian sausage, green pepper, and onion pizza and stopped checking email to enjoy the pizza with her scotch. Nicolette enjoyed this cheat meal; her workout regime and meal plan does not normally include pizza. When she completed the meal, Nicolette returned to her email on collarme.com. She had three new emails. None of the email warranted an in-depth response so Nicolette replied with one of her standard 'thank you, but no thank you' emails. She browsed through photos of the website and then logged off for the evening. Nicolette cleaned up her mess in the living room and got ready for bed.

The next morning, Nicolette woke up at 7:30 a.m. well rested and ready for a day of college football. She showered, dressed in Michigan gear from head to toe, and grabbed her keys to head out. Nicolette made it to Ann Arbor by 9:00 a.m.; three hours before game time. Being an out of conference game, the town was crawling with other Michigan fans. Nicolette parked at her house in the Washtenaw-Hill Historic District and started walking to the first of three tailgates that she was invited to. Her house was 1.5 miles from Michigan Stadium and each tailgate was on the way. The first tailgate was at the house of the fraternity that aligns with the chapter of her sorority. Nicolette arrived just before 9:30 a.m. and there already a number of people on the porch drinking and on the front lawn playing horseshoes. During her years at Michigan after crossing, she was chapter president, so she was very well known. As she walked up to the house, she was greeted by a few ladies in the classes after her with hugs. One of the new initiates came up to her and asked her if she wanted a beverage; Nicolette asked for a scotch. "Yes, Big sister, right away!" she exclaimed and jogged off to grab that drink. One of the alumni brothers from the fraternity that crossed when she was pledging ran up and hugged her and spun her around. "Nici! Wow, girl. I have not seen you in what ten years! How are you?" Nicolette giggled after being put down and while smiling very grandly, "DeVeon, I am well. How have you been? I heard you were moving and shaking in DC? How is the DVM?" DeVeon responded with his characteristic shrug, "You know how we do. You are fine as hell as usual. You have not aged a bit. How are you and Benjamin doing?" Nicolette continued smiling, "Thanks for the compliment. You have always been kind and sleek. Loving that silver streak – you dyed that or are you just a fox? As for Benjamin and I, he found pleasure with several groupies while I studying my ass off in law school. I do not share my things so, he gone!" Before DeVeon could respond, the young lady brought Nicolette her scotch. "Thank you, uh…" Nicolette said prompting the young lady for her name. "I am Danielle. I am the little sister of your first pledge's little sister. You are my grand big." "Thank you, Danielle. I appreciate the beverage. This is DeVeon Carter. He is a brother. He graduated in 1994 and is an aide to Senator Stabenow." Danielle perked up at the name of Senator Stabenow and shook the hand of DeVeon. "It is nice to meet you, DeVeon. I met her a couple years ago; she was amazing for the State of Michigan. I have always wanted to go into politics. Do you have any advice for me?" DeVeon replied, "Danielle, it is very nice to meet you. I want to catch up with Nici, but I would love to discuss my path into politics and also let you know about our internship program." He reached into his wallet and handed her a business card, "please call the office on Monday and we will discuss things in detail. It was very nice meeting you." Danielle took the card and walked away while tucking the card into her bra. DeVeon turned back to Nicolette, "Sorry to hear about you and Benjamin. He was a good guy, but easily distracted. I did not think he was ready to settle down, but I had heard that y'all were doing the long distance thing and was getting married. Hell, I was looking forward to my invite to my first NFL wedding." Nicolette replied frankly, almost short and cold, "well, I cannot and will not fight for something that is supposed to be mine. He has all the time and freedom to play; both with the ball and some pussy. What about you? Are you and Julietta still together? How is your son?" DeVeon's smile got very big and he replied, "Can you believe that little D is almost ten? He is getting big and has his own personality. J thinks he is just like me while I spend my days trying to not ring his neck. J and I just celebrated 17 years together; married for 14. I was one of the rare guys who married right before graduation. J is here; she is over..." Before he could finish the sentence, Nicolette heard her sorority's call echo across the yard in a familiar tone. It was Julietta; they crossed together and were very close friends, sister. Nicolette turned around and saw Julietta walking fast to her to hug her. They embrace and Julietta joins the conversation. "Nic, girl, how are you? It has been too long. I wish we could get away more often, but with sessions and little D's schedule, we are anchored in Maryland. I have missed you so much! When are you going to visit; I got used to seeing you once every few months when you were in Boston but now I am starving for my Nic time." "I know. I must do better, J. I miss you, too. I love you very much. I needed today." They ladies heard a familiar song and DeVeon threw up his sign and begun moving towards the other brothers who were stepping in the driveway. Nicolette and Julietta turned and watched the men step while sipping their beverages. Both swayed along with music while watching almost 40 men step. It was a beautiful sight of unity and brotherhood. "I see you!" Nicolette screamed out as the men continued to step in a circle up and down the driveway; Julietta took video and photos with her cellular phone. Two songs played that the men stepped to; there were a few that did not step but cheered on their brethren by repeatedly making their call. The next song that played was not one that men normally stepped to and after almost ten minutes of stepping, they were tired. Many of them hugged and high fived after stepping, continuing the camaraderie. The fourth song was a song that the ladies in Nicolette's sorority normally stepped to. The ladies started lining up in the driveway and started to stroll to the music. Both Nicolette and Julietta joined the group of ladies that were stepping in the driveway. The men, similar to the women, cheered them on as they stepped in the driveway. After strolling for two songs, Nicolette noted that she had been at the house longer than she expected to be. She did a round of good-bye and headed to her next tailgate.

Filled with joy from the time with her sisters and good friends, Nicolette moved to her next tailgate. It was a complete contrast to the first as it was with friends from her professional fraternity, Phi Alpha Delta. She arrived at the location of the tailgate and noted that people were out front in a sand volleyball pit playing an intense game. She laughed to herself that the game was too much for a tailgate. Nicolette went inside and found her friends playing drunken Jenga. She noticed that the friends that asked her to stop by and they were drinking the signature drink of the Campbell Chapter of the fraternity, the Elixir. "Oh, there's Elixir?" Nicolette asked with hope in her voice. "Yes, we made sure to save you some," Yon said as she handed her a beverage from the refrigerator nearby. Nicolette had a large smile come across her face. Nicolette jumped into the game as they had just started; she had to make three moves in a row. The first was to take a shot, so she opted for the fuzzy navel jello shots that were in the drunk Jenga fridge. The second block asked for an embarrassing moment, so Nicolette related the story about when she tripped up the stairs at the US Supreme Court when she was there taking photos after being sworn into the US Federal Bar Association. The third and last block to catch-up was a table shot. Everyone cheered and each selected their favorite jello shot from the trays in the refrigerator. After completing the shots, the game proceeded in normal fashion. Johnny Wu was next up, and he inadvertently touched a difficult block when looking to select a block; house rules require him to pull the block. He raised his hands and pleaded with the unyielding crowd. After a few moments of trying to avoid pulling the block, the room went very silent as Johnny made his approach. With a steady hand, Johnny was able to raise the block slightly so the weight would transfer to the other side before he slowly and deliberately had it lean on the blocks beneath the anchor he just drew. The pile was completely unstable now and Johnny got the piece out without the other blocks falling. He now had to place it on top of the pile which was sliding towards the uneven side. He finally started to place the piece to a chorus of disbelieving remarks ranging from gasps to swear words. Johnny placed the block and stepped back. Next was a young lady who was not a member, she went to take a block but was very sloppy in her approach and from leaning too much on the table, the entire pile fell. She was not content with the loss and refused to finish her drink which was the requirement of someone who loses. "That is utter bullshit. He left the most unstable pile. Anyone after him would have lost. I will reset the board, but I am not drinking all this drink. Nope. Utter bullshit." Nicolette was annoyed with the disregard for the rules and walked away from the table. Her friends called out to her, "Nici, where are you going? We are going to start another game. I thought you were going to play again." Nicolette replied, "I was, but I cannot bring myself to play with some random who does not adhere to the house rules. We are attorneys. Rules matter." As Nicolette made it to the porch to watch the volleyball game and finish her beverage, her friends joined her. "Wait. Why didn't you guys play your next game? I am not staying long anyway," Nicolette asked them as they sat in the chairs on the porch to watch the sand volleyball game. "You are right. If she is not going to play by the house rules and respect the game, then we do not need to play. I think all the members of the Chapter left the game. Which would leave her and perhaps the girl she came here with." Nicolette shrugged. "So when did the net go up and who are these guys?" The younger members in the alumni group answered some of her questions and they enjoyed the matches. It was a very competitive game; apparently a few of the guys in the fraternity were on club and varsity teams in their undergrad or before transferring to the University. Nicolette finished her cup and said her good-byes to her friends. While it was a professional fraternity, the brotherhood and togetherness were similar to that of a social organization. Being in both a professional and social Greek organization, Nicolette commonly compared them to each other. Being behind in her plans, she did not spend much time at the PAD house but enjoy the company of her friends while watching the younger members play a rowdy game of volleyball. Nicolette now headed to her third and final tailgate which was with the former student athletes. She, herself, was a coxswain for the Michigan Men Rowing team when she attended the University, which afforded her a Varsity Letter. She arrived at the student-athlete alumni party just in time to see the Michigan cheerleaders and Michigan Marching Band perform. Right inside the door was a bar so Nicolette got a beverage walked to a place where she could see the stand, watch the cheerleaders make pyramids, and chant along with "Let's Go Blue" and "The Victors." After the pep rally, Nicolette looked around for her ex-boyfriend, Andre. Nicolette and Andre dated when she was in high school briefly and they were always better friends with many interests in common, than being a couple. They dated at a time when Nicolette was not sexually active, so their relationship consisted mostly of going to sporting events, parties, and social gatherings together. Nicolette and Andre reconnected via social media when she moved back to Detroit and they reminisced about Cass Tech. They, also, had so many friends in common that it was easy to pick back up. As Nicolette was scanning the room looking for Andre, he walked up next to her and stated, "If I was a snake, you would have been bit." Nicolette turned in the direction of the familiar voice and hugged Andre. She said as they ended their embrace, "With all the women in here, I am sure someone would have screamed and started enough of a panic that I would not have been bit. How are you, Dre?" He smiled that familiar smile that she is used to and replied, "I am good. This is nice. Thank you for the tickets to the tailgate and to the game." Nicolette nodded, "How is the food? I know the drinks are quite yummy." Andre pointed to the back of the tailgate and replied, "The food is equally yummy. I thought the slider station in the back was the best. You have made to order customized sliders. Let's head back there." Nicolette and Andre start to walk towards the slider table, and she saw some of her former teammates. They waved at each other and exchanged a few pleasantries before Nicole and Andre made their way to the sliders. She ordered two sliders and some onion rings and ate before they made their way to the stadium. Her season tickets were on the south 30-yard line on the visitor's side. They made their way to the game right as the Michigan Marching Band (MMB) was being announced; the stadium was rocking, and all the fans were on their feet. The introduction of the team was new this year and the energy was palpable and electric. After the flyover, the crowd was ready kickoff. Michigan won the toss, so they deferred and kicked off the ball; Nicolette was excited for the start of the game with a defensive stand as that was always her favorite side of the ball. They cheered for a turnover, "Let's get this pick six!" "Ha! They are close enough for a safety." "True, a deep sack and we get two and the ball." And they were not disappointed as the Michigan defense caused a fumble that the defensive lineman recovered. The game continued in a similar fashion of our defense not allowing many yards and on occasion scoring points. The offense did not move the ball very well but did manage a couple scores including a field goal. The half time show performance by the MMB was a tribute to the musical history of UM including Nicolette's favorite the Hawaiian War Chant and the band did an amazing job. Andre and Nicolette seemed to pick up where they left off with their friendship. By the time the third quarter started Michigan was ahead by three scores and the stadium was only half full. The weather was beautiful, and the team was playing well. As the fourth quarter was starting, Andre asked Nicolette if she wanted to head out as well since the last score by the third string offense made the win to be a statistical guarantee. The stadium was now mostly empty. "No, I came to watch the game. I watch the entire game. I am enjoying myself. It is good to see the second and third string players do well and have real game experience. It will make injuries and late in the season easier for the Blue." "Seriously, Nic. I am bored. I do not want to sit here for another hour watching this. It is like watching paint dry and not the quickly drying water based. Vinyl paint. It is like watching vinyl paint dry," Andre stated frankly. "Well, Dre, I do not want to leave. You are free to go as we did drive separately," Nicolette stated. Andre sighed and started texting on his phone for a few moments. His gaze alternated between his phone and Nicolette; he stopped watching the game. "Dre, if you are not going to watch the game and you are this bored, please do not feel obligated to stay. After the game and MMB post-game show, I am going to Blimpy Burger before heading to my house here for the evening." "Oh, is that an invitation to stay at your house?" Andre asked in an inviting tone. "If you are asking me if I am inviting you to my house for something other than dinner then the answer is negative," Nicolette said flatly. Andre laughed. Nicolette looked at him with a stern, serious look and shook her head. After the game and post-game MMB show, they went for a burger. After they hugged, he left for evening plans that he had. Nicolette declined the invitation for a ride home knowing that walking would be faster than sitting in traffic, even with it being fewer people still in town post-game. Nicolette took her time getting to her Ann Arbor home, spending time at some of her favorite watering holes, making the acquaintance of random visitors and townspeople. She arrived home just before midnight, showered in her private bathroom, and curled up in her bed.

Chapter Eleven

Nicolette got up early to ensure that she would be home in Detroit in time for Mass. She cleaned the bathroom and bedroom and locked up her rooms before greeting the residents of the house and leaving Ann Arbor. Nicolette enjoyed keeping the home as a rental house since it afforded her a room for her travels to Ann Arbor which averages monthly each year. The drive home to Detroit was uneventful, but she could not help but thinking over her interaction with Andre. She could not quite put her finger on what was off with their conversation at the end of the game; she wondered if he expected to stay with her. Nicolette had assumed that the game was an outing as friends, not a date so she had not given him her normal 'I'm celibate' speech. She put the evening out of her head and prayed on the important things in her life including giving the debt of respect and understanding up to God during her Eucharistic prayers. A few month earlier during his homily, Fr. Dave had preached on the important of the Lord's Prayer and explained in detail that the debts from the line, "Forgive us our debts, as we also have forgiven our debtors," are not only financial. That those debts can be ones of time, respect, love, understanding, or any number of things. Reflecting on those words, Nicolette found freedom. She found peace as if a weight had been lifted off her shoulders when she no longer carried the weight or anger of disrespectful behavior or the pain of misunderstandings. After church, Nicolette prepared for the week with doing laundry, grocery shopping, and cleaning her house. She spent some of her downtime thinking about Andre. She decided to put up the debt of misunderstanding to

Jesus. "I never meant to lead him on, if I did. I think that he is a good person, but he is an ex-boyfriend for a reason. Please forgive me for my participation in the miscommunication." She prayed. Almost as soon as Nicolette completed her prayer, her phone rang. It was Andre. "Oh God, you are quick," she said as she picked up the call, "Hey Dre. What's up?" His tone was short, "So, are you better than me now? Or you this stuck up bitch now that thinks she is cuter than she is? You know that I've hit that before. It is not like that is new pussy. What gives?" Nicolette was caught completely off-guard. "Wow. Seriously? Is that really what you wanted to say to me? I am glad that I prayed for this." "Prayed for this? What are you talking about? You praying for dick, now? You are cuter than that. Just need to stop acting like that pussy is new," Andre replied. "Dre. Andre. Let me be very clear. I felt uneasy after our interaction and prayed to Jesus to take the debt of misunderstanding. Whether you want to call us not fucking yesterday being stuck up, being misguided about my cuteness, or acting as if my pussy is new, I do not care. I do not look at you as a mate anymore. We have not been together for years. I was what 19 or 20 years old when we were together. I am 30! That was a decade ago, Andre. I know that I have changed, matured in that decade. Sadly, it sounds like you have not. Have a good one, Andre. I think we should take a break from our friendship." Nicolette hung up the phone before he could answer. 'Wow. I guess I can add stuck up bitch that is not as cute as she thinks she is to the list of shit that people have said to me," Nicole sighed and walked from the dressing room, pausing in the mirror briefly. She noticed that she was smiling. Though his words were not true, they hurt none the less. She passed by the mirror, trying to not linger because she did not have anything kind to say to herself. She tried to focus on something that she was looking forward to, so she switched to the Hershey trip. It was odd that she was planning a trip the upcoming weekend since she usually only travels to away games during the football season. She was hoping for a productive work week with her new staff starting that Monday. She made a light dinner since she overindulged yesterday and drank water before reading a few briefs on the cases she will be prepping her staff on the following day. Nicolette went to bed earlier than normal on a Sunday, but it helped her wake refreshed early.

The drive into the firm on Monday was one traffic jam after another. Nicolette arrived at the firm 45 minutes after she intended, but luckily before her new employees arrived. Nicolette had just enough time to organize their projects and get their desk set up before they were done with Human Resources. Michael and Kamilah were brought to Nicolette's office where she greeted them with folders on the cases that they would be working on with an objective list and Gantt chart. Nicolette showed them to their desk and called I.T. over to get them set-up with their credentials. She allowed them a few hours to settle in before the all staff meeting where they would be introduced. It was no sooner that Nicolette completed their orientation, that Dich came looking for her. "Can I speak to you for a moment? I have some questions and I need advice." Nicolette nodded in agreement, ensured that her staff was comfortable, and walked over to Dich's office. As soon as Nicolette walked through the office door, she stopped Dich from speaking, "I cannot consult, advise, or help on your cases pending due to your employ with Compliance Assurance Testing Laboratory. Participating with you in any way, shape, or form is a direct violation of my contract with Oisin. The best that I can do is recommend someone who can sit on the counsel with your current attorney." Dich had made his way to his chair and sat as Nicolette was speaking about her limits, "Are you finished? This is not about those cases. I know you went to Michigan and my daughter is also looking to go into law and is looking at that school. I was curious if you had time to mentor her?" Nicolette was surprised by the question and stammered, "Uh. Yes. I do have time to mentor her. Please provide her with my phone number and email. I look forward to hearing from her." Nicolette made it out of the office before he could respond. Nicolette found herself releasing a sigh of relief. She did not like that feeling and said a small prayer in her head before returning to her office. Whether it was based on her ignoring the weirdness or things were returning to pre-lawsuit, the rest of the week went by uneventful and quite fast. Thursday arrived and Nicolette found herself driving towards Pennsylvania. She was excited for a few days at the spa and even more so to the days of being catered to 24/7. Arriving at the Hotel Hershey sooner than expected, Nicolette was not sure if she would be allowed to check-in to the suite. James got them the Catherine Hershey Suite for the weekend; it was perfect because it allowed them their own space, while, also, providing an opportunity for them to be together as it had a shared living room, dining room, and balcony. When she arrived at the valet, she gave them her last name and they commented that her room was ready for her. She checked in and the bellhop brought her bags to her room. Nicolette brought three bags, two of which contained play items for the hotel. She unpacked her clothes and toys and after getting settled, there was a knock at the door of her bedroom. "Yes", she called out. "Mistress, it is James. Is now a good time or should I come back?" Nicolette walked to the door and unlocked it to find James standing there holding a bouquet of flowers. They were hydrangeas, some of her favorite flowers. "Oh, thank you, James. Those are lovely flowers. How was your drive into Pennsylvania?" James placed the vase of flowers on the table in the seating area. "My drive was uneventful; I made very good time. I am glad I made the decision to drive because it allowed me to see a few clients before heading here. How about you? You had a much longer drive than me. You insisted. I was willing to arrange a flight." James responded as he brought in more items from the dining room including a cheese, cracker, fruit, and meat charcuterie tray. "My drive was easy as well. I made very good time. It was the same amount of time to drive as it was to fly; besides this allowed me to bring some very nice toys. I think we both prefer that I was able to bring some toys. "Yes, Mistress, I am glad that you were able to bring the toys that you wanted. Anything in particular you want to tell me about?" James commented, looking around the room for clues. "The fact that I made the trip should be reward enough. So, what is the schedule? I know tomorrow is a full day of spa treatments, but you did not give much details about tonight. What are your plans?" Nicolette stated ignoring his question and musing. "I figured that we both would be tired from all the driving to get here, that tonight would be low key. I have appetizers here, the charcuterie board, wine, and chocolate, and then later we can do dinner. In between, we can either get in-room treatments from the concierge or we can watch a movie. If you are very tired there is even time to nap." James outlined the options and she considered them all; "Well, let's start with the appetizers and perhaps you can tell me about the treatments tomorrow while you massage my feet." Nicolette went to grab the bottle of wine to pour herself a glass and James motioned that he would prefer to pour the wine, so she relented. James poured the wine and Nicolette reclined at the table. He addressed her, "So, Mistress, can I make you a plate of food? I would love to make your plate." Nicolette took a sip of the wine and nodded that she would make her own plate of food. "No, I would prefer to make my own plate, but thank you. Please have some wine with me." James pours himself a glass of wine and they both made a plate for themselves from the charcuterie board. James sat next Nicolette and the two discussed their drive in more detail and their plans for tomorrow in more detail. After finishing his plate of food, he took her foot into his hands and removed her shoes. His fingers felt amazing on her tired feet as he kneaded the knots that came from her long drive. She moaned slightly at his work on her feet and he made note of the things she enjoyed so that he could repeat them throughout the massage. His knuckles dug into the flesh and she could feel the pressure in her sole releasing. The massage felt so good that Nicolette stopped everything and just laid back against the couch and moaned in pleasure. James was clearly deep in subspace as he moved from her right foot to the left. All the things he noted as pleasurable on the right foot, he did immediately on the left foot. Nicolette was comfortable and falling into Domspace when her phone rang; it was almost like an alarm clock pulling her from the edge of pleasure back to reality. She slowly pulled her feet from James' lap and walked across the suite into her bedroom and grabbed her phone. It was her mother, Ernestine, "hello, mom?" Nicolette started. "Is everything okay?" Her mother explained that she was expecting her call, but because she had not received it, she was nervous. Noting that her parents are still hypersensitive to negative things, Nicolette apologized, "I am sorry mom. I just got in not too long ago. I should have called you." Nicolette provided her mother with her room contact information and reminded her mother of her itinerary. They exchanged pleasantries and her mother was once again content. Once she hung up the phone, Nicolette returned to James who was still teetering on the fringes of subspace. She sat back down on the couch and took a sip of wine and continued to snack on her appetizer. James reached for her left foot again and begun massaging it in the manner that she enjoyed. Nicolette laid back again to the melodic tempo of his finger working on her foot. The massage was heavenly, and Nicolette's moans exclaimed such to James. He had a growing erection that she could see clearly through the creases of his khaki pants. Nicolette ran her right foot over the length of his shaft which startled him out of his transfixed subspace, "I am sorry, Ma'am. I cannot help how aroused I get around you, thinking about you, touching you...you are such a natural turn-on for me." Nicolette felt badly that she knocked him out of subspace by rubbing his erection, but she felt that pointing out his sexual arousal should not have been so startling, so she wanted to address it quickly. "Do you not enjoy that you were sexual aroused by massaging my feet? Why did me rubbing your erection interrupt your subspace? Do you not equate your submission with service?" James stopped to consider her question and more importantly, his words. He replied, "Mistress Nicolette, I find you stunningly attractive. In the years that we have been speaking and the times you made for me both online, on camera, and in person has only made me yearn for you more. I am here to serve, nothing more, unless that is not what you truly want. You have told me that you are celibate. I, too, am not sexually active, but I would allow you to use every inch of me to your heart's desire. I practice tongue exercises so that I will never tire of orally pleasuring you. And it goes without saying that if you want to be penetrated, I guarantee I can make you feel amazing." Nicolette enjoyed the compliments of his speech, but wanted to know more about the why he stopped the massage or how he lost his erection that quickly, "Why did you lose your erection? Why did you stop so abruptly when I touched you?" James nodded his head, "I was embarrassed that I was erect. I am, literally, only touching your clothed foot and I should not have been so turned on. But in my defense, I have been dreaming of the day that I get you all to myself for several days and I get to please you in any way your heart desires." Nicolette nodded and finished her glass of wine. They both took another plate of the appetizer. "We should order in dinner as I think I am looking to get comfortable." Nicolette commented as she went into her bedroom to change out of the sweats that she wore when she drove to Pennsylvania.

She emerged from her room wearing a heather grey lounge shorts set and a bra; she felt that her natural breasts sagging below the tank top of the shorts set would not be a good look. James too changed from the khakis and polo shirt that he obviously had worn to work that day into sleeping pants and matching top; both were light blue satin. "I hope you do not mind that I, too, changed into something more comfortable, Mistress." James addressed her as she made her way back into the living room. "I have zero problem with you getting comfortable as well, James. I think we should order another bottle of wine and dinner soon. We can sit out on the balcony and have dinner if it will not be too cold." James and Nicolette both reached for their phones to check the low; it was forecast to be in the mid-50s. "Hmmm", Nicolette continued after checking the weather, "53° is a bit too cold for me to sit outside without a fire or several layers of clothes. That is too bad. I guess this place does not have a fireplace at all. Plan B of sitting inside and perhaps opening the patio for that cool, Fall breeze." James nodded in agreement, "I would sit in 53° for you Ma'am, but I understand that being too cold for you to enjoy the meal. Let me get the menu and we can decide on our feast." James handed Nicolette the menu and she looked through the options. After the appetizer, she did not want a salad so she opted for a simple pan-seared chicken with risotto, and baby carrots with a honey glaze. James got a cup of lobster bisque and a salmon dinner with rice pilaf and green beans. They order a bottle of sauvignon blanc to accompany dinner since they were halfway through the bottle that James brought with him. While they were deciding their dinner plans, Nicolette, also, looked through the online guide for a movie that they could watch. They each bounced some of the options off the other hoping that they could find a movie that they both would enjoy but it seemed to no avail. Just as they were giving up on the options, there was a couple television programs that they both watch regularly that they could enjoy together, even if in syndication. "James, so we are in agreement, Forensic Files and Law & Order: Criminal Intent will be watched?" Nicolette asked to verify their plan. "Yes, as I said, I do not watch much television, but the few times I have seen those programs; I have enjoyed them. It would be my extreme pleasure to sit with you, Ma'am, and watch these programs." James confirmed the plan. They sat on the couch in the living room and started watching an episode of

Law & Order: Criminal Intent. They had both seen the episode, so they spent some time during the commercial discussing the cinematography of the episode. Nicolette placed her socked foot into the lap of James, who begun massaging it again. As before, she fell directly into Domspace; his hands were bringing her to ecstasy. She laid back against the couch moaning as his fingers mechanically pleased her; he, too, was enjoying the massage as she could see his erection growing. James moved to massaging her calves which relieved some of the pain that she had from the hard braking in the Appalachian Mountains during the drive to Pennsylvania. James reached for her other leg so that he could massage them both at the same time, Nicolette obliged. Her problems seemed to melt away; she briefly forgot about the lawsuit that threatened Rockies' CEO, the disrespect that she experienced at the hands of Dich, and the constant nagging drone of the loss of her brother. Nicolette was able to relax, truly relax, and she found herself reaching climax, surprisingly. It would be the first time that she would orgasm from a leg massage and Nicolette found it slightly embarrassing, but she embraced the wave of pleasure that she was feeling. James begun working her muscles much harder, going deeper into the muscles and working the connective tissue and each knot that he worked from her legs brought her closer to climax. "James," Nicolette moaned, "I am going to come." As she announced her pleasure, James moved to her feet to ensure that she would reach release. Nicolette found her release and James rubbed her legs and feet lightly to give her a bit of aftercare. Nicolette stretched out on the couch and laid still for a moment enjoying the entire orgasm. James sat back and there was a noticeable stain on the front of his satin sleeping bottoms. Nicolette asked, "Did you come as well? You did not ask for permission to come." James looked a bit ashamed, "Yes. I did. It was quite unexpected, but the idea that I brought you to climax was enough for me. I apologize for not asking for permission, but I was so focused on guaranteeing that you were able to finish. Is foot fetish play a big thing for you? It was not on your collarme profile." Understanding the unexpected nature of the pleasure received from their play, Nicolette did not harp on the climax he received without permission. "I do not have a foot fetish, per se. I enjoy massages of all kinds. I have literally never come in this fashion; so you have that cherry. I lost my 'come whilst being given a foot massage' virginity with you. Speaking of which, I need to go to the ladies' room." Nicolette went to the bathroom off the seating area to wipe the come from between her legs and pee to relieve the pressure post-orgasm. As she was returning to the seating area, there was a knock at the door. She checked and it was room service delivering their meals. The young man placed the meals and the wine on the dining room table as instructed by Nicolette; James gave her some cash to tip him and he departed. James went to the restroom after Nicolette to clean himself up and to wash his hands. They decided to enjoy their meal at the table in the seating area instead of sitting at the dining room table which they both felt was too formal dressed in their pajamas post-orgasm. They reclined at table and enjoy their dinner and opened the white wine. The meal was rich and decadent without being heavy; it was a treat for Nicolette's taste buds. The mole sauce on the pan-seared chicken was made with 70% dark cocoa and it was balanced the heat of the barbeque sauce well. James seemed equally impressed with his meal. The salmon that James was eating was finished with a blood orange and beurre blanc sauce. Dinner was quite enjoyable; the flavors were perfect and paired famously with the wine. The dinner conversation was mostly in regard to the television program and quite playful. After completing the meal, they put the dinnerware in the hall on the tray that the hotel staff left for them. It was almost ten in the evening and both James and Nicolette were tired from the long days that were required to drive the distance and accomplish other tasks in the day. At that point, they had two open bottles of wine; James corked them both and put them away for the evening. Their treatments start at 8 o'clock in the morning and so they decided to turn in. Nicolette retired to her bedroom, which contained the king bed, while James returned to his bedroom which had two queen beds. Nicolette had prepared her bedroom for bed before joining James for the evening; he had done the same. Nicolette washed her face and brushed her teeth before doffing her clothes for bed. The sheets were a very high thread count and the felt glorious against her bare skin; she relaxed quickly and was asleep almost, as soon as, laying down in bed. Nicolette woke up at 6 o'clock in the morning and took a very hot shower to help wake herself up. After brushing her teeth and combing her hair, Nicolette wore a robe and went to see if James had awakened for the day. James was sitting in the living room when she walked out of her bedroom, he had already gone to the fitness center in the hotel, showered, eaten breakfast, and done some work that he had to complete for the Friday. "James, wow. You have had a very busy morning. I feel like a bump on a log compared to you. Gym. Work. Breakfast. I guess I should figure out my day before we are due in the spa," Nicolette teased. She looked over the breakfast menu and decided to go to the lobby for some fruit and walk outside prior to their appointments; it would, also, allow James to get some more work completed. Nicolette walked to the lobby and picked up a banana from the gift counter before taking a stroll on the grounds. The sun was high in the sky and the Fall air was amazing; Nicolette walked quickly around the hotel grounds enjoying visions of wildlife, landscape, and scenic views. There were other hotel guests out walking who Nicolette greeted along her path. After completing the banana, she discarded the peel. Nicolette walked the long route back to the hotel to gather James before their appointments. They made it to the spa for the first appointment which was a couple's massage. They met their massage therapists and went over the required medical history to get the deep stone massages that were scheduled. The 90-minute session started with them undressing and getting under the sheet and waited for the return of the therapists. "I cannot believe that I just saw you naked for the first time – and hopefully not the last time. Your body is stunning. Thank you for granting that permission." James stated as there was a knock on the door. "Enter." Nicolette commanded. She smiled at James and thanked him for the compliment. Both settled into their massages and both went directly into a mental state that was relaxing and comforting; speaking to the therapists and each other. It was clear from the questions that the staff was trying to ascertain their relationship but was not having any luck. The first stone that went onto James made him shriek in a combination of delight and surprise, while Nicolette loved the feeling of the heat radiating in her bones. Nicolette has had a number of hot stone massages in the past and she loved the feeling of the relaxation of the hot stone; it was like wearing a heating pad on every part of her body. After the massage, they were scheduled for a dual manicure-pedicure. The ninety minutes of the massage seem to fly by for Nicolette, whereas James felt that the time dragged as the stones were painful for him. When the therapists left the room for them to redress, Nicolette stretched out on the table and moaned deeply. "This has been an amazing weekend and it is only Friday morning. A Lady can get used to this. Thank you again for bringing me here. It is a dream come true." James nodded slightly but his grimace was obvious due to the pain that came from the combination of the hot stone and perhaps a heavy-handed massage therapist. They both adorned robes on top of their sparse clothing and made their way to the nail salon for their treatments. They were sat in massage chairs side and side one another and given paraffin treatments on both their hands and feet. They sat with a bag over their hands and feet while the wax was working to soften the skin on their fingers and toes. After the wax hardened completely, it was pulled from their skin and the traditional manicure-pedicure started. Nicolette had selected an orange color while James just wanted to be buffed. It took almost an hour to complete the manicure and pedicure. After, they had a two-hour break between treatments so they went back to their room to rest in between. They walked back to the suite in their robes; Nicolette was waddling like a duck so that she does not smudge her nails. When they reached the room, they had nearly two hours to kill before the next spa treatment. On the schedule was a sugar and cocoa bean scrub; Nicolette was looking forward to the exfoliating action of the scrub before soaking in a milk and chocolate bath. James had never experienced either of those treatments but was looking forward to the unique feeling of the scrub and bath. Back at the room, they poured glasses of wines and they laid around the living rooms in their robes. James handed her a glass, "Mistress, are you comfortable? Is there anything that I can do for you? Anything that can be done to relax you further or better?" Nicolette took a sip of her wine and looked at him pensively, "James, what are you asking? Do I want to be entertained by you? Why, of course, I do. The real question is how can I use in this limited time that would be enjoyable for me?" Nicolette knew that James would do almost anything to please her whether she wanted to use some bondage implements, corporal tools, and was prepared if they engaged in any forms of sexual intercourse. As she thought about how to use James, she went into her bedroom and got some bondage implements and decided to relax his muscles since the massage did not seem to accomplish that goal. Nicolette used some bed restraints to bind James to the dining table after putting on one of the extra, thick blankets beneath his body. The dining room table was sturdy and supported his weight well; Nicolette decided to explore what kinds of things would cause he pain and thereby her pleasure. Using a crop, Nicolette warmed his skin to her touch alternating between administering pain and making it feel surprisingly good considering the tool. James grunted but leaned into the pain soon into the session. "Thank you, Mistress." James groaned with each strike of the crop. He was noticeably erect and started begging for more. Nicolette teased and played with James, "Oh, you want more? You think you can handle what I can give you?" James was quiet briefly, contemplating her questions earnestly, "I want more. I yearn for your touch. Can I handle all that you give, probably not?" James chuckled. Nicolette put down her crop and picked up her bullwhip. She massaged oil into the whip recently so it was clearly moisturized and shiny; the sound of it cutting the air made James tense with anticipation. Nicolette ran her nails over his back and dug into his skin; James calmed down significantly in response to her attention. He was putty in her hands and it was apparent that he was deep in subspace; Nicolette cracked the whip against his skin eliciting a screech of pain which instantly made her very wet. She alternated between the whip, crop, and her nails bringing both herself and James to the climatic height of the scene. James begged for permission to come which Nicolette denied him because she wanted to keep him on the edge for as long as possible. Deep in Domspace, Nicolette slowly started bringing James out of subspace by providing scene aftercare which at this time consisted of massage the skin to ensure that there was not any skin damage due to the whip, whispering reassurances in his ear, and unbinding him from the table. James slowly returned from his deep subspace and Nicolette got him a glass of water to sip at his pace. She sat and caught her breath.

James came out of subspace well and was quite content. He stretched out on the couch and was hilariously masculine, "I am hungry. Are you hungry? Can you eat as well? I need a snack before the scrub." Nicolette laughed quite loudly considering they missed lunch, but James was not hungry when they left the spa for their room. They still had 40 minutes before their next treatments, so they got themselves turned around to grab lunch on the way to the spa. In the Circular Restaurant, James opted for the buffet lunch while Nicolette got a Cobb salad. James got breakfast food from the buffet, especially meats to help replenish the proteins that he lost during his early morning workout and the intense impact scene with Nicolette. They completed their lunch and made it to the spa five minutes before their appointment time. The scrub started with a brief shower to open the pores then the staff applied the scrub which was a mixture of invigorating and slightly painful for both Nicolette and James. After the scrub was applied and washed off using a high pressure water spray, the pair was instructed to the chocolate bath. Nicolette opted for the restroom before the chocolate bath then she joined James in a tub. They sat in a chest high bath of warm milk bath that was enhanced with chocolate. It was soothing and the smell of the chocolate essence made Nicolette settle down more than a milk bath normally would. The soak in the bath was relaxing; their skin was nourished and prune-like after the hour sit in the warm milk bath. James emerged from the bath first and went to the shower and washed with the aloe balm to soothe the small scratches from the scrub. His skin was renewed and he joked that it 'felt like a baby's skin – well the ass'. Nicolette did not step out of the bath until it started to drain; it was on an automatic cycle to start draining ten minutes after the end of the treatment end time. She walked to the shower and chose to only rinse with pure water. This was their last treatments for the day, so Nicolette opted to take a shower when she returned to the room. They donned their robes and made the walk slowly back to their room. "So, did you hate the entire experience so far?" Nicolette probed. James laughed, "I am not much of a spa person. This is mostly new to me and I am not as comfortable as one would be if they know what to expect." Nicolette paused and replied, "You did not answer the question. Are you not enjoying the spa treatments? How did you pick what we are doing?" James replied solemnly, "I picked the treatments on the advice of friends and some of my staff in the office. I am not hating this. I cannot hate something when I am with you. I have been looking forward to this since we met in Detroit. I know you are enjoying yourself and for me that is all I need. I did enjoy periods of all the treatments. I just am not a 'be pampered' kind of guy." Nicolette walked further, quiet for a bit considering his words. "I am glad that you do not hate the spa. I very much enjoy the treatments. The time being served by you is also something that I enjoy. Thank you." They reached the room just before 4 o'clock in the evening. Nicolette retired to her room to take a shower while James went to set-up for the evening dinner mystery cruise. Nicolette emerged from the shower relaxed and her skin was softer than she expected. She walked out into the common space looking for James, but he was nowhere to be found. Nicolette knocked on open bedroom door because she could not see him in the room. James was also not in the bedroom. Nicolette was curious where her companion had gone but retired back to her room. Nicolette dressed in a beautiful sundress and combed her hair even put a few curls in it; she decided to go for a walk around the small town. When Nicolette walked out of her room, James was still nowhere to be found in the suite so she left. She walked out of the hotel and strolled around Hershey. It was obvious that she was a visitor since 80% of the residents were white and she was obviously not. Nicolette browsed around some of the shops and spoke to some of the locals who were friendly. She loved the smell of Fall in the air that she did not even miss being at home. Checking her phone, Nicolette noticed that the Michigan night away game would be on soon, so she made her way back to the hotel. She walked into the hotel room within ten minutes of the game coming on television; James had nachos, drinks, and chicken wings laid out on the table in front of the television, which was tuned to the game. "Where did you go?" Nicolette asked of James as she entered the room. "I had things I wanted to get set-up. I apologize for not letting you know that I was leaving the room." James answered. "Thank you for setting up for the game, James." Nicolette said as she got comfortable after her walk around town. "No problem. I know that traveling in the Fall is not something that you do often, so I wanted to ensure that you were comfortable and got to see your game." James replied. Nicolette came back in the room just in time for the kickoff. She made herself a plate and she was surprised that the food was still hot; she was unaware of when the food arrived at the room. After making her plate and settling in to walk some football, James made a plate as well. As if he could read Nicolette's mind, he stated "I am surprised that you did not pass the waitstaff in the hallway as you arrived back to the room. The food is really fresh; it smells amazing." Michigan was playing another out of conference foe, but this team was much bigger than the MAC team that they beat last week. James sat next to Nicolette and they ate delicious pub fare and watched the football game. They sat on the couch and watched the kickoff. Nicolette was excited watching her team play well against Miami (OH) the week before after losing to Utah in a close game at home two weeks before. Now, at Notre Dame, Nicolette hoped that they could build on the win and make a season of it. She had high hopes because she was always a Michigan fan and wished the best for them. The game started without incident, but as the play progress Michigan was not faring well. Nicolette was trying to not be angry, but it was difficult given how poorly her team was playing. At halftime, Michigan was down two scores; Nicolette reassured herself that they were a second half time because it was the only thing she had to keep her hope in a victory. James blindly agreed with her; he did not watch television much nor did he follow college football. Nicolette watched the halftime program and poured another glass of wine; she had a need for the liquid courage to watch the second half of that game. The third quarter started well enough for the Michigan defense, but the offense could not find the endzone. The struggles of the offense to move the ball was just starting and they continued into the fourth quarter. It was becoming abundantly clear that Michigan was going to lose another game. Nicolette sat back on the couch, feeling dejected she commented, "Well, that was a huge bummer. I do not think we are going to have a good season if we cannot move the ball. The play calling is so damn predictable." James offered condolences on the predicted horrible season. It was almost 8 o'clock in the evening and they had just finished lunch and did not have any evening plans. Nicolette noticed that James was balancing the glass he was drinking from on his tongue. She laughed at him and asked, "What are you doing, James?" Caught off-guard he slightly jumped in his chair. "Oh. I was just doing my daily tongue exercises. I balance glasses, usually a shot glass, on my tongue for several minutes each day to build up my stamina and strength. My goal is be able to continually pleasure a woman orally for hours on end with having to stall or decrease my pace and, also, still being able to use all the techniques that she enjoys." Nicolette replied, "Yes, your exercises. I do recall you describing them. I think you showed me with a shot glass on video call once. That glass is way too big for you to be trying to balance. You will break something and that is not excluding yourself." James laughed, "That is probably why it looked weird because I was also using my hands and mouth to help balance it. But I have to stay ready. I am hoping to use my skills on a very lovely lady sitting next to me." He smiled at her and looked in her eye intently, "I would love to taste you, Mistress. We have hours to kill and I have a great way to spend it." Nicolette had considered using his mouth for several months; James describes his regimes and abilities in a manner that had fueled her imagination. Nicolette stood up and walked towards James' bedroom; it was tidy and clean. His items were laid out in the bathroom or hung in the closet. Nicolette allowed her sundress to drop to her feet and she climbed up on the bed. James entered his room and saw her laying on his bed and he just grinned and proceeded to walk towards the foot of the bed. He climbed up on the bed and crawled up the middle of the bed towards her waist. James proceeded to kiss lightly on her stomach and hips. He slid his finger under the seam of her underwear, lifting the fabric from against her skin. He pulled her panties slowly towards her ankles, planting kisses on her legs as he worked his way down her body. He removed her panties and dropped them on top of her dress. James crawled back onto the bed and begun kissing his way back up her body, licking occasionally on Nicolette's body. James took his time returning to her vulva area. He laid with his face just inches from her labia and took a deep breath, exhaling directly on the hood of her clitoris. Nicolette moaned softly at the pressure of his breath and she lifted her hips pushing herself into his face. James responded by kissing lightly on the shortly groomed mound just north of the clitoris. As Nicolette was lowering her hips, James places his hands underneath her on her buttock. He begun massaging her rump and he ran his tongue along her outer lips, partly them along his path upward. Nicolette was enjoying the combination of his hands deeply massaging her and his tongue on her lips. As she was relaxing into the feel of his tongue on her lips, Nicolette was startled by his tongue flicking her clitoris. "Oh shit", Nicolette growled, "That feels good, James." James enjoyed hearing his name being moaned from her mouth; he took hearing his name as encouragement and motivation. He took her clitoris into his mouth and sucked it softly at first and when she moaned louder he suction got harder. James felt her finger rubbing on the top of his head. He released her clit and returned to running his tongue along her lips, but instead of ending on her clitoris he darted his tongue into her vagina. He was making circular, O motions along her vaginal opening while he started rubbing on her clitoris. James seemed to be in a deep trance as he moved from sucking her clit, tonguing her hole, rubbing her clit, licking her lips, and kissing on her. Nicolette found herself nearing orgasm and she moved James' head from tongue fucking her vagina to her clit. He took the cue and started sucking and licking the clit and its hood. Nicolette vocalized her pleasure, "I am going to come." James remained on her clit and pushed two fingers into her vagina. When she began coming, James remove from sucking her clit to licking her vagina, literally eating her come. Nicolette orgasm lasted for almost a full minute and after she laid back and smiled. James kissed her lips once again and she ran her fingers along his head. He laid there pensively for a moment, "Do you want me to stop, Mistress?" Nicolette looked down at him and said, "I am very sensitive right now, so you can continue, but stay away from my clitoris." James smiled and replied, "Thank you, Mistress." He quickly placed his face back deep between her legs allowing her legs to engulf his head. He started making O and S motions along her vaginal opening while rubbing her perineum. James' mustache kept brushing against her clitoris which was still partial engorged. James breathed on her clitoris as he was repositioning himself between her legs. Nicolette was so turned on by his techniques and the feeling of his breath made her close to another orgasm. "Lick my clit, softly," Nicolette moaned and James complied. He licked, sucked, and kissed on her clit while rubbing her pubic mound. Nicolette felt the characteristic flush of pleasure and she held his head in place and was grinding against it until she finished coming. When she was done, she released his head and motioned that she was done. Nicolette laid on the bed for a few minutes; contorting her body to not lay in the wet spot. James stood next to the bed where Nicolette was laying on the bed; she was catching her breath. He smiled at her with moisture, her juices dripping from around his mustache and beard. "You look very happy," Nicolette said. James smiled at her and commented, "I am on cloud nine. I just fulfilled one of my biggest fantasies. Thank you so much, Mistress. I have imagined your taste and smell for years and I could not imagine how sweet you are and wonderful you smell." Nicolette smiled at him, "Thank you for my orgasms. We are at what? Three now." James went to clean up in the bathroom and Nicolette took her clothes so that she could also clean-up for dinner.

Nicolette donned a very simple, but elegant cocktail dress and James put on a sport jacket, polo shirt, and dress pants. They were schedule for dinner at The Circular in the formal gardens. They walked to their meal and were escorted to a private table in the garden which was set-up to have views of the lush grounds. The table was set with crisp white linens and was adorned with flowers from the garden. The waitstaff greeted them as James was pulling out Nicolette's chair for her sit. "Would you like still or sparkling water for the table?" James and Nicolette spoke in unisom, "Sparkling, please." The waiter nodded and left to grab the water. Nicolette sat in her chair and James sat opposite her. "This is a lovely setting, James. I hope we are able to get through the dinner before it gets too cold out here. At least, they have the portable heaters on." James nodded in agreement about the temperature and the waiter brought out the sparkling water. He poured it into the large wine goblets as he introduced himself and the specials. "Hello, I am Ian and I will be your server this evening. We do have a couple specials on the menu for this evening. We are celebrating the coming of Fall with some wonderful root vegetables medleys. The vegetables are available with either pan-seared Cornish hen, split duck breast, or slow-cooked Amish grass-fed roast. Can I start you with something to drink?" Nicolette was still looking at the drink list and had not selected her beverage yet, while James was sipping on the water. "Can you please give us a minute?" James asked. Ian nodded and walked from the table. James inquired of Nicolette what she was looking to order to eat and drink. "So what sounds good to you?" Nicolette was still considering the menu, "I have not had duck in some time so naturally I am considering that because the root vegetable sound good. What are you thinking about?" James smiled, "The roast and vegetables sound good. I might want to add some potatoes. So you want to share some red wine or grab a scotch?" Nicolette looked over the menu once again. "I think I will just do a scotch because I do not want to drink a lot of wine tonight." As she was completing her sentence, Ian returned to the table to take their orders. "So have you made any decisions?" James motioned to Nicolette to state her preferences. "I will have the duck with the root vegetables. Which are included in that medley?" Ian replied, "It is carrots, onions, celery, and beets." "Perfect. I will have a Glenfiddich to drink. Neat with a side of ice," Nicolette completed her order. James spoke next, "I will also have a Glenfiddich. I will then enjoy the root vegetables to accompany the roast. I would also like to add a baked potato with butter, chives, and sour cream on the side. We will also need some more water." Ian nodded and went off to get the beverages, bread, and butter. Nicolette hugged herself with each breeze; "I should have brought a sweater with me tonight." James took that as his cue; he removed his blazer and placed it on her shoulders. A gentleman came to the table and addressed them, "Hello, I am Henry. I am the manager this evening. How is everything going?" Nicolette and James looked at him while James responded, "We are doing well thank you. It is quite lovely out here." Henry nodded and replied, "Yes. The Garden dinners are highly sought after as we get several requests, but few are granted permission to dine in our formal gardens. Are you celebrating anything special with us this evening?" James started shaking his head in a negative manner, but Nicolette answered in a low, sultry voice, "Yes. We are experiencing a series of firsts this weekend." Henry looked from Nicolette to James and Henry's face turned a bit red. "I came out here to remind the gentleman that he must wear his jacket at all times. I see that it is a bit cold out here and I have turned up the temperature on the heat lamp. It will take a few moments. I will come back and check. It appears that Ian is on his way back out with your drinks." Henry turned and walked towards Ian and had a brief, quiet conversation with him. While they were speaking, James addressed Nicolette, "I cannot believe that you said that to Henry. He is probably thinking way too much about our sex life right now." Nicolette replied in a coy voice, "But, I did not once

172

mention sex. Nor did I imply it. He was too busy trying to be a dick that he was caught off-guard. They both laughed as Ian dropped off their beverages, bread, and butter. They thanked him and went to enjoying the views of the surroundings. The deck did increase in temperature quite nicely. Nicolette was comfortable sitting in James' blazer and looking and discussing the surroundings. It was like being on a stereotypical date with vanilla expectations and outcomes. Henry returned shortly before their meals to check on the couple. "So is it warm enough for you now? I would prefer if he was in his own jacket for dinner." Nicolette nodded, "I assure you that he will be wearing his own jacket for dinner." Henry smiled and walked on. Nicolette slid the jacket off and wrapped over her shoulder, stood, and motioned for James to add his arms effectively wearing his jacket and hugging Nicolette. They were hugged up closely on the patio which was closing in on 68°F. James was looking Nicolette in the eyes as he was only a couple inches from her face. "You like that," Nicolette whispered as she hugged into his neck. He moaned and started kissing on her cheek and neck. She giggled as his facial hair was tickling her skin and before they knew it, Henry and Ian were at their table with their food. Henry looked disappointed, "So now you are sharing the blazer?" Nicolette turned and looked at him, "Oh, our meals. Um, James, we cannot eat food like this." James complied and removed himself from the blazer. Nicolette handed him the blazer so he could be within the requirements of the dress code. Ian placed their meals in front of them and they went immediately to eating their meal and drinking their beverages. Henry and Ian wished them a good meal. Nicolette was trying to get done as quickly as possible so that she could return the warmness of inside, while James was taking his time to savor each bite. She ate some of the duck which was delicious and juicy; it practically melted in her mouth. The root vegetables were the perfect tenderness and were simply seasoned with butter, thyme, and cracked pepper. James was visually enjoying his meal as well. Nicolette took the last sip of her scotch and leaning back in the chair and hugged herself. She had reached an uncomfortable temperature. "At least, we know why this reservation was available. We are the only fools willing to sit out in this cold. I am ready to go back to the room. We can take the remaining food with us. Are you ok with that?" Nicolette asked and James nodded. They both stood and he gave Nicolette his jacket, "You should go inside. I will meet you back at the room." Nicolette smiled and nodded. Ian headed back to the table to ask if everything was going well with the meal. Nicolette overheard James comment that dinner was less than enjoyable with the temperature and the inability of him to provide his jacket to his lady companion. He requested that the meals get package so that he can take them back to their rooms. Ian and James continued to speak as Nicolette returned to the room. She placed James jacket on the bed and went and changed into fluffy sweats and then wrapped in a blanket and sat on the couch to await James' return. He walked in the room about fifteen minutes later and was clearly flush in the face. "What is wrong, James?" "I am ok. How are you? Are you warmer?" He asked her in reply. "I am warmer. But you did not answer what is wrong with you?" James sighed, "I wager my compliment of the gardens while also tendering my complaints. I asked why the dress code was not clear that a jacket was required as one can dress formally as a male without a jacket and tie. I said that, given the temperature, they were a bit unreasonable. I requested that they pack up the meals for our room." Nicolette listened intently and added, "I appreciate you standing up for me. I have yet to hear anything in that recounting that should have you all flush." James held up her finger, "Just wait. Well that Henry person got a bit too close and much too loud for the discussion that I was trying to have. I pointed that out to him and he seemed to be angrier. I explained that I am not into having conversation with yelling persons. I went to walk away and he grabbed my shoulder to continue yell at me and said something about being rude and disrespectful. I might have broken his fingers. Luckily, Henry has a history of being a bit over the top, Ian had called over the general manager who witnessed the last several minutes of the exchange. He apologized on behalf of the hotel for both the anal jacket policy in this temperature as well as Henry's behavior. He insisted on making a new dinner for us both and sending it up. We do not have to pay for any of dinner tonight." Nicolette sat back and nodded. "I see. I am sorry that I missed that." James walked into the bedroom to change and there was a knock at the door. Looking out, Nicolette saw Ian from the restaurant. She opened the door. "Yes?" "Ma'am, I was ordered to bring you a glass of scotch for each of you." She stepped to the side and motioned, and he placed the scotch on the table. Nicolette thanked him and he departed. James emerged from the bedroom and they toasted to the evening. "Here's to freezing and fighting!" Nicolette exclaimed before they clinked their glasses together. "I am so embarrassed. I tend to not be a violent person. But cheers. I need to shake this," James said shaking his head. They enjoyed the scotch and when their food arrived, the restaurant brought a tablecloth, flameless candles, and set-up a very nice candlelit dinner. Nicolette and James ate their dinner, enjoying their conversation. After they were done, they packed up the dishes and put them on the cart outside of the room. James thanked Nicolette for a lovely evening, and they retired to their rooms to clean up. After her shower, rolling up her hair, and brushing her teeth, Nicolette made her way to the common room where James was kneeling near her door with hands resting on his knees. "I am ready to serve you, Mistress, in any way you see fit. Do you have a use for me?" Nicolette smiled down at him. "I was hoping you saved room for dessert." James smiled at her and followed her into his room. "I always have room for your sweetness, Ma'am" he replied. James begun orally pleasing her, but after one very quick orgasm, Nicolette turned over. Without further prompting, James dove quickly between her cheeks and begun tonguing her asshole. His techniques were just as effective on her anus as they were on her clitoris and vagina. After her second orgasm, Nicolette laid in bed and motioned for James to join her. He smiled and made his way to the bathroom to wash his face first. After using the bathroom, James returned to the bedroom with a dancing, erect penis that was dripping pre-come. "You should probably do something about that, eh?" Nicolette teased. "It would be my honor to masturbate for you in front of you in person," James replied. Nicolette smiled and rubbed on his member, enticing more come to drip. He stood with his head leaned back with his eyes rolled back in his head. "Oh, Mistress. That feels amazing. I crave your touch. That is the best feeling." Nicolette removed her hand and James looked down and saw her invite him back to the bed with a tap on the bed. He sat down and she motioned for him to start to stroke and he complied. It did not take long for him to ask for permission to come, "Mistress, may I please come?" Nicolette wanted to edge him further so she denied him released. "No, not yet, James. Make it last for me. This is hot." James reduced the speed of his stroke and let out a deep breath. It was obvious that he was thinking of something other than the task at hand. Nicolette begun to tease him by nibbling slightly on his neck and whispering moans in his ear. "Oh, this is torture, Mistress." Nicolette started helping him masturbating by massaging his testicles. James released a throaty moan and his shoulders clinched tensely while he was fighting the orgasm that was imminent. "Ma'am, may I please come now?" James pleaded. Nicolette replied with an evil grin on her face, "Only if you drink it." "Yes, Ma'am. Thank you Ma'am." James replied and shot a large stream of semen which shot almost three feet into the air due to the pressure behind it; much of the product landed on and around his mouth. He quickly licked and swallowed a fair bit of the come. Nicolette watched and commented, "Good boy. Does that taste good to you?" James was still coming and he nodded his head 'yes'. When he was done, James again laid back on the bed and panted with come on his torso and chest. Nicolette went and got him a warm, soapy towel to clean up. "Have you ever tasted yourself before?" She asked. "No, I have not. It was not what I expected. It was much different than you...both your near and your rear." He said with a smile.

They laid on the bed together for a few moments before Nicolette walked slowly back to her own room. She sat on her bed for several minutes thinking about the connection and the relationship with James. He was many of the things that she sought in a man, submissive, and companion. They got along very well and had several things in common. She knows that he had hang ups about meeting her for years, but he seemed to have gotten over them or they would not be in this hotel together. The decision to be celibate was based on taking time to learn herself, love herself after the break-up with Benjamin. It was clear to Nicolette that she accomplished both of those goals; she accomplished them quite some time ago. Celibacy was easy for her; she was learning and playing in the lifestyle and since she was not in a committed relationship, she did not think about sex. Once she hit the five-year mark, it was like she had a new virginity that she had to think about giving away. Each time she was turned on enough with a person, she thought to herself 'is this person worthy of my new virginity?' She made her new virginity a prize and she was realizing that she painted herself into this corner that she did not want to be in. She had been wet, almost constantly, for three days now and while she has reached multiple orgasms so far this weekend, she was denying herself the pleasure of intercourse and did not have a good reason why. Nicolette, who was still nude, climbed out of bed and walked across the room to the bathroom. She looked at herself in the mirror and smiled. It was a meek smile, but a proud smile. "You are beautiful. You are desirable. You deserve to experience the pleasure of sex. You deserve to be pleased in all the ways you see fit.

Girl, why are trying to store your pussy away for a rainy day?" Nicolette nodded her head to her reflection then she made her way across the common rooms to the second bedroom door. James had left it open and he was reading in bed when he noticed Nicolette in the doorway, "Is everything ok, Mistress? Can I do anything for you?" Nicolette looked at him and smiled. "Yes, you can do me. Did you come prepared for sex? Intercourse, that is, not just oral sex." James stumbled over his words as he placed his book on the nightstand, "Wait. Yes. I mean, I was an eagle scout. But are you sure? You want to? Wow. Ok. Wait. Yes." James was smiling as he climbed out of bed with an obvious erection growing in his pants. He walked towards Nicolette and placed his hands on her shoulders; he composed himself and commented, "Mistress. I am prepared to please you in any way that you can think of and yes, I did bring protection if you are interested in making love to me. And I mean making love, not sex, as my fondness for you could not just be a carnal expression of lust." Nicolette smiled at James and kiss him lightly on the lips then on the neck, and shoulder. He began caressing her breasts and hips; moaning at her touch. Nicolette ran her nails down his back and held his hips as she moved him backwards towards the bed. James was running his hands over her body; pausing his hands only to massage her erogenous zones as he moved. At the bedside, Nicolette untied the drawstring on James' pajama pants, and they fell from his waist and dangled on his outstretched dick, which was engorged and throbbing. Nicolette looked at how impressive he was and commented, "It has been quite some time, muscle or not; you will have to be patient with me." James moved his pants beyond his dick, smiled and said, "I have all night." He placed a few kisses on her neck, cheek, and shoulder; nestling into the divot in her shoulder blade. Nicolette moaned and leaned into his advances; her hand was moving around the head of his dick tracing it with her index finger; her finger was coated in the oozing from his dick. James leaned Nicolette back onto the bed, lowering her slowly from her standing position. He followed laying on top of her still kissing and massaging various parts of her body but focusing on her neck and shoulders. Nicolette rolled over on top of James, straddling his nude body, and begun kissing on his chest with his arms pinned above his head. She crouched down to kiss down his body, but the steel-like nature of his dick did not budge. As she lowered herself to kiss upon his abs, pubic crest, and thighs, his throbbing, engorged member was positioned to thrust inside of her. She paused and jumped with a startle, "It seems your dick is trying to go spelunking." James laughed, "I could say that he has a mind of his own, but we are both thinking about being deep inside the sweet folds of you." Nicolette laughed and rolled off of him; James followed closely, quickly behind suckling on her breasts, flicking the nipples with his tongue and rolling the nipple that was not in his mouth with his fingers. James placed kisses from her breasts to her navel and was starting to indulge in the delight that was between her legs when she stopped him, "I want to feel all of you, not just your tongue. Indulge me." James spent only a few minutes sucking on her clitoris before he went to the nightstand for a condom. "Are you sure that…" James with his eyes lowered begun to ask for consent for the sexual encounter when Nicolette started to kiss him again and removed the condom from his hands. She opened it with her teeth, tearing into it; and then returned to kissing him. She was massaging his balls and she slid the condom down his entire shaft. She kissed him deeply again, before laying back on the bed, she replied, "I am sure. Now, come here." James climbed up on the bed and returned her kiss while positioning his self over her. He used his head to split her lips, rubbing the head briefly between them and on the clitoral hood. He pushed his girth past the first set of lips which caused Nicolette to arch her back and moan, partly from the pain and partly because of the stimulation. "Do you want me to stop?" James managed though it was clear that was hoping for a negative answer as he adjusted his depth.

"No. Don't stop," Nicolette gasped, trying to breathe through the pain. James was not prepared for how slow he would have to go for Nicolette to take all of him; he barely had the head inside of her and she was groaning and panting. He tried to push deep; he wanted to start a true rhythm but was denied access quickly with Nicolette clutching his waist with her thighs. James tapped her knees exclaiming, "Mistress, you are crushing me." Nicolette sighed and withdrew, "I am sorry. I did not mean to crush you." She turned away from his gaze and pushed back even further on the bed. She said, "This might have been a bad idea. I do not think I have come close to taking you and I am running and damn near crying. I feel stupid and this is ridiculous. You cannot be enjoying this." James laughed slightly and laid beside Nicolette to hold her; moving his still fully engorged penis out of the way. "Nicolette, I am having the best weekend. I enjoy your company. I love your body. And so far, the sex, both intercourse and oral, have been amazing. I, literally, have zero complaints. We could lay here for the rest of the trip and you would never hear a negative word from me." James placed his hand under her chin and began kissing her again. Nicolette decided that she needed to try to power through or at least 'woman up'. She rolled over and straddled James again. This time she lowered herself slowly, deliberately onto him. It took her almost ten full minutes and taking only very shallow breathes, but she made her way onto 80% of him. She rode him slowly, cheating by kissing him often so that more of him would slide from inside of her. James was nearing his orgasm, so he began trying to rub on Nicolette's clitoris, but she blocked his full access each chance she got since the more engorged and excited they both got, the tighter her muscles collapsed onto him. He noticed that she was denying him access and commented, "Mistress, I am so close, and I need for you to come. I want you to feel as amazing as I feel – for this experience to be perfect for you too." Nicolette laughed, but only slightly because each chuckle was felt deep inside her vagina and the pressure was excruciating. She said, "James, I am literally trying to get out of this without having to pack myself with ice. I am just proud that I was able to take all…what, 9 inches, of you. You are a block, but instead of a 2 by 4; I am fucking a 9 by 4." James seemed to consider Nicolette words closely and finally asked for permission to come again, "I would like to come, please. Is that acceptable, allowable?" Nicolette watched his face with was a mixture of his O face and the face he makes when he wants a compliment. She knew that he would not be able to resist his orgasm much longer, so she rode him slowly while she reached around to massage his balls. Nicolette enjoyed bringing him to the edge of his orgasm but denying him release. "Not yet, James. Make it last longer." She insisted. James clinched his teeth and thrusted slightly deeper, keeping pace with her. It was clear that he would not be able to edge much longer so she granted him permission. James seems to release his orgasm from the depths of his soul when she said, "James, you can come, now." He lost control of his stroke from the excitement and thrust balls deep inside of her, pushing his member completely and quickly into Nicolette. The depth and the convulsion of his ejaculate where too much for Nicolette, she literally jumped off his shaft while pushing him sideways and landed on the bed. He was still coming with his dick dancing and pushing its seed into the tip of the condom. He was confused and asked, "What is wrong? I do not know why you pushed off of me. Is everything ok?" Nicolette simply responded, "too deep". James, again, felt bad for the pain that he inflicted on Nicolette. The combination of the intense pleasure he felt and the deep pain he knew she was in combined for the best mindfuck he had in quite some time. James got out of the bed and discarded the load filled condom into the trash and returned to the bed where Nicolette was in the fetal position in pain. James caressed her and ran his fingers through her hair. He whispered, "Thank you, Nicolette, for one of the best nights this old man has had in quite some time. I vow to make you feel as amazing as I feel." Nicolette knew that he meant that vow, but at the moment all she could feel is the pain coursing through her that was reminiscent of the time she lost her virginity. James continued to caress her, and he kissed on her back, shoulder, and neck. He held her close and was cuddling her body; he asked "Do you want me to run a warm bath? I am sorry. I did not mean to lose my composure; you felt amazing and you are so wet. And I, I apologize. There is no excuse for going so deep when you clearly did not want me to or was prepared for me to be that deep inside you." Nicolette rolled and looked at James, who had a look of intense horror on his, and replied, "James, you can stop apologizing. I know that you were not deliberately trying to hurt me. You cannot help that you are endowed, turned me on, and thoroughly engaging in our sex. It would be insulting if fucking me did not make you lose composure on occasion. It will get easier for me. Pussy is, after all, a muscle. Mine is just out of shape." He smiled at Nicolette and was reassured by her words. "Well, it you let me, I would love to be her personal trainer." They both laughed and they laid in the bed for a bit. James drifted off to sleep soon thereafter. The pain was beginning to subside, and Nicolette decided to sleep there for a moment, as well.

James' alarm went off; Nicolette slept next to him all night. When she looked towards the clock, she noticed that James was not in the room. It was 4:30 in the morning. "Oh my God, do you hate sleep?" She asked to apparently no one. Nicolette turned off the alarm and sat up in the bed. The bathroom was empty so she made her way to the toilet; there was a dull throbbing pain still present that caused her to walk slower than normal, but no other reminder of the evening's activities. She walked out of the bathroom drying her hands looking around for James, joking to herself that he is horrible at one-night stands if all of this take several years. Nicolette left the room and was surprised by James in the living room stretched out on a yoga mat. "Oh. There you are. I was curious where you made your way to. Your alarm went off."

James opened his eyes and looked at her and smiled the biggest smile she has ever seen on him. "Good morning, Mistress. I hope you slept well and that my alarm was not too inconvenient. I forgot to turn it off when I got up." "Speaking of which, why are you up? It is only 4:30. Our seaweed treatment is not until 9:30 and the church you said you were going to take me to does not start for another three hours. What gives? You hate sleeping next to me?" Nicolette stated, half teasing and half annoyed. James laughed at the quip, "No, I am up at this time everyday to workout, whether yoga or handball. I did not want to overstep my line by waking you with oral sex this morning; therefore, I had to leave the room to no longer tempt myself." Considering his words carefully, Nicolette stated, "Consensual, non-consent. We have had most forms of sex that a man and a woman can have. We ended the night with intercourse. If you wanted to extend the scene by worshipping my vagina, then I could understand that. I enjoy your tongue and would not have found offense to that. But I do understand how both the D/s and rape lines were bolded." James nodded along to Nicolette's statement. She retired to her room for additional rest and he continued his workout. She emerged two and a half hours later showered, dressed, and ready for Mass. James, too, was ready to attend church. "Mistress, my mother would be happy to know that I am attending church this morning. It has been several decades as you know since I have been inside of a church. I will gladly escort you, but do not say I did not warn you if it goes up in flames when I enter." Nicolette laughed, "Well, I go every weekend and if they do not burn when I walk in, they will not for you. Besides, I am confident that one day there will be a scientist at the head of the Church, and we will make progress. It was not that long ago that a black woman, like myself, could not worship in the churches of this land. Gays, kinks, and transgender people will get their day." James just shook his head and they left the hotel. James opened the door for Nicolette, tipped the valet, and drove to St. Joan of Arc

Parish. They arrived early for the service and Nicolette picked a seat near the back, on the right-hand side of the altar. James and Nicolette sat very close to one another and whispered to one another as they waited for the Mass to begin; their closeness and the obvious differences drew a few eyes. Nicolette was disappointed that they sat in the church for almost ten minutes and no one addressed them. The priest emerged from the sacristy and the church became quiet as he walked to the back of the church. The Mass started in normal fashion and James seemed more and more uncomfortable as it proceeded while Nicolette sung the songs and recited the prayers. After the homily, the sigh of peace was disheartening as people walked up to them and gave a fake smile or skipped them altogether. Nicolette turned to James and said, "I wonder if it is that we are outsiders, an interracial couple, or the age difference. Either way, this is a shitty way to treat other children of God," James laughed. One of the deacons came up to them to offer peace and both were surprised and participated. "Welcome to St. Joan of Arc. Are you finding everyone kind and friendly?" He asked. Nicolette replied, "Peace be with you, Deacon. You are the first person to address us really, but we do appreciate the greeting. I was starting to think we had an arm growing out of our necks." The deacon laughed and extended his hand to James. He shook it without words and gave the deacon a brief smile. The Mass proceeded as usual and Nicolette went up for communion while James remained in the pew though she insisted that he could come up for a blessing. James, though a baptized Catholic, he was not participating member of the Body. Nicolette returned to the pew and prayed while the choir sung a selection. Mass closed soon thereafter, Nicolette felt refilled for the week and oddly more appreciative of her priest back home. James and Nicolette started to make their way to the exit when they were stopped by a Stepford-like couple. She spoke with a large grin across her face, "Hello. Welcome to St. Joan's. We are the Lewises. I am Jan and this is my wonderful husband Cameron. We are part of the Welcome Committee here and just wanted to reach out. Are you new to the neighborhood?" Addressing Nicolette before she could respond to the first group of questions, "Is this your grandfather? Uncle? Dad maybe? I could see you being a mixed mulatto." Nicolette looked at James, who had a very predictable and annoyed look on his face, and then she answered, "Hello. Thank you, Jan and Cam, for the welcome. No, we are not new to this neighborhood. We are in town just for the spa. And also, no, he is not my grandfather, uncle, or dad. He is my lover. We make animalistic, hedonistic love in our sin-filled romps. Lastly, not that it is your concern at all, I am not mulatto." Nicolette turned from their gape-mouthed faces to address James, "Let us make our way back to the hotel and have hot, monkey love. Might as well, I am going to Hell for addressing these prejudiced people as such in a Church of God." James through the best shit-eating grin stated, "Yes, Ma'am." He turned to the couple and stated, "Nice to meet you" as he exited the Church behind Nicolette. On the stairs of the church, the deacon addressed them again, "Would you like to join us for coffee or a pastry in the back of church?" Nicolette shook her head, "Deacon, I appreciate your offer, but I think we will pass as I do find that these parishioners are very closed-minded and offensive. Thank you for your kindness." The Lewises walked out of the church to watch Nicolette and James leave; the deacon turned and saw them and shook his head knowing who was rude. They walked to the car and drove quietly back to the hotel; James was grinning at the failure of the church experience while Nicolette was thinking about the lack of welcome she felt. "You can stop grinning now, James. Not all church people are like them. You forget that I am church people. I attend every week and speak to everyone. I do not judge anyone. Jesus didn't so I don't." James laughed and replied, "You are my kind of people, but it is funny that my first time back was so bad. I am not cut out for church." They made it back to the hotel and the valet open Nicolette's door and offered her his hand. She stepped out of the chair and James was a bit uneasy at the smile and attention of the young valet. Nicolette did not notice him or James' change in demeanor. She checked the time and noted that they have thirty minutes to change and make it to the spa. "Okay, James, we have to get turned around and make our wrap." They got to the room, changed, and back out to the spa quickly and made the reservations. Nicolette stripped down and got oiled down by the spa staff; they started wrapping her in wet seaweed that was rehydrated in hot water. The seaweed felt warm on her skin; she could hear James moan in appreciation of the temperature of the seaweed wrap. Once they were fully wrapped and laying on the table to dry, the staff added a charcoal facial and cucumbers to their eyes. Nicolette started to drift off to sleep, while James started to meditate.

An hour later after her nap and his meditation, the staff came and helped them get out of the wrap. They showered, dressed, and made their way to lunch. They had massages scheduled at the end of the day which was 4 o'clock. Before that they had a few hours to kill so they would have lunch and perhaps walk the town. They walked out of the hotel into town to have lunch with the locals. They decided on a hole-in-the-wall restaurant that had amazing reviews online. It was an Asian-fusion restaurant that served pho and other foods. They both ordered something filling, but light. They sat and discussed the weekend and reached the consensus that it was the best that they could have expected. After completing the meal, they walked around downtown, hand-in-hand and visited a few of the shops. The town was very sleepy, in that, it did not have a fair number of shops and things to do on a Sunday. Nicolette urged them back to the hotel, where with two hours to kill, she undressed and insisted he do the same. James was an anal virgin, but he was willing to do whatever would please Nicolette. She decided that she wanted to play with his ass, so she donned a finger cot and lubed up her finger-cot finger. She, then, bent him over the bed. She started by rubbing and massaging his cheeks, crack, and legs. When he tensed, she would massage his balls. When he was dripping pre-come, Nicolette eased her index finger into his ass. He grunted and spread his legs allowing her better access. She rotated her finger, massaging his prostate, milking him. James, with intense surprise in his voice, asked Nicolette, "Ma'am, is it possible that...that I can come from this? Oh my, I feel like I am going to come. Mistress, is this…" Nicolette focused on the prostate, focusing on milking him, "Yes, James. That is the point of milking." James grabbed at the bed beneath him and before he could ask for permission, he was ejaculating on the bed spread. "I did not want to make that mess." James said scurrying up the bed away from Nicolette, forcing her finger from his ass and off his prostate. Nicolette was very turned on by the anal play and James was not sure if he was into the anal play. "Ok, that was very different," James stated, "I did not know that I could come that way. I am…I do not know. I do not think I have reached orgasm this many times in one five-day period in my adult life. Does that turn you on? What do you get from milking?" Nicolette stated, "It is all about the power exchange. Last night, and probably tonight too, you held much of the power due to the nature of heterosexual sex." James look surprised and then smiled, "So sex tonight? Yes, of course." Nicolette laughed at him and went to the bathroom and washed her hands after removing the finger cot. "You know we have quite some time to waste, you should put your face between my legs. And if you can make me come quickly, I could also go for something filling and deep." James replied, "Are you still hungry? I can order in room service if you want." Nicolette shook her head and laughed that her comments went over his head. James sat quiet for a moment and eventually exclaimed his understanding. Nicolette started to undress and pushed James flat on the bed. She crawled up his torso and sat on his chest, pinning his arms to the bed under her feet and legs. He smiled at her and asked, "Where are you going? If you need, I have a place for you to sit. It would be helpful for me too since my nose is cold." Nicolette grinned and replied, "Be careful what you wish for." Nicolette settled onto his face and started slowly riding it, he quickly responded by licking and flicking his tongue allowing Nicolette to position his mouth where she wanted it. She arched her back and her head fell backwards in delight as she rode James' tongue. His exercises, she thought, were working as it was rare that a man can tongue her that long in this position without needing a break, usually within ten minutes. She lost track of the time while she was riding his face; her orgasm was epic and throbbing which lasted two full minutes, with several intense waves. When she was done coming, Nicolette dismounted from his face. She kissed him passionately tasting herself from his glistening face; Nicolette thought to herself how much she enjoyed her taste as she kissed him. The smile on his face was ever-present. Nicolette checked the time and they were due for their final spa appointment before checkout tomorrow. She dressed while he washed his face and crouch which were covered in come. They went for the couples' reflexology massage which focused mostly on the feet but also included a full-body component. James and Nicolette enjoyed the massage and felt extremely relaxed. After they returned to their room and ordered in a pizza, by Nicolette's request. She stated, "We have been eating too fancy for a few days now, I want to cheat with something bad for me and saucy." James laughed and stated, "That was too easy so I will just order a pizza." Nicolette agreed that pizza would be a fitting meal for the evening. She provided him with the toppings that she preferred, and James ordered the pizza. The pizza arrived within twenty minutes and they ate while finishing the wine that was left-over from earlier in the weekend. The medium pizza was the perfect amount for them as there were not any leftovers. They discussed the weekend and the plan forward. Each stated what they enjoyed about the weekend and that they wanted some more time to mull over the goings-on before they commit to something long-term. Their conversation was cordial and honest, and neither seemed upset or slighted at the end. Nicolette went to pack for the drive home; James returned to his room to organize and pack. Nicolette completed her packing and noted that James fell asleep on the bed before she returned so she allowed him his sleep and returned to her room.

Nicolette looked at her email briefly and decided that she did not want to read any of it. She rested well earlier and was not as tired as James. She decided that she was going to be very nice to James by letting him sleep. Nicolette decided to soak in a bath before bed; she turned off the light and turned on the flameless candles that were in the bathroom for that purpose and relaxed. The water was getting too cold for her in the tub, so she exited and dried off. As she was leaving the bathroom, she noticed that James was sitting patiently on her bed, "Mistress, I apologize for taking a nap when you are awake. I should have not gotten up so early this morning. I am a bit worn out." Nicolette felt bad for him, "James, you should go back to bed. Being worn out is not good, especially with you driving home tomorrow for several hours just, like me." James commented, "I would rather be worn out and tired when I drive home tomorrow than now when I am trying to soak up every second with you." Nicolette sat on the bed next James and started rubbing lotion into her skin. He reached for the lotion bottle and started to assist and take over for her by rubbing the lotion into places that she could not reach alone, or were difficult for her. When he was done and she was fully moisturized, James placed the lotion bottle on the nightstand. He just sat on the bed and looked at Nicolette. "What are you doing?" Nicolette asked with him just sitting on the bed staring at the wall. James rubbed his hands together and pensively looked at Nicolette, "I am here waiting to see if you want to use me. Whether with corporal again, or anal, or sexually…I am here to serve you and please you. I want you to be happy when you leave here." Nicolette smiled at him and she got in the bed next to him.

"Come here," she motioned him next to her, "I want you to rest with me. It is early for the evening, but late in our day." Nicolette laid down and spooned James, holding him to her body. James wiggled and laid very straight. Nicolette kept adjusting his body so that she could cuddle him easier and closer. Finally, after he moved out of her arms again she asked, "Is everything ok?" James cleared his throat and replied, "I do not think I have ever been held like that before. I am not used to being the little spoon. It is awkward and I also do not know what I am supposed to do in this situation." Nicolette laughed, "You do nothing, but lay here and let me hold you. Relax into my arms, into my caress. I have you." James started to whisper to himself 'She has me. She has me. I can relax. She has me.' It dawned on Nicolette at that time that he was not comfortable being vulnerable; all of their play and all their interactions only go as far as he can control. Nicolette again pulled James close and joined his whispers. She spooned him and she felt his muscles relax literally back into her arms. After about ten minutes of holding James closely, he settled completely into her arms. Nicolette whispered, "See. That was not that hard or that bad was it?" James did not answer, and Nicolette realized that it was because he was asleep. Nicolette slowly moved her arm from beneath him and got comfortable behind him with her body still against him and went to sleep as well. Nicolette was awoken due to James breath on her cheek. She woke up with a start and he was staring at her face. "How long have you been awake looking at me?" She asked him. "I just woke up about five minutes before you. We have been napping for four hours; it is eleven." Nicolette stretched, "Good nap. I feel refreshed, do you?" James' grin was undeniable, "I feel absolutely amazing. I did not realize that I needed to nap as bad as I did. You made me relax in a way that I did not think was ever possible." She smiled and rubbed her eyes; she felt refreshed and was hornier than she was before the nap. Nicolette looked James in eyes and rolled over on top of him. He started to kiss her neck and she kissed his neck and

190

chest. She was grinding on him; dry humping him like an adolescent discovering their sexual likes. As she grinded on him, the juices from her vagina begun to coat his midsection which turned him on even more. Nicolette worked her hips with the rhythm of his panting breath and his hands found her hips. He held his hands on her hips for a couple minutes, ensuring that he knew the pace that she was moving. He suddenly lifted her off his midsection and placed her rocking hips and dipping lips onto his mouth. Nicolette began riding his face as he opened his mouth awaiting her icing. His tongue impatiently lapped at her lips, parting them. She felt his tongue curl around her clitoral hood and she placed one hand on top his head the second was used for balance against the wall above the headboard. James' skills were unequivocal; he combined the experience of a man of his age with the glee of a first-timer. Nicolette was impishly alternating between riding his tongue for pleasure and face-sitting him to appease the sadistic thoughts in her mind. James focused his energy solely on enjoying her taste, smell, and weight on his face and tongue. He did not panic or struggle to gain breathe; in fact, he relaxed when she sat down fully on his face restricting his air. The only indication that she had that he was deprived for long enough to cause him pause was the decrease in the feverish pace of his worship of his vagina. Nicolette noticed that if she sat for ten seconds longer then he would start to move his arms towards a position where he could move his shoulders and gain air; that struggle and his skillset pushed her deep into Domspace. She was noticeably wetter than she had been in any of their encounters earlier in the weekend. James moved his arms so that he could use his fingers while he was suckling on her clit. He knew that she was close to her orgasm when she stopped smothering him and begun riding his fingers slowly, but with a constant rhythm. His tongue flicked against the tip of the clitoris while entire bud and hood where inside his mouth. Nicolette rocked away from his mouth abruptly and slumped over top him. The orgasm enveloped every inch of her causing muscles spasms from her back through her pelvis to her legs. She was vibrating on top of him and he was kissing lightly on her arms, breasts, and sides as those were the parts close to his face as she panted and moaned. When it was clear that she had regained some of the strength in her legs and core, he sat up on his elbow and made eye contact with Nicolette and spoke, "Mistress, that was intense. I have never been smothered like that before. Thank you for that experience. What do you call that?" Nicolette laughed to herself, "Face-sitting, James. That was face-sitting. I agree. It was a very intense, very sexy scene." She paused for a moment and looked down at his dancing, erect shaft. "Where was I?" She asked, "Oh, yes." She remarked and sat back on his midsection and begun grinding on him again. She felt his penis rubbing against her butt cheeks and the small of her back as she rode his stomach and pelvic crest. She could feel moisture dripping onto the crack of her ass; she knew that he was very aroused. James moved his elbows from beneath himself and placed his head on his pillow. "I did not know that bringing you to orgasm with my mouth was interrupting your grinding on me. I figured I was given you a much more enjoyable place to grind." James mentioned half moaning, half in a snarky tone. In an equally sarcastic tone, Nicolette replied, "That is what happens when you boys think." "Touche," James replied, very tongue-in-cheek. At that point, there was a very slick stream of James rolling down her backside and he went from dancing to being a rod that did not have any give as her cheek bounced against him. She looked down at James and raised an eyebrow, "I think we may have to do something about that...at the very least, get a flag for it." James chuckled at the statement and then pleaded, "I would rather a moist, warm place to stick him" Nicolette looked on the nightstand and then in the drawers, she located the condoms and prepared to straddle his oozing rod. She lowered herself onto him, taking her time to relax her muscles around his girth. Her pocket enveloped him well and she continued ride him deeper inside of her. He held onto her hips, grasping them periodically as the pleasure surprised him, overtaking his composure on occasion. She moaned as he worked deeper insider her; she was enjoying how he stretched her. Nicolette took her time, moving slowly and methodically down his shaft. She rocked her hips and moved in a small, circular motion as he pushed himself farther. Her breath was shallow at times as the intense fullness spread up towards her stomach. She felt his expanse swell and through her moans she barked at him, "You cannot come yet. I am not finished." James nodded, closed his eyes, and begun to murmur to himself. Nicolette leaned forward, withdrawing about half his length and started kissing on his neck, nibbling on his ear, and licking his lips. He opened his eyes just slightly to meet her mouth and kissed her passionately. Retuning his head to the pillow as she retreated herself onto the shaft, Nicolette continued to tease him with kisses and nibbles. James held onto her hips, his finger pressing into her skin, as he increased his stroke; the shaft moving deeper than it was previous. Nicolette could feel that she was taking almost all of him so she started rocking quickly on his lap, pushing the last bit into herself. Her right index and middle fingertips worked her clitoris, coaxing more natural lubrication and urging her muscles to relax around him. Contracting the muscles, Nicolette begun changing the sensation he felt and James grunted his approval. Again, she felt him swell inside her, the chant he was murmuring to himself got louder and more frequent. Nicolette barked at him, "Not yet." James sighed a long, throaty noise. She felt his entire exhale. His fingers replaced hers and she started to concentrate only on the sensations; she started to ride him quicker, almost matching the pace of his fingers on her clit. With each thrust, Nicolette felt him slide easier and deeper. The head of his penis was massaging her g-spot with each motion. The pleasure was overwhelming and he felt her tighten around his shaft, making the strokes harder to complete. "May I come, Mistress?" he moaned. Nicolette was engrossed in her own pleasure and managed only a nod as she continued to experience the completely titillating orgasm. "Thank you, Ma'am", James replied barely able to complete the sentence as his fingers moved from her clit to her hips and were pressed into the skin. He moaned his thanks repeatedly as he came. His body tensed beneath Nicolette and she could hear the joints in his toes crack as they curled. His entire orgasm lasted almost a full minute. When he was done, he slowly withdrew his partially erect member and placed it on his thigh. Nicolette laid on top of him for few moments before rolling onto to her side so he could clean their come off of himself. He returned a few moments later and cuddle up next to her. He placed multiple kisses on her shoulder, neck, and back and again expressed his gratitude. "Thank you, again, Mistress. I have had the most unexpectedly wonderful time with you. You have fulfilled so many of my fantasies. Just laying here holding you would have made this weekend amazing, but to experience so many different scenes with you. I am humbly yours." Nicolette smiled to herself and held onto to his arm which was around her waist and went back to sleep.

James woke up just before 7 o'clock and went to his room to shower, shave, brush his teeth, and pack all his remaining items. He also called into his office and instructed his staff on the tasks to be done in his absence. After completing the work, he ordered breakfast. Nicolette was starting to stir; he heard her in the bathroom. She was less sore than she was after their first tryst and Nicolette was relieved because driving for over 6 hours with a sore vagina would have been undesirable. She showered, brushed her teeth, and dressed for the day. Nicolette packed her last few items and placed them near the front door. "Good morning, James. I see you are up before the chickens again. I swear you hate sleep." James laughed at her quip, "It is late for me. I am usually at the gym for handball at 5. I ordered us breakfast. It should be here shortly. How did you sleep?" Nicolette nodded her head and replied, "I slept well. Good sex tends to do that. How about yourself; did you sleep okay?" "Mistress, I have not been able to wipe this grin off of my face. I slept quite well, too. I guess the most amazing sex I have ever had in my entire life will do that, too." Nicolette grinned at him as she made her way to join him at the seating room table. "I know it is too early to have this conversation, but since you mentioned it during coitus, I feel I must, at least, touch upon it. This was an intense weekend full of power exchange. It is difficult to not get caught up in the moment. As such, I must point out that you stated that I own you last night. I do not take ownership of someone lightly. Was that something you said in the throws of a mind-altering orgasm or do we need to start a serious conversation?" James sat back in his chair and sat quiet for a moment, "You are correct in your statement that this was an intense weekend full of power exchange. I have never been so moved like that before. And yes, while I did say it during arguably one of the best experiences of my life…" James was interrupted by his phone ringing. "I am sorry. This is my daughter. One moment please, Mistress." James answered the phone and, by the end of the conversation that Nicolette could hear, discussed with his daughter why he was not at work, tried to comfort her over the phone, and finally why he was sorry that he did that to you. He continued in a very circular conversation hitting on the three points repeatedly before sitting, sunken in his chair. He finally stated that his time with 'Nicolette was special, but not enough to bring up meeting the family'. He told his daughter how amazing she was, how much he loved her, and reassured her that he will be home that evening. While he was wrapping up his conversation, there was a knock at the door; it was their breakfast. Nicolette had the gentleman put the food onto the table and she tipped him, and he departed. Nicolette saw that James ordered a small assortment of the items she had eaten for breakfast throughout the weekend. She opted for an omelet and fruit. He closed his phone and stared at Nicolette.

He spoke, "Where was I? Oh, yes" Nicolette interrupted him, "I am fine. I have the answer to my question. Is everything okay back home?" James grabbed his bowl of oatmeal, toast points, and fruit. As he returned to his chair, he replied, "No. Apparently, my daughter, who is pregnant with her first child, just learned that her husband was cheating on her with someone he works with. She is obviously devastated. I am not there for her. I do not know what I can do from here." Nicolette tried to console him, "James, you will be home soon. Eat your breakfast and get on the road. I can check us out and we can talk later. You did what she needed already; he consoled her and reassured her that it is that asshole and not her." He nodded in agreement, but stated, "I know you are right. I am a dad. I want to fix everything for her. It is tough since her mother is no longer with us. It did not help that she stopped by my office and my admin told her I was off on cloud nine visiting my girlfriend at the spa." Nicolette hardened, "Your girlfriend?" James waved off the question, "I could not say I am going to meet the woman who will put my nuts in a vise. So, Angie had a million questions about the girlfriend she has never heard of and where I was because she wanted to meet her, etc. It is all bad." Nicolette agreed, coldly, "Yes, all bad." James looked at her trying to read her but did not know whether she was upset or just trying to change the subject. He hoped it was a subject change so he obliged, "I want to keep our day's plan and I will head home at a reasonable hour. Angie was going into work and then to see an attorney that Sue, my admin, recommended. So, we have another six hours or so together if you want, Ma'am." Nicolette did not want to change the subject and wanted to aid in providing information for his daughter. "It will be good for her to at least file a preliminary motion of divorce today. She can do that herself and with it she can request that he moves out of the home. Make sure she has a deputy serve him papers at work so the whore that is breaking up their marriage is aware as well as the rest of his office. What does he do? Some places have morality clauses. They both can lose their jobs." James nodded, "I know the attorney very well. She is tough, but fair. She will advise her on all of that. As for their living situation, I told her that she can move into the house if she wanted to get away from him, but she stated that the house they live in was hers before she met him and she did not add him to it when they wed so she changed the locks already when he left before going to find me at the office." Nicolette added, "But she cannot keep his things from him. That is the law in New York. Or are they in Canada?" James stated, matter-of-factly, "New York. I know that neither of us practice family law, but those years in law school come raging out when you are strategizing to help family." They both laughed, but Nicolette continued. "I am sure things will work out for her; her daddy would not have it any other way." James nodded and moved on to the breakfast, "I hope I ordered something that you would like. I tried to get a variety of things that I knew that you ate. I told them no mushrooms; that there was an allergy." Nicolette nodded and stated, "Yes, my breakfast is very good. You even remembered the wheat toast." "So, what do you want to do today? We already walked town and did the spa. There is the amusement park if you want to do that or we could go to one of the museums nearby, or on the way home." Nicolette sat back in her chair and stated, "Honestly, I think, after breakfast, we pack the cars, checkout, and head home. You have to help your daughter deal with this bombshell and Lord only knows what bullshit awaits me at home. Besides the sooner I get on the road, the sooner I can make my way home to get ready for the work week." James concurred, "I could make the afternoon schedule and see some clients and take Angie to dinner." They ate the rest of the breakfast in silence, but it was only slightly awkward. They did a final swept of their respective bedrooms and headed to the front desk to checkout. It was a quiet time at the desk, after the early morning rush and before the official checkout time rush. They both had their cars pulled around and went to settle their bills. Since they paid for the spa and tips after the procedures, they only had to cover the room and in-room meals. The bills came and Nicolette reached to pay for her own bill, but James refused to allow for that forbidding the hotel staff from taking her money. When she insisted that he, at least, allow her to pay him for her stay he would not allow that either. Once the tab was settled, he helped her load the items into her car and he loaded his own. Nicolette asked, "I can pay for my own bill. I am gainfully employed and make a decent living. Why did you do that?" James leaned in and kissed her politely on the cheek and whispered in her ear, "I could not allow the woman who opened my eyes and heart to pay for the vehicle that provided her sanctuary. This has been my absolute pleasure and I would not have traded this weekend for anything else in the world. Thank you, deeply and sincerely, Mistress Nicolette." James stepped back and opened her car door, "Your chariot awaits, my dear." He waved his arm towards the seat and once inside he kissed her passionately one last time. Nicolette drove off towards Michigan, confused and slightly annoyed. She, however, did not tell her face which was plastered with a grin.

Chapter Twelve

Nicolette pulled into her home just before 5 o'clock; delayed slightly by rush hour traffic. She was mentally exhausted by the weekend of play, but physically refreshed by the spa treatments and the power exchange. She started laundry and finished unpacking her suitcases. She cleaned and polished all of her implements that she had taken with her. After getting herself in a good place with organizing her items, Nicolette started dinner. Being away all weekend meant that she did not made it to the grocery store, but she had the staples in her home. She put a ribeye steak in the oven and opened a bottle of wine. Nicolette sat on the couch and browse through the DVR to see if there were any shows that she needed to watch for water cooler talk. She opted for some of the mindless reality shows. As the show was winding down, she put on a potato to boil and soften for mashing and picked a vegetable to microwave. Nicolette settled into the rerun of The Big Bang Theory while she ate her dinner. She enjoyed her meal as well as the television show, laughing and along to the jokes. Nicolette finished the meal and looked at her email on her laptop; there were 30 unread messages on collarme.com and 15 on her personal email servers. Most of the emails on her personal email were junk mail or things she only needed to note. She replied to a group message about the upcoming tailgate and moved on to the collarme.com email. She had an email from James which was a mix of thanking her for the wonderful weekend and ended with thanks for being compassionate about his daughter. Nicolette replied that she also had fun and the play was good. She wished the daughter well. There was a message from uwe checking in for the upcoming visit and seeing how Nicolette was doing. She replied that she was away for the weekend with a submissive that she had been speaking to for years. She outlined the play and weekend at both the spa and the sex. Ryan, Heinrich, ali, Jeff, and david all checked in with Nicolette as well. Mostly just asking about service and requesting her schedule. There was also a checking in message from MstrKat and slvkel outlining a party that individuals from the group that Nicolette frequents was attending. The other messages were either people who did not read her profile that she politely pointed in that direction or rude/inappropriate messages. Nicolette did not bother answering those messages even though that was uncharacteristic of her philosophy; she felt that if they took the time to write that she would take the time to respond. She spent time responding to racists, sexists, and straight-out assholes. After deleting all the messages, Nicolette noticed that she had a new message. It was from James. It read simply, "Mistress, I know that I claimed you as my owner without permission or discussion. I know you wanted to talk about it this morning when Angie called. I might have said

199

something mean or even rude about you in that conversation. I did not mean to say that you are not important or that this relationship was not important. I just spent the last three hours talking to Angie about you. She ended our conversation by saying, "Why is she not important enough to meet family? You sound smitten." I asked what she meant, and she said that I called you not important in our phone call. That must have hurt your feelings. I did not mean it in that way; I was trying to minimize the weekend since her relationship was failing. And frankly, I did not want to talk about what we are to her when we had not even had the conversation yet." Nicolette read over the message and debated herself about how to respond. She did not want a long-distance relationship and at nearly 60, she knew that he was not willing to move. She just turned 30 and was middle-level in her career; she would have to decide if she wanted to move that far from her family who just lost a member on the off chance of love. It all seemed overwhelming and decided to be noncommittal in her response to James, "First, I am glad that you and Angie had a few hours together to discuss her life and for you to comfort her. As for the slip of the tongue about me owning you, I know that you know that I do not and that we are not ready for that. There is no need for you to apologize or stress over a perceived slight." Nicolette smiled to herself, feeling better that he recognized his faux pas and felt it was important to correct it with her. After she hit send she received a message from uwe that outlined how hurt he was that she was seeing someone without waiting for him as he felt that he was perfect for her. Nicolette answered the message, "uwe, we have zero commitment and in fact, we have never met. I, currently, do not own anyone and outside of no longer being celibate, nothing has changed from when we first started corresponding." uwe responded almost immediately, "Okay. I guess I have to get over my jealously of you being with another man. Was he good? Was he bigger than me? Don't answer that, I can already feel my balls

200

shrinking." Nicolette laughed at the messages, "He was a patient, enthusiastic, and thorough lover. I very much enjoyed being with him though it was painful. Abstaining from sex for years makes it difficult to jump back in as it were. You are taller, more muscular, but I do not know what your penis looks like as you have not shown me it on cam/in photos. I love how your balls are affected by the mere knowledge of me having sex with another person." uwe sent a Yahoo! message requesting to open a camera chat session. Nicolette granted the camera session and she looked at uwe's smiling face. "Mistress, good evening. It is very good to see your lovely face. You look happy. Is that because of the dick? Was he big?" Nicolette laughed, "Wow. You seemed obsessed with his penis. It was quite adequate, and he used it very well. I would definitely fuck him again if the mood and opportunity present itself. If I look happy that must be because I am home and comfortable. I had a long drive home from the spa. You look refreshed; how's the season treating you?" uwe sighed a long exhale, "The pre-season is okay. I am not playing as much as I would like, but I am getting playing time which is important. It is weird to know you are better than others but just cannot find the way to prove yourself. I will get there. Difficult when you are not a player who played in the States before. Why are you changing the subject?" Nicolette raised an eyebrow at uwe, "I have not changed the subject, but I also do not think you have any say in what I decide to sit on. Well, that is, unless I decide to sit on you. Would you like that uwe? For me to sit down on your cock? Straddling you, riding you, taking all of you?" uwe visually blushed and was at a loss for words. "Oh, yeah, you like that idea, huh uwe?" Nicolette continued, "Are you excited thinking about fucking me deep? Are you imaging parting my lips with the tip of your penis, pushing slowly, deliberately into my small, tight, wet box? That sound good to you, boy?" uwe was licking his lips and moaning as he listened to Nicolette, "Oh my God, Mistress, are you trying to turn me on? This is not fair!" uwe responded. Nicolette laughed, "All is fair in love and war and if you want to be upset that I was fucking someone else then it seems we need to discuss us fucking. How is that dick? Is it hard for me? You want to fuck me? Let me see how turned on you are." uwe had no response for her, and she did not care enough to push seeing him displaying himself on camera though she was sure that he has done it several times before for others. Nicolette decided to change the topic to something that he would be comfortable with, "So, what did you do this weekend? Are you all settled into your place there? I know that moving from Germany was a process." uwe nodded along with her statements and said, "Yes, I left a girl behind that I was fond of, but I do not think she understands me. She is very strong, too, like you. Very pretty. You would like her. Wait let me send you a photo." Nicolette hid her surprise at uwe having a personal life, including a lady that he was attracted to. She noted to herself that she thought he was single and seeking a Female-led LTR; she confirmed in her own mind that he must have felt comfortable divulging the information that he also had other options knowing that she had sex. The image came through in Yahoo! messenger; the photo was of uwe in a tailored navy blue suit, standing with his arm around a petite black woman in a white dress. "Wow, she is stunning." Nicolette said, half surprise but completely honestly. "Is she from Germany, too?" uwe smiled that Nicolette found his taste acceptable, noting that a threesome may not be one hundred percent off the table. "Yes, she is, also, German. She is from a small town outside of Köln. We met through a friend of hers that trained with me in the past. You think she is pretty? Is she your type?" He asked with hope in his voice. "She is very attractive. Not my type, but still very stunning. So why aren't you two dating? You said 'she is strong like me', do you mean that she is dominant?" Nicolette wanted answers and her voice displayed such. uwe looked almost as embarrassed as he did when Nicolette asked if he wanted her to ride him slowly. He sat quietly for a moment and responded, "We were dating…we are dating. She and I met some time ago and we've been exclusive for some time; that photo is from a wedding we attended a month ago. She knew that I was leaving for the States, again. This is my third team in the NHL. It is somewhat my last chance. She did not think that it was a good idea for me to abuse my body with trying to play professionally. She feels that there are enough leagues and opportunities in Germany. We did not officially break-up nor did we officially say that we are exclusive still. I know that she went on a date or two; it started before I left. I do not know if she slept with them. No, no, she is not into the lifestyle. She, also, does not know that I am." Nicolette weighed his word and continued along her frank, cold line of questioning, "So, why did you reach out to me? Were you and her exclusive when you reached out to me?" uwe was shaking his head as Nicolette spoke, "Of course not. I would never try to enter into a relationship when I was in one already. When April and I, her name is April, started dating I cut ties with everyone on the collarme website. When things got rocky, I saw you. I am drawn to you. And obviously, it is more than sexual, or I would have dumped you when you cheated on me this weekend." uwe stated flatly. Nicolette looked confused and at a loss for words. Uwe continued, "I know we are not in a committed relationship, but you know as well as I do, that us males do not think others exist. In my mind, you were waiting for me to be ready to serve you. It is my male dominated thought process; it does not change the situation at all. But yes, you cheated on me." "I cannot cheat on someone I am not with. We have not even met. Seriously, there are a number of things wrong with that sentence, uwe. If you want to meet, which you affirm that you do, we can do that. If we mesh and you are done with April, then we can discuss a possible future. Will I be single by the time you make your decisions? – I do not know, but I will not collect dust waiting." Nicolette stated clearly, concisely. She checked the clock and noted the time. "It is late, uwe. I have to work in the morning. I need to let you go." She felt as if she had just gotten into an argument with her best friend. It was a weird, unresolved feeling. "Ok, good night, Mistress. I hope you have a good rest," uwe said and disconnected his camera. Nicolette cleaned up her dinner dishes and made her way to bed thinking to herself that she has dug a hole that she may not be able to emerge from with the number of noncommittal relationships that she was fostering. She shook her head, prepared for bed, and slept soundly.

Tuesday morning was not a welcomed sight. She was dreading going into the office as the cases against Dich would be coming to head, as well as her perceived insubordination for not wanting to be involved in the aforementioned. Nicolette dressed simply in some dress pants and a button-down shirt; she wore flats and her pulled her hair into a bun. She headed to the office and arrived slightly before 8 o'clock in the morning. Nicolette went into her office and sat at her desk which had a single letter placed on the center addressed to Nicolette Gruyere, JD. It did not have a stamp or any return information; the letter was sealed with tape. Nicolette sighed and opened the letter thinking to herself that having a peaceful, quiet week just went out the window. Inside the envelope was a subpoena; Dich and his attorney are calling her to the stand in his trial that very afternoon. Nicolette was annoyed at the lack of notice and the fact that the subpoena was not properly served. She turned on her computer and begun reviewing her email. Based on the emails, Nicolette was pleased to see that the new persons on her team jumped right into their roles and have been producing results. She smiled to herself, a silver lining to the firm. Nicolette had scheduled a staff meeting with her team at 8:30 to ensure that the two projects were running on schedule and to review billable hours. There was an email from George suggesting another project that Nicolette can undertake since he was confident that she was not overextended. George mentioned having confidence in Nicolette's abilities and he wanted to ensure that he was taking advantage of all that she could do. Nicolette read the company profile and summary of the potential business; it was a simple patent case. The potential client was a dental fixture company that deals only with Class I medical devices and want to research whether their content is unique in the United States and Canada. Nicolette replied to George's email that she was summoned to court on the Dich personal case so she will not have time to take on the new case. She also suggested someone who was also an attorney in Canada as the company wanted to patent in both countries. The response she received was almost instant, and in all caps, "YOU ARE NOT FREE TO WORK ON THE CASE FOR DICH. HE HAS AN ATTORNEY. YOU WORK FOR ME, NOT HIM." Nicolette replied to the email, "I was subpoenaed. I am not working in the capacity of attorney. I already declined that role on a number of occasions. I appreciate you reiterating what I already know. I have to meet with my staff on our current case load. Again, I suggest someone that has their license in Canada." Nicolette browsed through the email list and decided none of the remaining messages require a reply immediately. She walked out of her office to do a lap around the office en route to the conference room. Michael and Kamilah had the case files already in the conference room when Nicolette arrived. "Good morning, team." She said trying to sound upbeat. "Good morning." They replied in unison. Nicolette sat at the table opposite Michael and Kamilah. He begun going over the developments in the case when she was gone, "So, with the neuroscaffolding case, we had a major development. There is a competing patent. We have the application date, which is good. The patent competitor was a colleague of our client. In our conversations with the client, he waffles between the development not including the colleague to him having a minor role in a previous, unused model. I am at the point where I am ready to file a review with the competitor attorney." Kamilah added, "Bottom line, we have the application date by almost six months. Moreover, it appears that the competitor application was filed in order to prevent the competitor from having to spend a lot of money on suing our client." Nicolette took notes and replied, "I will reach out to our client and nail down his official answer. I will take a deposition and gather any proof of the relationship that he is alleging. Meanwhile, Michael, can you reach out to the competitor's attorney so that we can settle this overlap before we divulge any significant details in the application?" Michael nodded in agreement with the assignment. "Great. What about the stem cell case? Where are we with that?" Kamilah started, "I have been looking for precedent for this case in every developed country in the world. Thus far, I have not been able to find a case where a patient has been able to sue their physician if the doctor acted in good faith. We will have to prove that the doctor acted in good faith. Since using stem cells are not common therapy with well-known outcomes that should not be difficult." Nicolette asked, "Did you check with therapies in Canada and the European Union; they are, generally, leaps ahead of the States in medicinal therapies?" "I did find the treatment is being used in larger hospitals in Ontario as well as in four countries in the European Union. Both are considered experimental. It is not an approved treatment in the United States. There is a small Stage IV Clinical Trial in California State, currently." Nicolette took additional notes and asked, "Is there any information on the clinical trial? Is it something that could have been beneficial to the patient?" Michael answered, "No, that trial is for pancreatic cancer. They wanted to focus on the most deadly, seemingly incurable cancer. The patient in our case was looking to have heart valves rebuilt, if I remember correctly." "Yes, the patient needs to have heart valves rebuilt and wanted to have stem cells used for it. The physician suggested using pig organ and cadaver transplant which is common, but it did not work for the patient. The patient was given less than a year to live." Nicolette interjected, "Is that new information? That was not in the packet that I have." Michael nodded, "We received notice on Friday. It was a request to settle and/or accelerate the proceedings." Nicolette replied, "Did you reach out to our client? Kamilah shook her head, "No, we did not. We wanted to wait to hear from you on what you felt the best course of action would be. On one hand, we know that there are cases of the stem cells being used in the laboratory in South America, Canada, and a couple other places that were transplanted into patients as a last ditch effort. We do not have any good information on the outcomes yet as most of those patients signed a NDA. On the other, again that procedure, even experimental cannot be performed in the United States without a clinical trial and ample amount of follow-up." Michael added, "We have spoken to our client's malpractice insurance attorney. He was glad that he is not considered the lead attorney on the case. He wants to settle and sent over the packages that his company is willing to pay. It is boiler plate, but also included bonuses for us." Nicolette replied swiftly, "I am not concerned with settlement bonuses. Let's get our client in here and discuss the potential outcomes and review the cases that we found. If you could pull together the list of physicians that performed the procedures and have our research teams delve into their background as physicians. I know we all enjoy House the television program, but majority of his procedures are rogue, and would not fare as well in the real world. We need a physician to review both the procedures and information in the files that we are allowed to subpoena; see if we can get consent. We are willing to sign a BAA." Michael and Kamilah took notes on their assignments. "Anything else that I need to know?" Nicolette asked. Michael and Kamilah looked at each other but neither spoke. Nicolette sensed the tension that instantly came into the room. She continued, "How were your first several days? Are you two getting along with one another? Is the environment here something that you can handle? Case load doable? I want to ensure that you are here for time to come. Are you happy thus far?" Michael shrugged and commented, "Kammy and I are getting along just fine. I think the case load is good. I can handle it and like you said in the interview, I am able to make it home at a reasonable hour every night." Kamilah added, "Yes, Mike is cool. We understand one another and were able to quickly jump into the cases. We like that you are organized and efficient. We, both, enjoy being on your team." Nicolette added, "So, the problem is with the environment? Types of cases? Did something happened when I was gone? Should I bring in a HR representative?" Michael and Kamilah looked at each other and shook their heads no. Together, finishing each other sentences, they continued, "We feel that" "It is hard to work with the distractions" "Dich is very kind, but he is also bringing" "negative energy" "a negative presence really." Then together in unison, "He seems to want to undermine everything you wanted." "We completed your assignment. In the way you wanted," Michael added. "His requests did not make sense for our cases," Kamilah stated flatly. "It was uncomfortable. I spoke to George about it once," Michael added. "It only pissed Dich off," Kamilah replied. Nicolette sat back in her chair, "Is this something you can live with knowing that I am your boss and George and Dich are mine? Ultimately, I decided your path, but they direct the course of this organization. I will discuss with Dich and George about the incident. In the future, placate to Dich, but run any proposed changes by me. This way he is satisfied that he was heard, but I get what I need done for the cases. You do not have to justify any assignment to Dich or George. It is my job to do so." Michael and Kamilah seemed much more relaxed. "Yes, I think that course of action will work for me. I will forward you the log we created of all the changes that he wanted us to make in your absence," Michael commented. "Log?" Nicolette asked in a frustrated tone. She continued before he could answer. "Ok, I will review this log and have a discussion about it after our all-staff meeting. Anything else?" Kamilah smiled and ended their discussion and meeting with a simple expression, "And yes, we are happy here, working for you." They vacated the conference room for the large gathering of desks for all the research attorneys, associate attorneys, and paralegals. Each lead attorney's staff sat together in a group and those groupings were in a large open area in the facility that they nicknamed it the bullpen. In the bullpen, all the staff of the firm, which was twenty-five total, could gather briefly. The all-staff meeting was called by George to explain and outline the legal predicament of Dich and let the staff understand that it is separate from the firm. George wanted to reassure everyone that the case has no effect on the firm, and also allow for questions. Nicolette sat in the back on the pen and rolled her eyes inside her head as George maneuver around the landmine that was Dich's legal troubles. The staff mostly asked for Dich to stop bringing his legal troubles into the firm by asking advice of the staff and to stop directing the research team on his case. George, who appeared unaware that Dich was using the firm resources for his case, assured the staff that Dich will not behave in such a manner again. The meeting was dismissed, and Nicolette went to work on her case load. When she arrived at her office, George appeared in her doorway. "What did you think of the staff meeting?" he asked. Nicolette laughed as her only response. "That bad, huh?" George asked. "Well, I felt it needed to be spoken about because I have had three attorneys approach me to ask about his case after he insisted on help with his case. I guess I should have said something when he was first served here instead of letting it go for so long. Anyway, enough about Dich, why are you opposed to working that case for me? Do you feel comfortable enough in your role here that you feel that you should not perform work assigned to you by your boss?" Nicolette heard the threat in his voice. "Fine. I will work on the case," Nicolette said flatly and sat down at her desk. George looked at Nicolette stunned and did not speak. Nicolette sat at her desk looking at George who seemed to not know what to say or do in the current situation. "Was there something else you need from me,

George? I need to get quite a bit done before I have to go to court on this subpoena," Nicolette asked. "Is that it? All of a sudden you are content to work on the dental patent case?" George asked. "You made it clear that it was assigned to me. I perform tasks that are assigned to me. I do not understand what else you expect from me," Nicolette answered. George stood in the door briefly and looked at Nicolette dumbfounded. Nicolette maintained eye contact with George for a brief moment until he realized that she was not going to speak any further, then turned to exit her office. Nicolette breathed an exasperated sigh and read over the information on the new case that was on the copy server. As she completed reading the 200 documents in the file, she checked and noticed that she was running late for the courthouse. Nicolette updated her billable hours on her calendar and departed. The drive to the courthouse was not long, but since she was dreading why she was being called into this case, it seemed to take hours to arrive at the building. Nicolette parked and as she was walking to the courthouse she saw Dich and his attorney standing outside looking for her. "There she is," Dich announced as Nicolette approached the walkway. Nicolette saw a court deputy that she knew from her previous position. He waved at her in recognition and Nicolette took it as an opportunity to avoid Dich and his attorney. "Aaron, how have you been?" Nicolette called out walking in a brisk pace to meet him. He held out his arm to half embrace her and Nicolette hugged him. "Good, little lady. How are things? I see you made the big move." Nicolette laughed and walked with Aaron into the building side-stepping Dich and his attorney. "Yes, I am at a boutique firm in Troy, now. It is definitely a change of pace from the corporate law that I was doing at my last position. Different challenges, but it allows me the freedom I need in my personal life since my brother passed." "I heard about your brother. That was very sad. I have not seen you since that happened so my deepest condolences on the loss. So, what brings you to my neck of the woods today?" Aaron asked as he opened the door for her. "I was summoned due to my work on a similar, but conflicting case. It is strange. I do not think I will give the team that called me here what they are seeking, but you never know," Nicolette responded with a shrug. "Oh, you are a witness of sorts. Let me show you to the holding area. What courtroom?" Nicolette showed Aaron the subpoena and he walked her to the door which was only a couple feet away. "Alright, young lady. Here you go. Do not be a stranger," Aaron said as he held the door open for her. She entered and would not have to see Dich or his attorney until she was on the stand.

It was almost three o'clock when Nicolette was called into the courtroom. She was walked past Dich and his attorney to the stand. It was a jury trial, Nicolette noted to herself. She was sworn in and Dich's attorney asked her to state her full name and occupation for the court. "My name is Nicolette Guyere and I am an attorney for Rockies Law & Consulting," Nicolette stated plainly. "Great. And can you explain to the court your relationship with Mr. Richard Hansen?" His attorney continued. "Mr. Hansen is the CEO of Rockies Law & Consulting. I work for him and Mr. George," Nicolette started and was cut off by Dich's attorney. "Ms. Guyere, I did not ask about anyone else but Mr. Richard Hansen." Nicolette nodded, but rolled her eyes in her head noting that Dich's attorney was treating her like a hostile witness. She resolved to only answer yes, no, and briefly. He continued, "Are you aware of why you are here today, Ms. Guyere?" "No," Nicolette responded. Dich's attorney turned his back to Nicolette and made a smart-assed comment in her opinion, "No? And you are an attorney. You are here because you were subpoenaed." The prosecution objected to the line of questioning calling it irrelevant and immaterial. It was sustained. "Mr. Coleman, this is a witness you called. You seem to not want her here. Either ask the questions you have or dismiss her," This judge warned. Nicolette thought to herself that Dich's attorney seem to be fumbling, but she knew he was only 'Elle Woods'ing' her à la Legally Blonde. She was prepared for him to strike, and she did not take his comment that downplayed her knowledge as an attorney seriously since she knew he was only setting doubt in the jury's mind about her abilities. The judge saw it that way too, and instructed the jury to disregard his statement. He continued, "Ms. Guyere, are you aware of a case against Mr. Richard Hansen and Mr. Oisin Chua?" Nicolette answered, "No, I am not aware of a case against both Mr. Hansen and Mr. Chua as co-defendants." Dich's attorney addressed the court, "Permission to treat this witness as a hostile witness." The judge responded, "On what ground, Mr.Coleman?" Dich's attorney replied, "Ms. Guyere defended Mr. Chua in a case where he was the defendant of the same charges that my client is being tried for here. She is aware of the details of both cases as she works for Mr. Hansen. She is privy to information that would make her client look guilty of crimes that this court alleges my client committed." The judge replied, "Sidebar." Both Dich's attorney and the prosecution approached the judge and argued amongst themselves for nearly five minutes. After returning to their respective places in the courtroom, the judge cleared the jury. "Ms. Guyere, I will question you on the facts of this case and the case you defended Mr. Chua against. Once I am satisfied, I will provide a summary to the jury. Do you understand?" Nicolette replied simply, "Yes." The judge began, "Ms. Guyere, is that which Mr. Coleman stated true? Did you defend Mr. Chua and Mr. Hansen in a case?" Nicolette replied, "No, that is not true. The case that I defended was against Mr. Chua, solely. Mr. Hansen was not named on the case, nor did I ever discuss details of the case with Mr. Hansen or his attorney." The judge continued, "What was the nature of the case?" Nicolette replied, "Mr. Chua was being prosecuted for falsifying laboratory tests." The judge looked over the charges against Mr. Hansen and turned to Dich's attorney, "Mr. Coleman, Mr. Hansen is before this court with several counts of defrauding the government; a crime that Mr. Hansen has already served time in federal prison, prior. How are these charges even remotely related?" Dich's attorney replied, "The charges against Mr. Chua are tied to the fraud case because the fraud was committed *by* the person who falsified the laboratory tests. This court is alleging that it was my client who did that crime. We are maintaining that it was Mr. Chua. Since Mr. Chua had this manipulative attorney get his charges dropped, he fled back to Singapore leaving my client holding the bag." The judge continued, "I see. I am calling recess for the evening so that I can review the testimony in the case against Mr. Chua. Bailiff, please escort Ms. Guyere to her holding room. I will dismiss the jury. We will reconvene tomorrow morning at 9 o'clock in the morning. That includes you Ms. Guyere." The judge banged her gavel, stood, and exited. The bailiff escorted Nicolette to the witness room from which she left immediately so she could avoid Dich and his attorney. She went back to the office to instruct her staff and to inform George that she will not be present tomorrow morning either due to the orders of the court. Nicolette went to the gym as was customary after work. She was so in her head about the events of the day, Nicolette did not socialize as much as usual. She put in her earphones and did twenty minutes on the elliptical stair stepper, and thirty minutes of weight lifting before heading home. The drive home for Nicolette was similar to running down the stairs to the living room on Christmas morning as a child. She was looking forward to being in her house with a glass of scotch and letting the cares of the day melt away. She was annoyed at Dich and his attorney for wanting to blame the case on Oisin. She knew as his attorney, she would have to brief him on the details of the case and Dich's defense. She, also, knew that this would jeopardize the future of the laboratory and its staff since Oisin will likely pull all his funding from Dich's projects. They were all trying to rebuild their reputation and many of them were named in the news stories about the dry-labbing.

It would be difficult at best for some of them to find work in this area of science again. Nicolette pulled into the garage at her house and walked up the back staircase on to the deck and through the backdoor. She placed her briefcase by the backdoor because she knew she would not be using it or any of the contents that evening. Nicolette played with the idea of working from home that evening earlier in the morning, but after the day she had she left the firm at the firm. Nicolette was looking forward to a mindless night of personal email, kinky photos, and television. She undressed, let down her hair, and climbed into the shower to wash off the sweat from the gym. As the soap rolls down her body into the drain, the stress of the day went with it. She emerged from the shower a new woman. Nicolette dried her body and walked into the dressing room and donned a pair of fuzzy house shoes. She walked down the stairs to the kitchen where she poured herself a glass of Glenfiddich and went through her snail mail. It was mostly junk mail for her brother and sister-in-law. She discarded it and opened the two bills that were for her. She noted that she had them set to pay automatically and sat on the couch to do relaxing, mindless tasks. Nicolette opted for catching up on her DVR while going through all the emails and Yahoo! messenger away messages she received over the weekend. There was a checking in message from Ryan; he was always freer in the fall due to his job with the power company, which is the complete opposite of Nicolette who was the busiest in the fall due to her sports' schedule. Ryan had looked at the Michigan football schedule and had proposed something for each of the next three away/bye games. Nicolette laughed since her free weekends tend to fill up quickly. She replied that she was not sure if she was going to be able to find time to play with him, and regretted that she had to postpone their play due to her trip to Pennsylvania. Ryan had the most endurance out of all the persons that Nicolette has ever smothered. She enjoyed using him in that fashion since he was eager and skilled at all aspects of the play, and received such a cathartic release from the power exchange. After introducing James to the fetish over the weekend, it would be a welcomed return to play with the pet who introduced her to it, Nicolette thought. She looked at the next away game, it was a month away, and it would be a huge test for her time. Ryan was looking to go to the game the weekend before; making it two weeks of him in a row. The trip to the game would be a vanilla outing which do not always go well since Ryan was a huge pothead and Nicolette did not like being around drugs. Nicolette decided to only allow one weekend; which she gave Ryan the option. He chose the away game and 12-16 hours of face-sitting. As she was reviewing her tentative plans with uwe and Heinrich, Nicolette noticed that she was well into November with her plans. Before she made any final decisions, Nicolette needed to have a conversation with James about their expectations. The last thing she wanted to do was to assume the course of their relationship. Nicolette got up to get another glass of scotch and to decide upon dinner. She had a few options and decided upon the chicken breast with brown rice and broccoli. She began cooking her dinner and returned to the email and DVR. When she returned to the laptop, she had a message from James. Nicolette opened the email and it read almost like a 'Dear John' letter. "Ms. Nicolette, I very much enjoyed our weekend together. I have not been able to figure out how you found it in yourself to deem me so very lucky to have you. I have been trying to understand what you found in me to allow me to pleasure you and serve you. While, you are absolutely perfect for me in the lifestyle and our kinks align so well, I do not think we would be able to have a strong, vanilla connection. Mind-altering sex with a physical specimen as perfect and edible as you can only satisfy my physical self for so long before my mind and soul seeks more from you. We are at such different places in our life. Do you know that my daughter, Angie, is your age? I found myself trying to explain our acquaintanceship and I failed at every turn as she kept asking about our age difference once she found out. I could not imagine how it would go if you ever met Angie; which if we dated and you owned me, you would meet. I could not explain how this woman that I am more twice her age wanted me, and what she wants. I know it is not money as you have your own. I know it is not the father figure as you have a dad who is active in your life. I have nothing to explain why you are entertaining me. I cannot spend my life trying to figure out what is wrong with you, what I have that you desire, or worse yet, the questions from my family and friends. This was a mistake. I should have left us… this… as a fantasy. I am losing so much by writing this, but I cannot have the alternative. I cannot have this fantasy ruin my reality. I hope you understand and that you do not hate me. Please keep in touch as I do very much enjoy all our conversations. James." Nicolette looked at the screen and felt tears fill up in her eyes. "Are you fucking kidding me?" she screamed at the top of her lungs. She re-read the message again and started to build her response in her head defending her position. Nicolette realized that she was lawyering the response and she declined to respond. Nicolette finished the second glass of scotch and went to finish dinner. She poured another glass of scotch, made her plate, and ate dinner watching *How I Met Your Mother* on her DVR. After completing the show and dinner, Nicolette finished the third and last glass of scotch. She cleaned the kitchen and retired to her bedroom after cleaning up for bed. Nicolette was looking forward to a new day and put the stress of the day to bed with her.

Chapter Thirteen

When her alarm clock went off on Wednesday morning, Nicolette was excited for the day. She decided that Wednesday would be the redo of Tuesday that she needed. Nicolette prepared for work in an upbeat fashion; choosing an outfit that flattering to her figure as well as comfortable. Nicolette made a small breakfast since she would not be able to eat in the courthouse. The drive into work was light and relaxing; Nicolette made it to the courthouse fifteen minutes prior to her call time. She was pleased to see that Dich and his attorney were not outside or in the hallway as she made her way to the witness cloistering room. Nicolette was not in the room long before she was called into the courtroom. She returned to the witness stand, the judge dismissed the jury again, and the judge summarized what she read from the Oisin Chua deposition. "Ladies and gentlemen, I read over the court proceedings of the case of Oisin Chua. I did not find any connection to this trial nor did I see any evidence that point to the guilt of Mr. Chua in falsification of the laboratory results. I know that he was not in the country at the time and he did not have access to the files remotely as evidenced by the records of the prosecution of that case. Mr. Coleman, I caution you against wasting the time of this court. I will be bringing the jury back into the room and explaining the case against Mr. Chua. Then it is your witness." The judge had the bailiff return the jury to the courtroom and she explained the case against Mr. Chua. She, also, outlined that the aforementioned case has zero impact on the current proceedings. Dich's attorney was using Oisin's case as his Hail Mary and it failed. He needed to know what Nicolette learned during Oisin's case, but he knew that she would not share without being compelled by the court. "Ms. Guyere, my apologies for the long delay. I know that you research the matter of the dry-labbing. Can you explain to the court what it was and what you learned?" Nicolette took a long pause hoping and expecting an objection, but did not receive one. She continued, "Dry-labbing is when laboratory results are reported without laboratory tests being run. Mr. Oisin Chua invests in a laboratory that recently admitted that they dry-labbed some samples. Mr. Chua was a silent investor and therefore did not have any say or input in the laboratory itself. The case was eventually dropped against him." Dich's attorney continued, "Was that the only thing that you learned during the course of this case?" Nicolette replied quickly, "Yes. All the other details are under privilege of attorney-client conversations." Dich's attorney objected to her answer and asked to treat Nicolette as a hostile witness again. The judge allowed it. "Ms. Guyere, did you learn during the course of your investigation who reported the dry-labbed samples?" Nicolette answered, "Yes." The eyebrow of Dich's attorney raised and he asked, "Who was the person that release the dry-labbed samples?" Nicolette started to answer the question, but she was interrupted by the prosecutor who objected to the question and asked for a sidebar again. After the discussion, Nicolette was instructed to answer the question. She replied, "The results were released by Richard Hansen. It was originally thought that one of the employees of Compliance Assurance Testing released the result since he is currently serving time and confessed, but he has an appeal and proof of his innocence." Dich's attorney walked through the opening that Nicolette deliberately left. "And you saw this proof of innocence and support for your statement that Dich released the sample?" Nicolette replied, "The subpoena of the laboratory information system does have the proof." Dich's attorney walked back to his table and had a brief discussion with Dich. "Your honor, this is new information for our defense. May we have a brief recess?" Dich's attorney requested a continuance. The judge granted the continuance. During the recess, Dich's attorney reached a plea deal and Nicolette was dismissed. She returned to the firm and worked on her case load. Dich returned to the office late in the afternoon after settling the case. The government collected damages of nearly $3, 000, 000, effectively crippling the laboratory. Dich walked into Nicolette's office and looked at her from the door and did not say anything. "Nicolette, do you really think that I am guilty of this crime? Would you work for someone that is the criminal that they say that I am?" Dich finally asked. "Dich, I really do not know what to think about this case, but the facts and science do not lie. Your computer and login information were used to send that information. There are emails that outline you telling the prosecuting attorney that you will guarantee results within their timeline even though you knew that you could not make it. It is not my place to determine your guilt or not. But you did plea guilty. This is the second time that you plead guilty to defrauding the government. As for the question of whether I can work here, this is not Compliance Assurance Testing. This is a legal firm that does not have any blemishes. We should keep it that way." Dich laughed. "I like you. You can help keep us above board." Dich left her office and Nicolette continued to work on the caseload on her desk. She logged into Yahoo!, where she had a note from James. It was a simple checking in message where he hoped that she did not take offense to his email. Nicolette did not respond to that message either and just looked to get home for the evening. She completed her tasks for the day and headed home. Nicolette argued with herself on the ride to the gym about whether or not to talk to James again. She was celibate for so long that she felt akin to jilted woman after giving a man her virginity. She knew that his actions were out of insecurity due to the over thirty-year age difference because they had many interests in common outside of kink. They had been friends online taking about every topic under the sun for over five years. Nicolette wanted to have a Female-Led relationship that included physical expression, mental fulfillment, and all the kink that she could handle. She thought that she had found that with James but was proved wrong. As she was told to not "pass go and to go straight to jail" to start over, Nicolette could not help but feel all the abandonment of losing her brother come crashing down. After a workout that was much more physical than normal on the Wednesday, Nicolette met Dana for a drink where they reminisced about Charles. Nicolette walked into the bar, "Hey, D. I feel like I was rode hard and put away wet…and not in a good way. How are you?" Dana laughed hard and replied with a smile, "Rode hard, huh? James in town? When do I get to meet this silver fox?" Nicolette's smile faded fast, "Uh. Never. That shit is done. It was probably done before it started. Apparently, he is afraid of what his daughter would think." Dana's smile also faded, "Ouch. Why does that bitch matter? Does he not like you? Hell, why did he fuck you if he was afraid of his daughter? I thought his generation was supposed to be the best generation – chivalrous, kind, well-off, professional…fucking baby boomer. Baby is definitively the correct term." Nicolette giggled at her anger, "Oh D! Thank you for captioning my hell so well. I just do not know why he is living his life for his child. He is a grown ass man. Very grown as he is older than my parents. He should know that he cannot live his life by others' standards. His daughter would love me. I would totally make a *great* stepmother." Dana raised an eyebrow and spit some of her beer onto the bar, "Mommy dearest, indeed." Nicolette dropped a napkin on her mess and pumped her, "NO WIRE HANGERS." Dana laughed again, "Seriously, you want to talk about it?" Nicolette took a long sip of her long island, "I guess. I am just so frustrated. I let down my guard. I do not let down my guard often and I feel like I was duped. Yes, he mentioned his daughter and the hang-ups with that before, but why would he fuck me if he was that unsure. Blah blah blah, I know. *I know.* I hear myself and at the end of the day he is male. But even with this shit, I do not think that James can be lumped in with other guys. He was…is different. He wooed me. He is still wooing me, even in the middle of this bullshit. I do not know if my picker is just off. Or if I should hang it up. I am going to be alone the rest of my life." Nicolette wiped away a tear that she was trying to hold back as she voiced the greatest fear of her life. Dana placed a soft hand on her back, "Nicolette, you will find someone. You will be happy. Fuck you might even have some ugly little motherfuckers running around soon enough. This is a set-back, but not even that great. I mean, how did you expect introducing that old ass nigga to your parents was going to go? Uncle A and Auntie Ernie are not kind to normal niggas, but an old ass Canadian? C'mon." Nicolette laughed, "Why that nigga gotta be old though? Plus, my parents don't give much of a shit about me. I am like their sixth or seventh favorite child." Dana look perplexed, "Sixth or seventh? There are only three of y'all." Nicolette explained seriously, "Charles was my father's favorite and my mother's second favorite. Steve is my mother's favorite and my dad's second favorite. Then you and Brig are third and fourth. Order is unimportant. My godbrother is definitely fifth for my dad. De'Andre for my mother. So that makes me sixth at best. Shit, I am being generous. I may not crack top ten. Who knows how many outside kids are out there." Dana just stared at Nicolette. "You cannot be serious. Nici, your parents love you." Nicolette shrugged, "Dead serious. I never said I was not loved, but that is debatable. I think that I serve purpose in their lives. I think they feel like they have to love me, but I do not think either would go out of their way to do anything for me. I am, just, not *that* kid. I am ok with that." Nicolette took a long sip from her drink. Dana did as well. Dana broke the silence, "So back to that old nigga. Are you done or are you going to try to make it work? You said that you enjoyed the sex." Nicolette choked slightly on her words, "Oh no. I am done. I was rejected. There is no coming back from that." Dana sipped her beer, finishing it. She pointed to order another round, "How are things going with people treating you like Charles?" Nicolette shook her head slowly 'no', "It is slightly better. But I also yelled at a number of people. It is sad. I am not my brother. I know I am a tomboy and can relate like a male in many situations, but I am not Charles. My calls have decreased, too. Apparently, word got out that I do not want to role play Charles." Dana replied, "I get it. Mourning loss is difficult. People wanted you to be a stop gap. That is not fair to you. They were wrong. By the way, Charles and I used to come here all the time and play pool. Want to play a round?" Nicolette shot Dana a dirty look. Dana laughed hard. "Naw, bitch, I don't. Besides it is getting late. Let me grab this check." Dana and

Nicolette finished up at the bar and go through respective ways. After, Nicolette headed home where she sent James a message that stated, "It's cool. No hard feelings. You do not want something long term with me. I understand. But do not put it off on me or make it some bullshit insecurity you swear you have. No need to try and appear as a good guy; I do not have a negative opinion of you. Take care." Drained, but feeling as if she got a monkey off her back, Nicolette walked to the bathroom and took a long, relaxing shower. Nicolette dried herself and stood in the mirror of the dressing room, she felt a wave of emotion come over her. "You are loved by the most important person in your world," she said with tears running down her face, "you cannot live your life with what-ifs. This chapter is closed, but a new one just opened. Write those pages you incredible woman." Nicolette stared at herself for a moment, catching her breath. She nodded as if accepting the pledge. After lotioning herself, Nicolette crawled into bed. She was spent and it was only Wednesday evening.

Nicolette did not have a great night of sleep. She tossed and turned most of the night when she was not crying. She wanted to simply blame the tears and the lack of sleep on James, but she knew that she was working through mourning of Charles. Each day, Nicolette awakens to seeing Charles' name still partially scrolled across her ceiling. "Fuck. I need to remove that from my ceiling." She stretched in the bed and walked slowly to the bathroom. Nicolette sluggishly moved through her morning routine. Work was a welcomed distraction from the sadness overtaking Nicolette's mind. The cases that Nicolette and her team were working on were moving swiftly along. The stem cell case finished up in the research department and the team was not able to find any legal precedent in the United States to cause their client to not proceed with the jury case. The team had a call with the client. Nicolette started, "Hello, Dr. Smith? This is Nicolette. We have completed all our research, interviews, and wanted to touch base on your case. Also, thank you for the review of the cases that we found abroad." Dr. Smith replied, "Hello Nicolette. I am joined with Drs. Jones and Schmidt. While you are only representing me, they were also sued by this same patient. I was, also, just informed that this patient filed a complaint against my license. My hospital has suspended me because they do not want the bad press; she has taken to social media. I think this is slanderous." Nicolette nods at Kamilah, who was taking notes, "My staff was not aware of this development. We will file a few briefs today before the close of business. Instead of holding out for a jury trial, we can probably resolve this in chambers/deposition. Do you need me to draft something for the hospital?" Dr. Smith was agreeing along as Nicolette spoke, "I have to wait for a committee. It will be in a few weeks, but if we can resolve this by then that would be perfect. I am still being paid so I am using this time to catch up on my writing for a journal article that I am working on. Do you think it will be helpful to get their lawyers involved?" Michael interjected before Nicolette could answer, "No. I spoke to their attorneys already and their approach is much different from ours. We think it would be best to keep these cases severed. We are, however, sharing notes and ideas." Nicolette added on, "Kamilah and Michael are, also, on this call. So, to fill you in, we were not to find precedent here in the United States. Also, based on the information you provided, the stem cell transplants that were successfully performed abroad were not to repair whole valves like in this case. There is not a clinical trial, research study, or surgery where embryonic stem cells were formed into a complete structure. In all cases, cells were made into healthy heart cells and transplanted as synchronized cells. I think we will be able to submit our research and rationale, along with the laws that ban the use of human embryonic stem cell research in the United States to the judge. We may have to argue a few points, but I can see this being dismissed." Dr. Smith exhaled an excited sigh. "Thank you very much for this update. How soon can we get before the judge so that I can submit these results to the American Board of Surgery?" Nicolette looked from Michael to Kamilah. Kamilah replied, "I already have a tentative date in front of the judge next week Wednesday. We will have the briefs and motions off to the plantiff' team tomorrow via courier. We can have a decision by this time next week at the earliest." Dr. Smith sounded happy and felt better about his situation, "Thank you, again. I look forward to next week. Kamilah, I will look for the schedule in my email. Otherwise, unless you need anything, I guess we are done?" Nicolette closed the conversation, "Yes, Dr. Smith, I think we are good. Kamilah will follow up in the next few hours with briefs, our filings, and our strategy. Dr. Smith, we will get through this together." They disconnected the call; Michael and Kamilah left the conference room to work on getting everything filed and off to their respective parties in preparation for the hearing on Wednesday. Nicolette sat in the conference room for a few moments to take a beat and relax. She checked her watch; it was 3:00 o'clock. It was almost the end of the day and Nicolette only had a few things to accomplish for the week before she was schedule. Nicolette returned to her desk to check email and review the motions that her team prepared. There was nothing of note in her email; Nicolette laughs that the send/receive refresh button is similar to the grim reaper. "I am glad that the reaper did not destroy my afternoon. Nothing that I have to respond to! BINGO!" Nicolette laughed further. The remainder of the day closed without incident. All the required briefs and correspondences were remitted as necessary. At 5:30 p.m., Nicolette changed from her heels into boots and donned her coat. She started her car, remotely and checked out with the reception. Her trip home was quiet and she tried to stave off the thoughts of Charles.

Nicolette walked through the door, removed her boots, and disarmed the alarm. She walked up the stairs to the dressing room and changed into something comfortable to sit around the house. She was too emotionally drained to go to the gym.

After getting undressed, Nicolette made her way to the kitchen to make dinner. She had thawed chicken breast for the meal. She breaded the chicken with parmesan, bread crumbs, and flour and started it on the stove stop to brown in olive oil. Nicolette decided to make chicken parmesan with whole wheat pasta in a garlic-onion Ragu sauce. While the meat cooked, she poured a glass of red wine. The wine was rich and helped pull Nicolette away from her mourning; she savored the rich aroma and pepper aftertaste of the Zinfandel. She sat on the couch and pulled out her laptop to check her email on collarme. There were several emails in her inbox. The emails were from ali, James, uwe, and Heinrich. Nicolette was annoyed by the senders of half of the messages, "What do these bitches want, now?" She opened the first message from Ali which was another plea for her to reconsider because "he had a taste for her." She deleted the message and did not respond. James message was almost an entire page long. It started with an apology; he apologized for hurting her feelings, leading her on, and breaking her heart. He then took back all his apologies and stated that he was only sorry for not taking a chance on them. "I have never felt as amazing as I have with you. My deceased wife was amazing, but there is not a word for how wonderful I felt with you, around you…inside of you. I will always cherish those moments. I am not some guy that was just using you. In an ideal world, my daughter's opinion would not mean as much to me. I would not yearn for you as much as I do. I want to you like I cannot describe in words, but at the same time I know that I can never be everything that you need. I am an old man flirting with Father Time; trying to steal a few more moments with a wonderful woman like you. You trusted me with your heart, your dreams, and your amazing body. I want another day, week, month, year, lifetime with you. Please do not discount me. I am not rejecting you. I am trying to convince myself to take a bet on myself. Even if you do not trust me for intimate things anymore, please allow me to continue to be your friend. You are one of the brightest people that I know and I need you in my life. If I was a young male, I would argue that I love you. I know how cynical you are with love so I know that it is more lust, infatuation than love, but I go to bed thinking of you and I wake up thinking of you. I cannot explain it any other way, but love. I am in love with the idea of you. I am in love with how you make me feel. I am in love with the touch of you, the taste of you, the smell of you. I know that you probably have already written me off, but if you find it fit please email me back." Nicolette read through his email, sipping her wine. She did not delete the message but she did not answer it either. She moved on to the third message from Heinrich. It was inquiring if she was going to visit Germany, on his dime since he does not have any plans on coming to the States any time soon. Nicolette replied that she could not travel in the middle of the case that she was working. She also noted that the holidays were coming, but it was the first holiday without her brother. She did not think that she would be traveling during that holiday season. The final message was from uwe. It included all the details for his game at Joe Lewis Arena. It had a link to the tickets and parking pass. Nicolette noted that he sent two tickets on the glass. She replied, "Wow. I did not know that the visitor's tickets were on the glass. I generally do not like sitting on the glass because you do not get a great view of the entire ice. I am wearing my Wings' sweater. Will you have time outside of the game to meet and etc?" After Nicolette sent the message, a chat request popped up. She ignored the chat to check her food. The breading of the chicken was brown on both sides so Nicolette put the skillet into the oven to cook the meat throughout. Nicolette poured a second glass of wine and returned to her laptop. She checked the chat request and it was from James. She sighed and decided to ignore the request. Before she could respond to his message her phone rang. It was James. She answered, "Stalker much?" James sounded hurt and startled, "I hope that you know that I am not stalking you. I do not want you to hate me. Your last message was quite harsh. I am scared. I am scared and I do not think that I am what you want or need. I just…" Before he could finish his thought, Nicolette interrupted, "No, James, I was not serious when I called you a stalker. There is no need to be scared as I already told you that you and I can remain friends. But you, also, need to adjust your expectation of my time. I am seeking a relationship; a Female-led relationship. You do not want that, so I am forced to continue to look." James' tone was quiet, but stern, "I understand. I am disappointed, but I cannot expect you to wait for me. You are allowed and entitled to seek the perfect one for you. I just wish that I meant more and you were willing to pause for me. I need to go." The line went dead. Nicolette was confused. "Why would I wait for someone that does not want me," she said aloud. Nicolette decided to clear her mind and respond to his comment in an email response. "James, I do not understand your statement on the phone…you want me to wait for you? You have stated in no uncertain terms that you were looking for anything long term. You, also, stated that you could not have anything long term with someone 'younger than your daughter'. So, I do not understand how you can even act as if you are hurt. I was the one discarded quickly and randomly. You CANNOT put this, whatever this is, off on me. That is some bullshit." Nicolette walked away from her laptop and put on the pasta and removed the skillet from the oven. She added the pasta sauce to the skillet and topped it with mozzarella. The skillet was returned to the oven. She looked at the available bread in the refrigerator to decide if she wanted to make garlic bread. Nicolette grabbed her fat and decided against the bread and closed the doors. Nicolette drained the noodles and added pasta sauce to the noodles. Once her food was done, Nicolette made herself a plate and settled at the dining room table. After a moment of sitting there alone and watching the steam stream off her plate, Nicolette got the candlestick with beeswax candle in them off the shelf and lit them. She turned off the overhead light, rejoined the table, and watched the candles dance in the air. Nicolette took a sip of her wine and started in on her dinner. The food was delicious and satiated her. As she enjoyed her dinner, Nicolette heard her phone ring in the living room. She allowed it to go to voicemail as she ate her dinner. There were leftovers once Nicolette ate her fill; so she packed her dinner for lunch on Friday. She blew out the candles and proceeded to clean the dining room and kitchen. Nicolette grabbed her phone and retired to her second floor. She cleaned her face and walked to the dressing room to get comfortable for the evening. As Nicolette placed her phone on the nightstand, she noticed that the call was from James. She snorted and cleared the missed call from her phone. Nicolette climbed into bed, sighed at Charles' name on her ceiling, and went to sleep.

Friday was a rough morning. Nicolette was hoping that it was Saturday, but she needed to finish another work day before she could relax into her weekend. She got ready quickly, hoping that starting her day optimistically would make it better. Nicolette arrived at work before all her staff and most of the other attorneys. She had a lot on her plate at the firm working to get all the information together for the stem cell case. Nicolette received response from the plaintiff in the stem cell case requesting early access to the documents that the firm would be presentation in front of the judge. She laughed aloud at her desk and called in his team. Kamilah and Michael entered her office and Nicolette directed them. "So, I received a response from the plaintiff in the stem cell case. They are asking for a sneak peak at our defense. Do not remit anything else to them. If you receive a subpoena, please bring it by me *before* you respond to it. Does that make sense?" Kamilah asked hesitantly, "We are legally bound to respond to subpoenas. Are you asking me to not abide by that?" Nicolette shook her head no, "I am not asking you to disobey the law. I am asking you to run all requests, formal and otherwise, by me. Does that make sense?" Michael added, "I know that we do not want to give away our strategy. They must think that we are stupid. Kamilah, you know that Nicolette has morals. She would never steer us wrong. I got your back, boss." Kamilah continued her questioning, "Dich's cases are public. I do not want people to think that we are shady due to association. Are you going to respond to the subpoena that you received?" Nicolette sat back in her chair and replied, "Kamilah, you are misunderstanding. We have not received a subpoena. I doubt that a judge would sign one where the plaintiff is asking for the basis of the defense's approach. That being said, my license and reputation is above reproach. I plan on keeping it that way. This conversation was strictly for me to tell you my expectation. Do we have an understanding…an agreement? Or do we need to go into details? Do you have any additional questions? Michael? Kamilah?" Michael shook his head no. Kamilah looked from Michael to Nicolette then she sat back in her chair. Nicolette noticing how uncomfortable she was started again, "All the briefs and motions were filed in the case. We are set to be in front of the judge on Wednesday on this case. We have responded, timely, on ever subpoena and request for information. The request that I received today asking for all the research that we did and our approach on the case will not be granted. I *will* let them know that we decline this request. It was not a subpoena signed by a judge; it was an email from the lead attorney. He is fishing. We are not easy fish to catch and that is ok." Kamilah sat up in her chair, "Ok. So you are going to respond and it was not a subpoena. I am ok with this approach." Nicolette wanted to rub her head, but just smiled and moved on to the other case that they are working. "Ok. So, we are all on the same page with Dr. Smith's case. Where are we with the scaffolding patent?" Michael replied, "I am still waiting on research to provide me with the patent search. I have inquired a few times, but they do not respond well with me. I was going to ask if you can drop a inquiry as well to see if that will hasten the response." Nicolette nodded in affirmation, "I will look in on research with that case. Thank you both for your time." Kamilah and Michael left the room quietly talking amongst their selves. Once they were out of the room, Nicolette took the opportunity to massage her temples. "Shit, that was rough," she said aloud as Dich appeared in her doorway. "Got a moment?" he asked with a shit-eating grin on his face. Nicolette recited a silent prayer as she responded, "Of course. What's up?" Dich walked into her office and closed the door behind him. "First, I would like an update on your cases. Most people come to me, dance outside my door to tell me about their cases – both victories and failures. They value my input. You seem to too self-sufficient. Is that a thing? I enjoy your independence. I really appreciated it when Julie was out mourning her daughter. But now, you seem to think you run this place. Must I remind you that I am your boss?" Nicolette wanted so badly to massage her temples more, but chose to pinch herself in the thigh under her desk to keep her face and tone in check, "I apologize, Dich, if you felt like I was not providing you with enough updates. When I started, you informed me that updates are done in the attorney meetings on Mondays. How often would you require updates outside of the Monday meetings? And for the record, I am aware that I work for George, Julie, and you." Dich sat up in his chair, visibly turning red, "You work for me. Please make that clear. You interviewed with me and I alone can release you of your position." Nicolette knew that that fact was not true, but also knew that Dich was pulling rank so she just half nodded. She continued to answer the unasked question, "The stem cell case is going before the judge on Wednesday. We expect the case to be dismissed at that time. The plaintiff is pulling at straws at this point. I think that the plaintiff is near the end. The neuroscaffolding case is stuck in research, I just learned. I was going to motivate them when you came in." Dich nodded along, "And the Canadian case?" Nicolette realized with those words that this conversation was a setup. "I have no update on that case as it is very new to my team." Dich shook his head no and continued, "George is very invested in that case. Perhaps you should prioritize that case." Dich stood and left the office before Nicolette could even acknowledge his words. She sighed and setup her out of office reply. It was 4:00pm and she was leaving for the day. Nicolette stopped by the research group's team leader's office and inquired about the neuroscaffolding case. He admitted that he did not have any additional information. "Hey, Nic. Thank you for checking in. I am sorry that my team has not been able to get to all your cases. We think that they are interesting and want to ensure that we give them the most attention and focus that we can. I will have information for you this time next week. Is that acceptable?" Nicolette was happy to get a deadline and nodded her agreement, "Thanks, Jacob. That works for me. This case is very important for the firm and it is a high priority for Dich and George." Nicolette grabbed her coat from the hook behind her office door and headed to the lot with her car. Nicolette made her way quickly to her car; the crisp in the air is unmistakable. Winter will be there soon. "I cannot believe Charles has been gone almost a year", she muttered to herself. Nicolette felt a familiar feeling start to sink into her body. She took a moment to gather herself before starting the drive home. She glanced up at herself in the rearview, "Girl, pull it together" she counselled herself. It was not a particularly trying week for Nicolette at work, so she did not know why the rug was being pulled out from beneath her feet. "Fuck, c'mon Nicolette!" She screamed at her reflection. Nicolette felt the tears were close behind the exasperated sigh. The sound of heels on the pavement broke her gaze and concentration; it was Kamilah, Michael, Julie, and an administrative assistant walking to their cars. Nicolette did not want them to see her breaking down in her car. They would never understand; more is always expected of her at the firm. Nicolette took a deep breath and thought about her nephews and niece. Their smile pulled her back to center, back to where she could fake a smile. Nicolette flashed her best fake smile, started her car, waved at the group, and drove towards home. As she approached her exit, Nicolette decided that she needed a drink first. She called Dana and Bridgette. "Hey. I am in need of some sister time and a stiff drink. Can y'all get away?" Nicolette asked with a slight crack in her voice. "Ah. I am actually in the City visiting my mom's so I can meet y'all pretty soon." Bridgette replied. "I'm down," Dana replied, "Where do y'all want to go? Union Street?" "I am open. Someplace, where if I break out in an ugly cry everyone won't be looking at me left." Nicolette replied half-serious, half-joking. "Nic, if we are ugly crying, let's order in because I just got my wig straight. I am looking to be seen, not be embarrassed." Dana interjected. "Fine. I will ugly cry in a bathroom if the need arises. You and your damn hair. Bitch, you got that half-German good hair. I am over here looking like I am one z from Kizzy." Nicolette said. Bridgette just laughed loudly at their interaction. "Fuck, I feel better already. I need this. See you in ten minutes at Union." Nicolette disconnected the call and headed for Woodward. Union Street was busy with the typical happy hour crowd. Nicolette found parking on Woodward in front of the Majestic Theatre. She felt lucky as the meters stop at 6:00pm so she only had to pay a dollar to park. Nicolette was not thinking that she would go to happy hour when she dressed for work that morning therefore, she did not have a change of shoes. As such, Nicolette made her way across to Union Street jogging across Woodward in 3.5" stiletto heels. She was the last to arrive; Dana and Bridgette were sitting at the bar. Dana had an empty glass in front of her and half a plate of nachos. Bridgette was being handed a frosty mug as Nicolette walked up. "My sisters!" she said as she embraced both their shoulders. Nicolette removed her long overcoat and placed it on the back of the chair next to Dana; Bridgette was on the other side of Dana, flanking her.

"So, Dana, Union Street must have a secret portal to your office, eh?" Nicolette asked. "It might have been a little more convenient than I originally led you to believe. What got you out in them heels? You *never* wear heels to happy hour." Nicolette shrugged, "I was not planning on coming to happy hour when I left my house this morning. But as you know when you are a black, successful, professional woman, you cannot be yourself around 90% of the people in your life and I needed to be around my people. And you ladies are my people." Bridgette, who worked in law enforcement, commented, "Try being the only woman, black woman, in a male dominant field. Hell, those motherfuckers have weapons." Nicolette laughed while Dana added, "Seriously, I am an engineer. Yes, there are more woman in the field now, but when I started over a decade ago, I was the only woman in my department for YEARS. I was told recently that I did not get the promotion that I wanted because 'I am too emotional when my subordinates do not abide by my orders, in lieu of the orders from a male group leader from another department.' Trust me that I understand that bullshit. I cannot smile, nod and hold onto my hood hard enough for this mess." "Each day it gets a little bit harder to keep my Eastside of Detroit at bay", Nicolette added, "And soon, I will just let go and let the true 48205 all over Troy." Bridgette laughed, "Nici, take a vacation. You have been working so many extra hours that you have to just be burned out. Do not let those people knock you off your mark. Do not lose yourself or go 'hood' because you will end up in jail with a crooked ass mugshot." "True." Dana added, nodding along with Bridgette. "Mental health days are for the weak…and the white. But after this case next week, I should take a couple days off. I cannot drink with you hoes every day." Nicolette commented. She then addressed the bartender, "One more round and we will also take a sampler platter." The bartender brought Bridgette another beer and Nicolette a long island. He then addressed Dana, "Do you want another Coke, water, or did you want to order a drink?" Dana shook her head no and replied, "No, I will just take a club soda. Thanks, Mark." Nicolette and Bridgette both gave Dana a look and before either of them could speak, Dana smiled and exclaimed, "We are *finally* pregnant!" Bridgette screamed, "I knew it! You are glowing AND have a huge plate of carbs in front of you. Congrats, Dana!" Nicolette hugged Dana and wiped a tear of joy from her eyes, "I'm gonna be an aunt again! How far along are you? Is this why you have been sleeping instead of partying the last few times I tried to get you out?" Dana nodded, "We are just entering the second trimester. I did not want to say anything until the doctor was certain that we would not lose the baby. I do not think I can take another miscarriage." Nicolette still beaming, "Well, mommy, you do not have to think about that. You have your blessing. I told you that over the summer that it would happen for you and Erich. That you need to be patient and wait for God's timing. This is perfect." Dana laughed, "You know it was hard to wait for this to happen. After all the miscarriages and negative pregnancy tests, I thought that I was barren. Hell, we were thinking of starting IVF and went to all the doctor appointments to get started. They did a pregnancy test and said, 'it looks like you don't need us after all'. I was thrilled, Erich was confused. It was great." "That is great. I am here if you have any questions. My second trimester was the best, but I know several with horror stories. I never really got too huge with my pregnancies. But I was also working out, running, still training. It was no fun being put on desk duty after the second trimester. Being a pregnant trooper is not a good look," Bridget commented. Nicolette smiled at both of her cousins. "I am just happy. I needed something to lift my spirits. I was hyper-focused on Charles today with winter setting in, but this, this news and having you ladies in my life have lifted me out of the dumps. Thank you." Dana and Bridgette smiled back Nicolette. "We are here for you." Dana said as the food was set in front of her. "Sweet. I was hungry." Bridgette said as she started putting food on her plate. The ladies toasted to the new life growing in Dana and started eating the appetizers. The ladies finished their drinks and food, hugged, and went their separate ways.

Nicolette jogged back across Woodward and made it to her car quickly. She drove home quietly, thinking about her day and the interaction with her cousins. She steered her car down Mack making it the few miles in about ten minutes. Nicolette backed up her car and parked. Her emotional high from an hour ago was gone. She gathered her purse and briefcase from the car and made her way into the house. Nicolette kicked off her heels and jogged to disarm the alarm. She opened her front door and checked her mailbox. She had no mail; it was rare for her to receive any mail except for bills. Nicolette wanted a slow night since she had a home game tomorrow; it was the Big Ten opener. Her team was playing a very good, ranked Wisconsin team. She made her way to the dressing room to disrobe and get comfortable. Nicolette paused in front of mirror. She was sad, but it was no longer about Charles. While Nicolette was truly happy for Dana, her being pregnant meant that of all her 51 first cousins, Nicolette was one of four not married or without kids. The cousins who are a decade younger than Nicolette were starting to get married and have children. At thirty, she was starting to feel like being unmarried and childish made her the black sheep of the family. Nicolette sat in front of her mirror and could help but to mutter the thought that was bouncing around in her head, "why are you so hard to love, Nici?" On some level, she started to recap all her break-ups. DeShawn, her first love, stole from her and stood her up on prom after she bent over backwards with her mother to go to his prom the night before. He thought nothing of not even telling her he was not coming to take her to prom; it was fun being forced to wait at home past their dinner reservations while her entire family took pictures of her and guessing that he might be late. They were together for almost three years when he dropped her without a second thought. Then there was Desmond, the guy she had a crush on freshman year. He was an intelligent, kind, and generous upperclassman that she met almost as soon as she moved into Bursley Hall at Michigan. They were good friends and she spent a lot of time in a mutual group of friends with him. She tried to flirt and let him know she was interested, but Nicolette found out through the grapevine that he did not 'want to hurt her feelings by rejecting her so maybe she should crush on someone else.' She was so devastated but rebounded by dumping all of their mutual friends. In the end, that move only hurt her because it left her friendless and without her crush. Nicolette poured all her attention into marching band and her studies. Then there was Benjamin, he was the greatest love of her life. They were supposed to be married, but after nearly five years together things ended between them. Nicolette found out that he was unfaithful, and her world was shattered. She mourned that loss hard; she gave back the princess cut, two-carat, platinum engagement ring. All her friends called her stupid for not looking the other way because he made 'a mistake that most men make.' They thought that she should begin to endure 'a little cheating now in order to be setup for life.' Nicolette refused the idea that she had to share the man who supposedly wanted no one, but her. She refused to go through life not trusting the man she loved. She left. Benjamin never would tell Nicolette why he cheated and that was all she could think about for the first few years following the break-up. Benjamin did try to reconcile for the first six months but had given up thereafter. He moved on and was married within two years. Nicolette did not have any animosity towards him; in fact, she traveled to see him play on his dime a few times since their break-up including a Super Bowl in New Orleans. They have tried to be friends, but their lives eventually diverged. And though not a great love, Nicolette was just rejected by the first male that she tried to establish a Female-led relationship. Her mind was swirling about what made her so difficult to love; in a way she thought "shit, I am the worst. My parents do not even rank me in the top five amongst their three kids. I have to do something," she quipped. At that moment, Nicolette looked herself straight in the eye and she decided that it was time to work-out her personality. After staring at herself for a couple minutes, Nicolette washed up and headed to bed. It was a home game tomorrow and she needed to be fresh as she was meeting Carol at the bar in Ann Arbor to accompany her.

Chapter Fourteen

Nicolette met Carol at the Brown Jug in Ann Arbor two hours before the game. Carol was not a big sports fan, but she was great company and fun to be around. It was a game that Michigan was not expected to win, and Nicolette had a hard time finding someone to accompany her. Carol was a great stand-in as she was like a sister to Nicolette; plus she understood the game and would scream along Nicolette; even when the game was not close. "You have to show up and play your best," Carol states often as she cheering for sporting events. The Jug was very busy on gamedays and today was not any different. They found a seat at a two-top table near the kitchen door, ironically under a photo of Nicolette as a child eating a large plate of pancakes with strawberries and whipped cream taken in 1985. They both order drinks and shared a plate of chicken wings. There were a fair number of Wisconsin fans in the bar, luckily, they were friendly. A group of guys struck up a conversation with the ladies. "Hello ladies. What does a couple of co-eds do when unescorted to a football game?" Carol smiled and replied vey sarcastically, "Why we are looking for big, strong mates to give our lives meaning, of course." One of the guys in the group of five, who was not sober enough to know that she was not serious, replied, "Well little lady today is your lucky day. I love your accent by the way. Where are you from?" Nicolette took a sip of her drink to keep from laughing in their faces. Carol looked from the guy to Nicolette. Nicolette replied," She is from Michigan. Look guys, as flattered as we are that you have interest in talking to us, we are just trying to catch up with each other." The tallest guy amongst the group reached out his hands and continued, "I apologize for my friends being rude. My name is Neil. We are just excited about the game today. It is our first time on your campus. We would love to have two lovely, and so far nice, even if a bit sarcastic, ladies to help show us around. Keep us from making too many stupid mistakes." He continued while pointing to his friends, "The sarcasm oblivious one is Marc. The short one here is Jeff. The quiet one there is Avery. And finally, the charmer that brought us over here is Henri." Nicolette could see his sincerity, so she shook his hand and replied, "I am Nic and this is my sister Carol. There are very few places to go on campus that are not safe. Even if you venture off campus, Ann Arbor is a very safe town." As Nicolette was speaking, she reminded herself that she wanted to revamp, work-out her personality. She smiled at the group who were exchanging handshakes with her and Carol. "So…", Henri started, "have you ever French kissed a French man?" Carol and Nicolette exchanged a horrified look as Neil tried to pull him back away from the table. Carol replied, "Mais, bien sûr. Je suis la Macédoine. Je parle français et J'embrasse français." Nicolette added, "Elle embrasse lentement, tendrement." Henri seemed surprised, but not enough to be silent, "Je suis impressionné. Votre accent est bon. Très bon…êtes-vous tous les deux francophones?" Before they could answer all the other males in the group interrupted, "English, Henri." He apologized, "Sorry, sorry. Are you both fluent in French? How did you learn?" Nicolette replied, "Carol is Macedonian. She has been speaking French most of her life. Her family speaks it exclusively at home. I have studied French since third grade. I do not speak it as often as my sister." Avery asked," So play sisters?" "No, real sisters. Her family adopted me and I them," Carol said, and then added, "And I could not be happier. She is, also, my brother." Nicolette grinned. "Yes, you are also my brother." Jeff remarked as he walked away, "Dude, these chicks are weird and being difficult. Much nicer looking talent over here." Nicolette and Carol both laughed loudly. Avery and Marc followed Jeff. Henri and

Neil continued to talk to Carol and Nicolette. "So are you ladies single?" Neil asked. Nicolette could see that he was fishing for a reason to leave, but on a much kinder note than his friends. Carol answered, "No. I am dating a wonderful man that Nic introduced me to a few years ago and she…" Nicolette finished her sentence, "is not single either. She is dating a wonderful woman that she thinks that she might love." "Nice meeting you ladies," Neil stated as he went to join the rest of his friend. "Enchanté." Henri replied with a wave as he followed close behind Neil. After the men were out of ear-shot, Carol inquired of Nicolette, "you're dating someone? You think you are in love?" Nicolette laughed, "Yes, I am dating myself. I am trying to learn to love myself. I am going to start taking myself out, date myself. I have to figure out why I am not lovable." She shrugged and took a sip of her drink. Her eyes watered over slightly. Carol pointed at Nicolette in a scowling tone, "you are definitely loveable and fuck anyone that does not see how amazing you are." Nicolette just nodded her head and looked away. Carol just rubbed her hand and stated simply, "I love you, so you are obviously not unlovable." Nicolette was fighting tears, so she just looked at her friend and mouthed thank you before taking another sip of her long island. Their wings arrived to break the tension of the conversation. Nicolette ordered a purple rain long island and Carol ordered a vodka tonic. The wings were demolished readily by the women and there was about 90 minutes before the game. They asked for their check but were informed that was already paid by the group of five guys that they were speaking to earlier. The ladies verified that the server was tipped and went to thank the group before leaving for the stadium. "Merci!" Nicolette popped her head into the conversation the men were having. Neil replied, "Oh. You are welcome. I noticed after we left that you two were having a very heavy conversation. I saw the tears and her comforting you. I apologize we interrupted. I guess life does not stop for gameday. In hindsight, you two were very polite to some very rude men. It was the least we could do. Wait. Are you leaving already? How far away is the stadium from here?" Nicolette replied, "Yes, we are. It is a little longer than a mile. There are a number of random house parties that can be hit, or you can watch the band do inspection and walk to the stadium." Neil nodded, "Thanks ladies." He turned to his friends, "Two-minute warning, gents!" Nicolette and Carol walked out the Jug and started south on South U towards the stadium. The ladies enjoyed the walk, the weather was mild. They paused to watch the Michigan Drumline perform their step show before walking to further to the stadium. The game itself was quite competitive. Nicolette was among those surprised in the stadium that Michigan was holding own against the highly ranked team. As the game was winding down, it was looking like Michigan might win the game. Nicolette spirits were lifted significantly. It was a two-point Michigan victory. The stadium was rocking, and Carol and Nicolette were dancing together celebrating the victory. After watching post game, the women walked almost two miles back to Nicolette's house.

Her room was neat, clean but it was not heavily decorated. She usually does not host people at her Ann Arbor home but knew that Carol would sit on the floor in an empty room with her. Nicolette and Carol did not discuss if they were staying in Ann Arbor or traveling their separate ways after the game. Nicolette sat on the bed next to Carol and started to catch up, "how's law school? You are in your last year?" Carol nodded, "Yes, this is a scary time for me. Classes are going well, but I have the bar soon and then I need to decide where I will practice. Joshua and I spoke about the future. We are talking marriage, kids, and what kind of jobs we should do. I have been encouraging him to ask for a raise at Arbor. He is making good money; six figures, but soon I will be making a quarter of a million. If I am making two-thirds of the money, I will make most of the decisions." Nicolette stated, "It is good that y'all are setting expectations now. What did he say? Josh is quiet, but he still is a man. He has a strong pride. Being the only son and the youngest in his family, he struggled as a child to always assert himself. But trust me, he is quite prideful." "He did assert himself. He stated that he will always make a contribution to our family. He stated that he would continue to support me, which he does right now. I have very little income, and he supports if I ever have shortfalls." Nicolette nodded along. "It will work out, Carol." Carol agreed, "I know. I just want him to do more for himself. He is so passive. But that is who I fell in love with." Carol continued, "Ok. I should be able to make it north now. I am going to Josh's house for the evening. I stayed there last night. You are more than welcomed to join us for dinner." Nicolette thought about it for a moment but did not want to be the third wheel and declined. "I appreciate the invite, but I have been drinking and just want to take a nap. We will hang out soon. There are a number of additional home games so we will get together after a game soon." Carol, who parked at Nicolette's house hugged her friend and left for her evening plans. Nicolette locked the door behind her and laid on her pillow and stared at the ceiling. She enjoyed this bedroom because it did not have Charles' name scrolled across the ceiling. Soon she was blinking slowly and she was asleep before she realized. Nicolette rowed over and checked the clock. It was 11:42pm. She had slept away the rest of her day. She was hungry and did not have food in the house. Nicolette went to the bathroom and brushed her teeth. She decided to get a burrito from Pancheros. When returned to Michigan from Boston, Massachusetts, she dated a man whose family managed, worked, and partially owned the restaurant in Ann Arbor. She loved the food and whenever possible she would have a burrito. Their relationship ended mutually and amicably. Nicolette was outgrowing their relationship and Mario had begun to wander. Nicolette walked the five blocks to the restaurant. It was very busy with the post-game, pre-nightclub traffic. The line reached the door. Nicolette was not good at waiting in line at Pancheros because she was always able to skip ahead. Valiente, Mario's younger brother was at the register. Valiente smiled at Nicolette. He waved her in the register and turned to his staff, "haz un burrito de pollo." He then turned to Nicolette, "¿Frijoles? ¿Queso? Salsa?" Nicolette replied, "Arroz y Frijoles Pinto. Si, queso. Verde y pico de gallo. Guacomole. No crema." Valiente waited on the person at the front of the line then the staff brought him the burrito they made for Nicolette. Valiente handed her the burrito and said, "bueno noches, Nic." Nicolette smiled and placed a twenty into the tip cup and replied, "Gracias, Valiente. Gracias. Buenas noches." As she walked out eating her burrito people booed at her for jumping the line. "It is really good." She said as she sauntered by the line with a wink.

Nicolette walked home cutting through the alley behind the houses on South Forest. It was a well-known short cut and it was usually well lit and safe. As she was walking along eating her burrito, Nicolette heard footsteps behind her quickening in pace. She instinctively reached for her hip; Nicolette carried a Glock 9mm when she was out alone at night when she was not planning on drinking. She had been a concealed pistol license carrier since she passed the bar. After unsnapping the holster strap, Nicolette placed her unfinished burrito in her jacket pocket. The footsteps, clearly that of someone taller than her, were coming up on her faster. She spun around, ready to take evasive action, if needed, and ready to draw her weapon to see the familiar face of one of her neighbors. "Hey." He said with a wave as continued to power walk past Nicolette. "Hello" She stammered before she cut across the lawn of the fraternity house off the alley and across the street. She could see her house from where she was and made it home quickly. She walked into the bedroom, walking past some of the renters who she acknowledged. Nicolette locked her weapon into its safe in the closet; it was mounted in a hidden drawer. She finished her burrito and curled up to watch some television before turning in. She wanted to make it back to Detroit for Mass in the morning.

The beginning of the week was a blur, coming and going so rapidly that, Nicolette felt like it should only be Monday. She had been working to establish all the last-minute facts and details for the negligence case. She knew that the patient was not faring well and was afraid of a last-minute stunt from their attorneys. At the close of business on Tuesday, there were zero surprises that Nicolette was afraid they built a case that she was not prepared for; or managed on some information that her research department or legal team thought of. She was so nervous inventing boogeymen that she even had weird dreams. Nicolette woke up Wednesday morning nervous about the case. She knew that her team had prepared well and was ready for whatever they thought could be thrown at them. She got an almost eight hours of sleep the night before and decided to eat a hearty breakfast before leaving for work. She was dressed simply in a grey suit with navy blue pinstripes; it was tailored for her body so the suit fit her perfectly. Having a suit that fit her like a glove made her feel shapely and sexy while being professional. She decided to wear a white shirt with navy and light blue stripes. Nicolette's hair was pulled into a tight bun and she wore zero jewelry. After eating a bowl of farina with butter and honey, Nicolette gathered all her notes and files, then donned her overcoat. Her purse, keys, and phones were sitting at the backdoor. Nicolette made her way to the courthouse. Michael and Kamilah were meeting her there. She pulled into the closest parking structure and sat in her car for a moment. She caught her breath and looked into the mirror and gave herself a brief pep talk. "Okay, Nici. You got this! Your team provided you with everything you need for this case. You are smart and prepared. You got this! Go show them why you are so widely regarded. Go flex on them, Nici!" Nicolette felt good about the case, herself, and she got out of the car and walked the parking structure to the courthouse. In her mind, she was walking through a decade of the rosary. Michael, Kamilah, George, and Dich were already in the courthouse when Nicolette arrived. She shook her head but was thankful that she said a decade on her way into the courthouse. She smiled at the team and sat behind the defendant's desk and waited on Dr. Smith to arrive. He scurried in a couple minutes after Nicolette. "I apologize for being late. I was served with a plea deal offer." He handed paperwork to Nicolette. It was not a plea deal, but a way to push him down a path towards a plea instead of trying the case. Nicolette raised an eyebrow and addressed Dr. Smith, "You did not accept this, did you?" He shook his head, "I have a lawyer. That would be your job if you think it is the best option for me." Nicolette breathed a sigh of relief, "Good. I am glad. This is not a plea deal. But it would make it so that you could only take a plea or enter a plea of guilty. We are going to win." Dr. Smith took his seat and smiled at Nicolette. Promptly at 9:30am, the bailiff called the court to order. Nicolette, in her head, was very angry at the opposing counsel for such a cheap tactic. She kept her composure and the case was called. Jury selection was not required as the pool was only 14 persons therefore the case would proceed with all persons, the twelve plus two alternates. Mr. Silanis, who Nicolette recognized from law school, as he was a year ahead of her, was the lead attorney for the plaintiff. He opened by explaining that his very sick client could not be with them because they were denied care by the defendant. Mr. Silanis painted a story as if my client was the uncaring, industrial medicine complex. "My client is a mother, sister, daughter, aunt, and wife. She was a hardworking teacher; she has taught kindergarten for fifteen years. Some of her students are here today to support her though she, herself, could not make it. Mrs. Silver is not here because she is in the hospital, dying. Dying – not because she was not willing to fight. Dying- not because she does not have great insurance. Dying – not because she did anything wrong. Dying – not because of anything within her control. Dying because of HIM!" Mr. Silanis pointed at Dr. Smith. His face was horrified, and he looked at Nicolette to object. She whispered reassurances to him. Nicolette and Michael, her co-counsel, were taking copious notes during his nearly twenty-minute opening statement. It was very riveting, both Nicolette and the jury were drawn into his speech. She knew that she had to be on her A game to defect his charms and charisma; this case would not be about the facts if Nicolette could not neutralize his charms and wit. He continued, "Is this a bad man? A murder? A rapist? No, he's a doctor...someone sworn by an oath to do no harm. Someone sworn to help the sick. Well, Mrs. Silver was sick when she met Dr. Smith and now, she is on *death's door.* All we are asking for is for Dr. Smith to live up to the oath that he took. As doctors and hospitals make money hand over fist, Mrs. Silver is struggling just to afford her medicine. Here someone that teaches our future does not even know that she will see that future due to money hungry doctors like Smith. I, personally, hope that I have doctors who believe in that oath. And will uphold the oath if I am ever as sick as Mrs. Silver." When Mr. Silanis finished, he flashed a grin at Nicolette. She stood and took note of the jury; it was mostly white like Dr. Smith and Mr. Silanis. The jury contained two women, presumably mothers, and three minorities (two black and one person who appeared to be Indian-American.) Nicolette knew that she had to tread lightly and inject the things that would not offend, but turn persons like her parents, grandparents to Dr. Smith's side while remaining jurors were probably in the top 1% for income. Nicolette understood that those jurors would not be swayed by the same opening statement so she had to shape the statement in a way that would appeal to both. She started, "This case is not about a doctor that chose to harm his patient. Dr. Smith is a beloved cardiac surgeon; he has been practicing medicine for several decades and has never had a complaint. Not only has he not had a complaint, but his patients refer him 87% of the time. Moreover, his work and research is ranked amongst the top in the world." Nicolette could see the probable one-percenters nodding along to her sentences. She knew that they would have an open mind during the case so she turned the rest of her opening statement to the minority. "The Hippocratic Oath states that the physician will help the sick within one's ability and judgment. Dr. Smith is NOT a stem cell surgeon – in fact no one in the United States has performed the surgery that Mrs. Silver required of my client. Not only no one in the US, but no one in the world has used stem cells in the way that Mrs. Silver required. Would it do harm if my patient injected unknown cells into her body? Probably. Would you want to take the risk of injecting unknown cells into your body? Better yet would you take that risk with your mother, your sister, your daughter, your aunt, or your wife? Dr. Smith is a great physician who would not want to risk the life of his patient. So, she sued him?!" Nicolette walked back to her table slowly, deliberately letting it hang in air the questions that she just posed. She got to the table and turned back to the jury and ended her statement, "Dr. Smith is very sorry that Mrs. Silver is ill. He is a gentle, kind, loving physician, who wants the best for all his patients. But he does not need to be punished because he did not want to hurt her in an attempt to give her something that would *not* cure her." Nicolette looked to Michael to ensure she touched on all the things in the plaintiff's opening statement that they wanted to address. He nodded and Nicolette sat in her chair. The judge asked the plaintiff to present his case. Mr. Silanis called a stem cell researcher from the University of Toronto, Dr. Hans Messner. Dr. Messner is a pioneer for stem cell implantation and very well respected in the community throughout the world. Mr. Silanis started by getting Dr. Messner certified as an expert in stem cell implantation before the court. Nicolette did not have any objections to his certification. Mr. Silanis started his examination of Dr. Messner, "Dr. Messner, first, thank you for coming here today for us. Can you please overview how stem cell implantation works?" Dr. Messner answered,

"In the case of stem cell implantation, either differentiated or non-differentiated cells are placed inside the body to combat a disease." Mr. Silanis asked about the success rate of the transplant. "Allogenic stem cell transplants are 62% successful; with many being up to 85% successful. We used to lose 100% of patients to blood cancers." Mr. Silanis nodded, "Thank you, Dr. Messner." Nicolette was instructed to cross-examine the witness. "Thank you, Dr. Messner for your work and research on bone marrow transplant and blood cancers. You have single-handedly saved hundreds of lives. My first question, are there any complications for bone marrow, stem cell transplants?" He replied, "Of course. On the most severe end, you have death from rejection, graft vs. host, and a myriad of infections. Moreover, you can develop other cancers as undifferentiated cells can start growing into other cells uncontrollably in the body. Finally, you can have organ damage or infertility." Nicolette listened to the long list of life-altering complications and continued, "And are the complications the same for using stem cells to repair the human heart?" Dr. Messner shook his head in a negative manner, "I have never used stem cells to repair an organ. Blood is a tissue, but not an organ. I do not know how that would work without first differentiating the cells, building a structure that needs to be replaced, and transplanting it similar to a whole organ." Nicolette knew that she had to drive home the point she was making, "So, the 62-85% successful implantation rate that you are speaking of is *not* for the type of surgery that Mrs. Silver requested of Dr. Smith?" Dr. Messner replied simply, "No, that success rate is for bone marrow transplants that I perform." Dr. Messner went to stand, but Nicolette had another question, "I am sorry, Dr. Messner, I have one additional question. Can you please let me know the success rate of heart transplantation and rejection?" Dr. Messner replied, "Well whole organ transplants have a one-year success rate near bone marrow, but they do have a rejection rate of 40%. I do not know of anyone who has used stem cells transplantation for hearts."

The judge asked if Mr. Silanis wanted to re-cross Dr. Messner. He asked only one follow-up question, "Dr. Messner, is there a large difference between organ and bone marrow transplants in terms of technology, risk, or science?" Dr. Messner answered, "The science and risk are similar between the two, but the technology is different. It can be vastly different; bone marrow transplants are quite mature in terms of use as opposed to stem cell transplants or organs developed from stem cells." Dr. Messner left the stand and the courtroom. The plaintiff next called Mr. Silver, his client's husband, to the stand; hoping that his testimony would help achieve a high payout. His testimony was factual about his wife, her contribution to their life, their children, and the impact her illness has had on their family. Nicolette did not cross-examine Mr. Silver. Nicolette felt confident that she had won the case without calling any witnesses, but she felt it would be preferred that Dr. Smith testified. Dr. Smith took the stand in his own defense as the first and only planned witness for his defense. Nicolette first certified him as an expert in both cardiology and cardiac surgery. Mr. Silanis did not object to his certification. "Dr. Smith, I only have one question for you," Nicolette started, "can you outline for me why you felt that the treatment with stem cells did not work for Mrs. Silver?" "It was simple," Dr. Smith stated, "Mrs. Silver has a congenital defect in her heart that made her heart decrease in function over the years. The stress of childbirth made her heart essentially non-functioning. Her heart was only working at 55%. She could live with that heart for a period between a few months to several years depending on factors including weight, lifestyle, and stress. Adult stem cells have not been proven to differentiate into heart cells. Moreover, they have not been able to form complete organs. Mrs. Silver was added to the transplant list for a new organ, but one has not been made available yet. Cells, more than likely, would have caused more problems than they solved." "Thank you, Dr. Smith", Nicolette said as she rejoined her table knowing that she wanted to see the hand the plaintiff was holding, "your witness." Mr. Silanis stood and made his way to the witness booth and started his line of questioning, "Dr. Smith, so you felt that Mrs. Silver desired to die?" Nicolette objected, "Objection. Argumentative, your Honor". It was sustained. "Dr. Smith," Mr. Silanis started again, "you felt so strongly about your opinion that you felt it was appropriate to condemn Mrs. Silver to death?" Dr. Smith was visibly rattled, "I consulted experts in the stem cell field from the University of Michigan, University of California, the Centers for Disease Control, Mayo Clinic, and King's College in London. I did not take this decision lightly. I do not enjoy losing patients whether it is to their disease, to the treatment, or of natural causes. I tried to help Mrs. Silver, even suggestion a number of things including losing weight, but she only wanted an easy fix – stem cells." Mr. Silanis continued, "Easy fix? You think that Mrs. Silver was not trying to live?" Nicolette objected again, "Speculation, your Honor." It, again, was sustained. Mr. Silanis retracted, "I have no additional questions." Defense rested and Dr. Smith left the stands. Mr. Silanis did not have any additional witnesses. The judge's aid drew two names to dismiss two alternates. The jurors were then excused to deliberate. Nicolette took Dr. Smith out of the court to have lunch and to wait for the jurors to reach a verdict. At the restaurant, Nicolette, Michael, George, Dich, Kamilah, and Dr. Smith discussed his impression of the case. "I think we won", Dr. Smith said with a shrug. "I am confident that I left enough doubt in the minds' of the jury." Nicolette stated. They ordered food and enjoyed lunch discussing minor things including weather, their respective families, and their careers. It was almost two hours after the jury was excused that Nicolette received word that the verdict was reached. They made way back to the courthouse. Order was called in the courtroom and the judge instructed the defense to stand. The jury foreman stood and rendered their verdict, "We, the jury, have found that the defendant, Dr. Smith was not negligent in his decision to not refer Mrs. Smith to stem cell treatment. On the second count of medical malpractice, we, the jury, have found that the defendant, Dr. Smith performed his duties in the best interest of the plaintiff, Mrs. Smith." Nicolette turned to Dr. Smith and shook his hand. The Judge thanked the jury for their time and dismissed them. He, then, informed that Dr. Smith was free to go, and that his bond was released. "Thank you, Dr. Smith for the work that you do. You are free to go. My office will produce a letter for your licensure board. Thank you, counsel." He struck his gavel. Nicolette asked Dr. Smith if he needed anything else, but he shook his head as he smiled. Dr. Smith shook the hand of his colleagues and then hugged his family. Michael, Nicolette, and Kalimah started to pack up. Mr. Silanis walked to Nicolette and shook her hand and complimented her work on the case. Nicolette inhaled a deep breath and released it. The courtroom cleared and Nicolette walked to her car. Once inside, she drove away from the courthouse. When she was sure that she would not be seen by another she knew she screamed, "Yes! I flexed on those bitches!"

Chapter Fifteen

The weeks passed quickly for Nicolette. Things were going well for her at work since winning the case for Dr. Smith; there was zero negligence found in the case. The judge drafted a letter for him to file with his license. Her team was on pace to close out all their cases before the close of the year. The neuroscaffolding case patent was almost complete and the Canadian case was weird, but simple. Things were going very well at work and George and Dich seem to calm down after all the cases were closed. Similarly, things are home had relaxed as well. Adrianna was doing well in school and was enjoying not being known as the kid that lost her dad. Jude's grades were slightly better than average, but socially he was not fairing as well as Adrianna. He missed his sister being in school with him and made a point of seeing the guidance counselor daily. Sebastian had turned one and there was a large party in his honor. Everyone gathered around and Nicolette alone took two hundred photos. Financially, Nicolette was working to pay off Andrea's debt on the Seneca home. Though stressful at times, Nicolette was on pace to have majority of the debt gone within five years if nothing major happens. Michigan was on a several game losing streak; it was embarrassing. They dropped all of their final games except one. This will be the first year in over three decades that they do not make a bowl game since they did not win six total games. It was nearly the weekend of the game that uwe purchased her tickets. She decided to take Kat to the game with her because it would give them a chance to hang out during the fall without either of them having to play host. Nicolette was looking forward to meeting uwe; they have been talking about their mutual interest in the lifestyle for almost two years. She knew so much about him and his life outside of the lifestyle. In fact, Nicolette was convinced that he was vanilla with a slight kinky streak. He definitely did not think that he was interested in a Female-led relationship. Saturday morning before the 7:00pm game, Nicolette woke up earlier than expected since Michigan was done for the season. She stared up at Charles' name on the ceiling until she was motivated to start her day. She spent the morning cleaning her bathrooms. Nicolette, also, put a load of clothes into the washing machine. Right before noon, Nicolette grabbed some lunch and sat on the couch in her living room to watch some college football playoff games. Tablet in hand, she multi-tasked between nourishing her body, watching the game, and scrolling on collarme.com. Nicolette had three new messages: one from an administrator, one from Heinrich, and one from uwe. She noted that James had not emailed her in three weeks. The email from the administrator was about changes coming in the following weeks to collarme.com and how the site relies on advertisements. The administrator was encouraging clients to click on the ads around the margins of the site. "Meh, no thank you." Nicolette said as she deleted the message without replying. The message from uwe was on logistics for that evening. It provided her with links to her parking pass and which will-call to pick up her lanyards. It, also, included a message of excitement to meet her and Kat. Nicolette answered the email, "I am excited to watch you play. It will be great to meet you as well." At that moment, they did not have plans to hang out after the game. uwe did not have the team's travel itinerary yet. Due to being off on Sunday, it was possible that the team did not leave Detroit until Sunday morning. If he had the night off, then they were going to have dinner in Birmingham, where the team was staying. The message from Heinrich was a check-in message. He was not traveling to the States in the near future and wanted to be used by Nicolette. She replied, "Hey Heinrich. I, currently, do not have much on my wish list at the moment. I will spend some time tomorrow looking at Amazon and adding new things. I am going to a hockey game tonight with a girlfriend. We have good seats and will be making a night of it. I am excited. What is new in your neck of the woods?" Nicolette had two new messages after she sent the reply to Heinrich. One from James and one from uwe. "Shit. I talked him up, apparently." The message from James was short. "Hello, Mistress. I have missed you. I hope you are well. Please do not be a stranger." Nicolette replied, "I am well. Hope you are too." The message from uwe was simply an emoji of a smiling face. She deleted the email. Nicolette's phone chimed. It made her realize that she left it upstairs. She finished the sandwich that she was eating. Nicolette walked into the kitchen and placed the plate into the sink and went to retrieve her phone. The chime was a notification from PayPal; it was a note that she received money. Nicolette checked and she had received $1000 from Heinrich with the note "Tonight is on me. Enjoy your hockey game." She laughed to herself, "That man must have been really needy to PayPal money for tonight." Nicolette transferred the money to her banking account and texted Kat that her finslave is funding their evening. Nicolette took her phones downstairs to the couch. Nicolette sent Heinrich an email thanking him for the pocket money and noted that they will be able to enjoy themselves on his dime. She also commented that "you are one hard-headed ass slave. Every time I tell you that I do not like random money sent to me you find a new way to send me random money." James replied to her email, "I am as well as an old man who passed on the best thing that could have happened to me can be. One of these days, I will learn to live my life for me and not care what my daughter thinks. But, alas, I am not there yet. I still think of you quite fondly, my dear. I still compare every woman I see to your beauty, charm, and grace. I fear that I will be alone forever trying to find someone who measures up to you." Nicolette read the email shaking her head, "That is one thing about James, the man had a silver tongue." She replied, "Thank you for the kind words." She did not want to say anything that would encourage the conversation, nor did she want to allow him to think that the door for a relationship was still open. She was moving on. Heinrich replied to her email, "I do not understand why you are denying me. I am trying to be the best financial slave you could ever hope for. You will not allow me access to your bank records so I can pay your bills. You do not like when I send you cash. You only like gifts and I thought that providing you with the gift of a wonderful night was acceptable. I am not nearby to drive you to and from the game and open an account for you to buy food and beverage. This was the best I could do on such short notice. Well, the money and the car that I sent for you. My driver will pick you up at whatever time you request, just give Sam a call at 800-336-4646, he works for Carey and will drive you wherever on my account. He is expecting your call. Tomorrow, we can talk about you using me properly." Nicolette was not certain if she should be annoyed or impressed. But she did call Sam. He asked for the details of evening, which she provided, and he made arrangements for a car to pick up her and Kat. Nicolette thought about Heinrich's complaint again and re-read his email. She replied, "You are correct. I am not using you properly. I will remedy that. I will spend some time tomorrow outlining my expectations and will share with you then. I will warn you now that the adage to be careful what you wish for will become your mantra." Once she sent the message, Nicolette logged out of collame.com and went to be productive with her laundry.

At 5:00 p.m., Nicolette started to get ready for the game. She showered and donned her favorite pair of jeans, tank top, and Red Wings sweater. She knew that she only needed ID, cash, and keys for the evening since between Heinrich and uwe everything was covered. Nicolette put her items in her pocket, grabbed her phones, and went to the car parked out front. As she walked out the front door, Sam got out of the car and walked to the steps to meet Nicolette. "Hello, Ms. I was instructed to make this evening as comfortable for you as possible. I have stocked the car with drinks and my associate has picked up your friend. We are taking you both to a private dinner." Nicolette nodded, "Thank you, Sam." Sam opened the door and held Nicolette's hand as she climbed into the car. She sat directly behind the driver's sit and poured herself a Macallan 18. Nicolette reclined and enjoyed the scotch while Sam took her to the dining table. They arrived at a closed library where another car was parked out front. Sam parked and opened the door for Nicolette. When she stepped out of the car, she saw Kat waiting outside of her car. "Hey, Lady," Nicolette addressed her, "I guess Heinrich setup a private dinner for us here." Kat replied, "Well, this is fun so far. I have kel at my house cleaning and tending to the cats. And we have a nice dinner, drinks, and game to enjoy." Sam escorted the ladies to the doors of the library which he opened. "I will be here when you ladies are done with your meal. Just walked straight ahead towards the light." Nicolette and Kat walked through the doors and there was a slightly illuminated path to a dining table with a server and chef standing alongside the table. Nicolette looked at Kat and smiled, "I have a good finslave, eh?" Kat smiled, "Very good!" "Hello, Ladies. Which one of you is Nicolette?" Nicolette smiled and replied, "I am. Why do you ask?" The chef stepped forward, "Ma'am, I am Chef Matthew. I was hired to make this dinner and it apparently is based on your favorite things. Susan, here, is your server. She and I are at your disposal. As I understand it, you have a hockey game at 7:30pm so I only made two courses for your enjoyment. So, unless you have any questions, let's get this party started." Kat and Nicolette took their seats at the table, assisted by the chef and server. "No, I think we are ready for our meal," Nicolette stated. Susan placed two long islands onto the table, "Are these long islands acceptable ladies?" Nicolette picked up her beverage and tasted it, "This is perfect for me. Kat?" Kat sipped her long island, "I usually do not drink these, but this is quite yummy." Susan smiled and walked away. "So, Kat, what is new for you?" Kat replied, "Things are good. Nothing new. Work has been going well. kel and I are going well. I cannot believe that I have found my soulmate this early into the scene. I met him amongst the first people that I met when learning about BDSM. He is such a good person, slave, and lover. So, is this Heinrich person a keeper?" Nicolette laughed, "He is a very good guy. He is wealthy and has such a financial domination fetish. He only checks one of the many boxes that I have, but I do enjoy him. He did explain that I am not meeting his expectations because I do not spend enough of his money. I must figure out the future path of our relationship. It sucks because he is a great to me, but he wants more than what I think I can give. I am glad that things are going so well with you and kel. I am envious of your relationship; I want to have what you guys have." Chef Matthew brought out the dinner course of petit filet mignon, garlic mashed potatoes, and asparagus. "Ladies, dinner is served. Mr. König said to make a simple steak and potatoes. I hope you enjoy. Susan, can you bring the Malbec out for their dinner?" Susan nodded. Kat and Nicolette toasted with the long island glasses as Susan gathered the wine. "Cheers to the fiercest bitch I know!" Kat laughed, "You are very fierce, too. You are a great lady, dominant, and woman." The steak was done well and quite juicy. Nicolette noted that Heinrich even sent the temperature to the chef. The wine was delicious as was the perfectly paired dinner. It was approaching 6:45 p.m. and the ladies were done with their meal. Nicolette went to tip the pair who served them, and they declined. Chef Matthew insisted, "We have been generously compensated already. But thank you, Ma'am, for trying to tip us. Here is my card if you ever need my services...cooking or otherwise." Nicolette and Kat exchange a knowing look, thanked Matt, and then exited the building. Sam was waiting. He opened the door to his vehicle for the ladies. Once inside, Sam drove them to Joe Louis Arena. Sam dropped them in front of the player will-call; Nicolette showed her ID and receive two lanyards and an escort into the building. Inside, the ladies where lead to a spot directly on the glass. Nicolette sat on the aisle and Kat was seated inside her seat. The players were doing their warm-up skate. Nicolette spotted uwe; he was grinning from ear-to-ear when they took their seats. One of his teammates skated up to him and pointed at Kat and Nicolette. Nicolette noticed the conversation and turned to Kat and said, "It appears as if our presence is known." Kat laughed as she removed her jacket and got comfortable, "Ok, Nici, well, we did come to be seen and it is nice to be noticed – good thing I wore my sweatshirt. I do not know very much about hockey so you will have to help me." Nicolette noted that she was wearing a Michigan sweatshirt. "You want me to get you some hockey gear because that can be arranged?" Before Kat could answer, a server was at Nicolette's side. "Good evening ladies, my name is Bella and I am the rink side server. Is there anything that I can get you?" Nicolette turned to address Bella to her face, "Hello, Bella. I am Nicolette and this is my girlfriend, Kat. I need a long island iced tea and..."

Kat answered, "I will have a vodka tonic." Bella noted their orders, "Ok ladies. I will grab your drinks. Do you need anything else?" Both ladies shook their head no and Nicolette turned back to Kat to finish their conversation, "We can get you decked out in some gear, you need?" Kat chuckled, "no, no, no thank you. I have so little space in my walk-in as it is to take it up with something I would probably never wear again." Nicolette was laughing when a body banging against the glass startled her. With a slight jump, Nicolette turned to see the blue eyes of uwe burning into her. She made a kissing face motion towards him which he smiled at her and skated away. It was less than ten minutes to the puck drop. The players from both teams skated off the ice. Bella brought them their drinks and a menu for dinner. Neither lady was hungry, but they toasted "Here's to a great game, great friendships, and awesome fights. Let's go Red Wings!" Kat smiled, "Let's go!" Kat pulled out her phone and took a couple photos and texted them to Nicolette and kel. Nicolette added some of the photos on Facebook; her profile was new, and she wanted to add more content. When she was done adding the photos and tagging Kat; the lights dropped for the team introductions. The players were introduced and skated onto the ice then National Anthem was sung. The puck was dropped and the faceoff was won by the Wings. Like most hockey games, the players started skating fast. Nicolette tried to give a partial play-by-play for Kat. "So, the wings won the faceoff, they control the puck. This side of this blue line", she pointed, "is the Red Wings' offensive zone. And they play defense in that one in front of their goalie. The reserve is for the visiting team, the Jackets." As she was talking the referee called off-sides on the Wings. Kat looked at Nicolette, "What does that mean? Why are they moving the puck over there?" Nicolette explained, "That player over there crossed completely over the blue line in the offensive zone for the Wings before the puck. That is called off-sides. That is why the referees had his arm straight up in the air when he blew his whistle. There will be a

faceoff and it will right outside the zone because that is
neutral ice." Kat nodded her understanding. One of the
people sitting behind them tried to strike up a conversation
with them, "So, you are not down here a lot...I see your
friend does not even understand the game. What brought you
here tonight and with such great seats?" Kat pointed, "She is
here as a guest of one of the players. Besides that, she knows
hockey well and *is* a season ticket holder." Nicolette took a
drink of her beverage and saw that uwe's line, their second
line, was on the ice. He was skating well, fast. Nicolette was
impressed with his puck handling skills, but she could only
admire him on the surface as she was learning his playing
style. Besides he was playing for the enemy, the opposing
team, she thought. uwe was checked into the glass right in
front of Nicolette. She did enjoy that. His teammate picked
up the puck and uwe turned to Nicolette and she stuck out
her tongue. He laughed, shaking his head as he skated after
the puck, play. uwe's line changed soon after. Kat asked,
"Why is he leaving the ice, already? He did not get hurt by
the hit, did he? Was it a legal thing that happened?"
Nicolette shook her head, "No, most shifts – the times that
the players are on the ice are not long. Most are less than two
minutes. They push themselves hard for those couple
minutes, but you will do your team more harm than good if
you are on the ice much longer." Kat nodded, "Need fresh
legs?" Nicolette nodded, "Yes. Need to always be matching
personnel and making sure no one skates until they're tired."
As they were talking, the Wings score easily. She stands and
claps; some of the Jackets' bench shook their head. Nicolette
knew that the team and some of the players knew that she
was uwe's guest. She made it clear that she would cheer for
the Wings and was allowed the tickets regardless. After the
faceoff at center ice, the Jackets got the puck and were
skating hard. They accessed the zone easily and had an odd
man rush; the first shot was ricocheted by Osgood. The
rebound was picked up by uwe; he was at the left-wing side
of Ozzy. uwe passed to the point, but they did not shoot. The

puck was cycled from the left point to the right back to the left and down to uwe. He shot a one-time wrist shot which slipped by Osgood due to a screen in front of himself. The Jackets on that sequenced played like they were on power play. The goal tied that game. Nicolette stood and clapped for uwe and cheered his name. He turned and smiled at her after celebrating with his team. Kat high-fived Nicolette when she returned to her seat. The chatty man behind her started to question her motives, "So, do you not understand how the game goes or are you just happy to see the puck go in the net?" Nicolette, partially annoyed and partially enthused at his constant chatter, replied, "No, I understand hockey. I am a Wings' fan. I am also a fan of uwe. I am his guest. Besides, that was a killer fucking goal, Ozzy had no chance of getting it." Bella returned to check on the ladies, Nicolette flexing her dominance ordered beverages and snacks, "I will get another round for us and the gentleman behind me. Also, let's get them a snack. Pretzels with nacho cheese?" The chatty guy grinned and exclaimed, "I'm having Labatt's. And a pretzel sounds good." The first period ended soon after the Jackets goal and the players left the ice. Nicolette did not pay much attention to the on-ice entertainment, but she did enjoy watching the zambonie drive around the ice. Bella returned with their drinks and the pretzels. "Ah, thanks for this…," he paused for her to inject her name, but Nicolette didn't, "I am Dale. This is my buddy Trevor. We are from Windsor. We are huge Wings' fans and do not get here often. These are our company seats. Normally, we are up in the nose bleeds. But if beautiful ladies like you are down here, I might have to start saving now for next season." Trevor laughed, "Cheers, mate." Nicolette replied, "thank you for the compliment Dale. Nice to meet you, Trevor. This is Kat and I am Nici. Like she said, I am here because of uwe. My seats are higher." The second started fast, the Wings' scored two goals quickly. It was very clear from the poise and control of the game that they were the defending Stanley Cup Champions. The Jackets' bench table, "Tough go of it tonight, guys. But welcome to Cheli's. He will be out in a moment to say hello. But in the meantime, what can I get you?" Nicolette looked slightly confused and ordered a long island, Kat ordered a vodka tonic with a lime twist, while uwe and his teammates all ordered two pitchers of beers." Great, I will work on that for you." Their drinks arrived much quicker than Nicolette was used to which impressed her. She chalked up the fast service to the presence of the Jackets' players. uwe led a toast amongst their table, "Here is to good friends, lovely ladies, and the greatest sport a man can play." They clanked their glasses together and started sipping their beverages. A couple people in Jackets' jerseys noticed the table and walked up for autographs. The guys indulged their request for photos and autographs. The table conversation was general and polite. uwe's teammates asked about Nicolette and Kat's careers. Kat asked a few questions about hockey; most of her questions were follow-up questions to the things she learned earlier talking to Nicolette. uwe leaned over and kissed Nicolette on her neck. He whispered in her ear, "I wish we were alone. I would love to serve you right now. You are so amazing, Herrin. Ich möchte deinen Arsch anbeten." Nicolette replied with a smile, "Du bist so ein guter junge. Mein Arsch? nuttiger kleiner junge!" uwe chuckled, "Ihre nuttiger kleiner junge, Herrin." Jay laughed, "Are y'all flirting in German?" Nicolette turned to him, "Just a little. Why? What did we miss?" Jay laughed, "I do not think I have seen uwe smile this much since I met him." uwe blushed, "She is an amazing woman." Chris Chelios walked up to their table and shook the Jackets' hand again, "Hey guys, I was not certain if any of you were going to come by tonight. When do you return to Ohio?" Chris replied, "Our plane was being cleaned at DTW, so they put us on delay. Most of the guys scattered, but uwe had a guest at tonight's game, so we joined him on his date." Jay laughed, "Yeah, this smiling gent is usually mostly frowning." Nicolette nudged him, "Do I make you smile, junge?" Steve moved into the booth to offer Chris Chelios a seat, "Take a load off." Cheli sat down and raised his finger into the air and the bartender brought him a beverage. "So you ladies live here? I see the Michigan sweatshirt and the Wings' sweater." Kat replied, "Yes, Nici is a huge Wings' fan and she was teaching me. We both are Michigan alumnae." Chris nodded, "That is cool. Do you guys come here often? To the Joe?" Nicolette replied, "I live close to here. Indian Village area. I have season tickets to the Wings. Kat has not been to many games. She lives west. But we have been friends for years. I do not know if she comes here…" Kat replied, "No, I do not come downtown often at all. I try to spend time in and around home." uwe leaned in and kissed Nicolette on the shoulder and again on the neck then whispered, "I will have to come back in a few weeks around the holidays." The group completed their drinks and Cheli picked up their second round and departed. As the table drank their second round of beverages, Nicolette excused herself from the table. She went to the bar to pay the table's tab. uwe was close behind her. He placed his hand on the small of her back and followed her to the bar. She turned to uwe, "I am paying this tab and I am not taking any arguing." uwe leaned into her and complained, "I am not allowing you pay for my friends drinks." Nicolette turned and looked him deep in the eyes and said sternly, "It is not *my* money. My financial slave has been paying the night." uwe turned a bit red and there was a bit of edge in his voice when he replied, "My balls! I cannot allow another man buy my drinks when I am out with you. I can feel my balls shrinking. You like torturing me. I did not even know what to do with you." Nicolette turned from him and handed cash for the entire check plus tip to the bartender, "Thank you for the great service." As her back was turned to him, uwe groaned his displeasure. He leaned down to her ear and groaned, "My balls are so tight and high. I am such a cuckold." Nicolette turned from the bar and leaned into uwe and whispered close to his mouth, "Naw. Only a cuckold if I was fucking him. That was the other guy." uwe stepped backwards as if the wind was knocked from his lungs, "Ouch. Maybe one day I will have the pleasure of being a good cuckold." Nicolette whispered in his ears, "Cream pie and all." Nicolette rejoined the table with uwe a couple steps behind her. uwe sat back at the table and Nicolette addressed the group, "We should probably get you back to the team bus. I would hate to be the reason that you are late." The men checked their respective time pieces and agreed. The six of them loaded into Sam's vehicle and he promptly got returned to the Joe. When they pulled up other players were loading into the bus. Their luggage and gear were being loaded. "Perfect timing, Nici." Steve said as he piled out the car first. He was followed by Chris and finally Jay. Kat waved and said good-bye as the men left the limo. uwe was the last to get out of the car. Nicolette stepped out of the car behind him to hug him good-bye. He placed his arms around her back, and he was tall enough that his arms wrapped around her back more than once. He hugged her, gripping her in his arms clasping his own wrists. "Thank you, Herrin, for coming to see me play. For the drinks and for the cream pie thoughts. This was such a wonderful night and I am so glad that I went outside my comfort zones, put off my fears to see you. This was amazing." His arms slipped down to where his hands grip her buttock. "uwe, it was great for me to see you play. Amazing goal, by the way. I was highly impressed with that wrister. It was so good meeting you. I am glad you got me tickets and came out for drinks." uwe had one hand on her right buttock and one on her lower back, "I do not want to leave, but I see some of my friends watching us through the window. So, I will keep this simple." He leaned in and kissed her neck again sensually. Nicolette enjoyed his lips on her neck, "junge, you are trying to turn me on. That's not good. You are leaving. I cannot use you." He laughed and kissed her passionately on the lips before ending their embrace. "Goodnight, Herrin. We will talk soon. I will probably text you as soon as I get on the bus." Nicolette turned at the cat calls and whistles of his teammates, "You mean after you are heckled. Luckily, I am cool and adorable." Nicolette stuck out her tongue and walked back to the car. uwe held her hand as she climbed into the car. He waved at Kat, closed the door, and walked to the bus. Sam drove Kat home first before dropping Nicolette at home. When Nicolette got home, she had a text from uwe; he had boarded the team bus. The text was short and complimentary including a note that stated that his teammates thought very highly of her.

Nicolette woke up on feeling refreshed. She looked at Charles' name on her ceiling and felt a little sad. The holidays were in full swing and she could not help but feel a little lonely. It would be different, she thought, if she was in a relationship. Nicolette checked her phone and had a message from both Kat and kel; kel thanked Nicolette for taking Kat to the game and teaching her about hockey. Kat's message was expressing similar sentiments. Nicolette texted both back letting them know it was her pleasure. "It might just be an in-bed morning." Nicolette stated to no one and opened her tablet to collarme.com. It loaded a weird page; it was not the normal loading page. It was a simple text screen explaining that the owners of collarme.com were fighting. Apparently, if you believe the page, the person who owned the page was a silent partner who was not being compensated based on the advertisements on the page. This person, who owned the domain, felt like the operating owner of the page was taking advantage of her. "Well, oh shit. Cannot have shit!" Nicolette laughed. Nicolette checked her email; there was a message from collarme.com administration who suggested that the members try a new page which added a number to the typical collarme.com address. Kat, kel, and several others have been trying to get Nicolette on fetlife.com; she was reluctant. Nicolette did not want to join multiple fetish sites, but everyone explained to her fetlife was the Facebook of the fetish world. She was a recent additional to Facebook so since collarme.com was done she decided to just take a break from all the sites. Everyone she spoke to often had other ways of contacting her and she felt it was time for a clean slate…in all her life. Nicolette climbed out of bed; it was nearly a year since Charles died and her whole life changed. "I need to do for Nicolette." She went and looked in her full-length mirror and had a pep talk with herself, "Nicolette Guyere. You are fierce. You are deserving of a wonderful life. You are going to have a good life. You do not need a man. You do not need a slave. You do not need anything or anyone but yourself. You are the best person for you! Be a better lawyer, the best lawyer. Be a better aunt, the best person that your nieces and nephews will ever have. Be a better Dominant, no one can wield a whip, crop, or single-tail like you. Nicolette motherfucking Guyere, you are a fierce ass woman. Do not let one bad day, one bad event, one death, one negative stop you from being you best self!"

Ok, now to get Charles' name off our bedroom ceiling!

Angelique Clemens is a speaker and writer from Detroit, Michigan. She has had passion for writing since she was a young child. She published poetry as a teenager in English and French and co-authored murder mystery short stories with her mother as a pre-teen. She has continued to love writing throughout her life.

Outside of writing, Angelique enjoys traveling with her husband and attending sporting events. She is an avid fan of both professional and collegiate sports.

www.angeliqueclemens.com